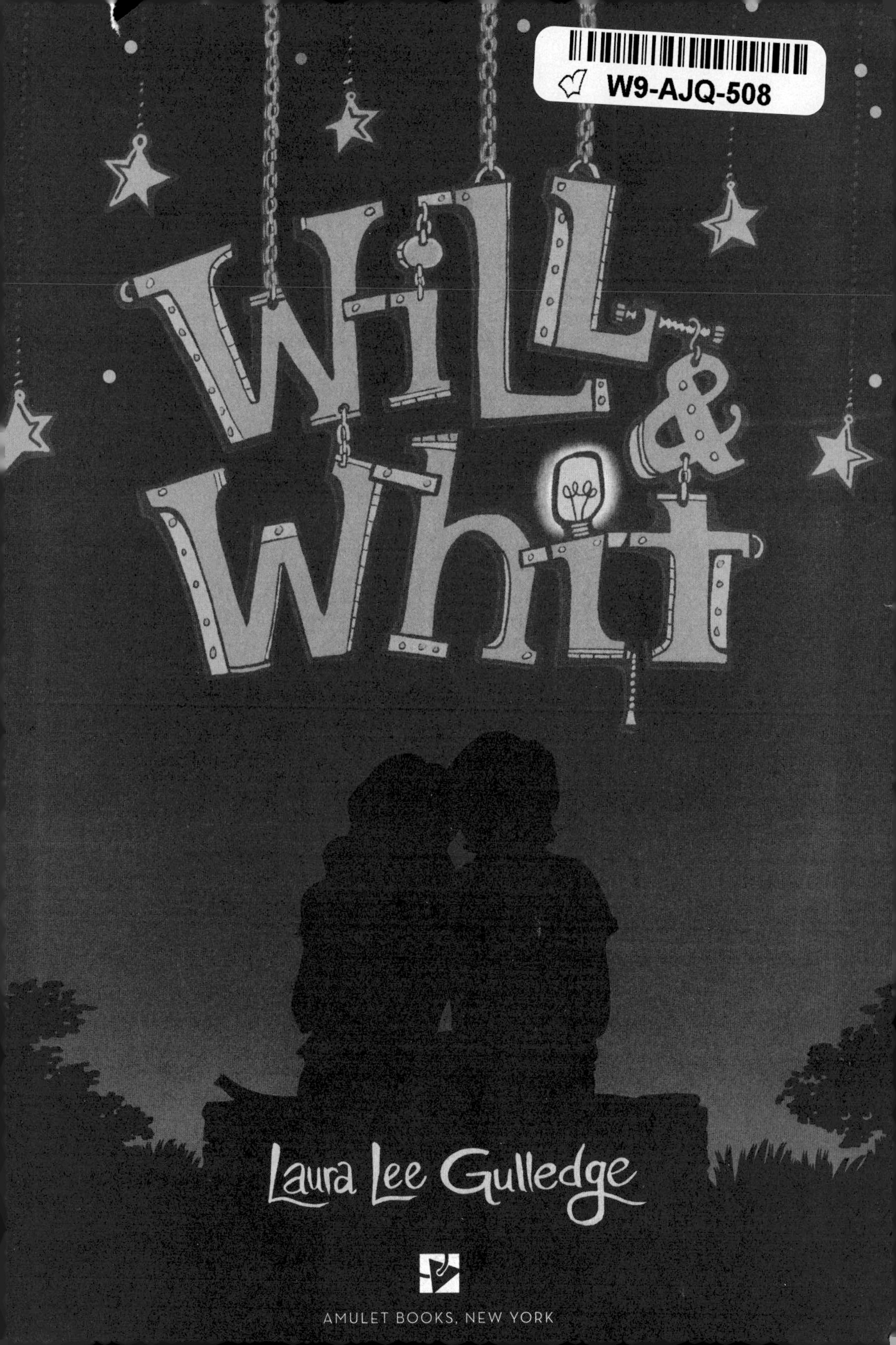
Will & Whit
Laura Lee Gulledge
AMULET BOOKS, NEW YORK

Sparks

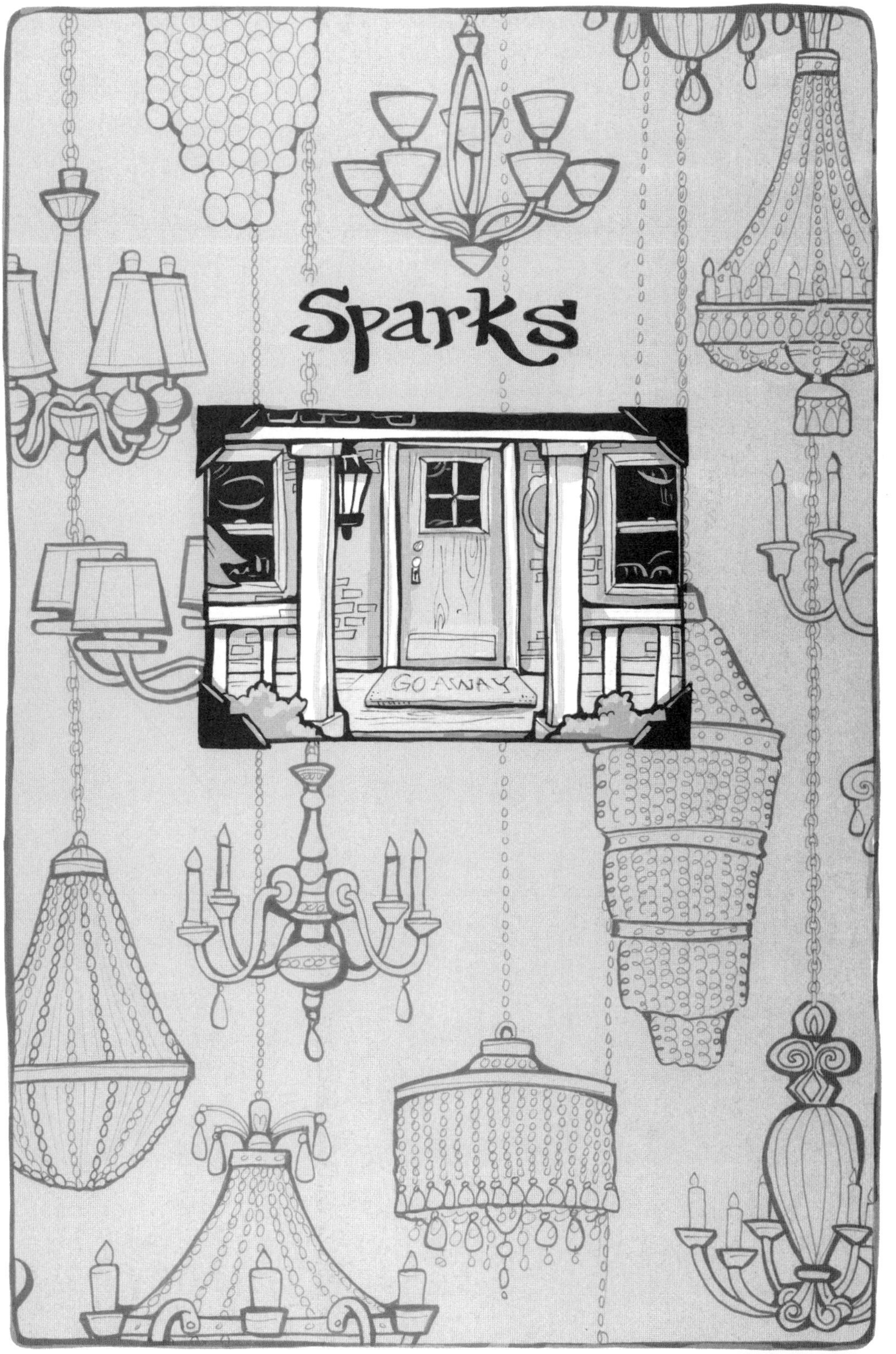
GO AWAY

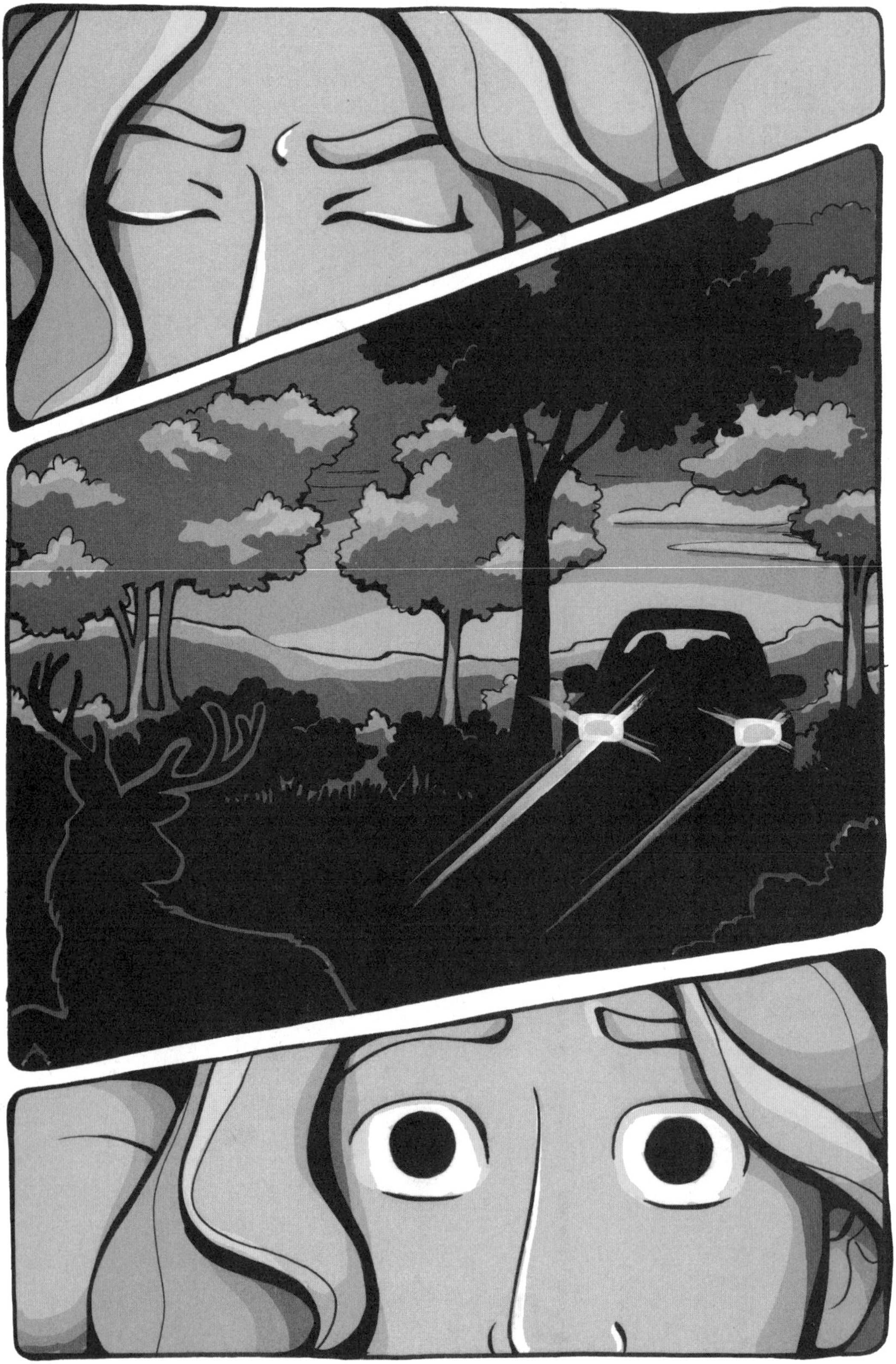

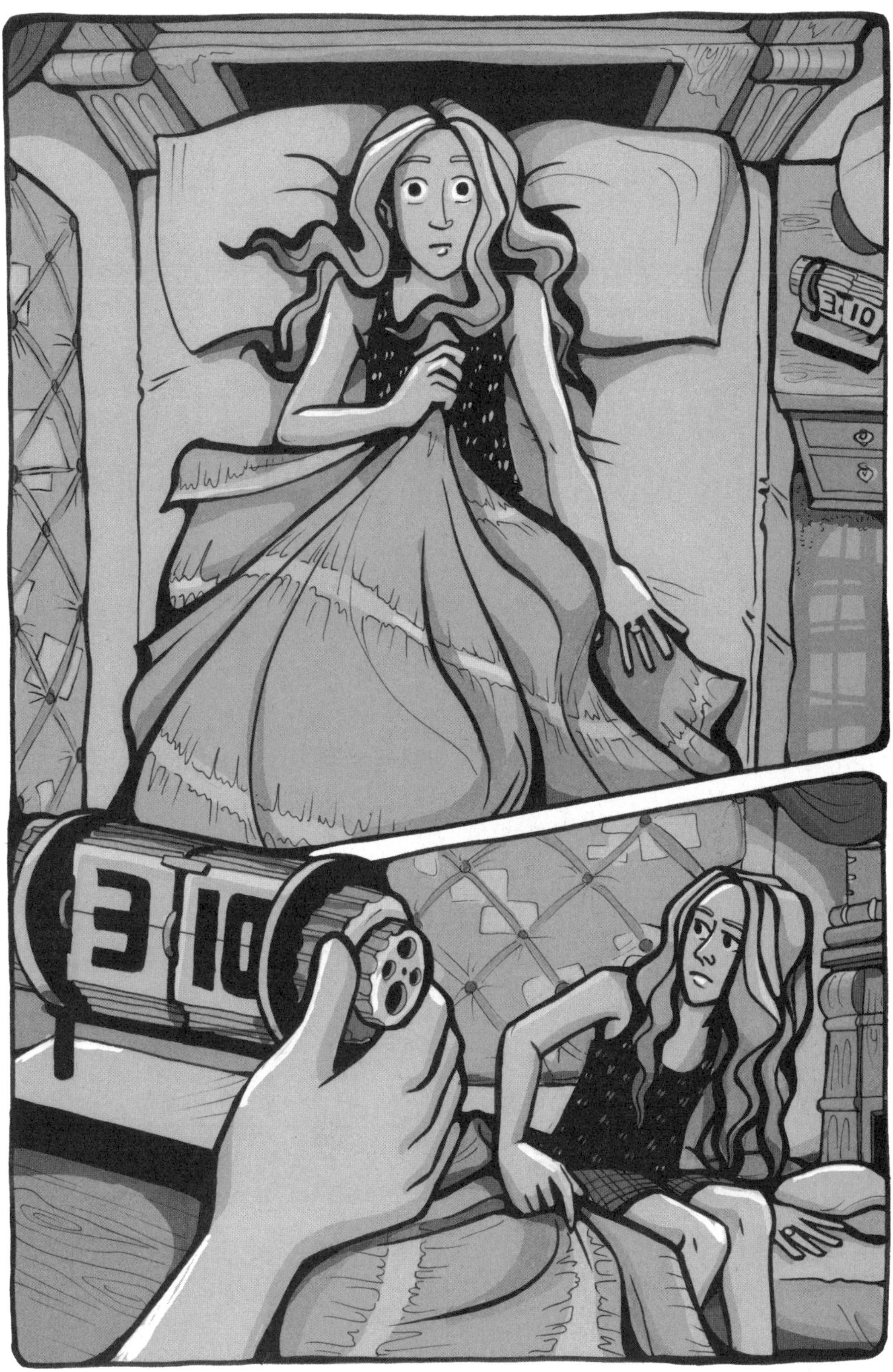
3 10

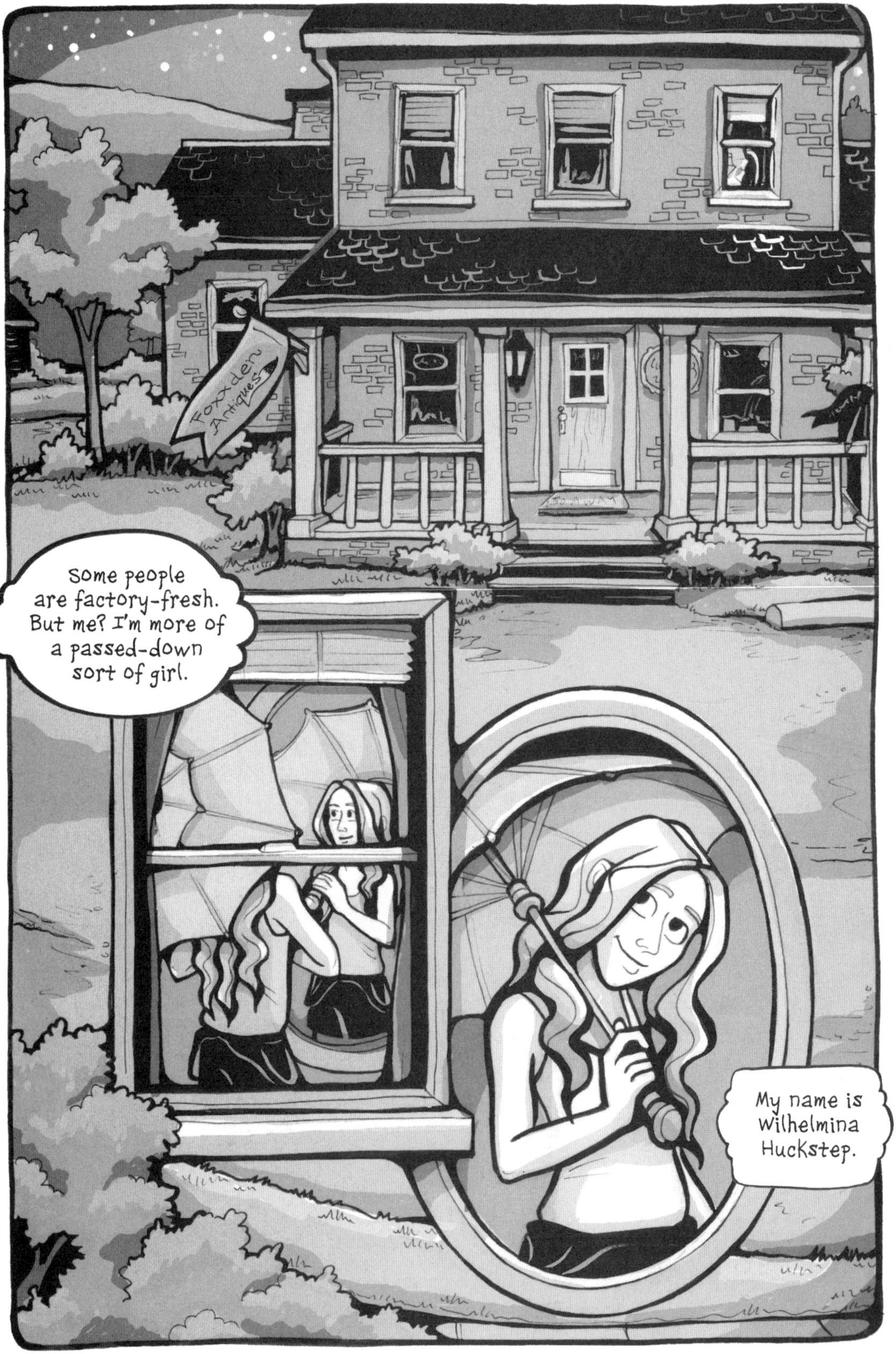
Foxxden Antiques
Some people are factory-fresh. But me? I'm more of a passed-down sort of girl.
My name is Wilhelmina Huckstep.

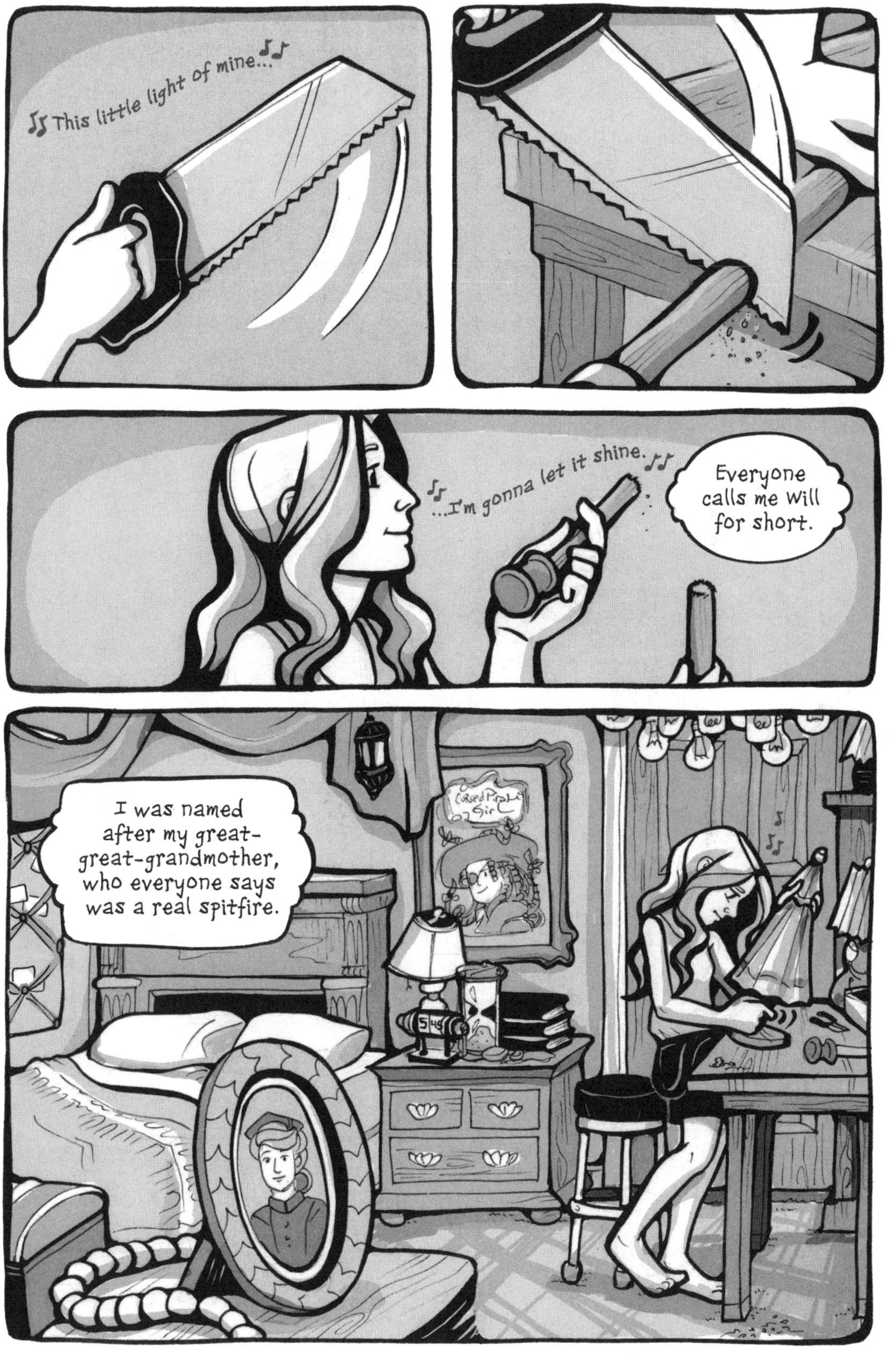
This little light of mine...
...I'm gonna let it shine.
Everyone calls me Will for short.
I was named after my great-great-grandmother, who everyone says was a real spitfire.
Cursed Pirate Girl

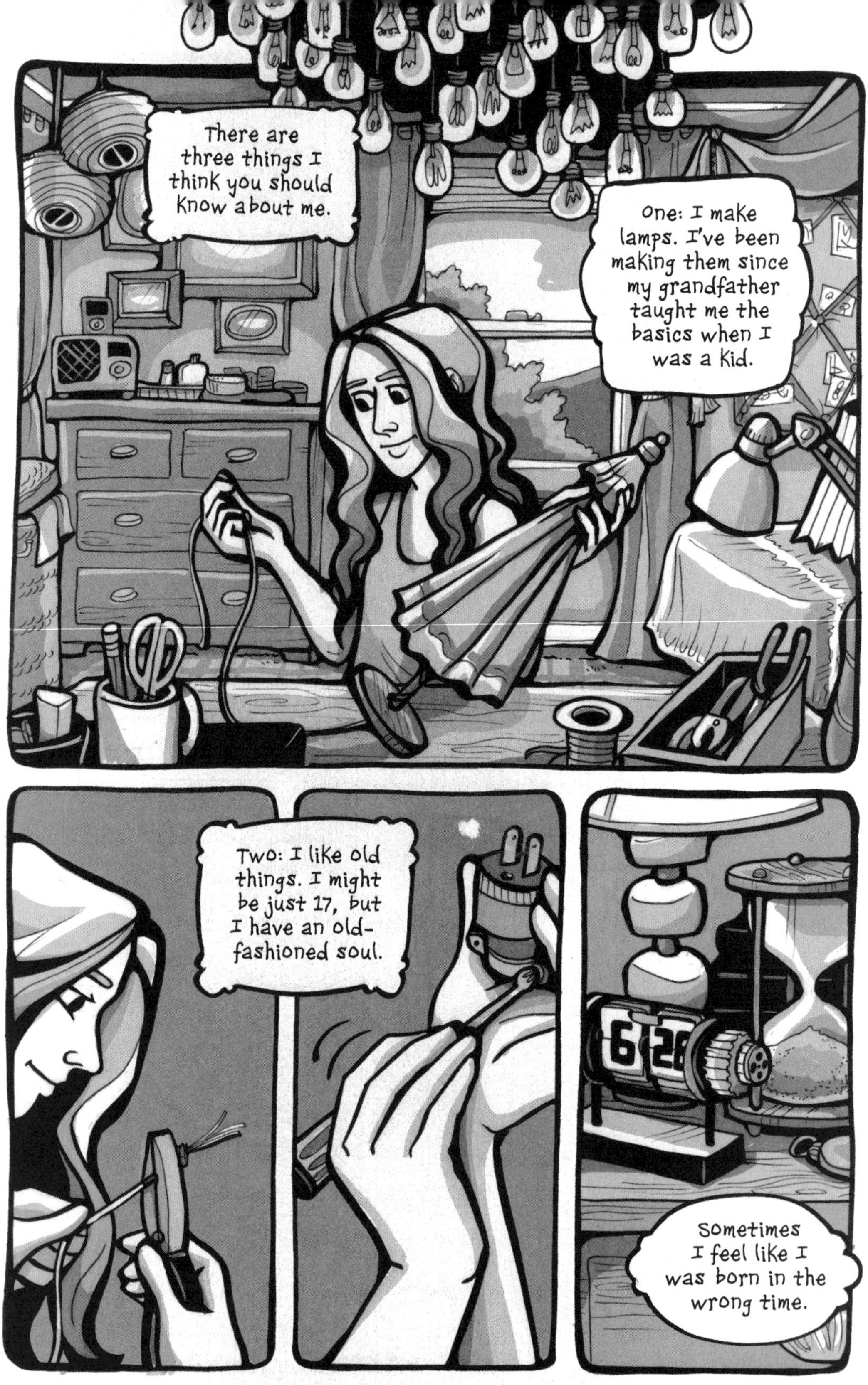
There are three things I think you should know about me.
One: I make lamps. I've been making them since my grandfather taught me the basics when I was a kid.
Two: I like old things. I might be just 17, but I have an old-fashioned soul.
Sometimes I feel like I was born in the wrong time.

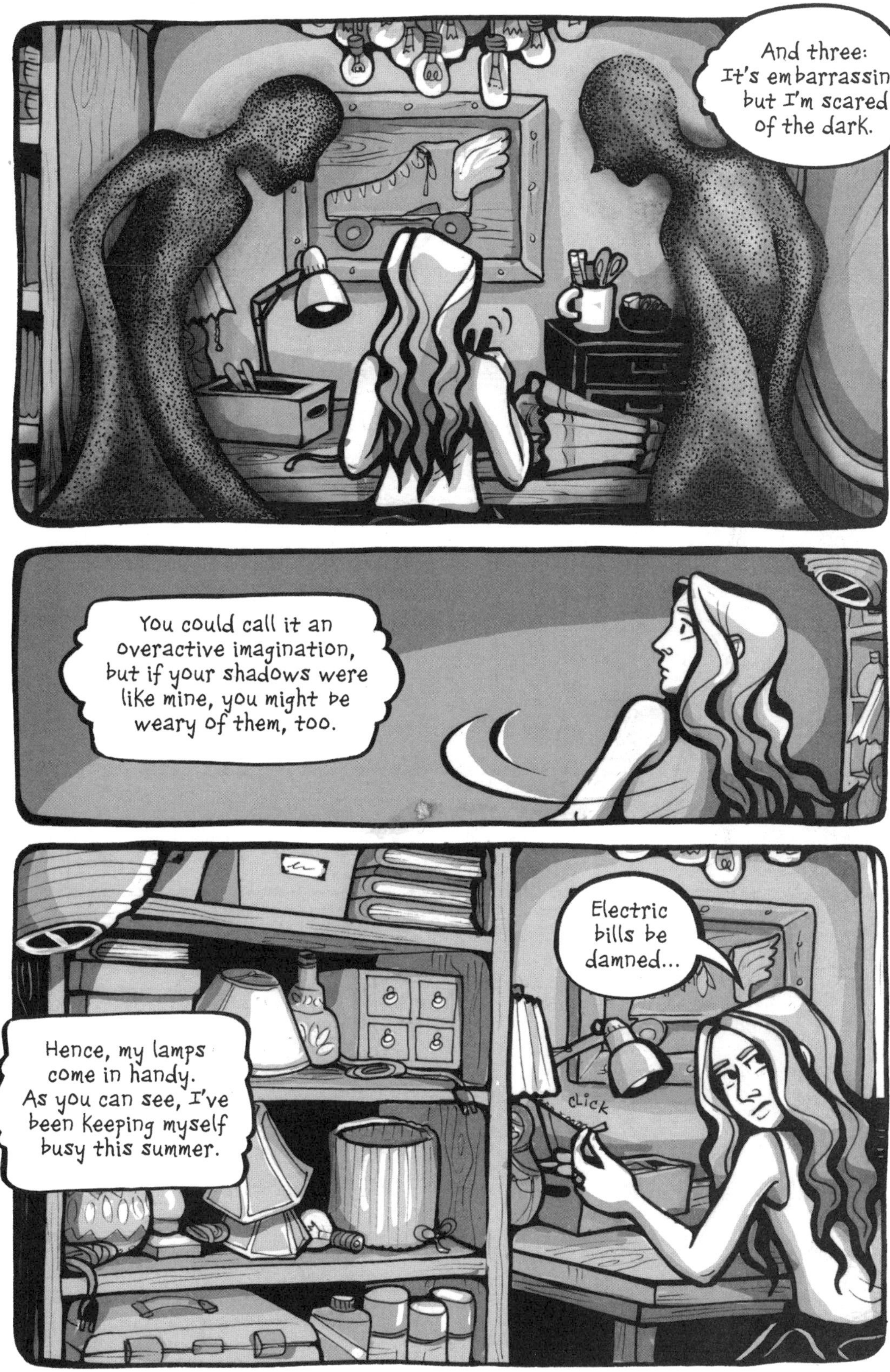
And three: It's embarrassing, but I'm scared of the dark.
You could call it an overactive imagination, but if your shadows were like mine, you might be weary of them, too.
Hence, my lamps come in handy. As you can see, I've been keeping myself busy this summer.
Electric bills be damned...
CLICK

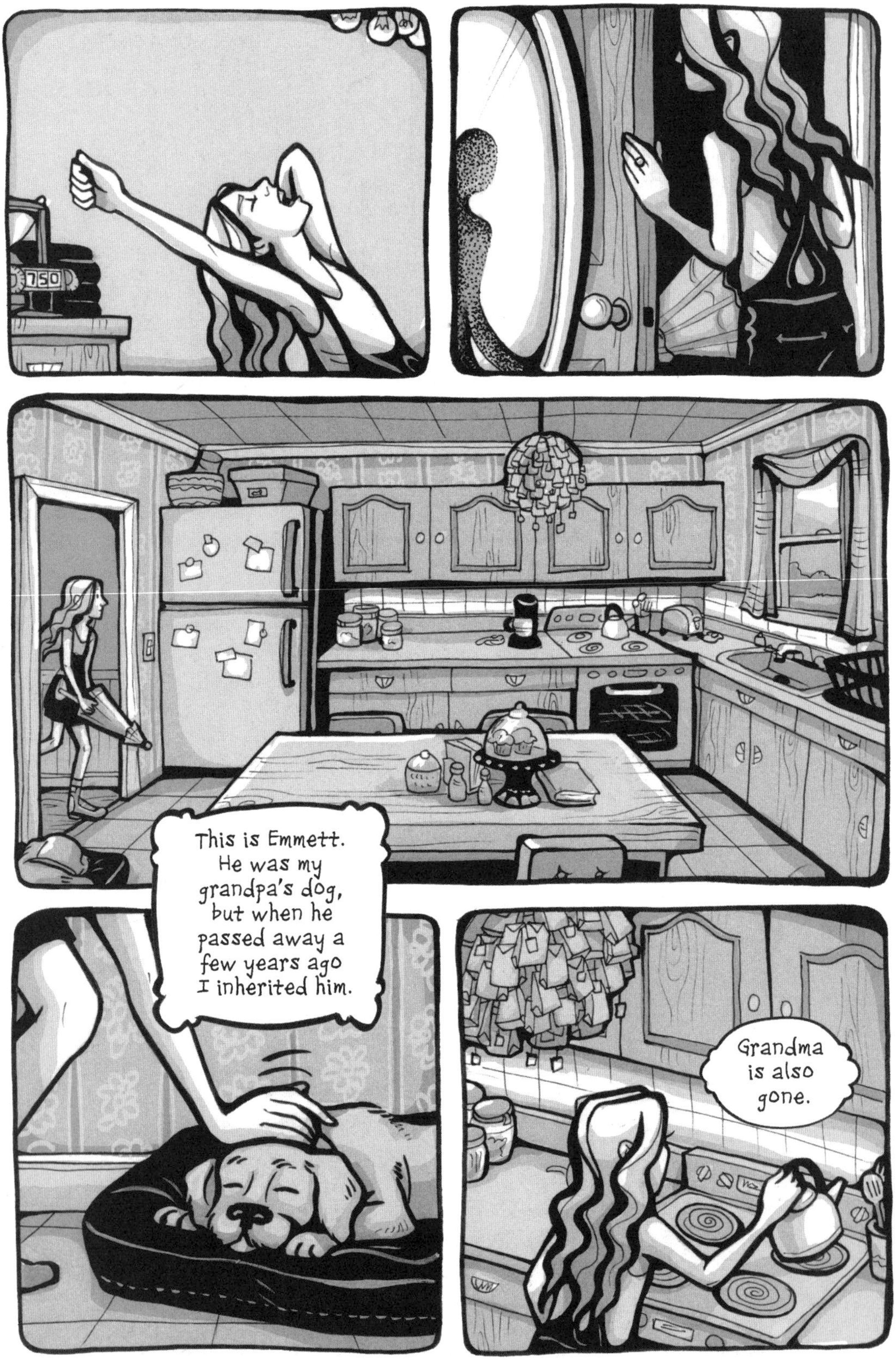
7:50
This is Emmett. He was my grandpa's dog, but when he passed away a few years ago I inherited him.
Grandma is also gone.

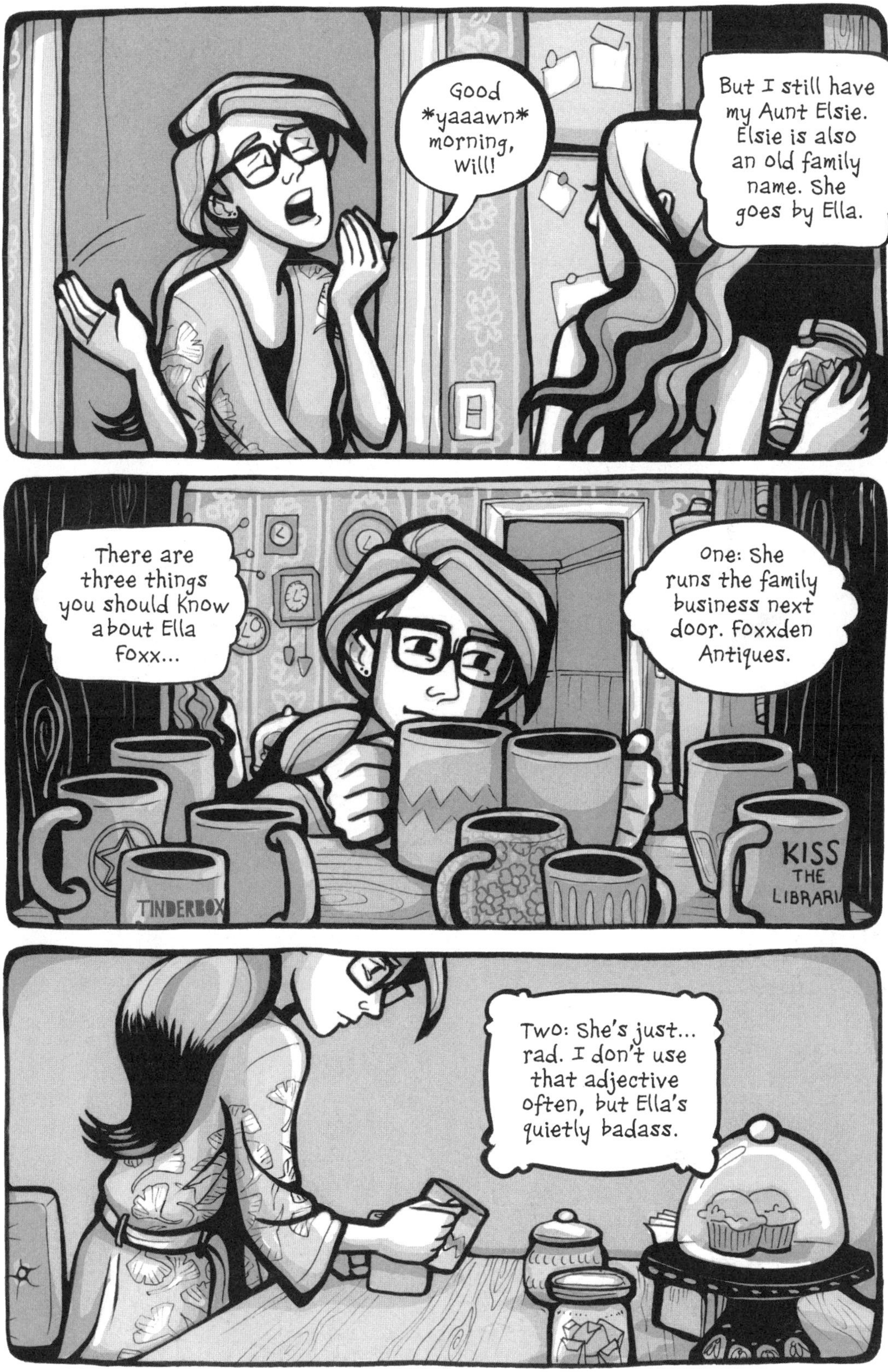
Good *yaaawn* morning, Will!
But I still have my Aunt Elsie. Elsie is also an old family name. She goes by Ella.
There are three things you should know about Ella Foxx...
One: She runs the family business next door. Foxxden Antiques.
TINDERBOX
KISS THE LIBRARI
Two: She's just... rad. I don't use that adjective often, but Ella's quietly badass.

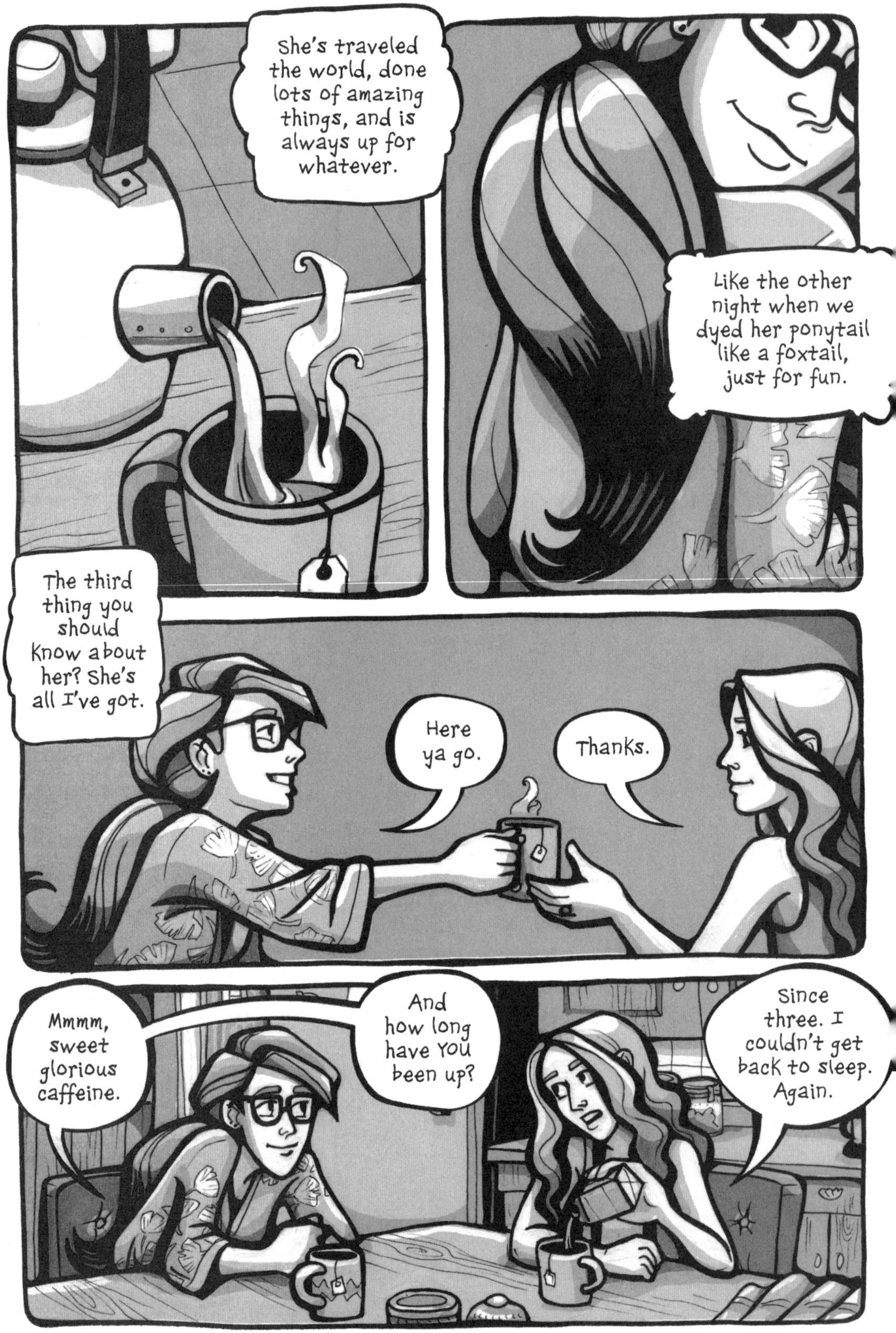
She's traveled the world, done lots of amazing things, and is always up for whatever.
Like the other night when we dyed her ponytail like a foxtail, just for fun.
The third thing you should know about her? She's all I've got.
Here ya go.
Thanks.
Mmmm, sweet glorious caffeine.
And how long have YOU been up?
Since three. I couldn't get back to sleep. Again.

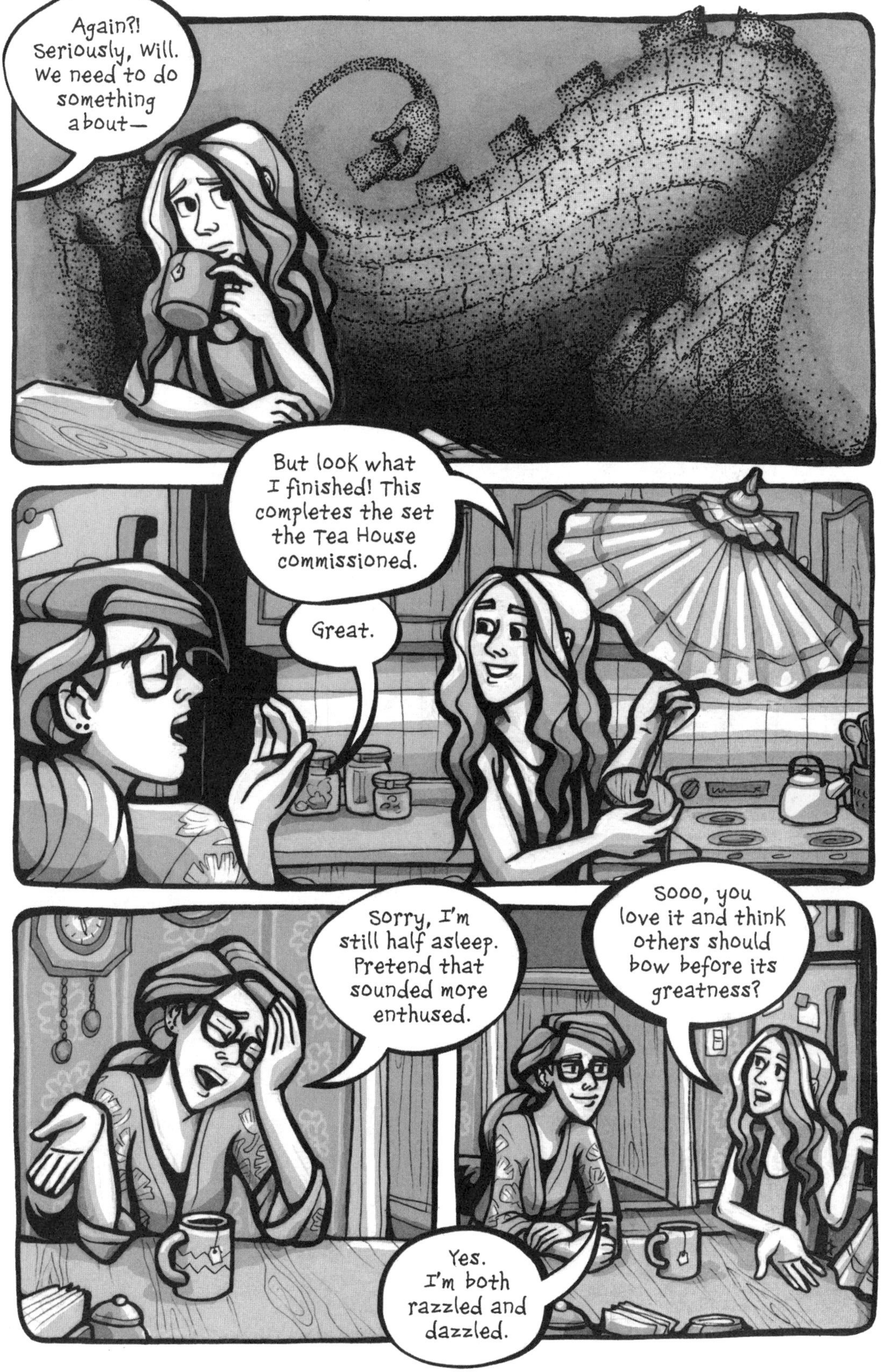
Again?! Seriously, Will. We need to do something about—
But look what I finished! This completes the set the Tea House commissioned.
Great.
Sorry, I'm still half asleep. Pretend that sounded more enthused.
Sooo, you love it and think others should bow before its greatness?
Yes. I'm both razzled and dazzled.

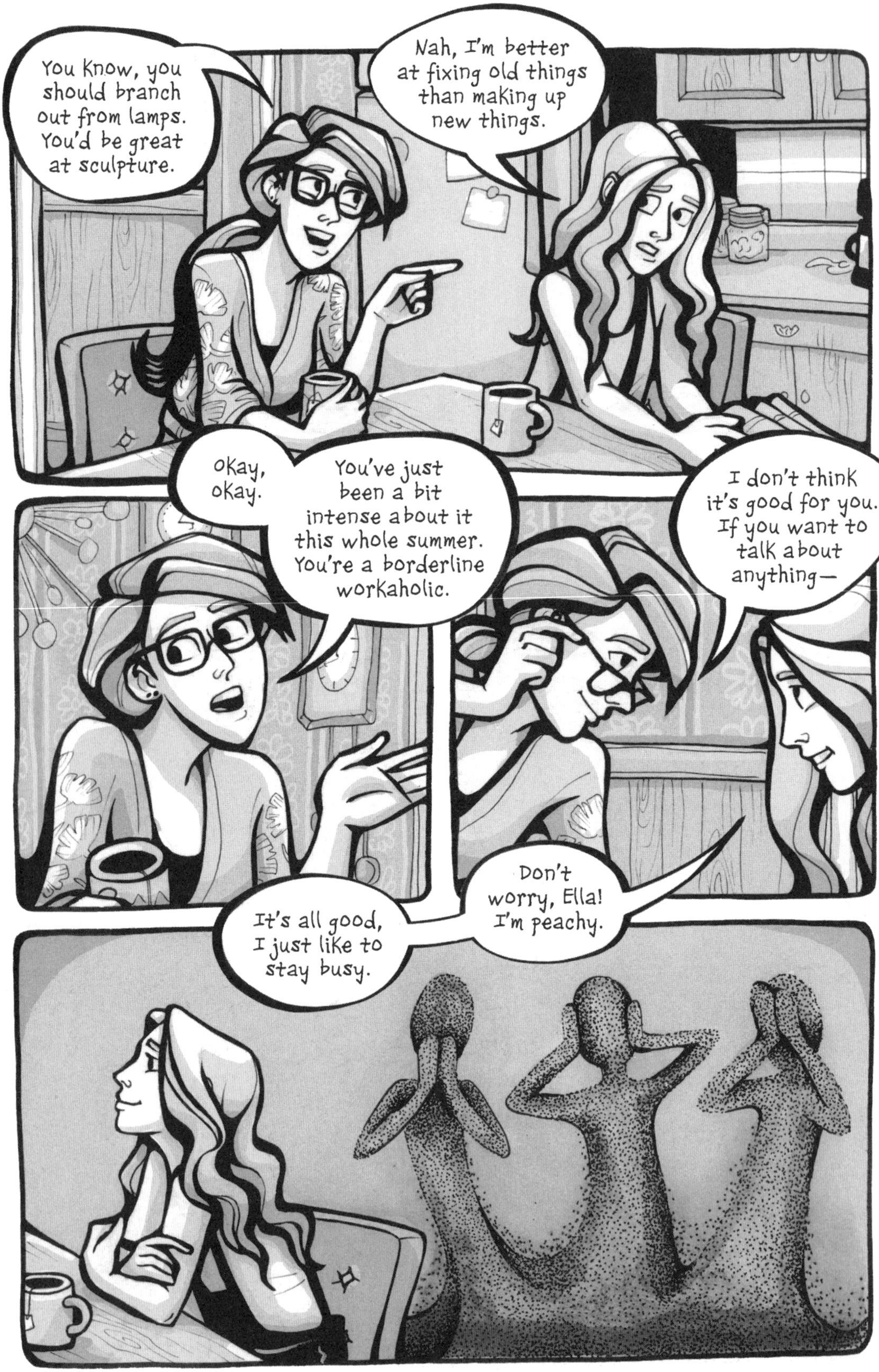
You Know, you should branch out from lamps. You'd be great at sculpture.
Nah, I'm better at fixing old things than making up new things.
Okay, okay.
You've just been a bit intense about it this whole summer. You're a borderline workaholic.
I don't think it's good for you. If you want to talk about anything—
Don't worry, Ella! I'm peachy.
It's all good, I just like to stay busy.

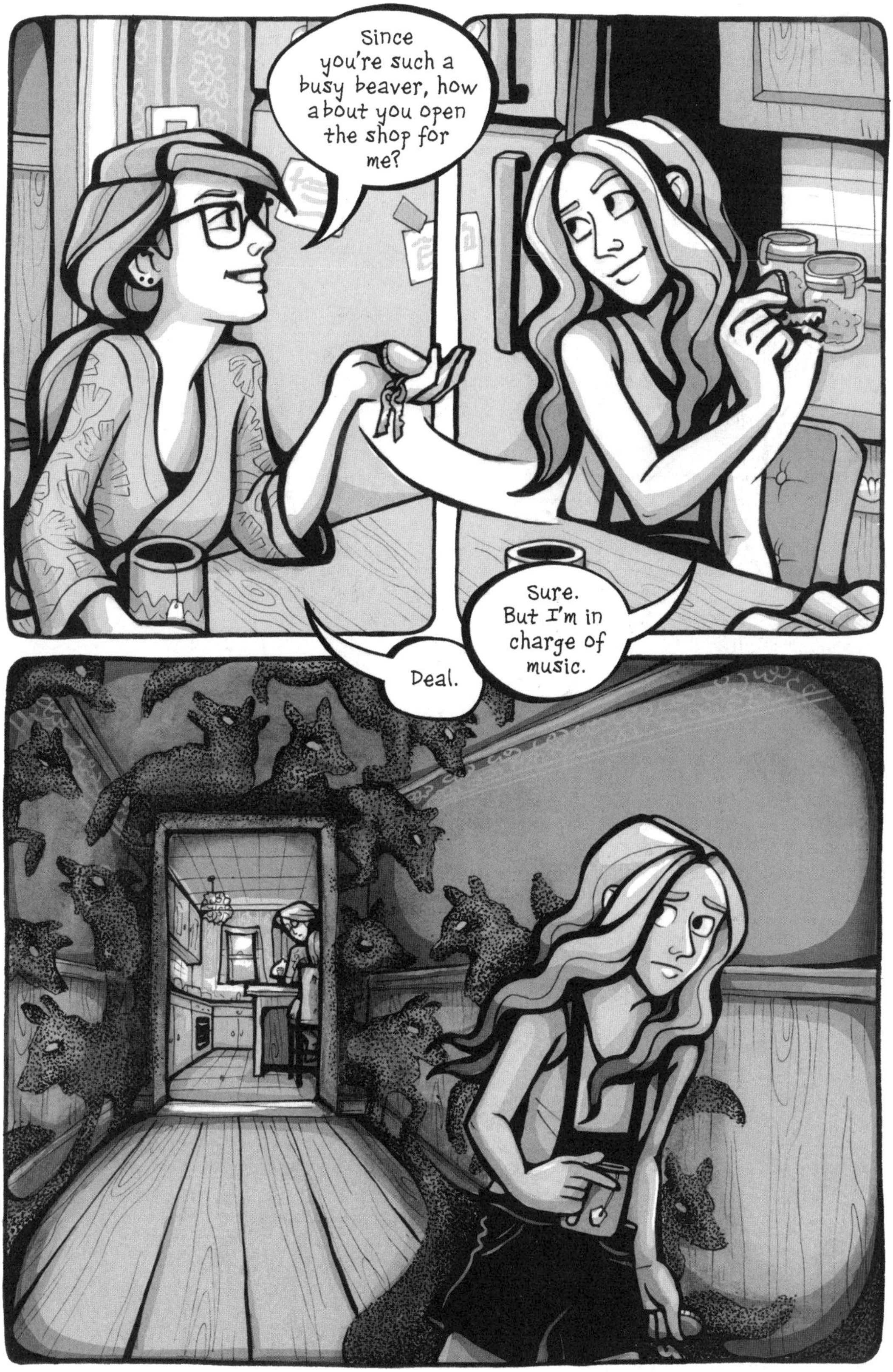
Since you're such a busy beaver, how about you open the shop for me?
Sure. But I'm in charge of music.
Deal.

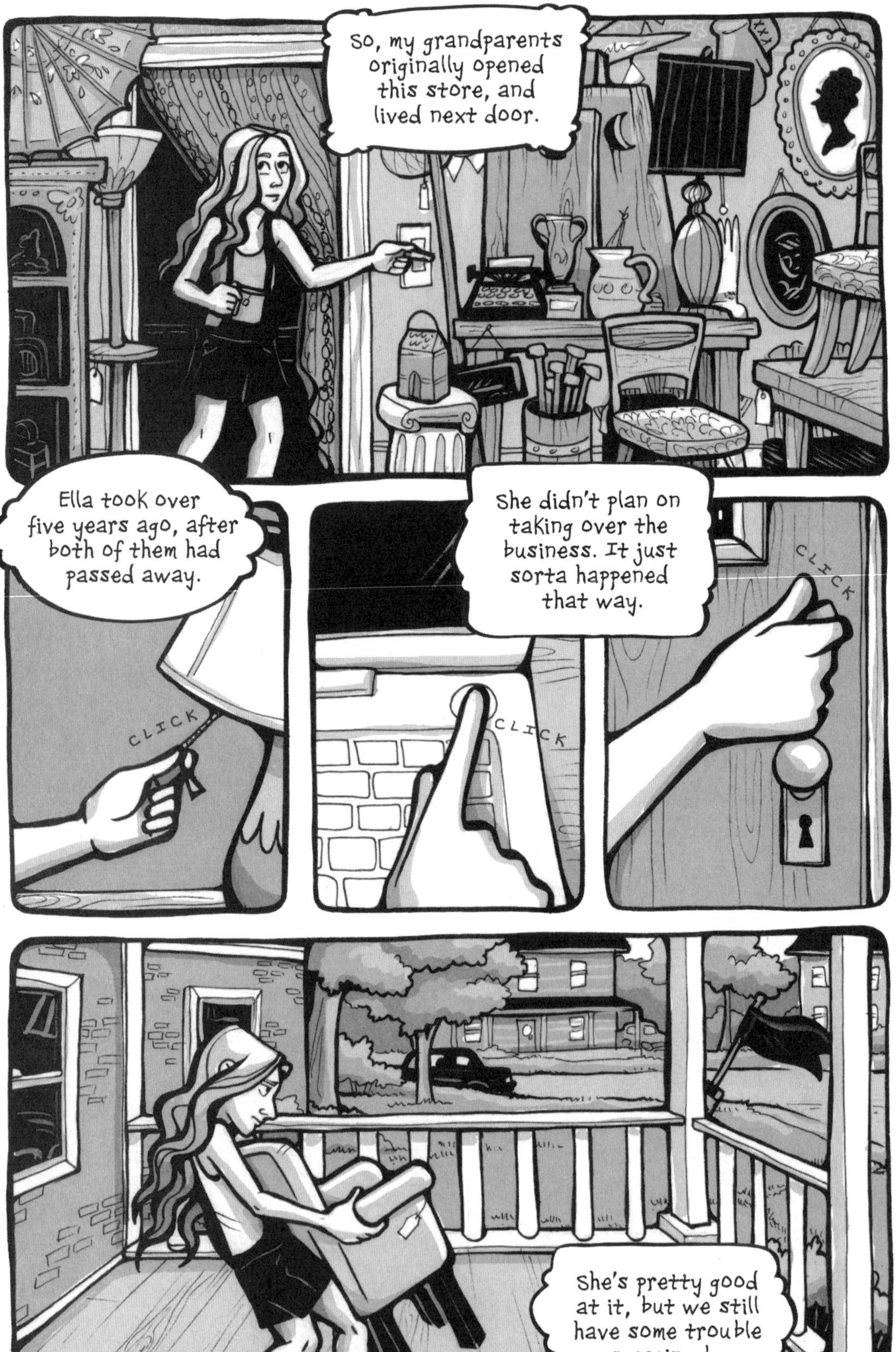
So, my grandparents originally opened this store, and lived next door.
Ella took over five years ago, after both of them had passed away.
CLICK
She didn't plan on taking over the business. It just sorta happened that way.
CLICK
CLICK
She's pretty good at it, but we still have some trouble scraping by.

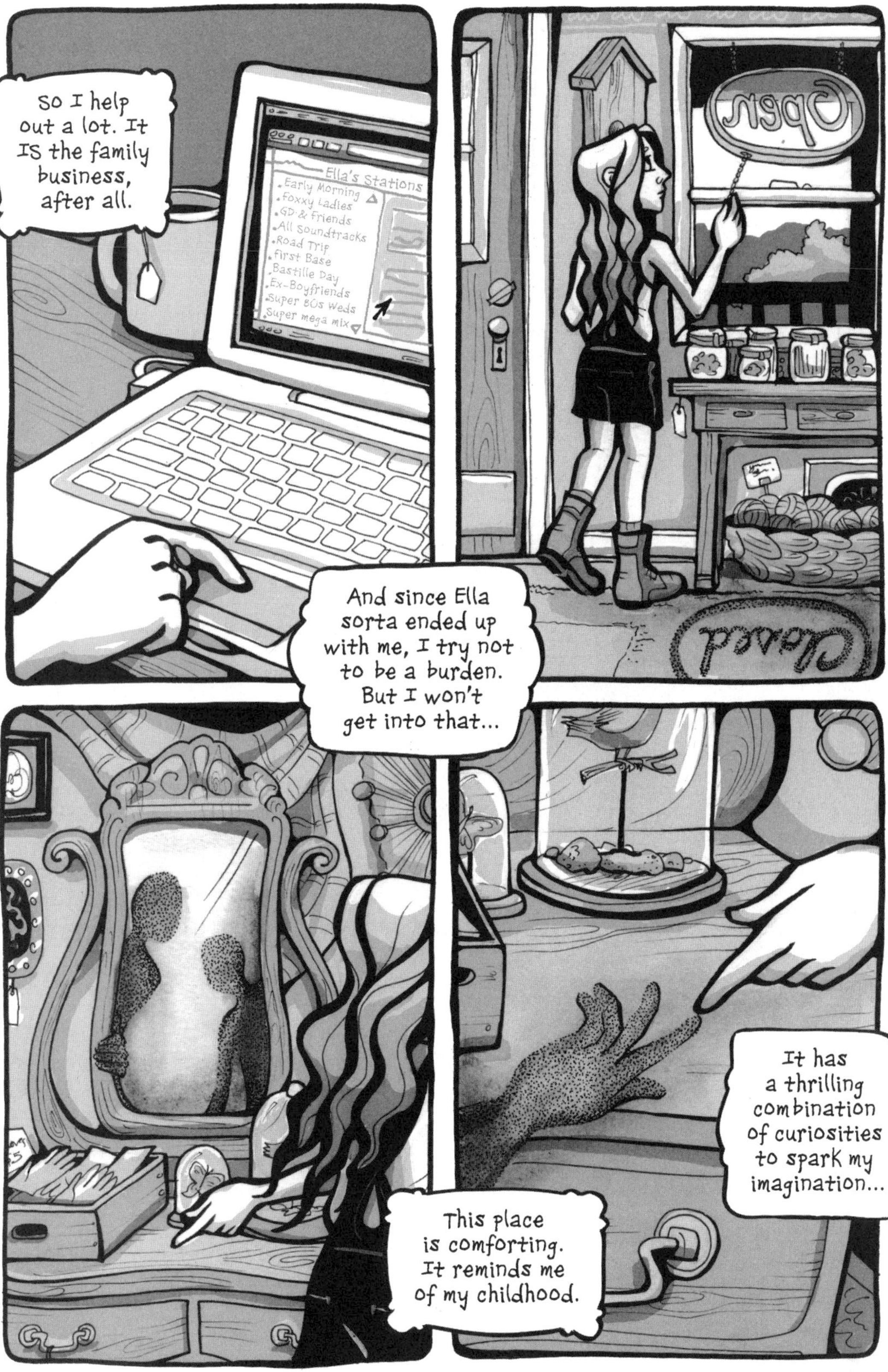
So I help out a lot. It IS the family business, after all.
Ella's Stations
Early Morning
Foxxy Ladies
GD & Friends
All Soundtracks
Road Trip
First Base
Bastille Day
Ex-Boyfriends
Super 80s Weds
Super mega mix
Open
Closed
And since Ella sorta ended up with me, I try not to be a burden. But I won't get into that...
This place is comforting. It reminds me of my childhood.
It has a thrilling combination of curiosities to spark my imagination...

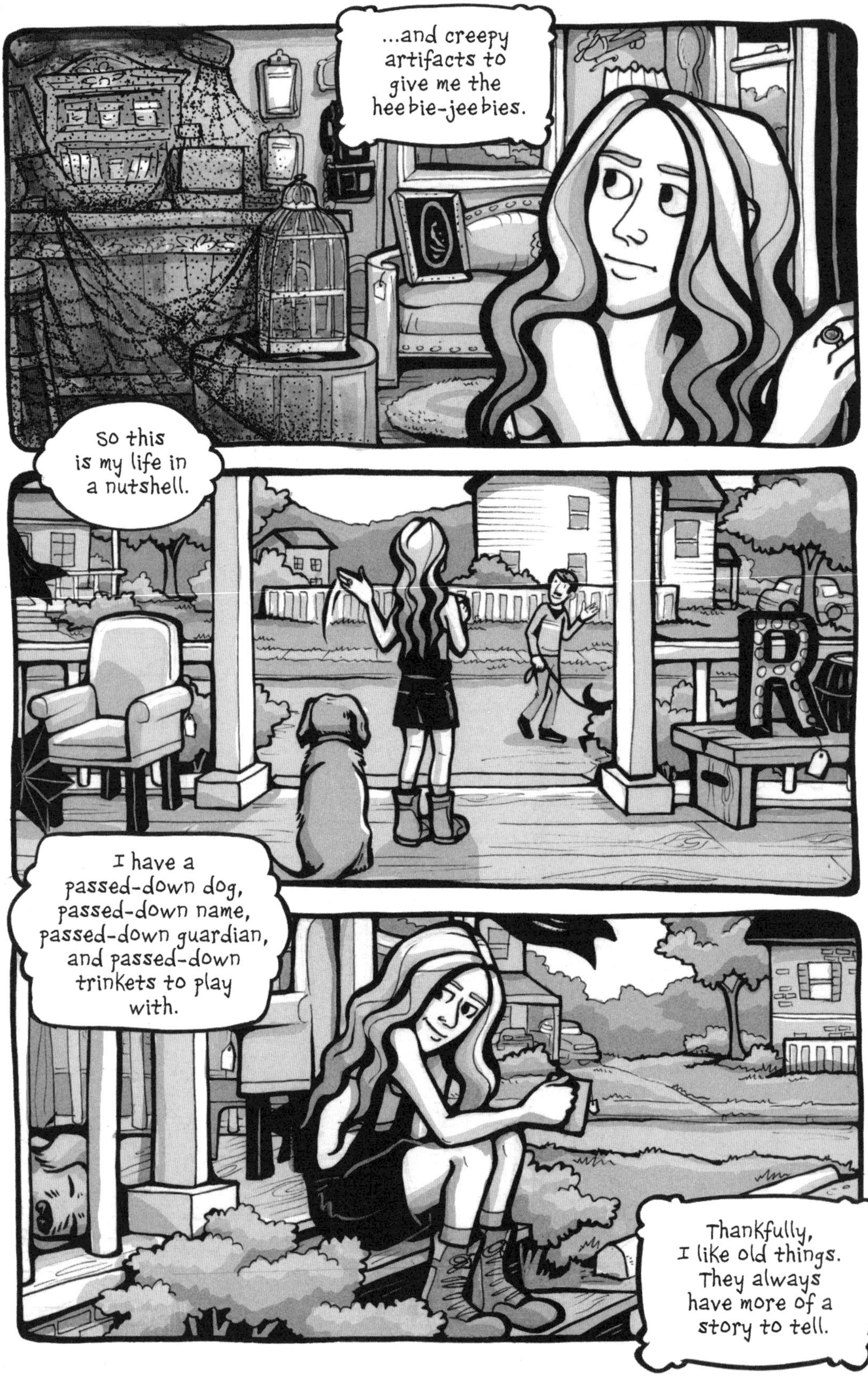
...and creepy artifacts to give me the heebie-jeebies.
So this is my life in a nutshell.
I have a passed-down dog, passed-down name, passed-down guardian, and passed-down trinkets to play with.
Thankfully, I like old things. They always have more of a story to tell.

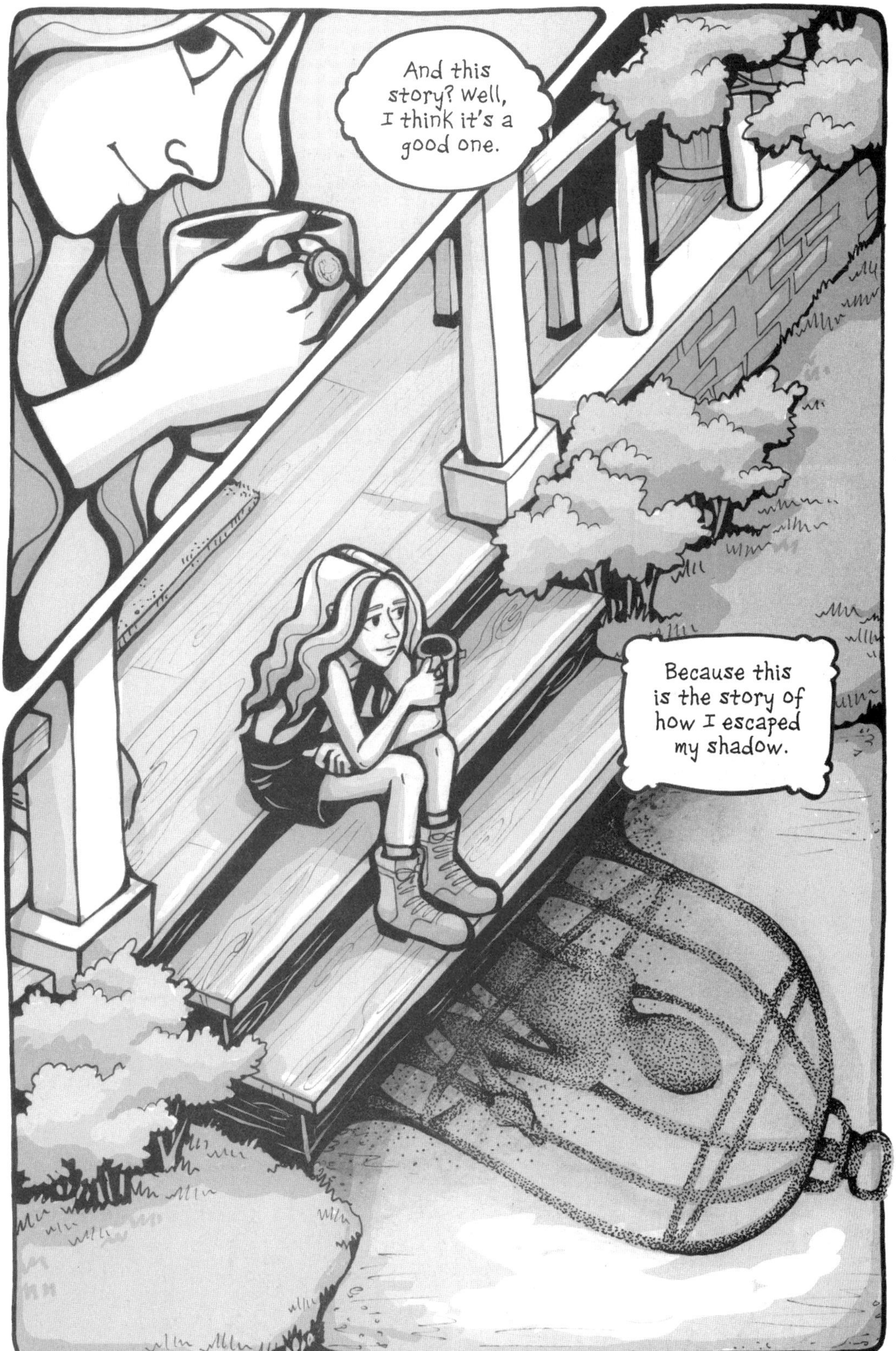
And this story? Well, I think it's a good one.
Because this is the story of how I escaped my shadow.

Bright Ideas

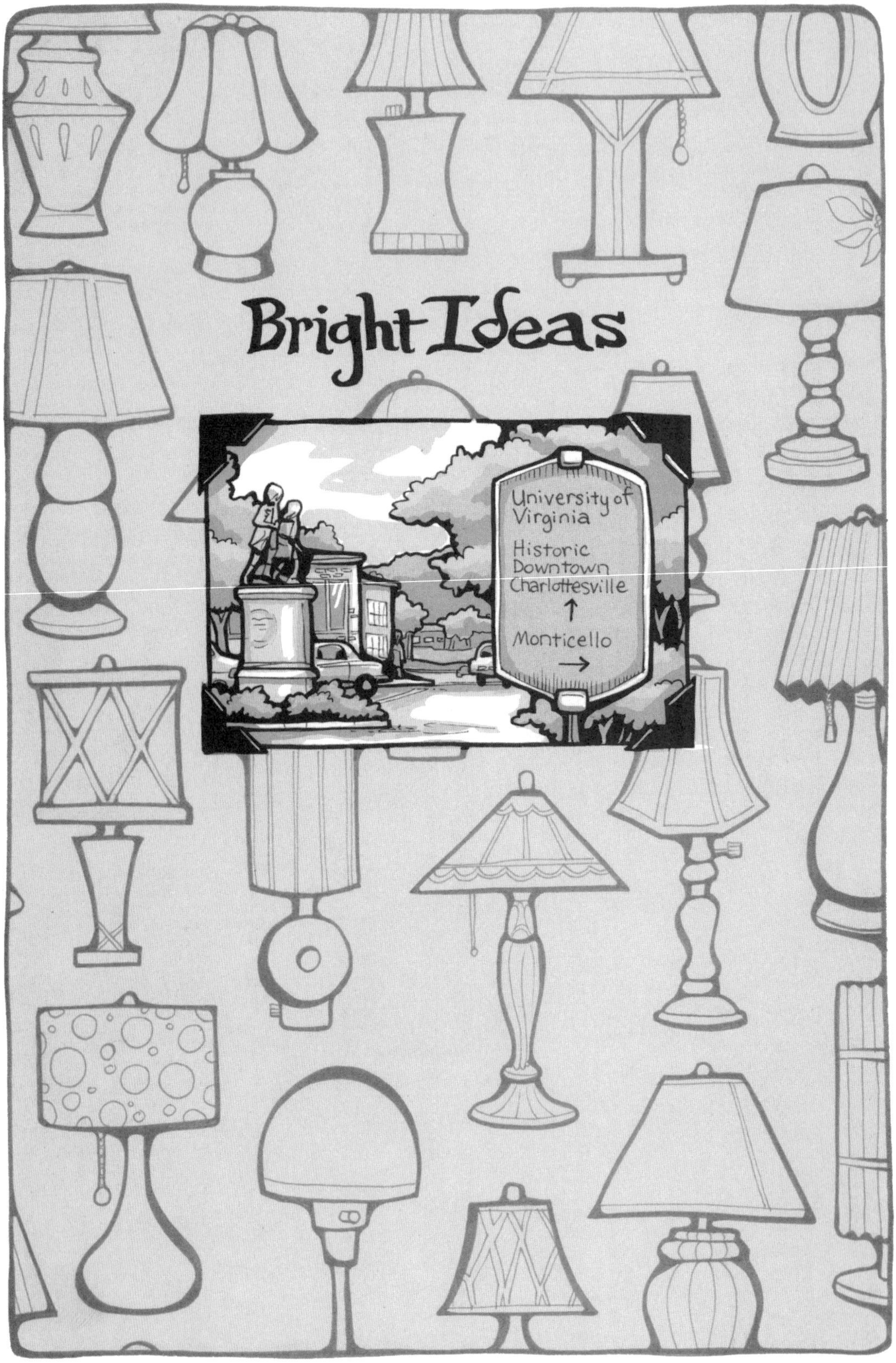
University of Virginia
Historic Downtown Charlottesville ↑
Monticello →

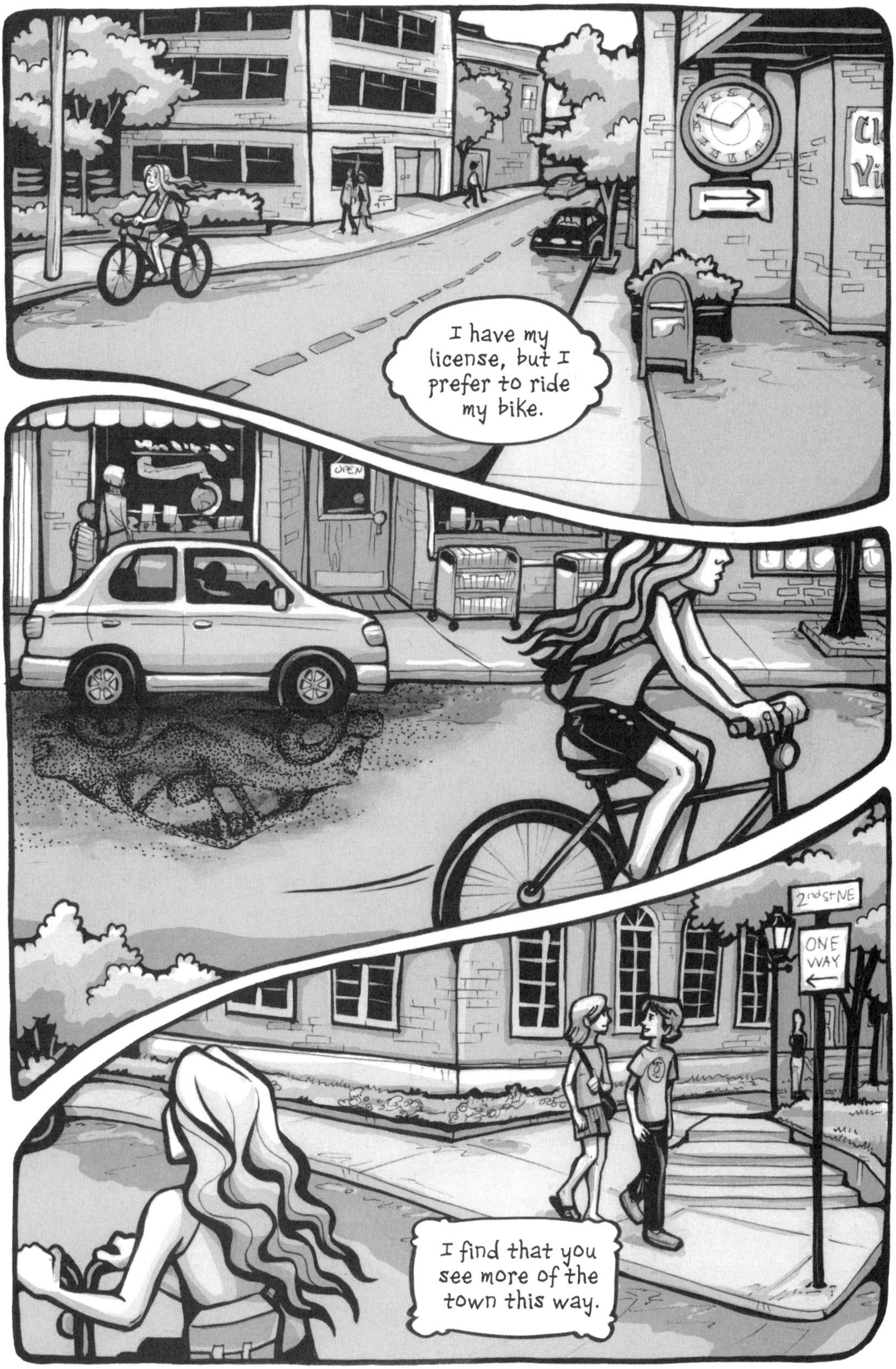
I have my license, but I prefer to ride my bike.
OPEN
2nd st NE
ONE WAY
I find that you see more of the town this way.

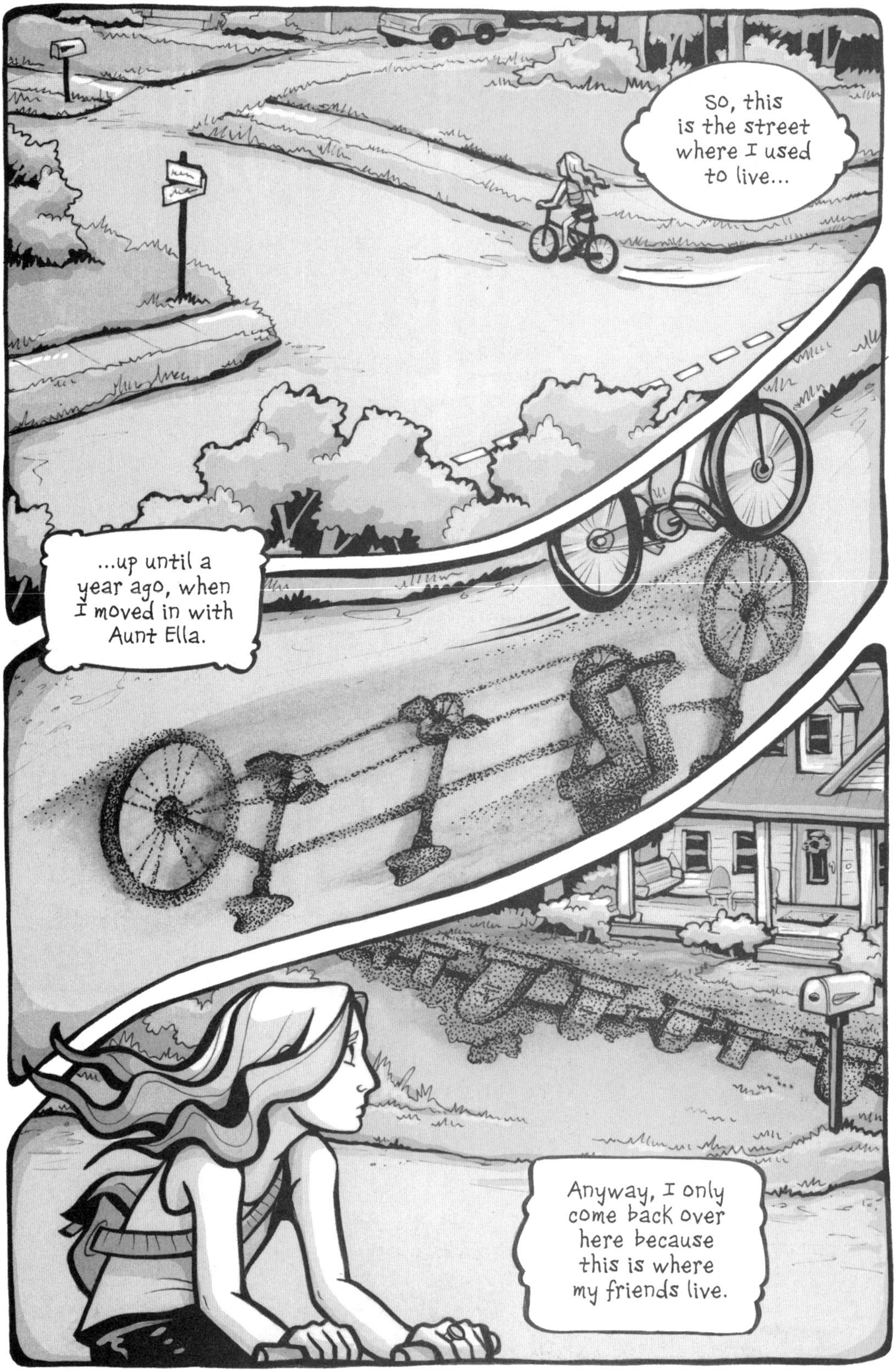
So, this is the street where I used to live...
...up until a year ago, when I moved in with Aunt Ella.
Anyway, I only come back over here because this is where my friends live.

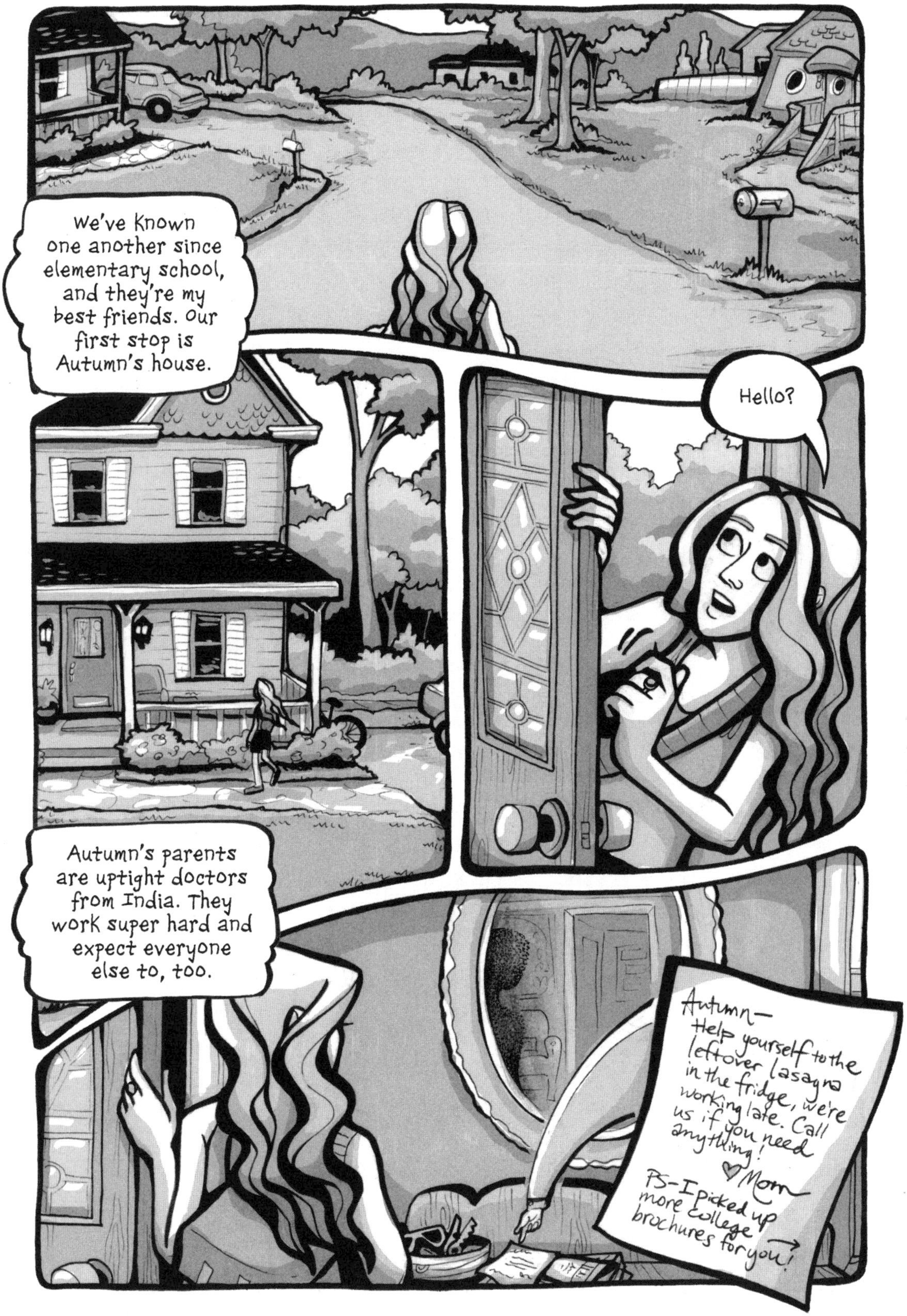
We've known one another since elementary school, and they're my best friends. Our first stop is Autumn's house.
Hello?
Autumn's parents are uptight doctors from India. They work super hard and expect everyone else to, too.
Autumn— Help yourself to the leftover lasagna in the fridge, we're working late. Call us if you need anything! ♥ Mom
PS—I picked up more college brochures for you!

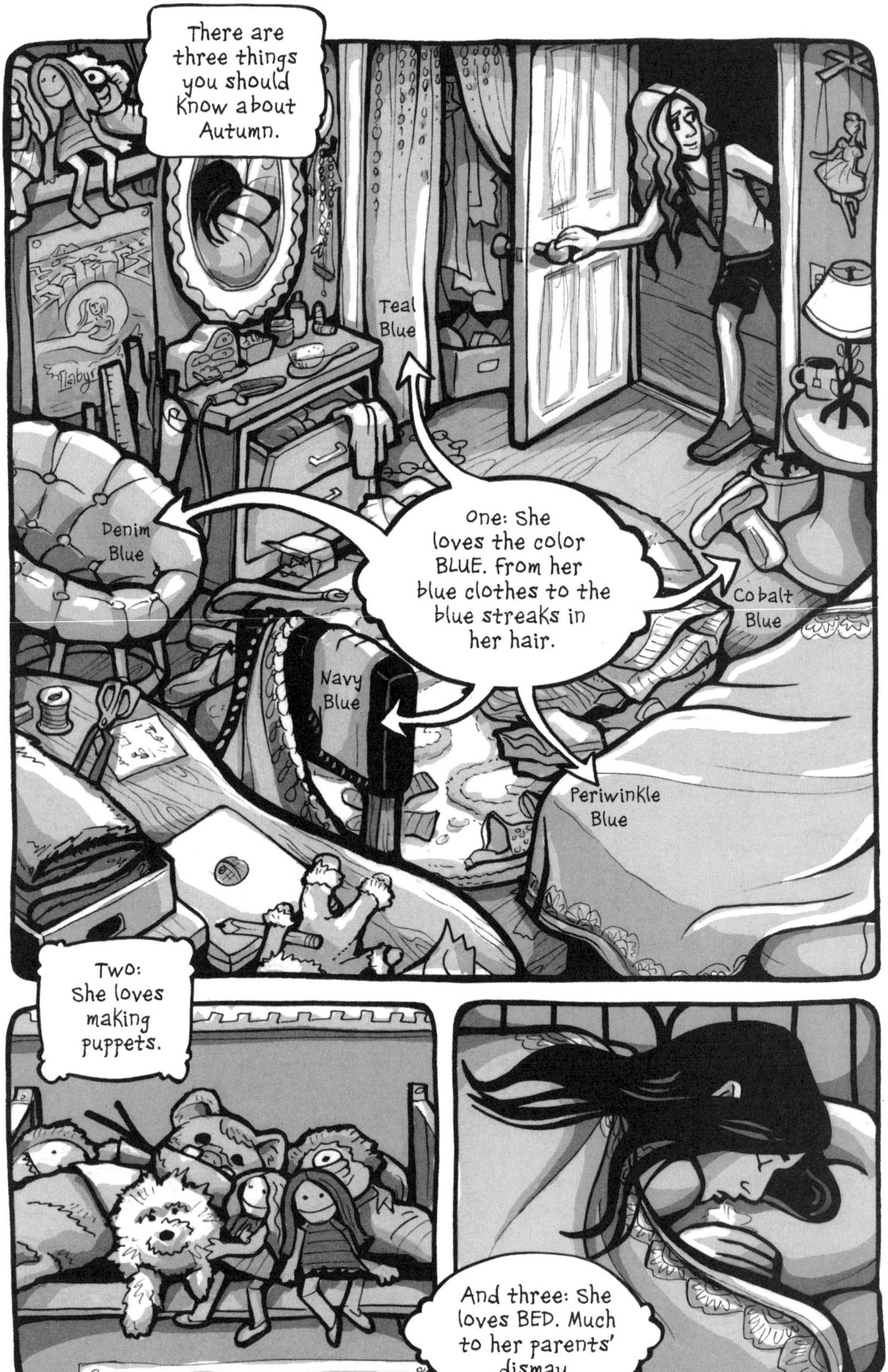
There are three things you should know about Autumn.
Teal Blue
Denim Blue
One: She loves the color BLUE. From her blue clothes to the blue streaks in her hair.
Cobalt Blue
Navy Blue
Periwinkle Blue
Two: She loves making puppets.
And three: She loves BED. Much to her parents' dismay.

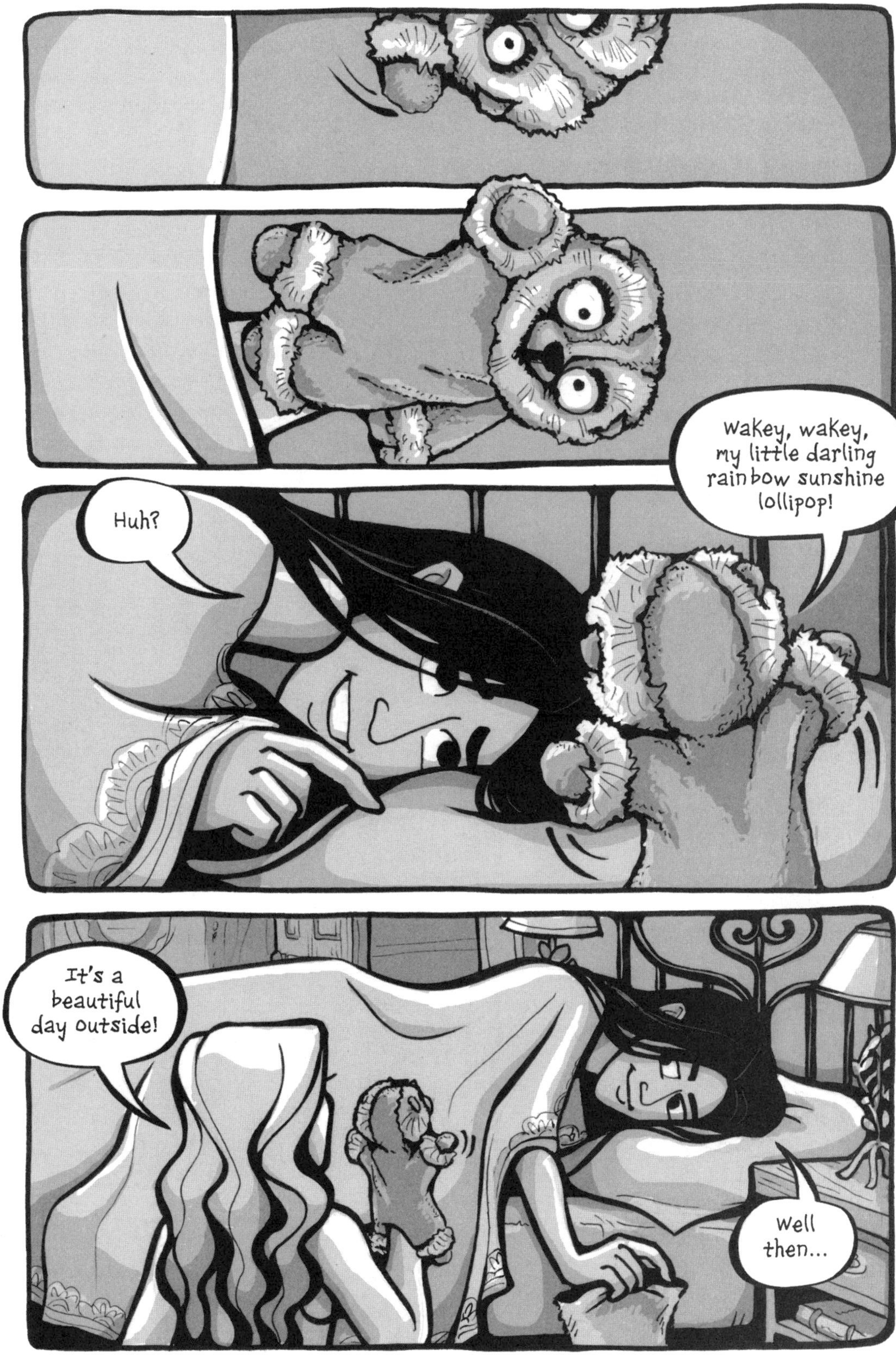
Wakey, wakey, my little darling rainbow sunshine lollipop!
Huh?
It's a beautiful day outside!
Well then...

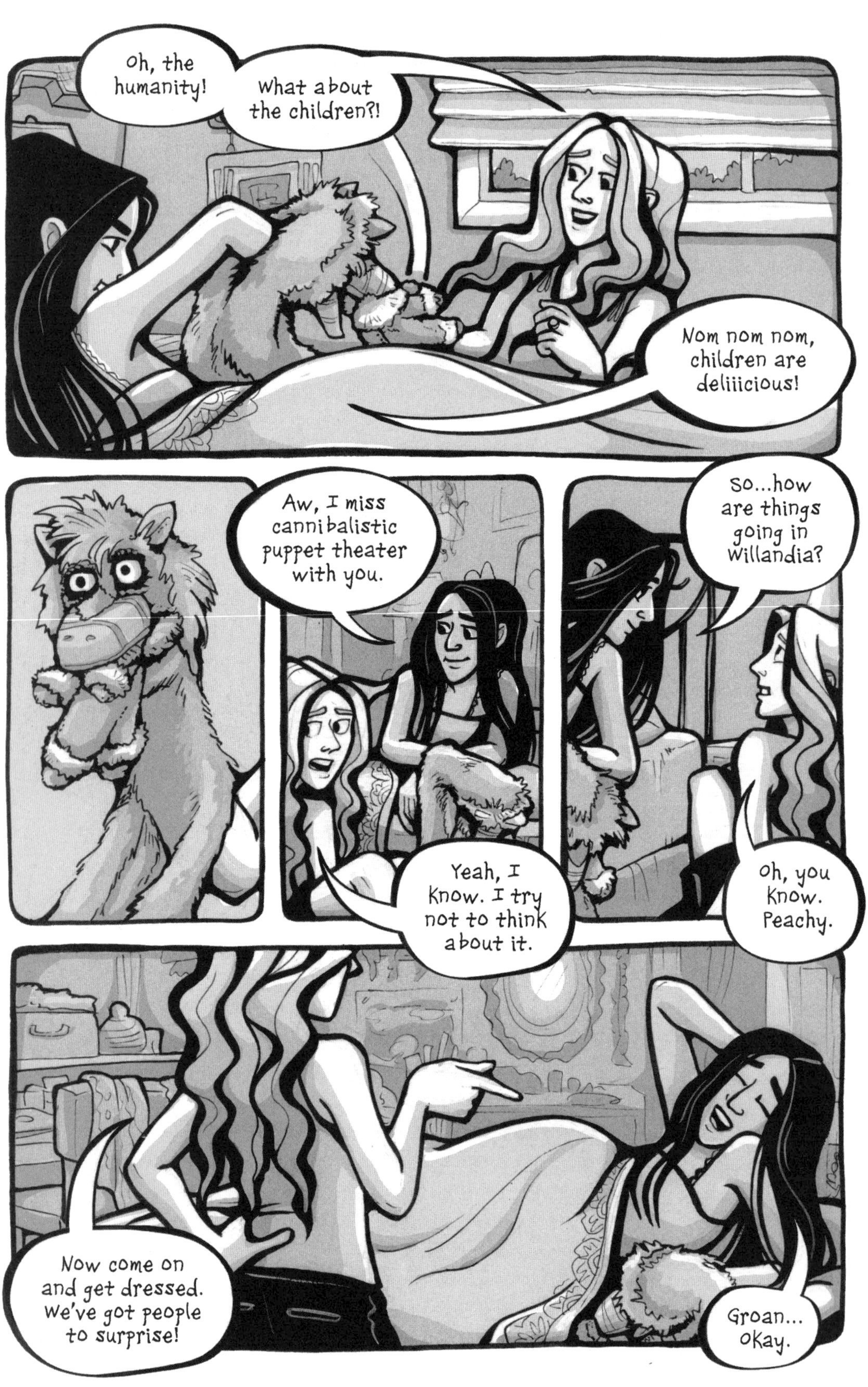

Oh, the humanity!
What about the children?!
Nom nom nom, children are deliiicious!
Aw, I miss cannibalistic puppet theater with you.
Yeah, I know. I try not to think about it.
So...how are things going in Willandia?
Oh, you know. Peachy.
Now come on and get dressed. We've got people to surprise!
Groan... Okay.

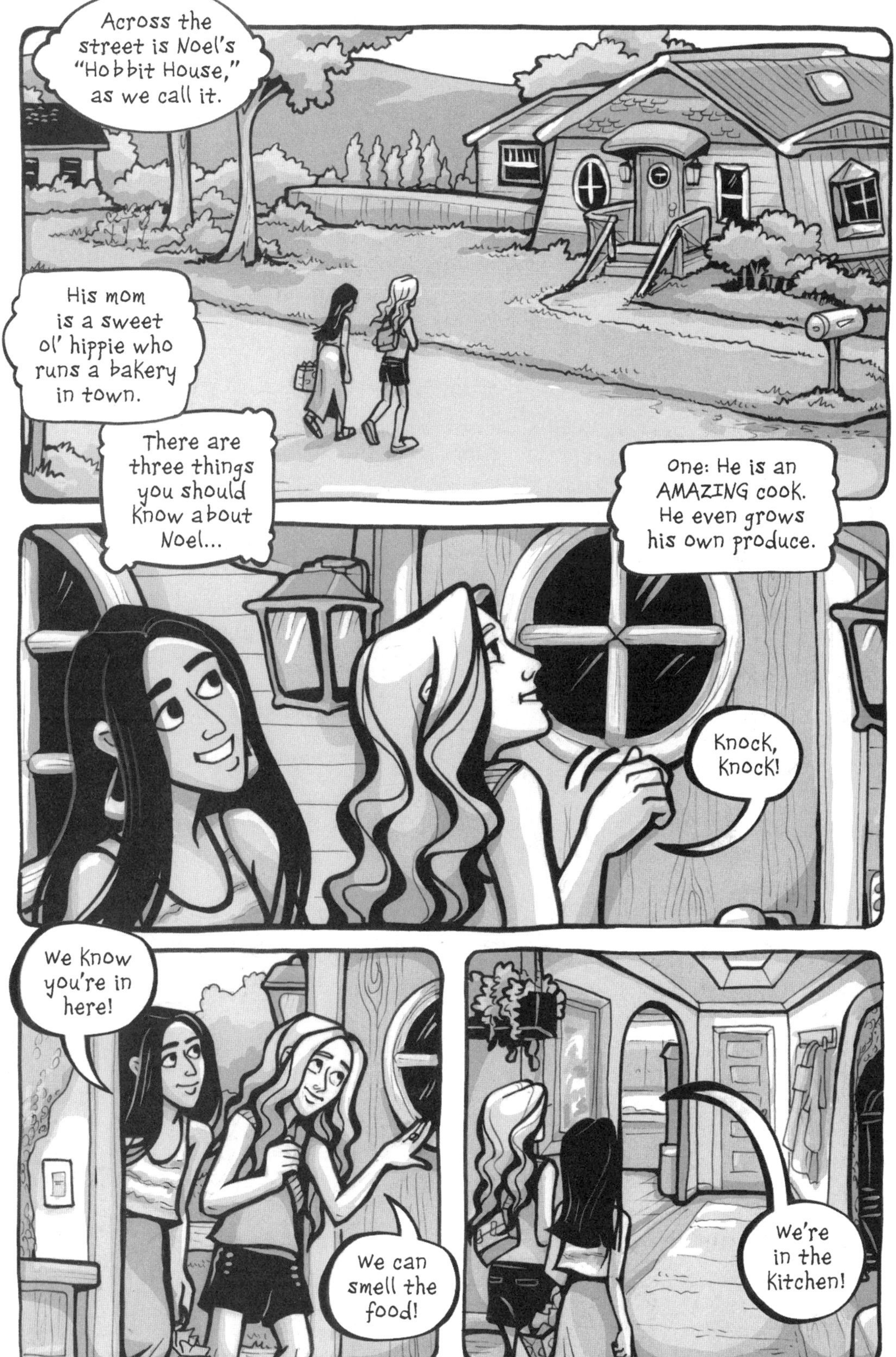
Across the street is Noel's "Hobbit House," as we call it.
His mom is a sweet ol' hippie who runs a bakery in town.
There are three things you should know about Noel...
One: He is an AMAZING cook. He even grows his own produce.
Knock, knock!
We know you're in here!
We can smell the food!
We're in the kitchen!

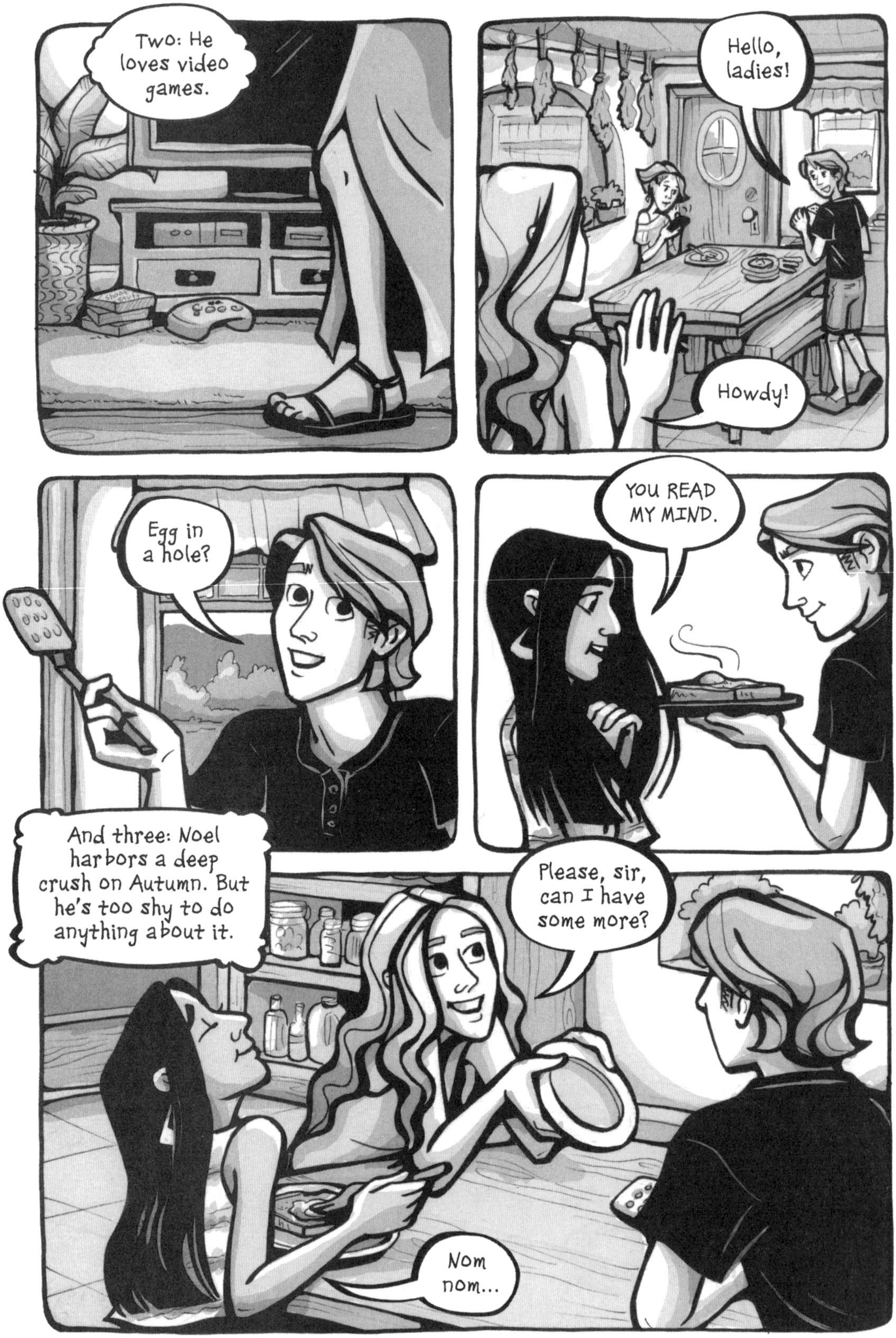
Two: He loves video games.
Hello, ladies!
Howdy!
Egg in a hole?
YOU READ MY MIND.
And three: Noel harbors a deep crush on Autumn. But he's too shy to do anything about it.
Please, sir, can I have some more?
Nom nom...

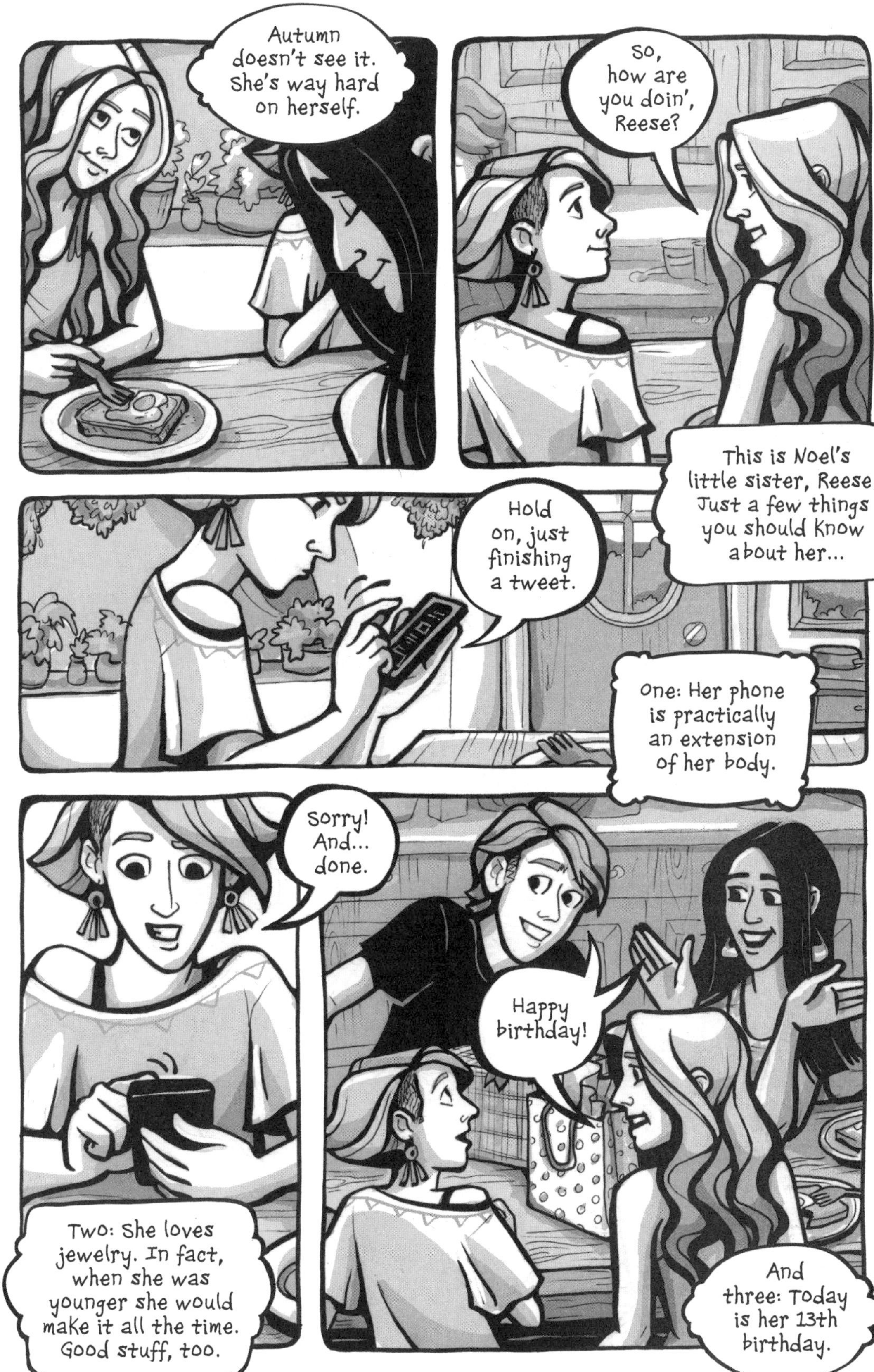
Autumn doesn't see it. She's way hard on herself.
So, how are you doin', Reese?
This is Noel's little sister, Reese. Just a few things you should know about her...
Hold on, just finishing a tweet.
One: Her phone is practically an extension of her body.
Sorry! And... done.
Two: She loves jewelry. In fact, when she was younger she would make it all the time. Good stuff, too.
Happy birthday!
And three: Today is her 13th birthday.

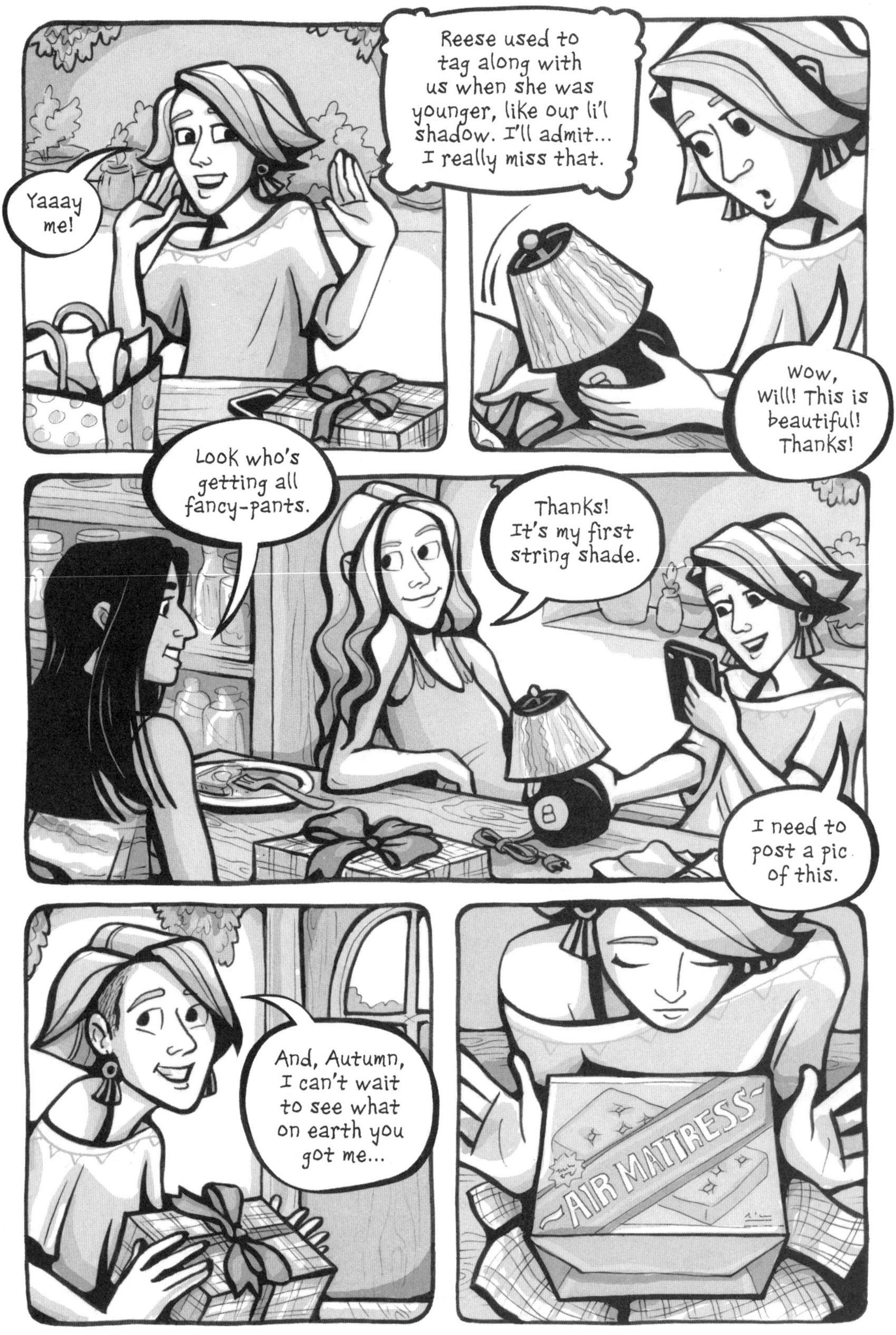
Yaaay me!
Reese used to tag along with us when she was younger, like our li'l shadow. I'll admit... I really miss that.
Wow, Will! This is beautiful! Thanks!
Look who's getting all fancy-pants.
Thanks! It's my first string shade.
I need to post a pic of this.
And, Autumn, I can't wait to see what on earth you got me...
AIR MATTRESS

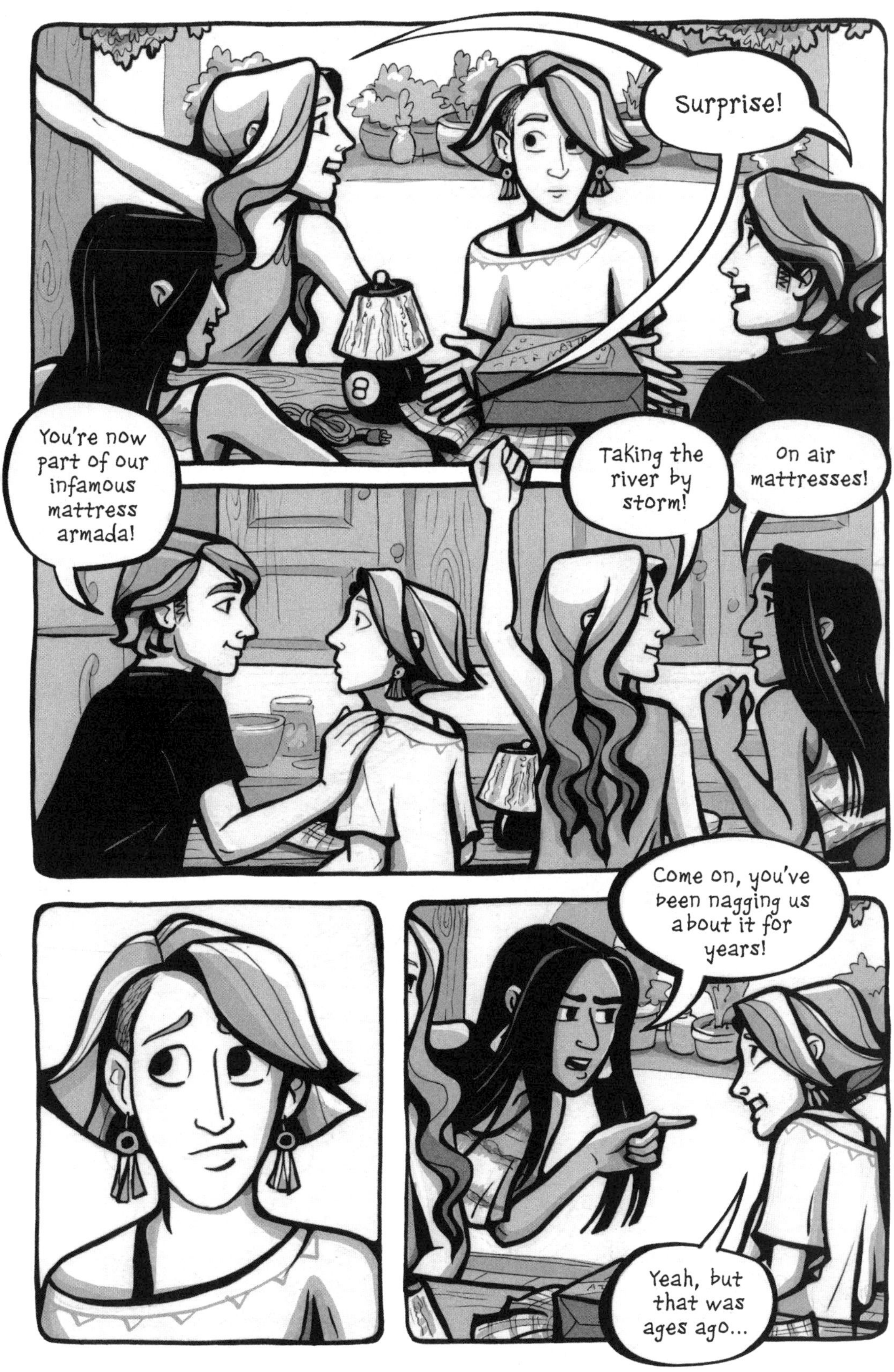
Surprise!
You're now part of our infamous mattress armada!
Taking the river by storm!
On air mattresses!
Come on, you've been nagging us about it for years!
Yeah, but that was ages ago...

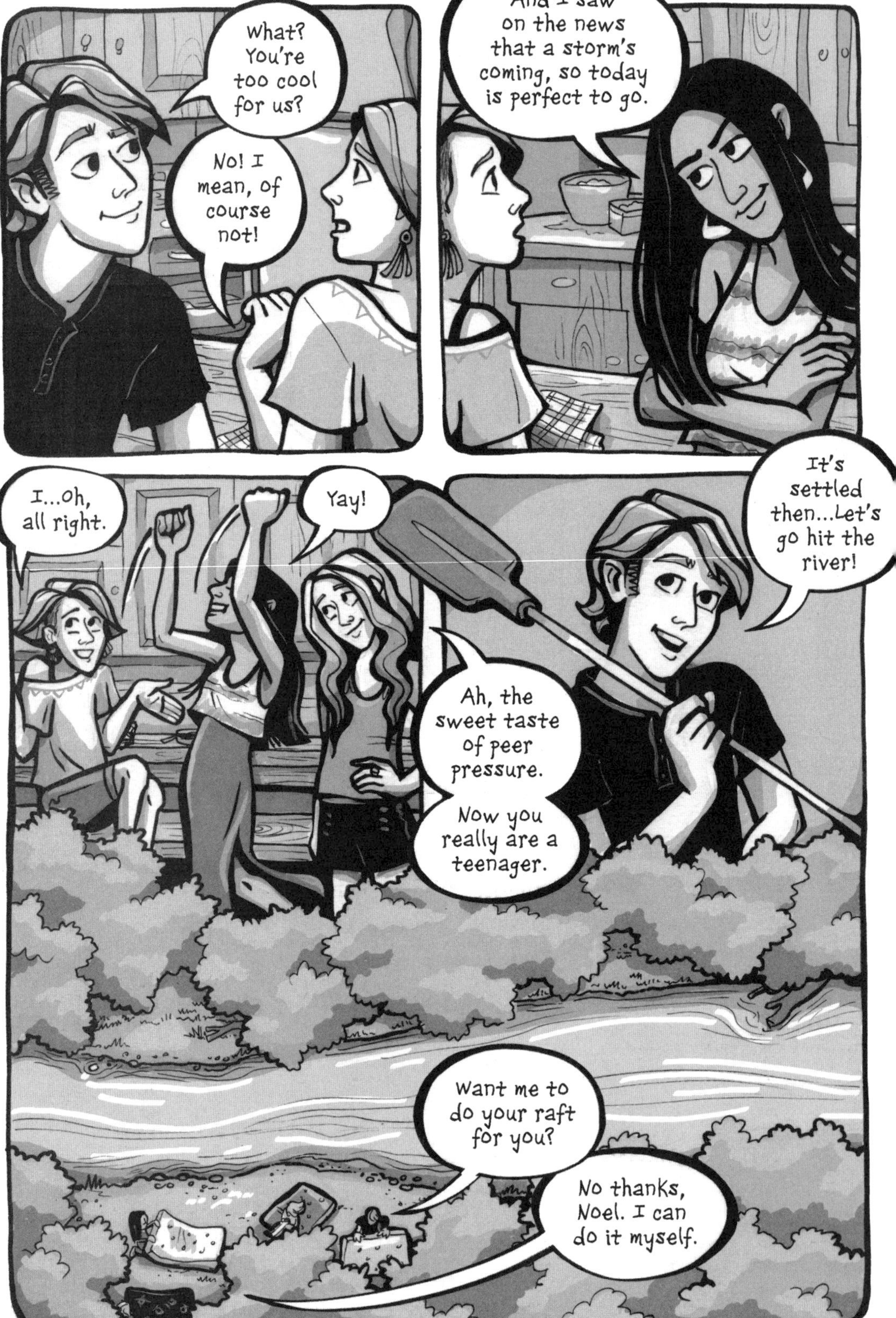
What? You're too cool for us?
No! I mean, of course not!
And I saw on the news that a storm's coming, so today is perfect to go.
I...oh, all right.
Yay!
It's settled then...Let's go hit the river!
Ah, the sweet taste of peer pressure.
Now you really are a teenager.
Want me to do your raft for you?
No thanks, Noel. I can do it myself.

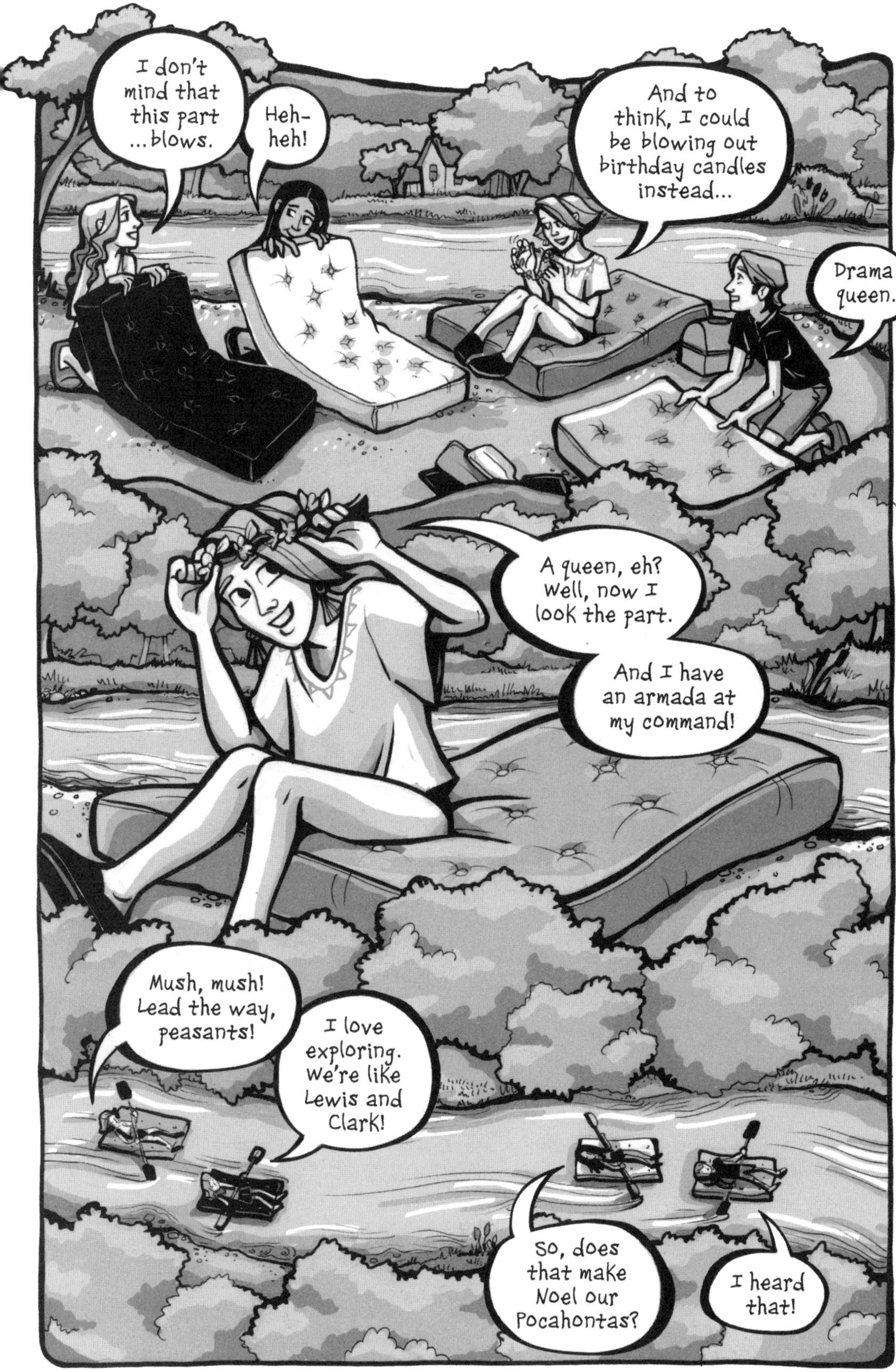

I don't mind that this part ...blows.
Heh-heh!
And to think, I could be blowing out birthday candles instead...
Drama queen.
A queen, eh? Well, now I look the part.
And I have an armada at my command!
Mush, mush! Lead the way, peasants!
I love exploring. We're like Lewis and Clark!
So, does that make Noel our Pocahontas?
I heard that!

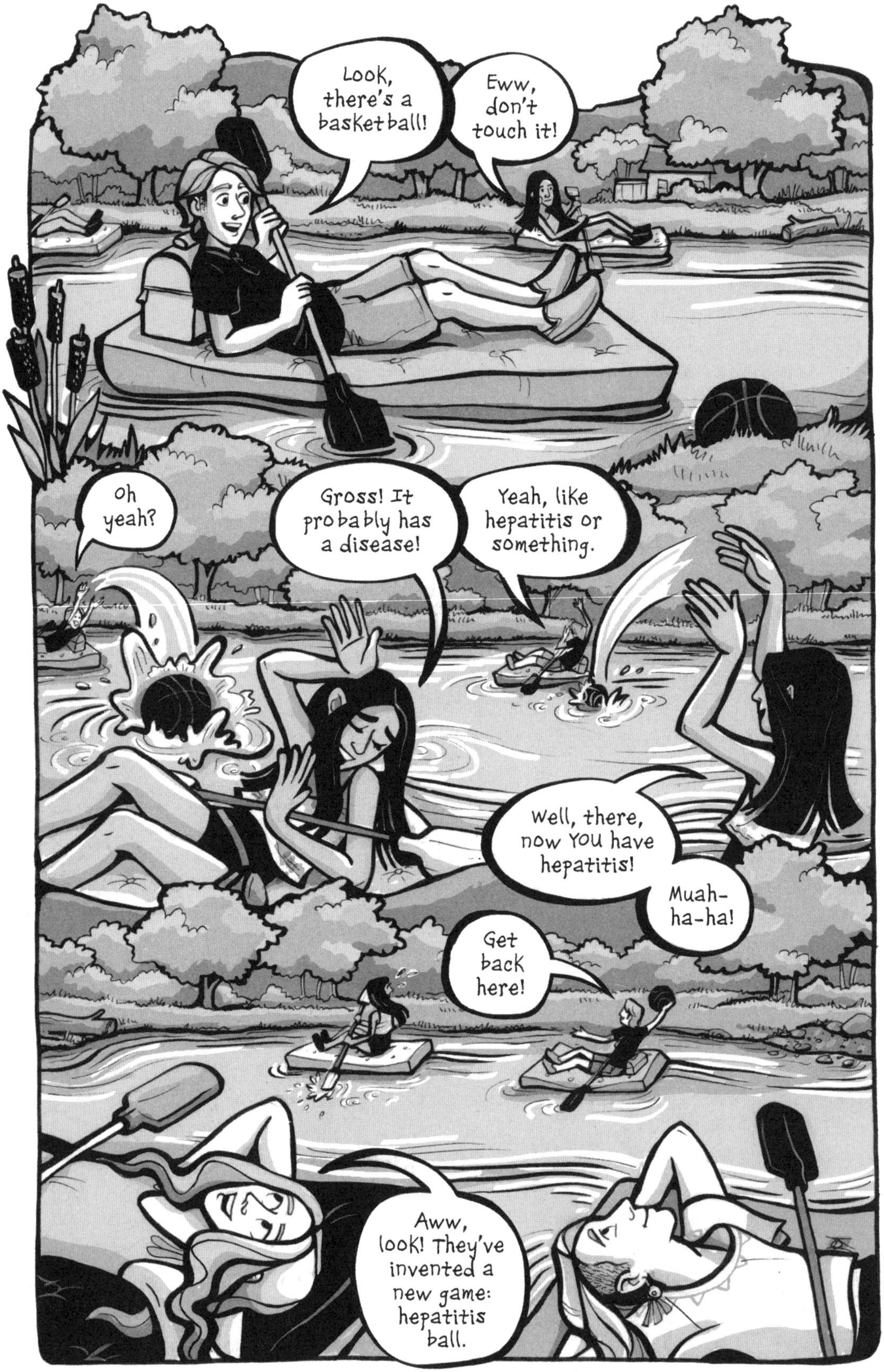
Look, there's a basketball!
Eww, don't touch it!
Oh yeah?
Gross! It probably has a disease!
Yeah, like hepatitis or something.
Well, there, now YOU have hepatitis!
Muah-ha-ha!
Get back here!
Aww, look! They've invented a new game: hepatitis ball.

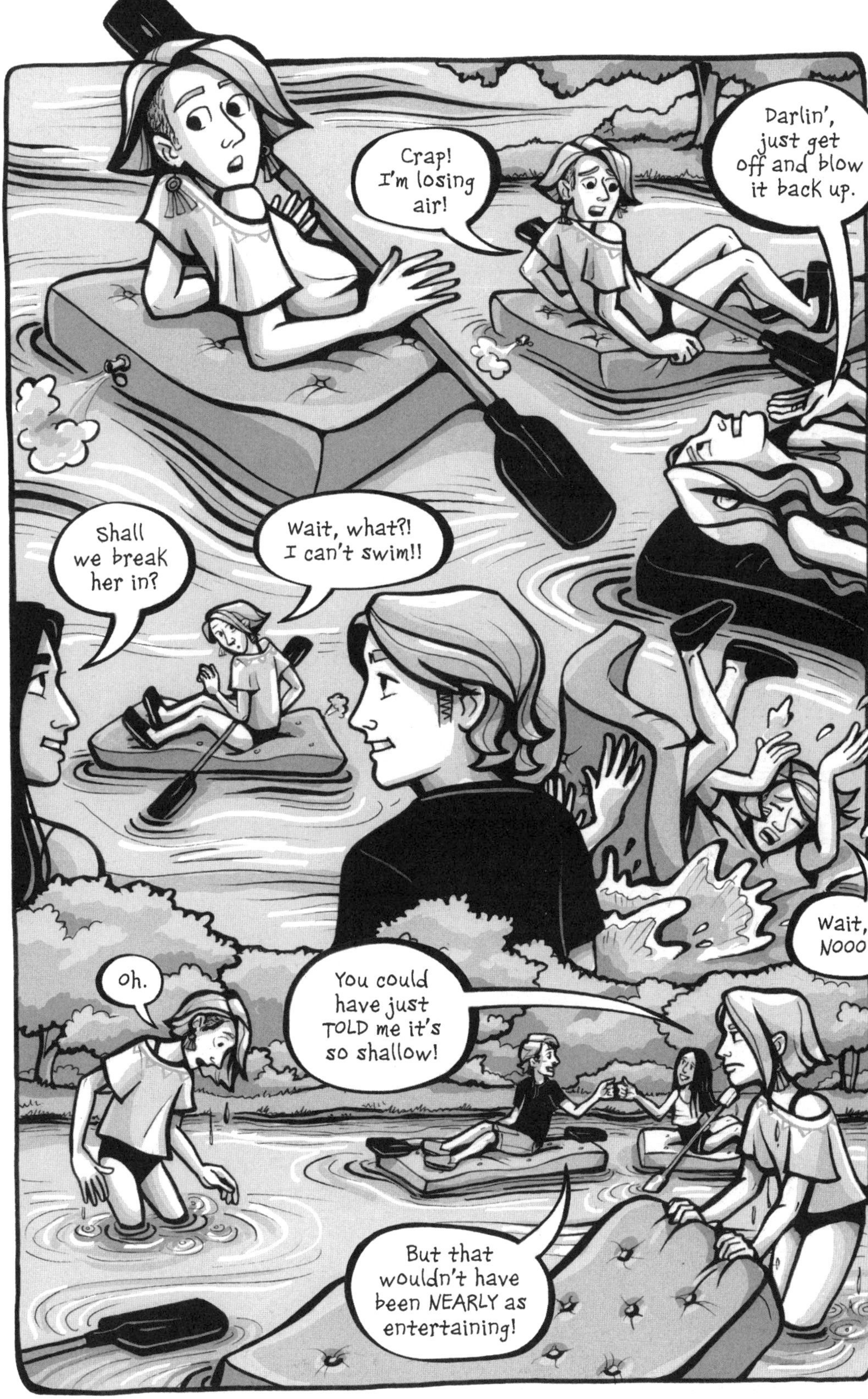
Crap! I'm losing air!
Darlin', just get off and blow it back up.
Shall we break her in?
Wait, what?! I can't swim!!
Wait, NOOO!
Oh.
You could have just TOLD me it's so shallow!
But that wouldn't have been NEARLY as entertaining!

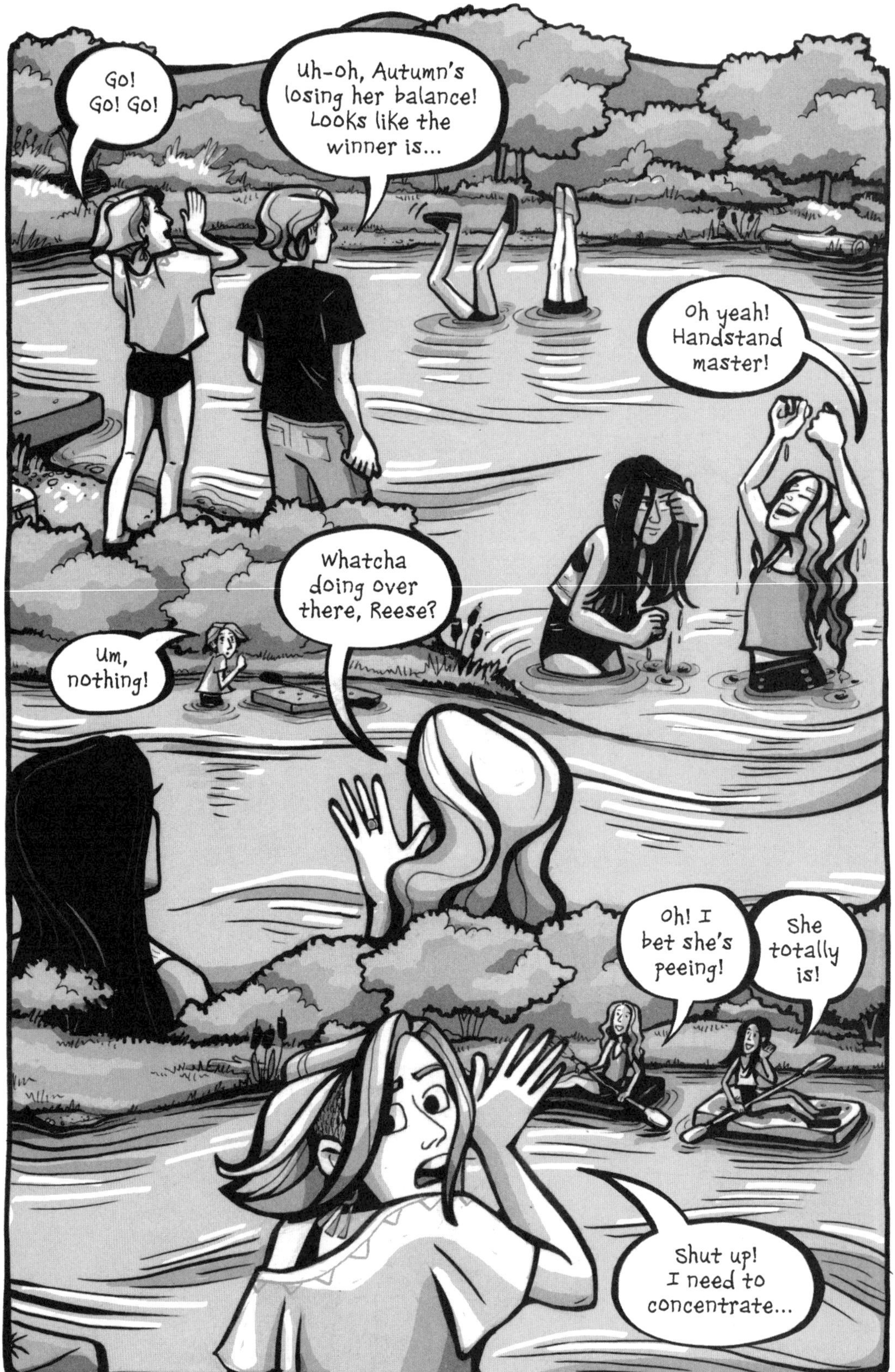
Go! Go! Go!
Uh-oh, Autumn's losing her balance! Looks like the winner is...
Oh yeah! Handstand master!
Whatcha doing over there, Reese?
Um, nothing!
Oh! I bet she's peeing!
She totally is!
Shut up! I need to concentrate...

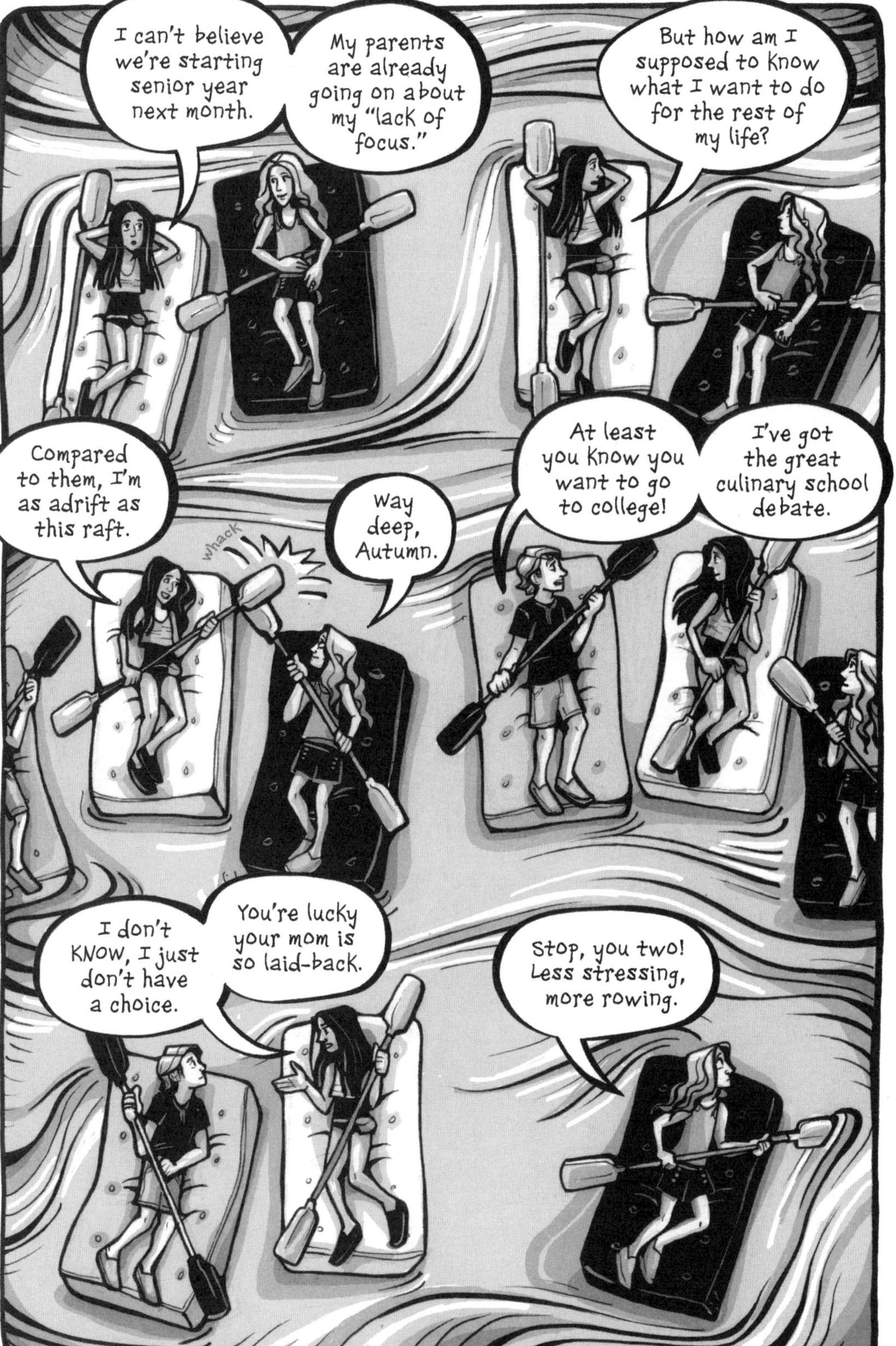
I can't believe we're starting senior year next month.
My parents are already going on about my "lack of focus."
But how am I supposed to know what I want to do for the rest of my life?
Compared to them, I'm as adrift as this raft.
whack
Way deep, Autumn.
At least you know you want to go to college!
I've got the great culinary school debate.
I don't KNOW, I just don't have a choice.
You're lucky your mom is so laid-back.
Stop, you two! Less stressing, more rowing.

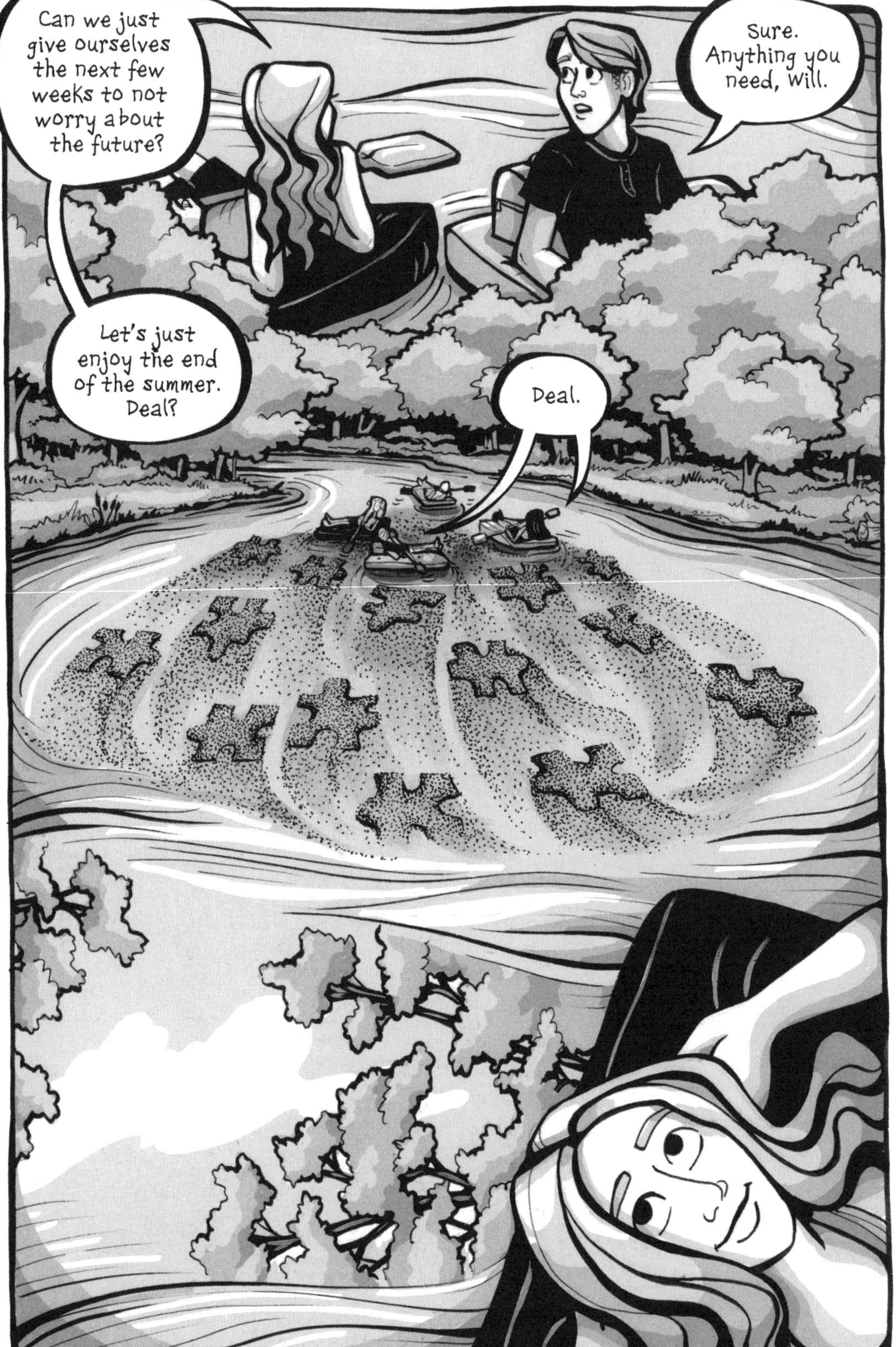
Can we just give ourselves the next few weeks to not worry about the future?
Sure. Anything you need, Will.
Let's just enjoy the end of the summer. Deal?
Deal.

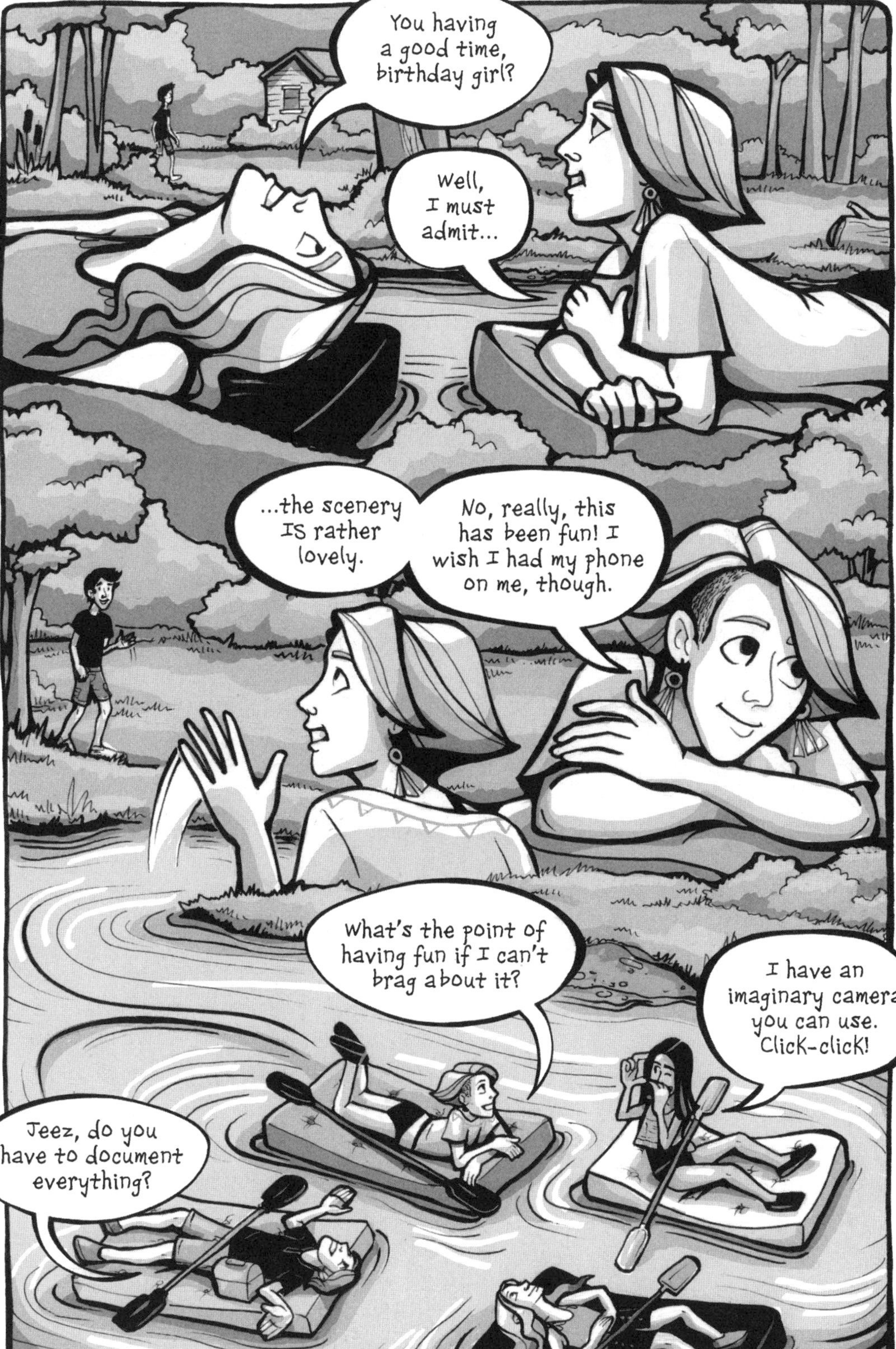
You having a good time, birthday girl?
Well, I must admit...
...the scenery IS rather lovely.
No, really, this has been fun! I wish I had my phone on me, though.
What's the point of having fun if I can't brag about it?
I have an imaginary camera you can use. Click-click!
Jeez, do you have to document everything?

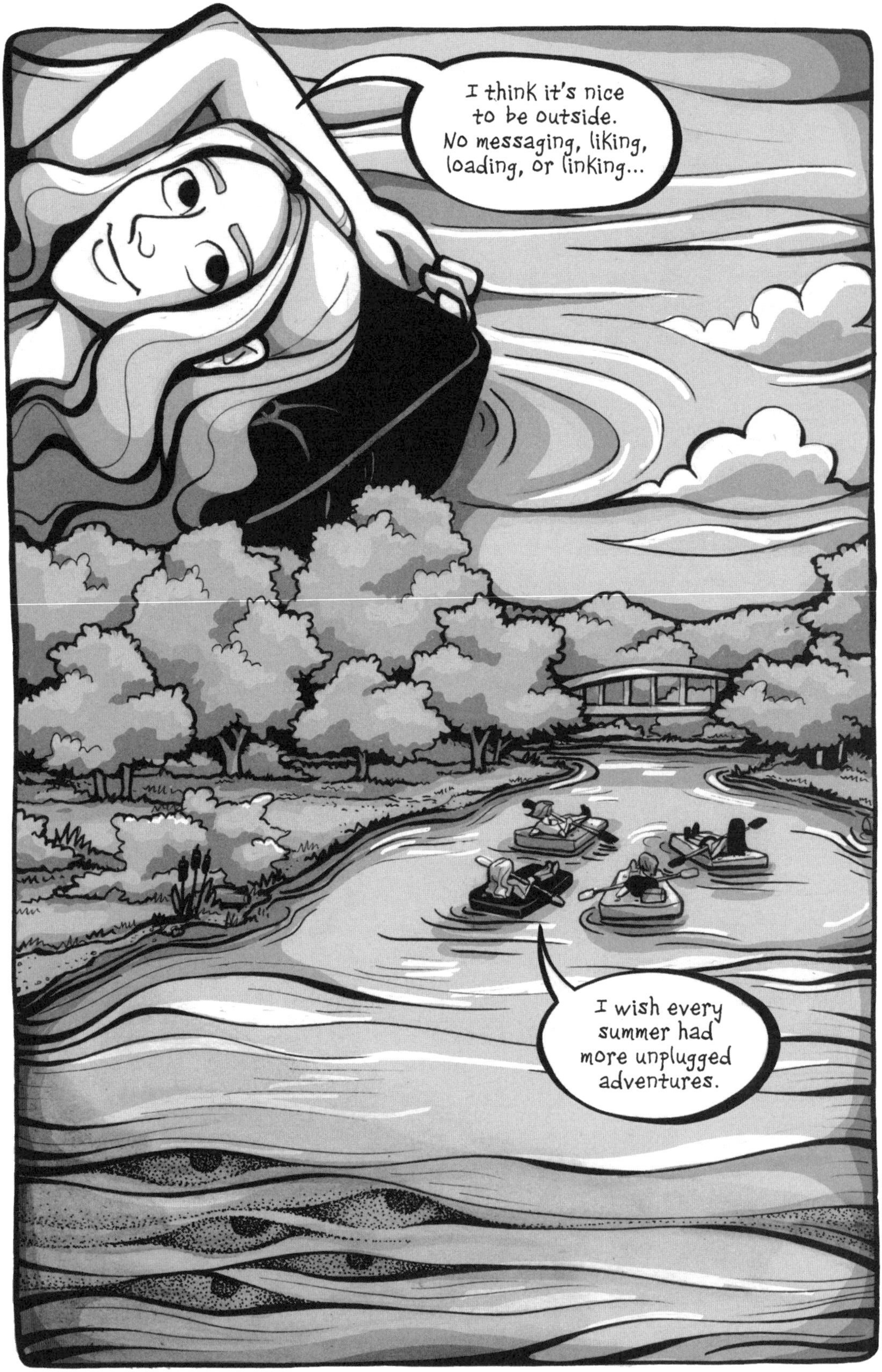
I think it's nice to be outside. No messaging, liking, loading, or linking...
I wish every summer had more unplugged adventures.

Shedding Light

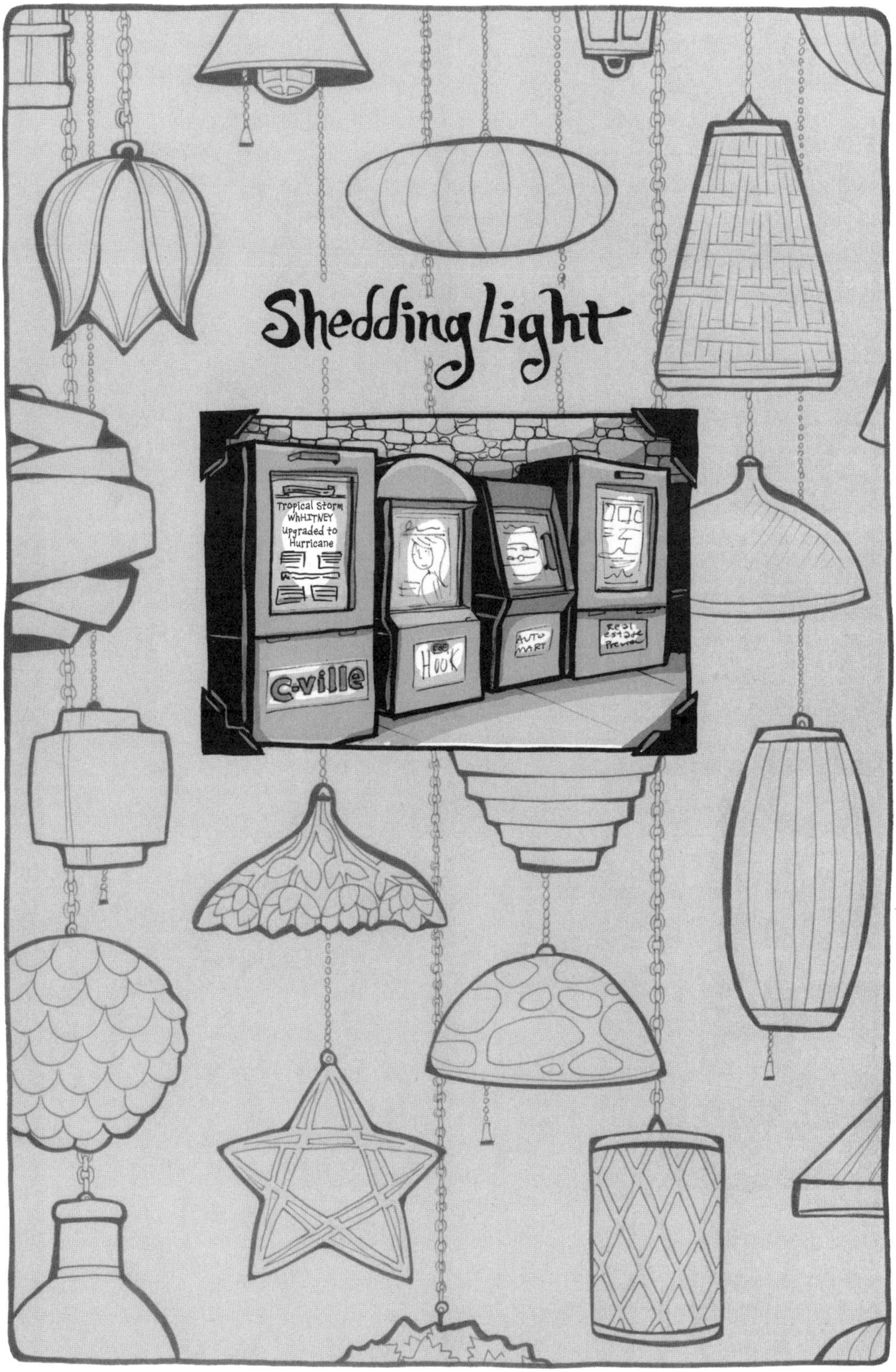
Tropical Storm WHITNEY Upgraded to Hurricane
C-ville
Hook
AUTO MART
Real estate Preview

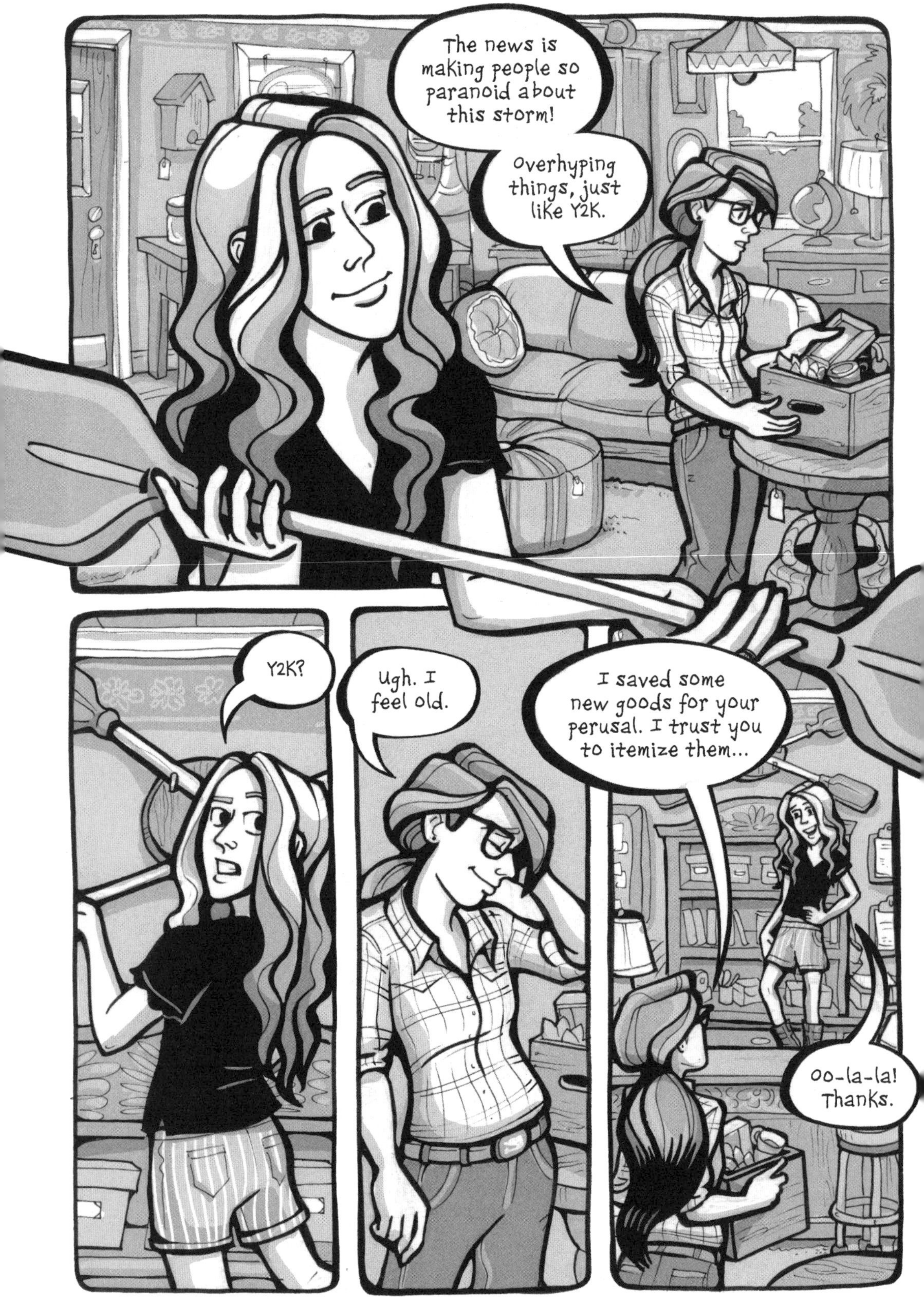
The news is making people so paranoid about this storm!
Overhyping things, just like Y2K.
Y2K?
Ugh. I feel old.
I saved some new goods for your perusal. I trust you to itemize them...
Oo-la-la! Thanks.

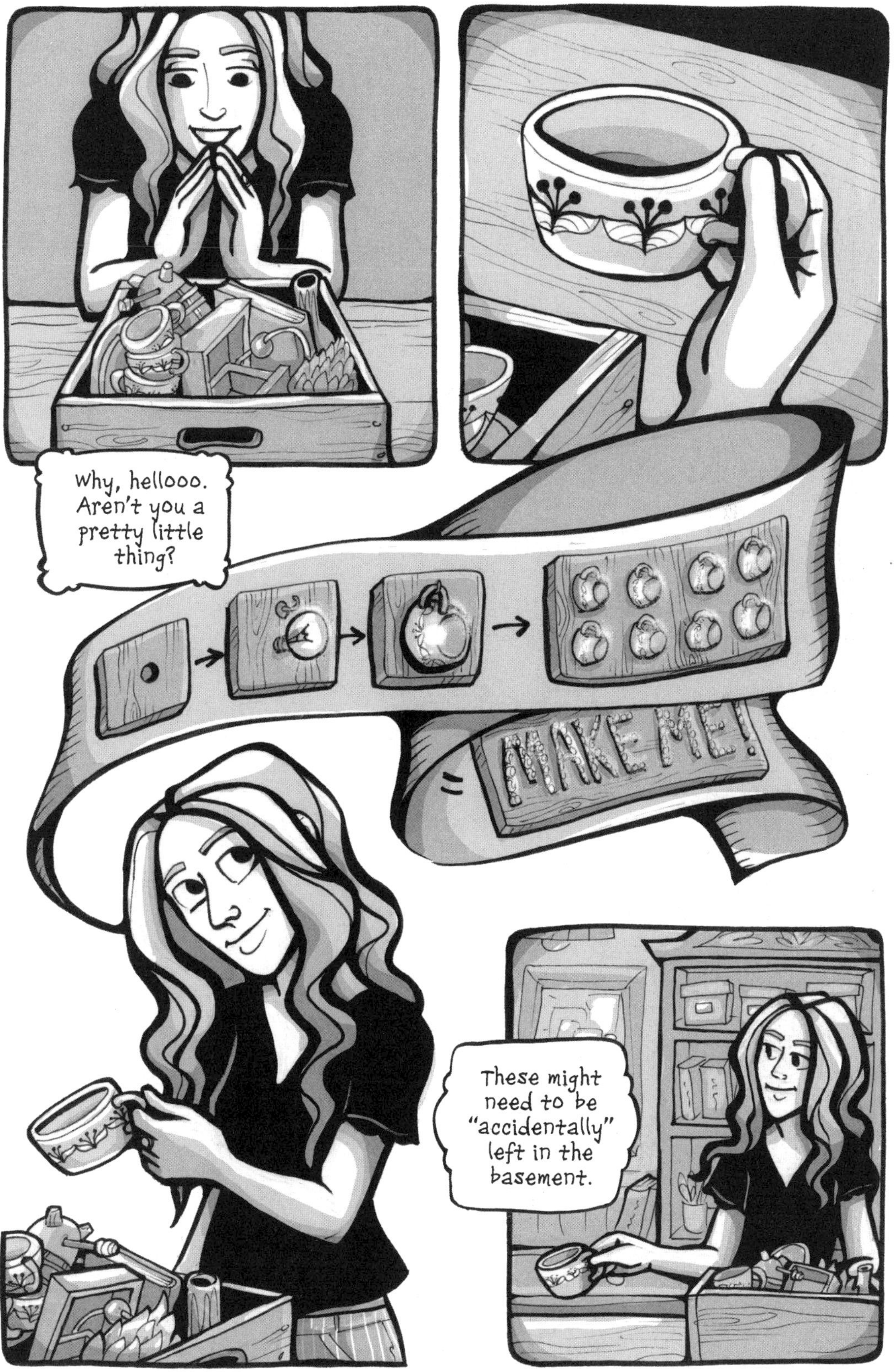
Why, hellooo. Aren't you a pretty little thing?
MAKE ME!
These might need to be "accidentally" left in the basement.

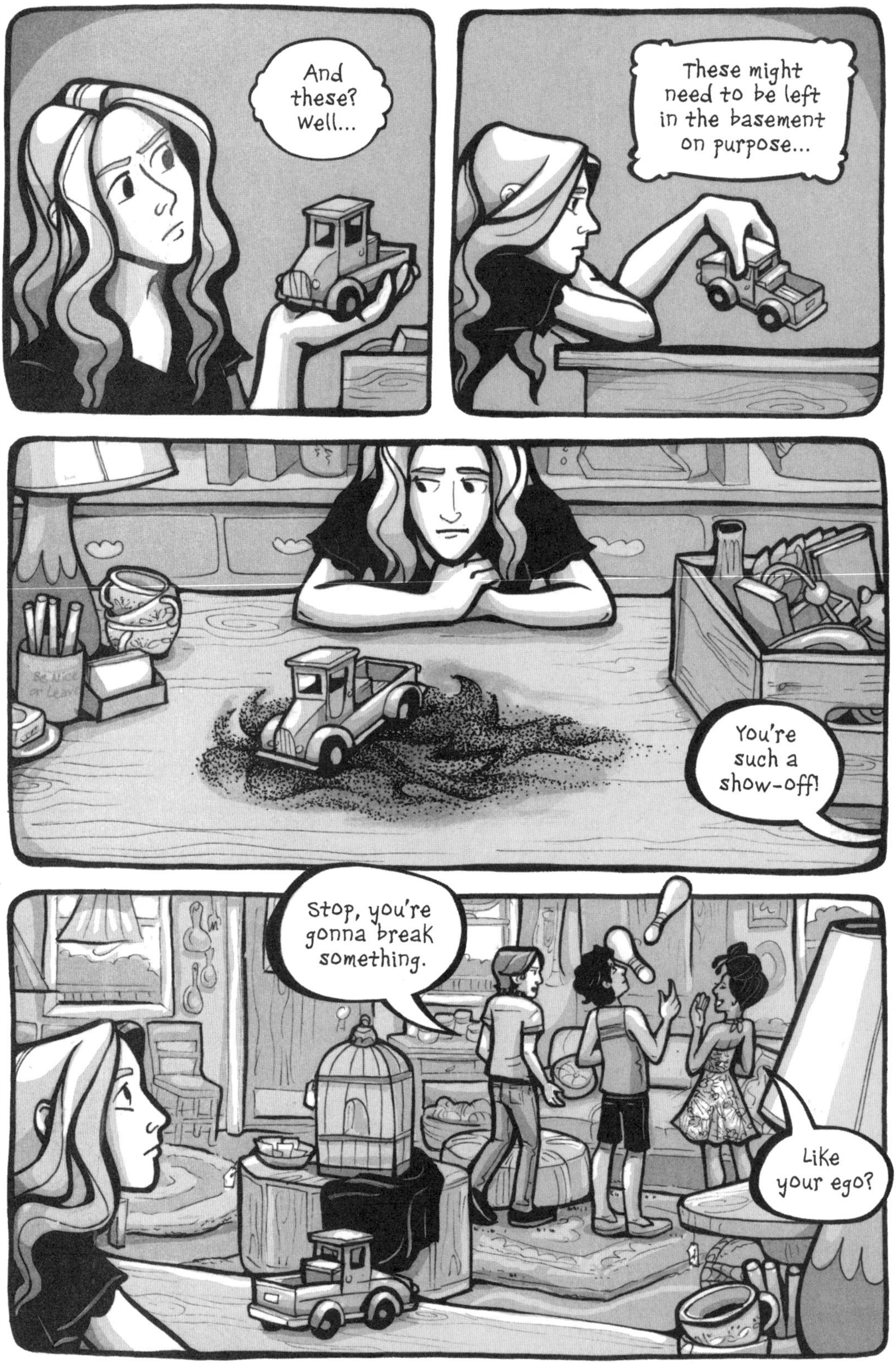
And these? Well...
These might need to be left in the basement on purpose...
You're such a show-off!
Stop, you're gonna break something.
Like your ego?

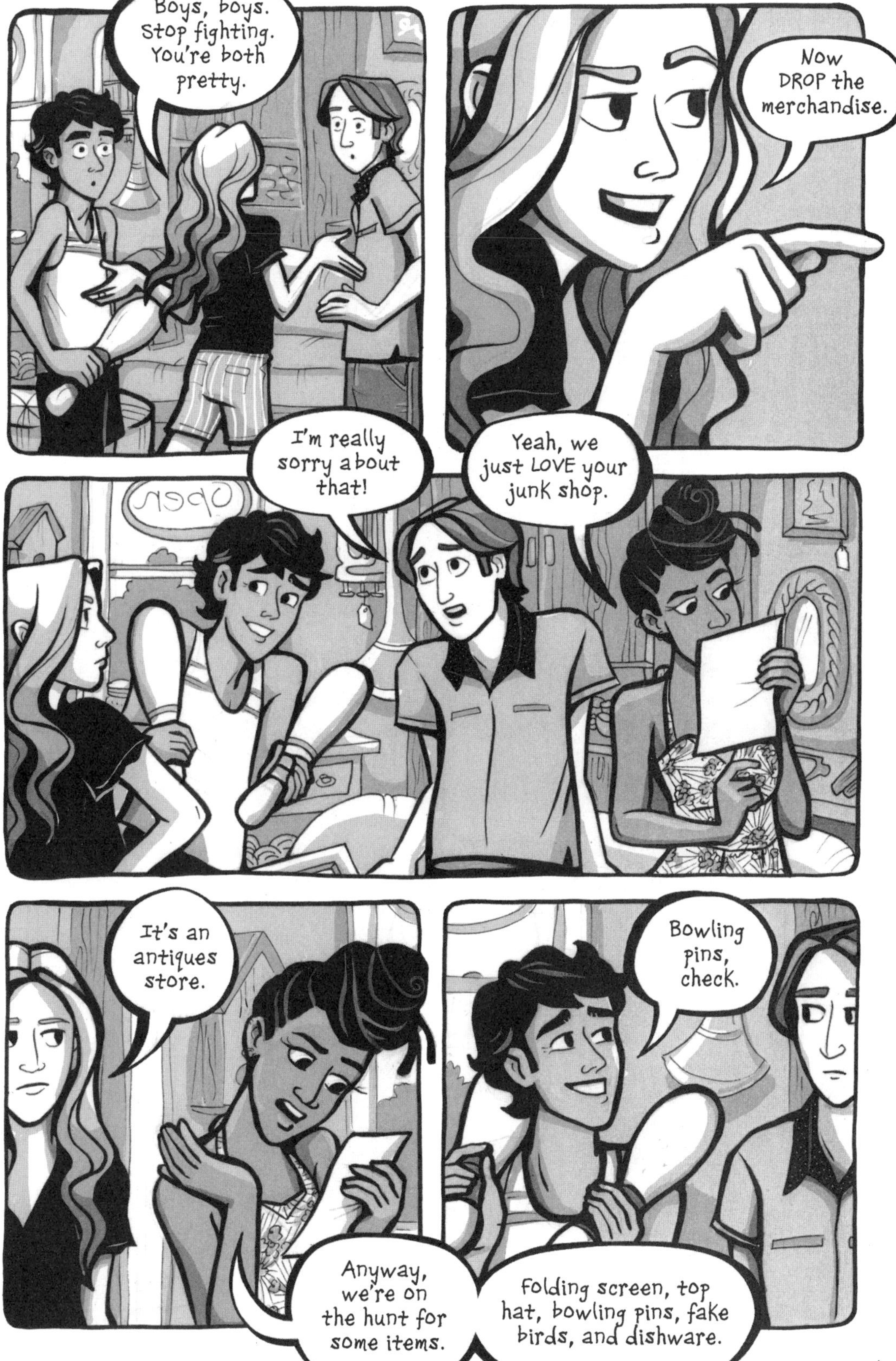
Boys, boys. Stop fighting. You're both pretty.
Now DROP the merchandise.
I'm really sorry about that!
Yeah, we just LOVE your junk shop.
It's an antiques store.
Anyway, we're on the hunt for some items.
Bowling pins, check.
Folding screen, top hat, bowling pins, fake birds, and dishware.

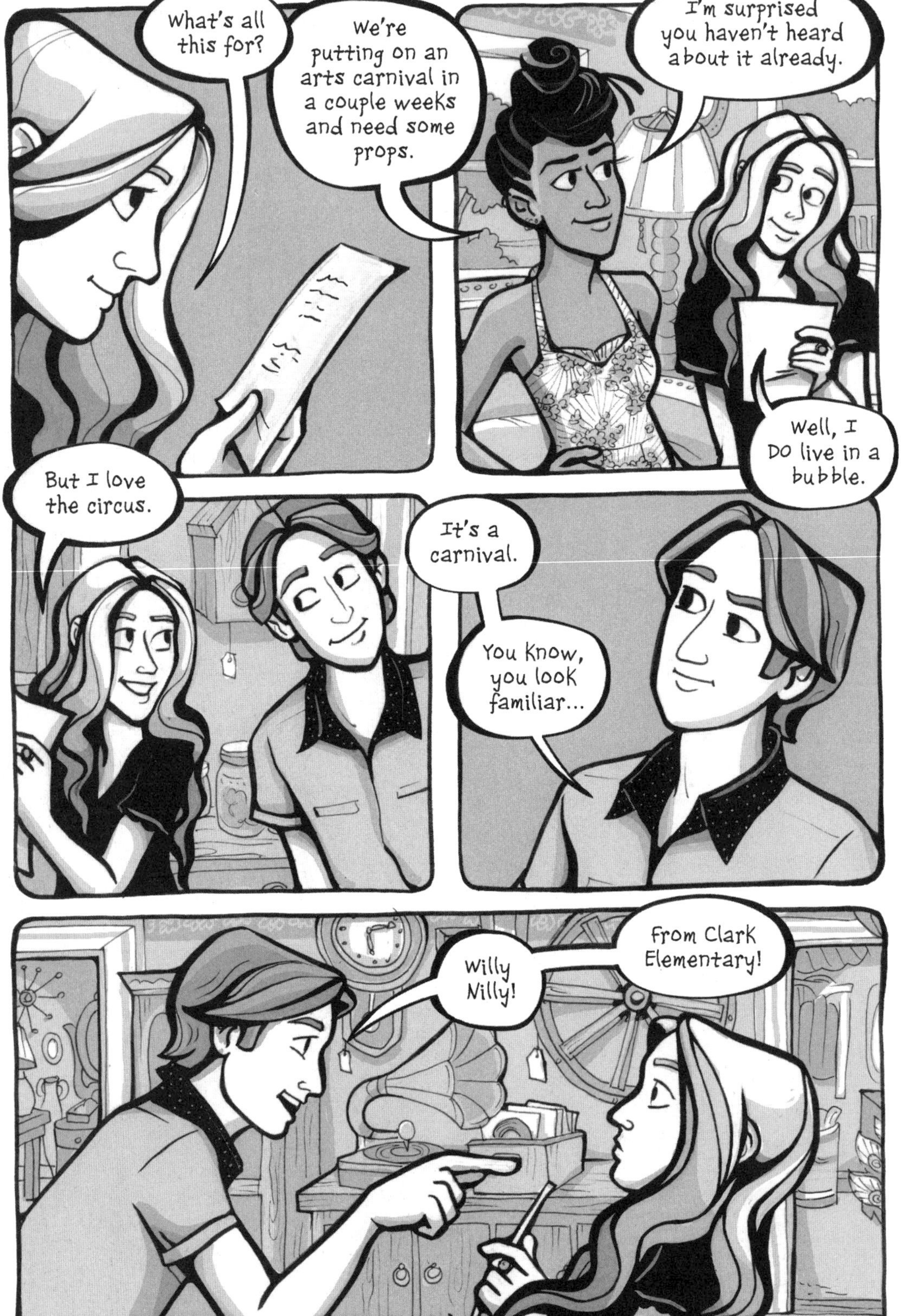

What's all this for?
We're putting on an arts carnival in a couple weeks and need some props.
I'm surprised you haven't heard about it already.
Well, I DO live in a bubble.
But I love the circus.
It's a carnival.
You know, you look familiar...
Willy Nilly!
From Clark Elementary!

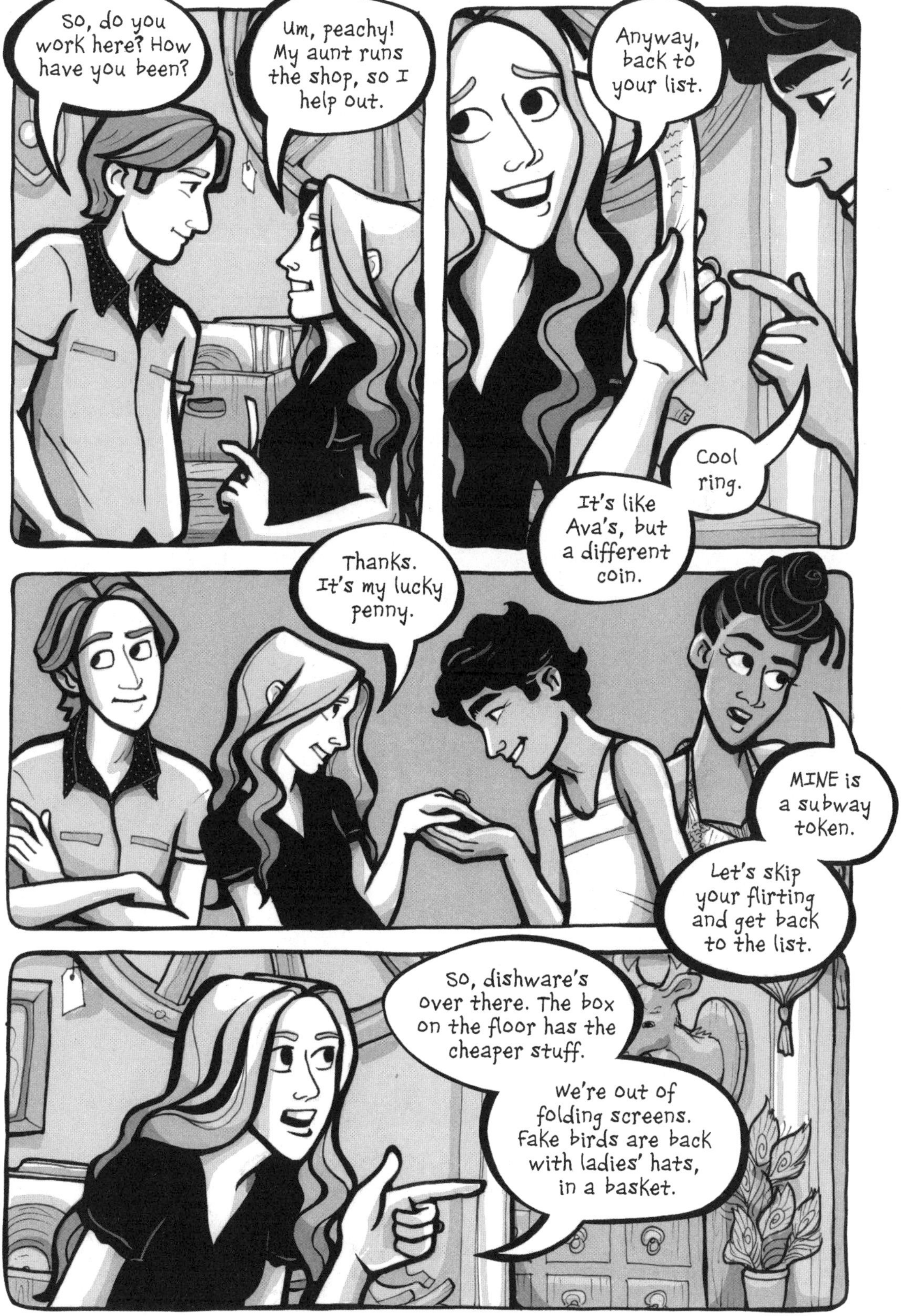
So, do you work here? How have you been?
Um, peachy! My aunt runs the shop, so I help out.
Anyway, back to your list.
Cool ring.
It's like Ava's, but a different coin.
Thanks. It's my lucky penny.
MINE is a subway token.
Let's skip your flirting and get back to the list.
So, dishware's over there. The box on the floor has the cheaper stuff.
We're out of folding screens. Fake birds are back with ladies' hats, in a basket.

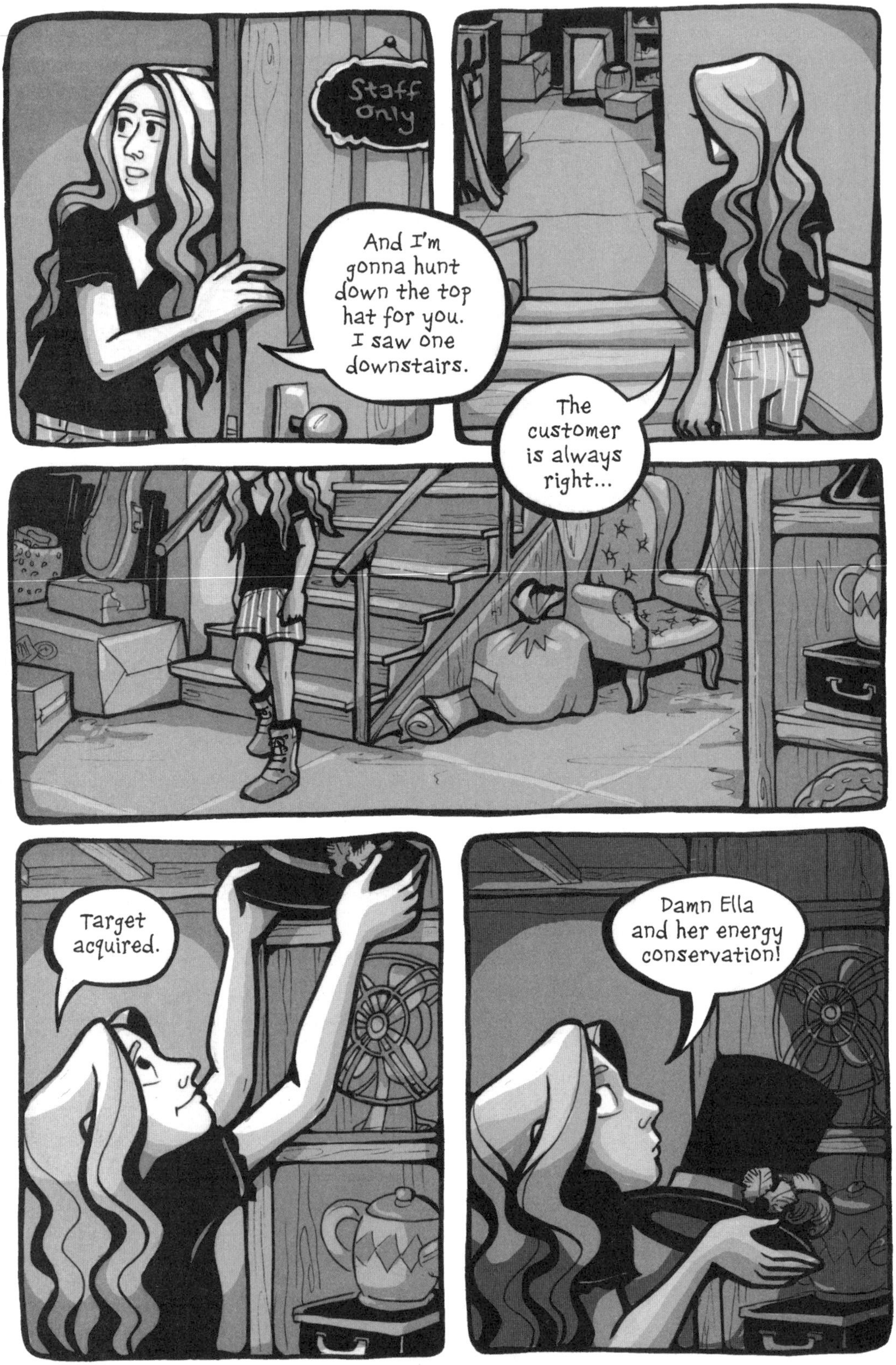
Staff Only
And I'm gonna hunt down the top hat for you. I saw one downstairs.
The customer is always right...
Target acquired.
Damn Ella and her energy conservation!

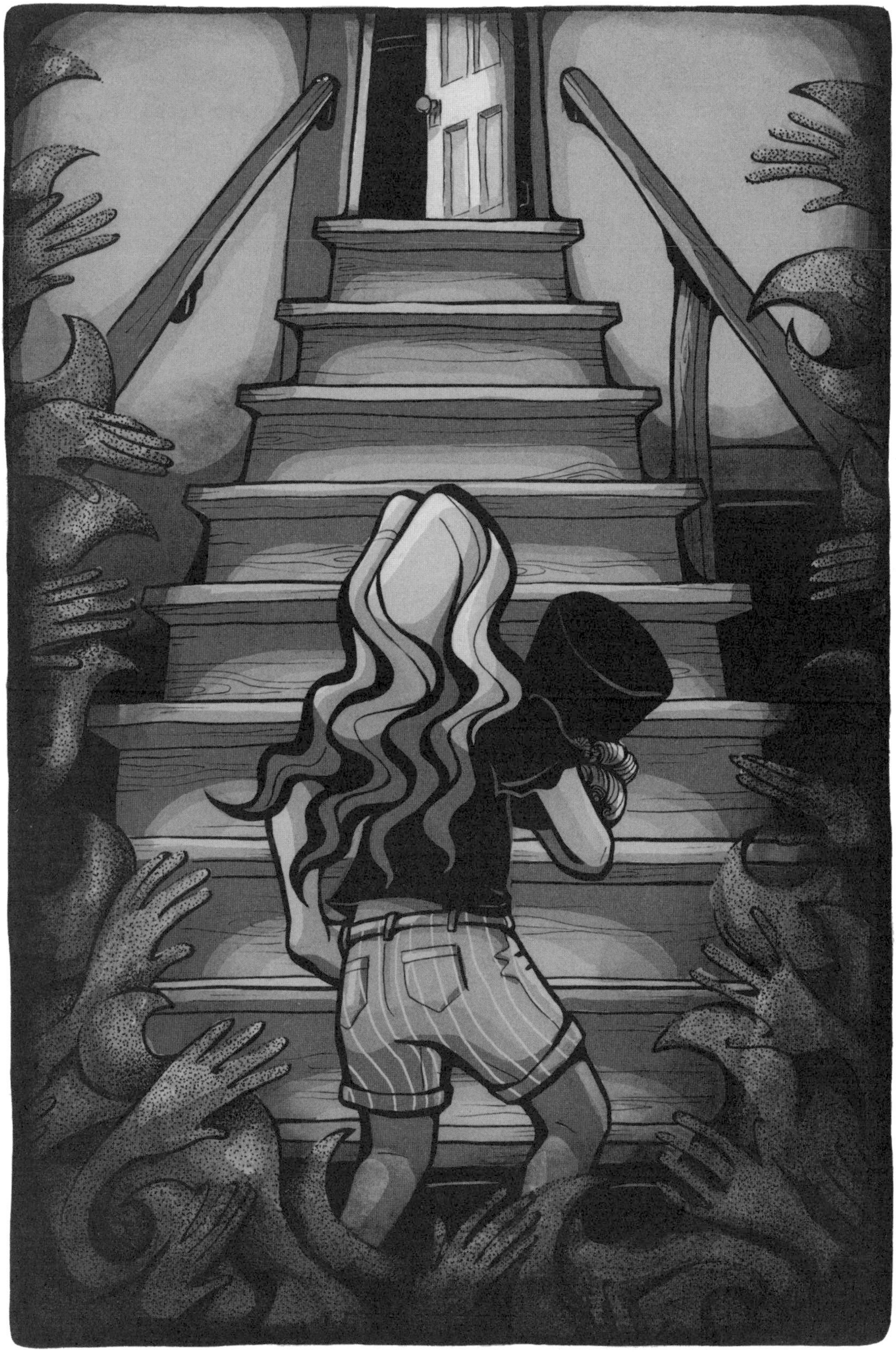

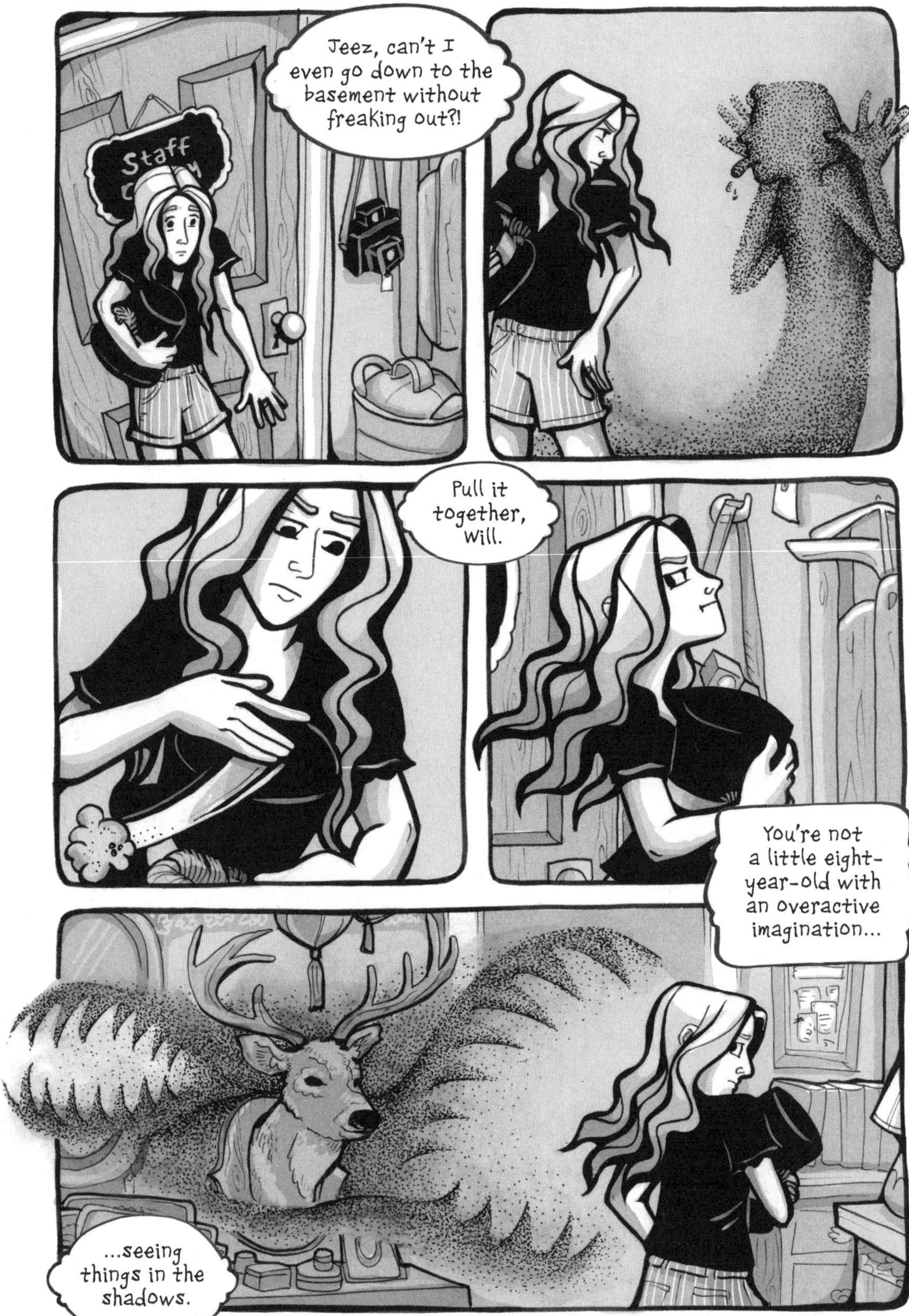
Staff
Jeez, can't I even go down to the basement without freaking out?!
Pull it together, Will.
You're not a little eight-year-old with an overactive imagination...
...seeing things in the shadows.

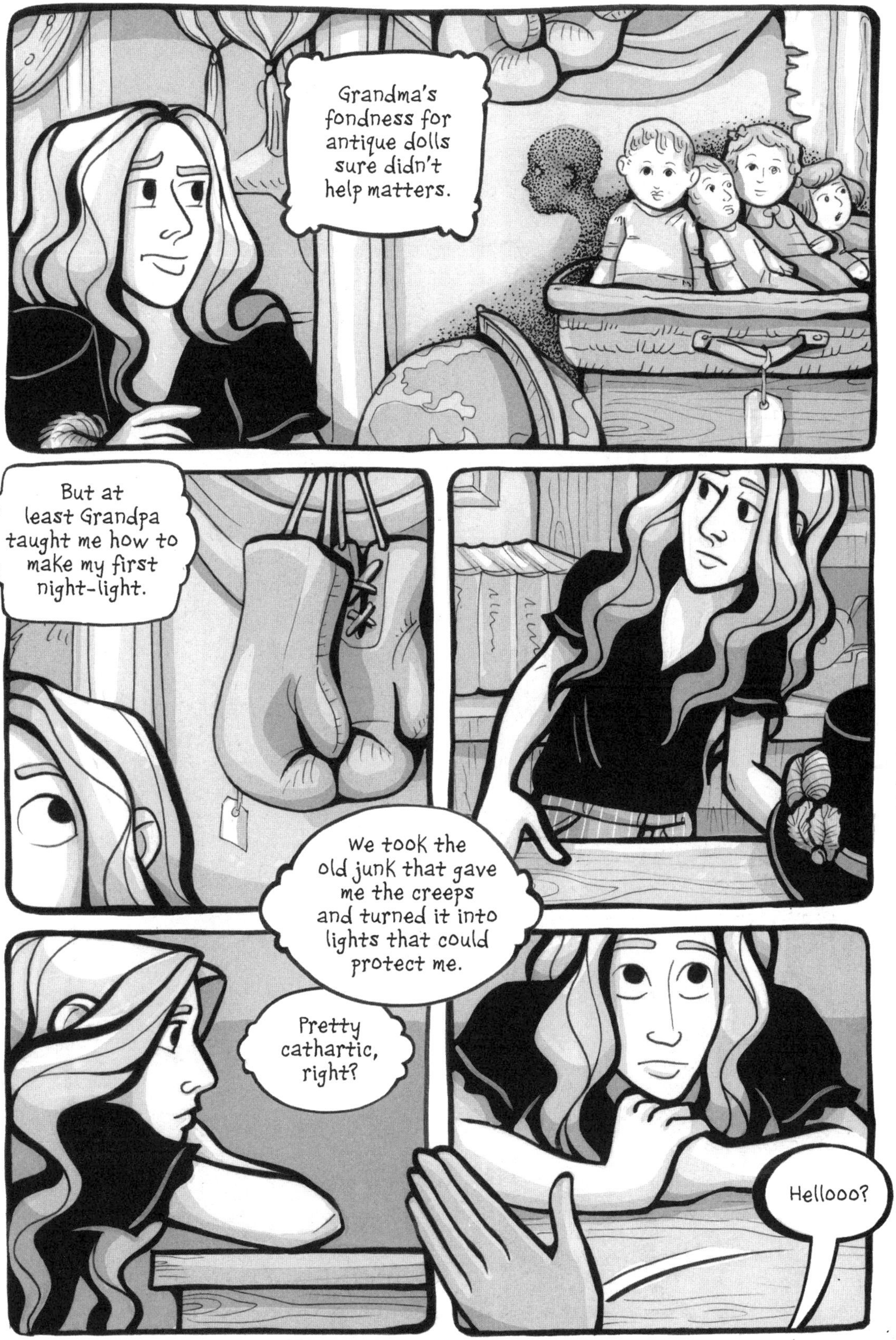
Grandma's fondness for antique dolls sure didn't help matters.
But at least Grandpa taught me how to make my first night-light.
We took the old junk that gave me the creeps and turned it into lights that could protect me.
Pretty cathartic, right?
Hellooo?

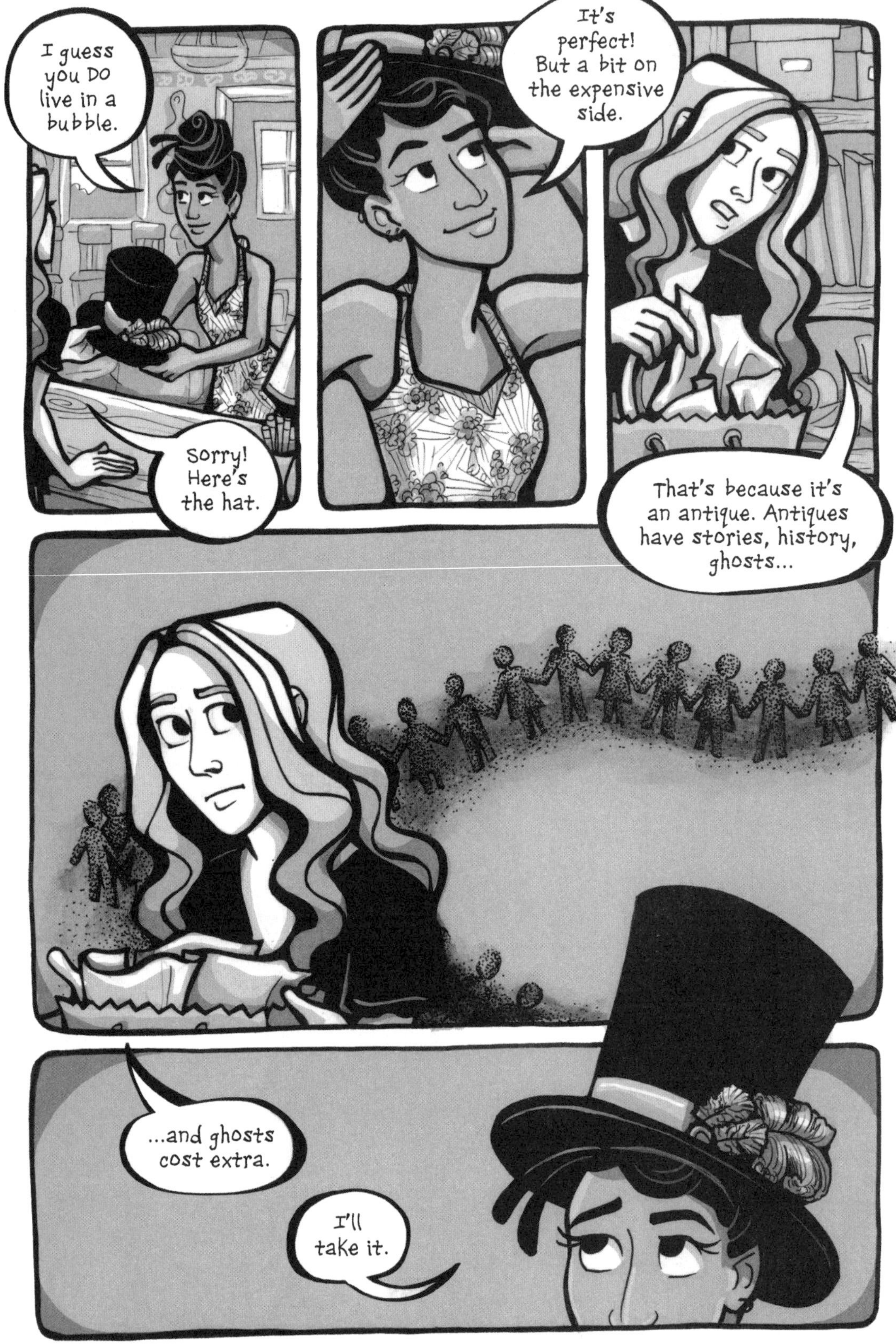
I guess you DO live in a bubble.
Sorry! Here's the hat.
It's perfect! But a bit on the expensive side.
That's because it's an antique. Antiques have stories, history, ghosts...
...and ghosts cost extra.
I'll take it.

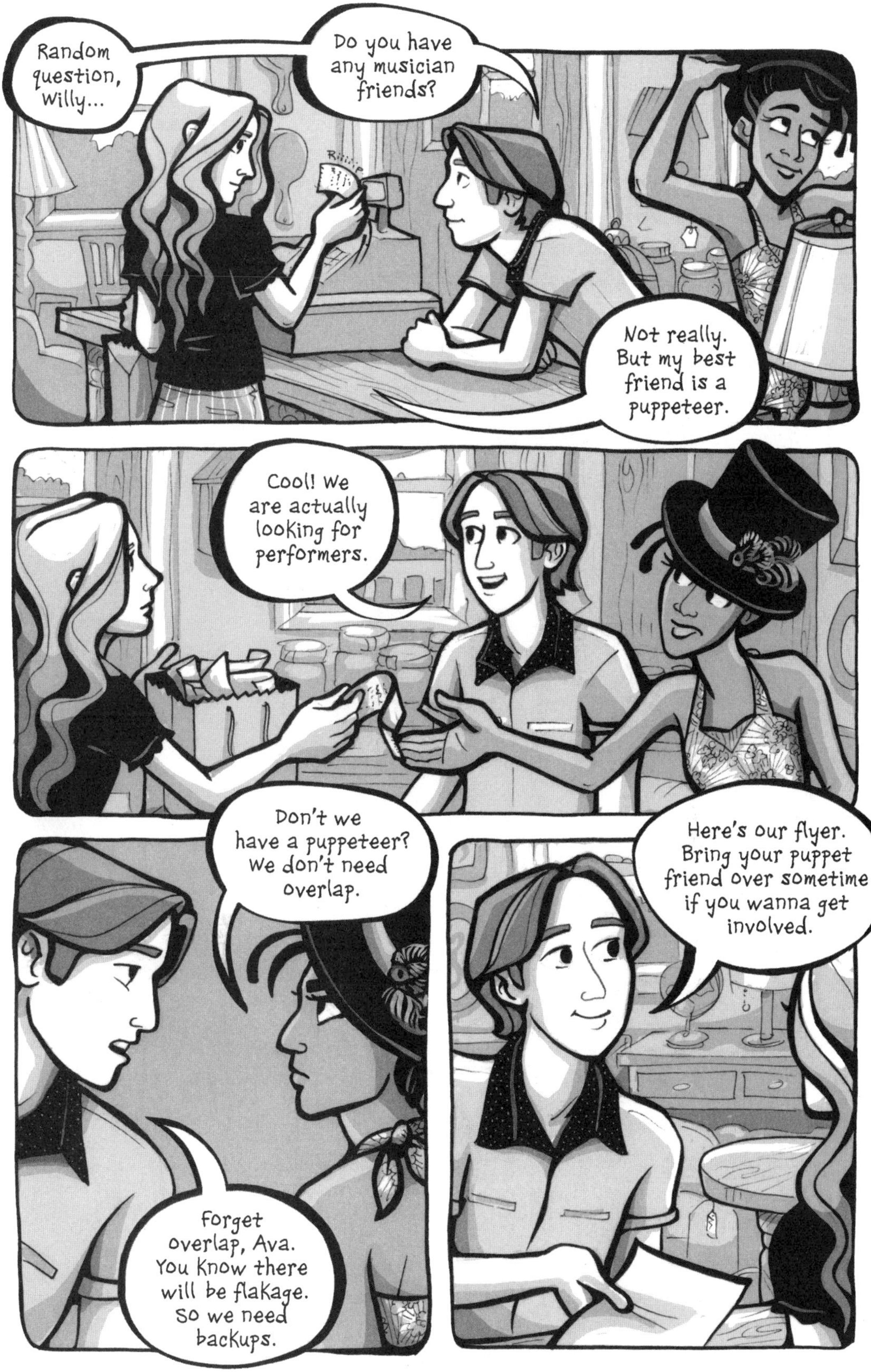
Random question, Willy...
Do you have any musician friends?
Ritiiip
Not really. But my best friend is a puppeteer.
Cool! We are actually looking for performers.
Don't we have a puppeteer? We don't need overlap.
Forget overlap, Ava. You know there will be flakage. So we need backups.
Here's our flyer. Bring your puppet friend over sometime if you wanna get involved.

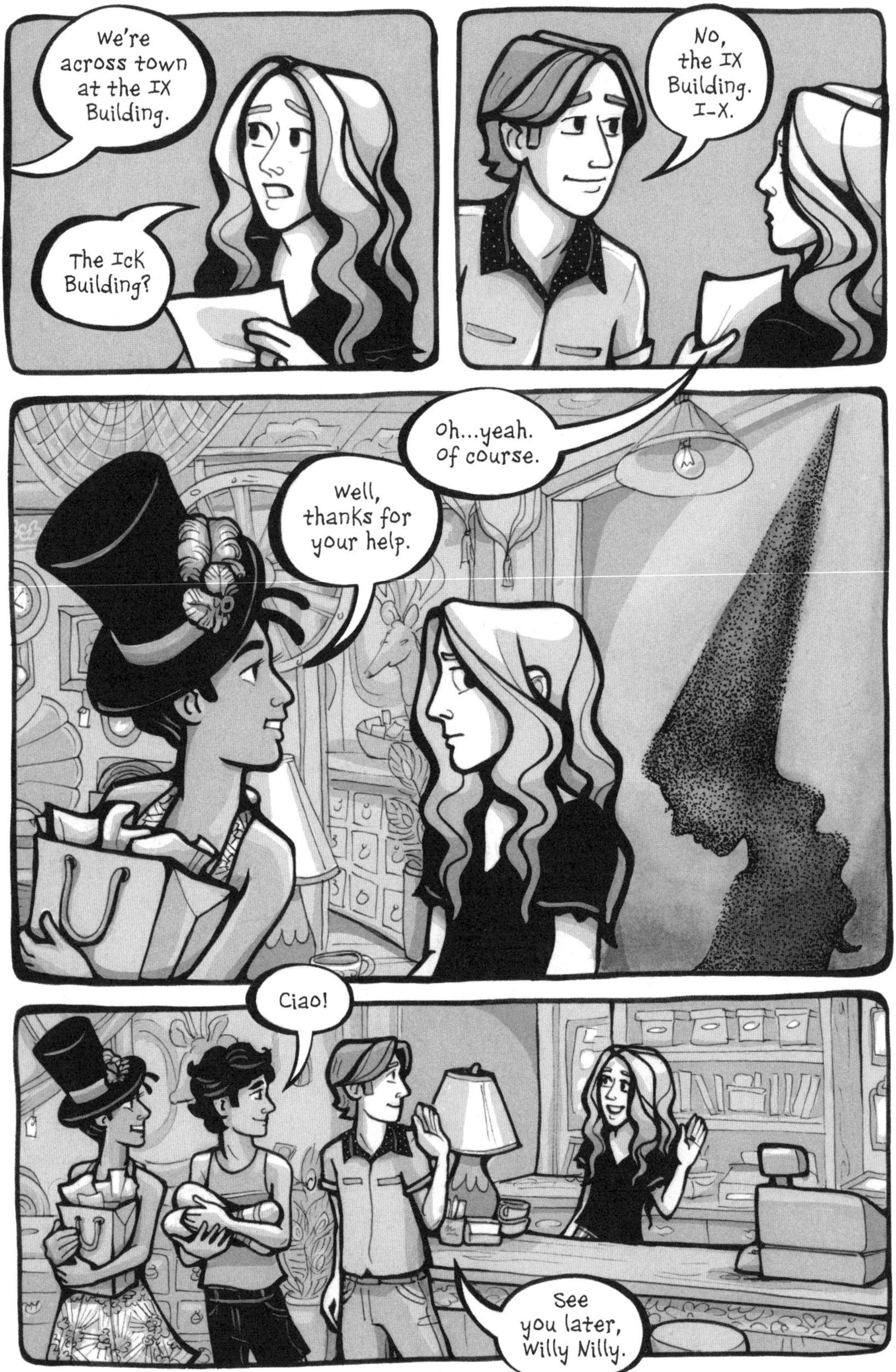

We're across town at the IX Building.
The Ick Building?
No, the IX Building. I-X.
Oh...yeah. Of course.
Well, thanks for your help.
Ciao!
See you later, Willy Nilly.

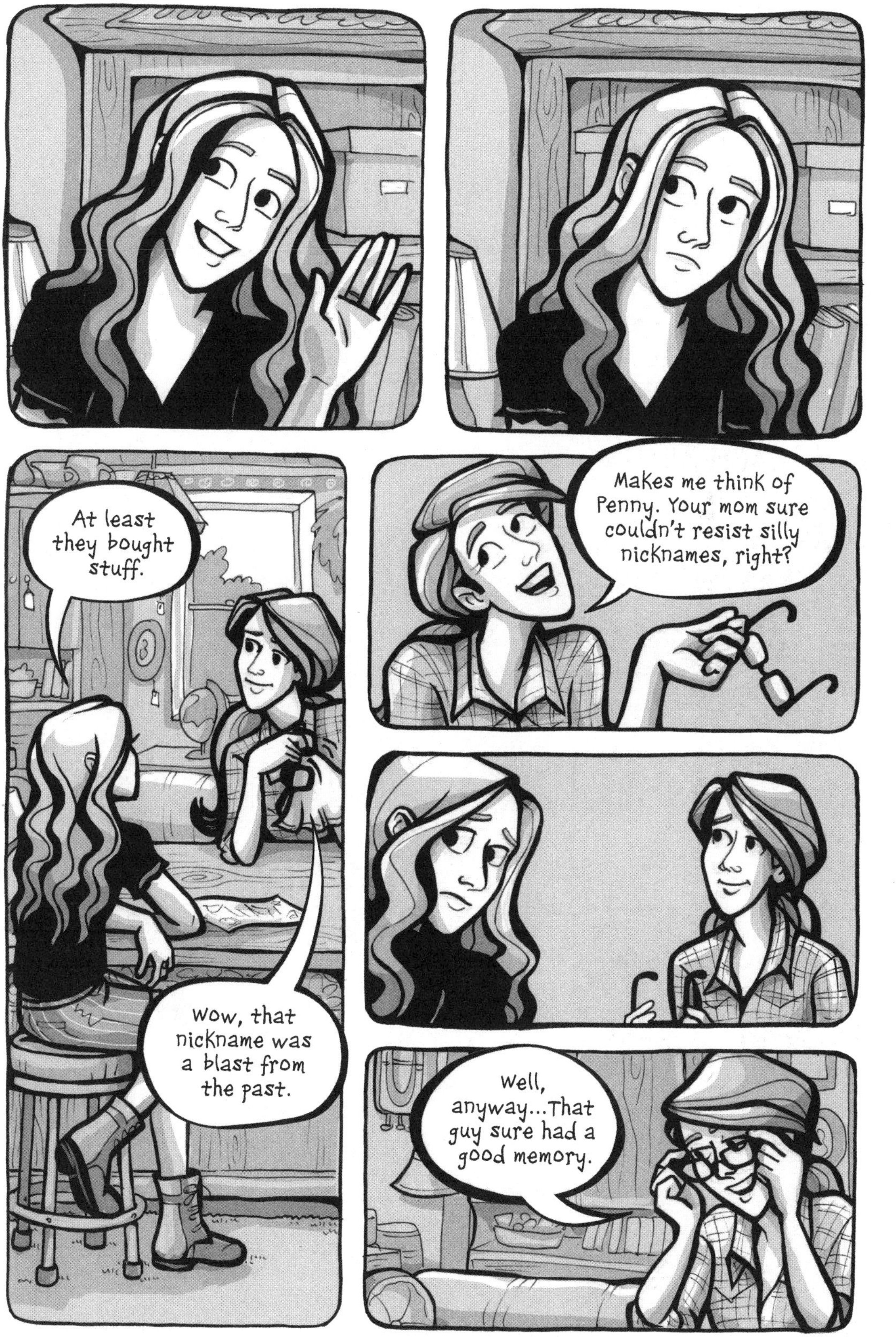
At least they bought stuff.
Wow, that nickname was a blast from the past.
Makes me think of Penny. Your mom sure couldn't resist silly nicknames, right?
Well, anyway...That guy sure had a good memory.

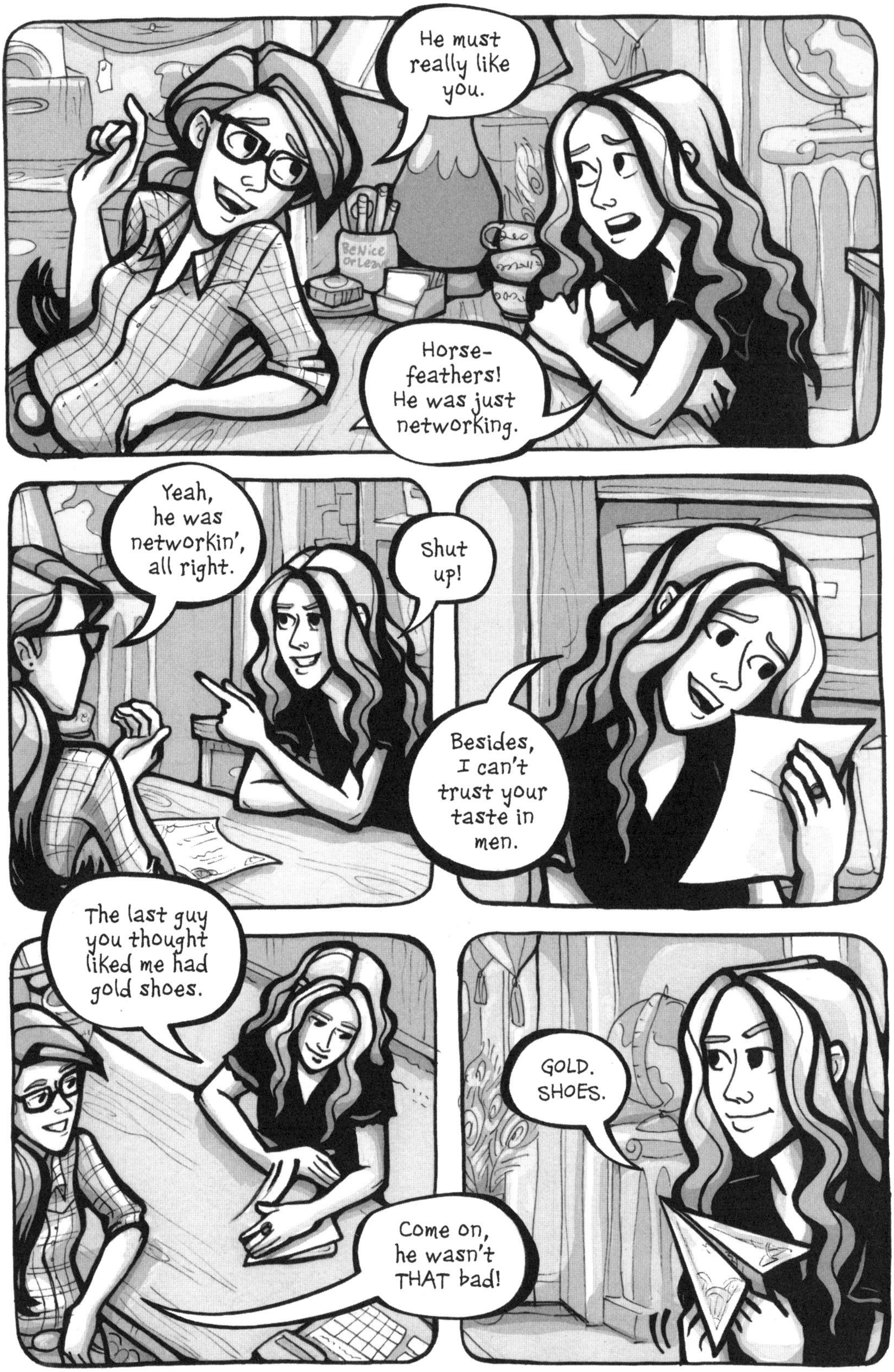
He must really like you.
Horse-feathers! He was just networking.
Yeah, he was networkin', all right.
Shut up!
Besides, I can't trust your taste in men.
The last guy you thought liked me had gold shoes.
Come on, he wasn't THAT bad!
GOLD. SHOES.

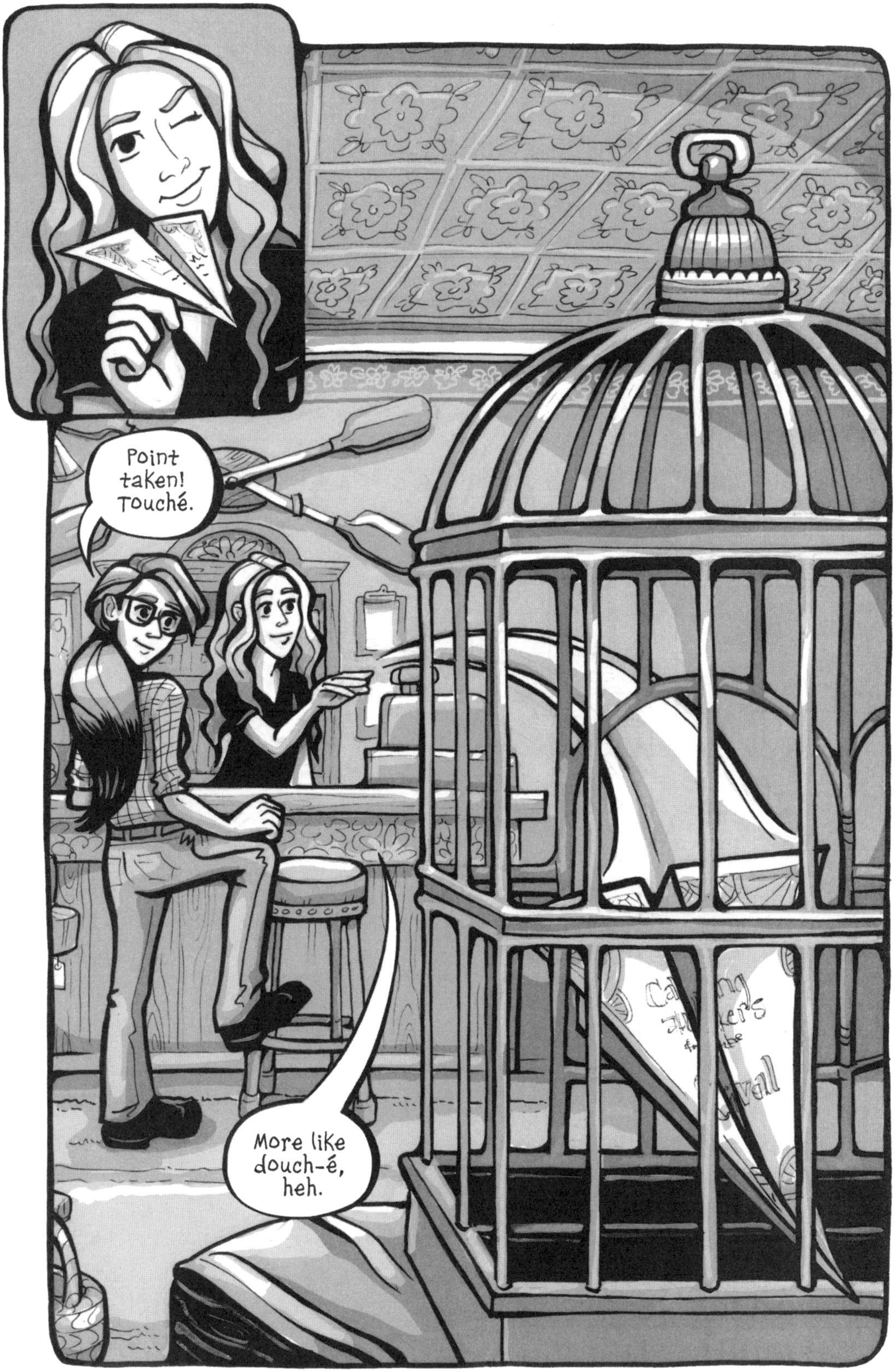
Point taken! Touché.
More like douch-é, heh.

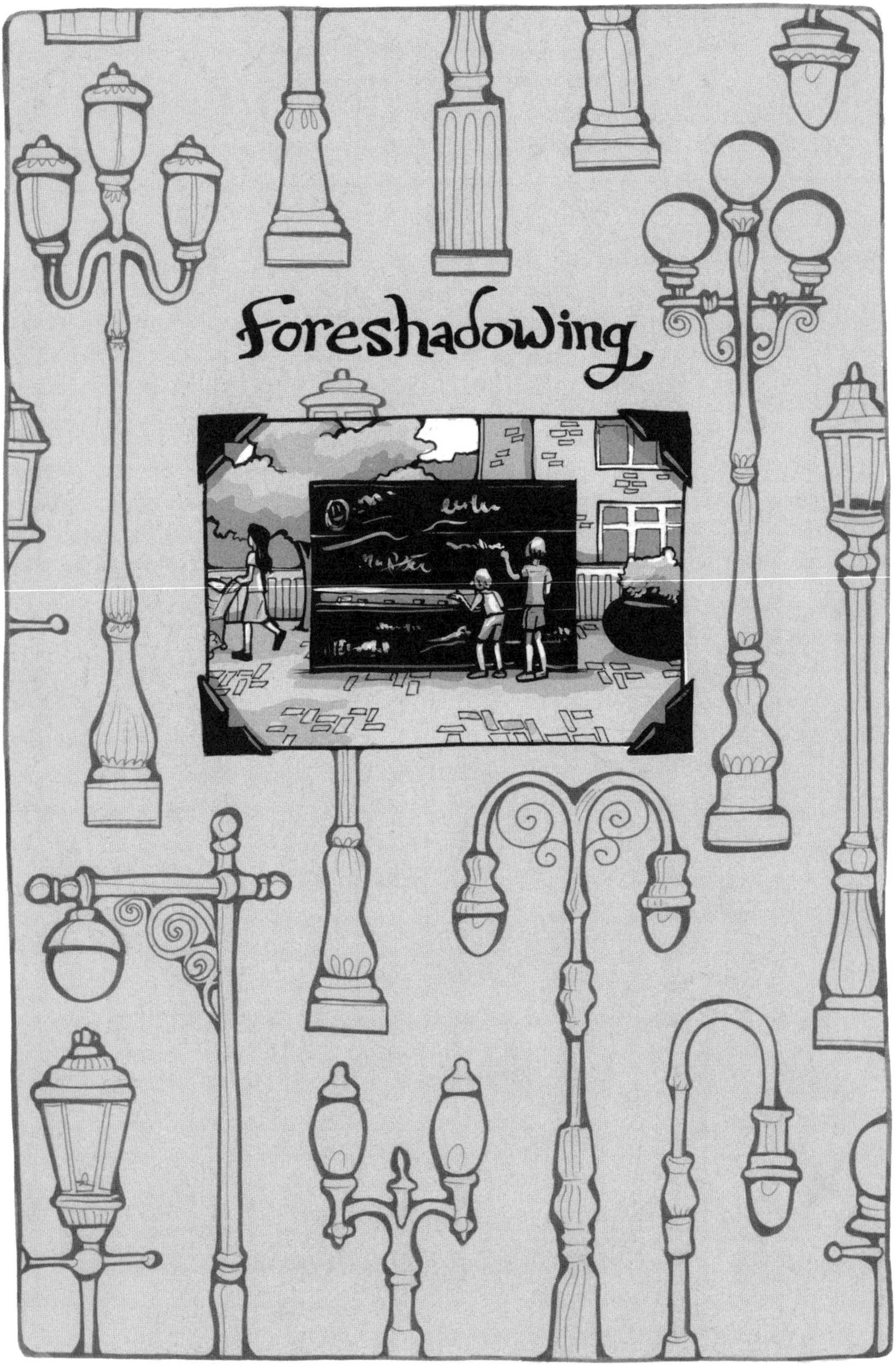
Foreshadowing

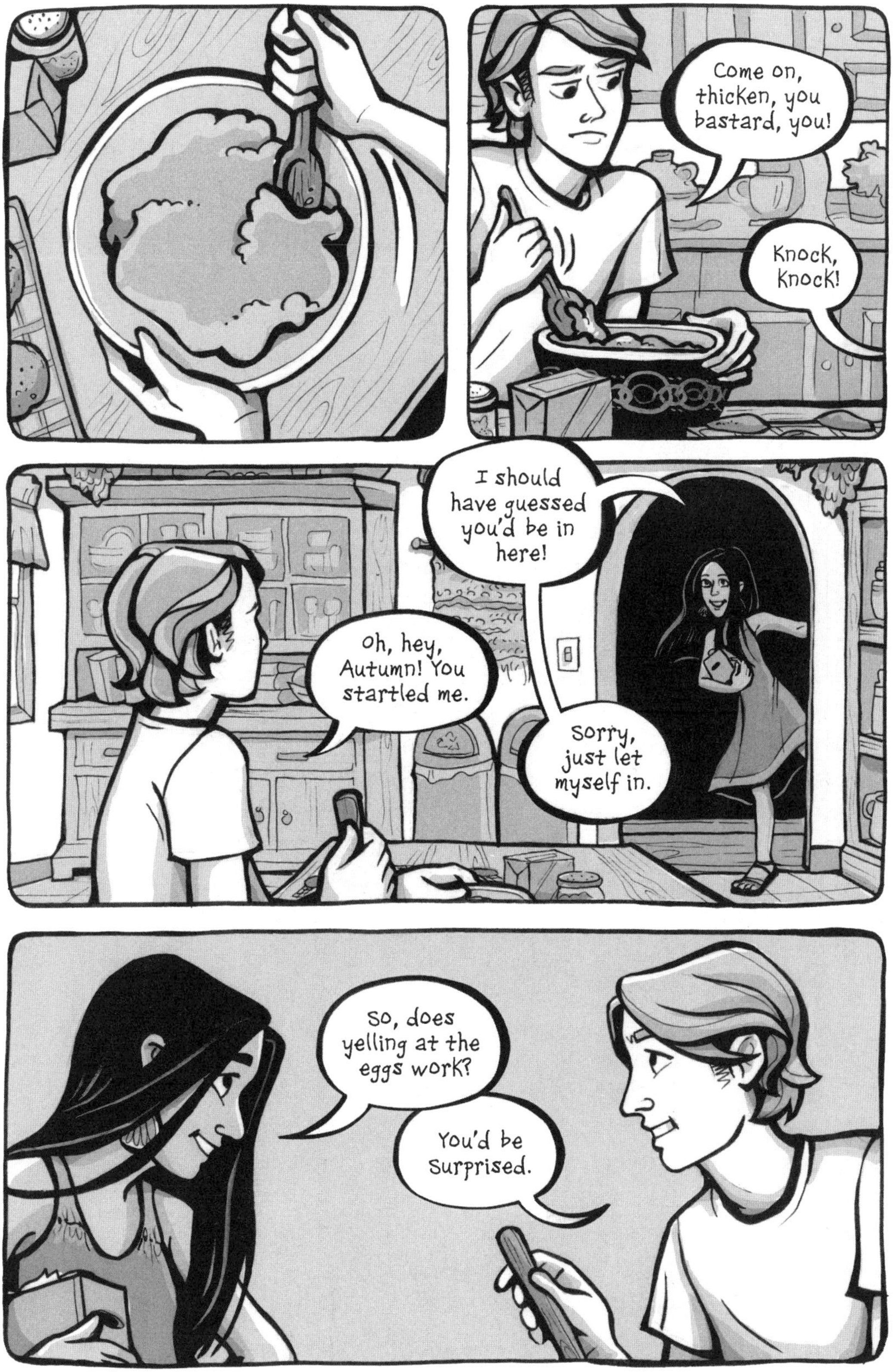
Come on, thicken, you bastard, you!
Knock, Knock!
I should have guessed you'd be in here!
Oh, hey, Autumn! You startled me.
Sorry, just let myself in.
So, does yelling at the eggs work?
You'd be surprised.

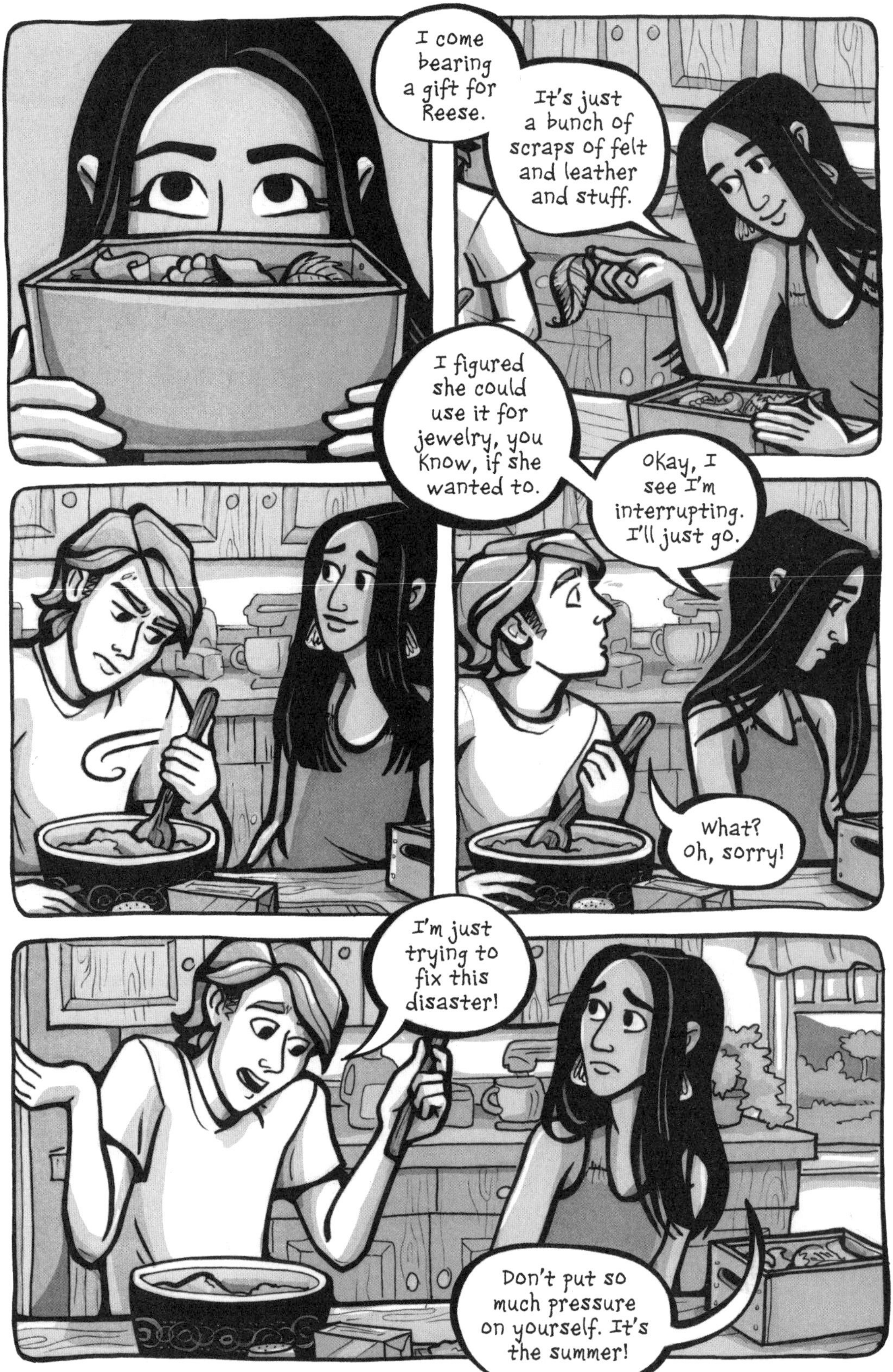
I come bearing a gift for Reese.
It's just a bunch of scraps of felt and leather and stuff.
I figured she could use it for jewelry, you know, if she wanted to.
Okay, I see I'm interrupting. I'll just go.
What? Oh, sorry!
I'm just trying to fix this disaster!
Don't put so much pressure on yourself. It's the summer!

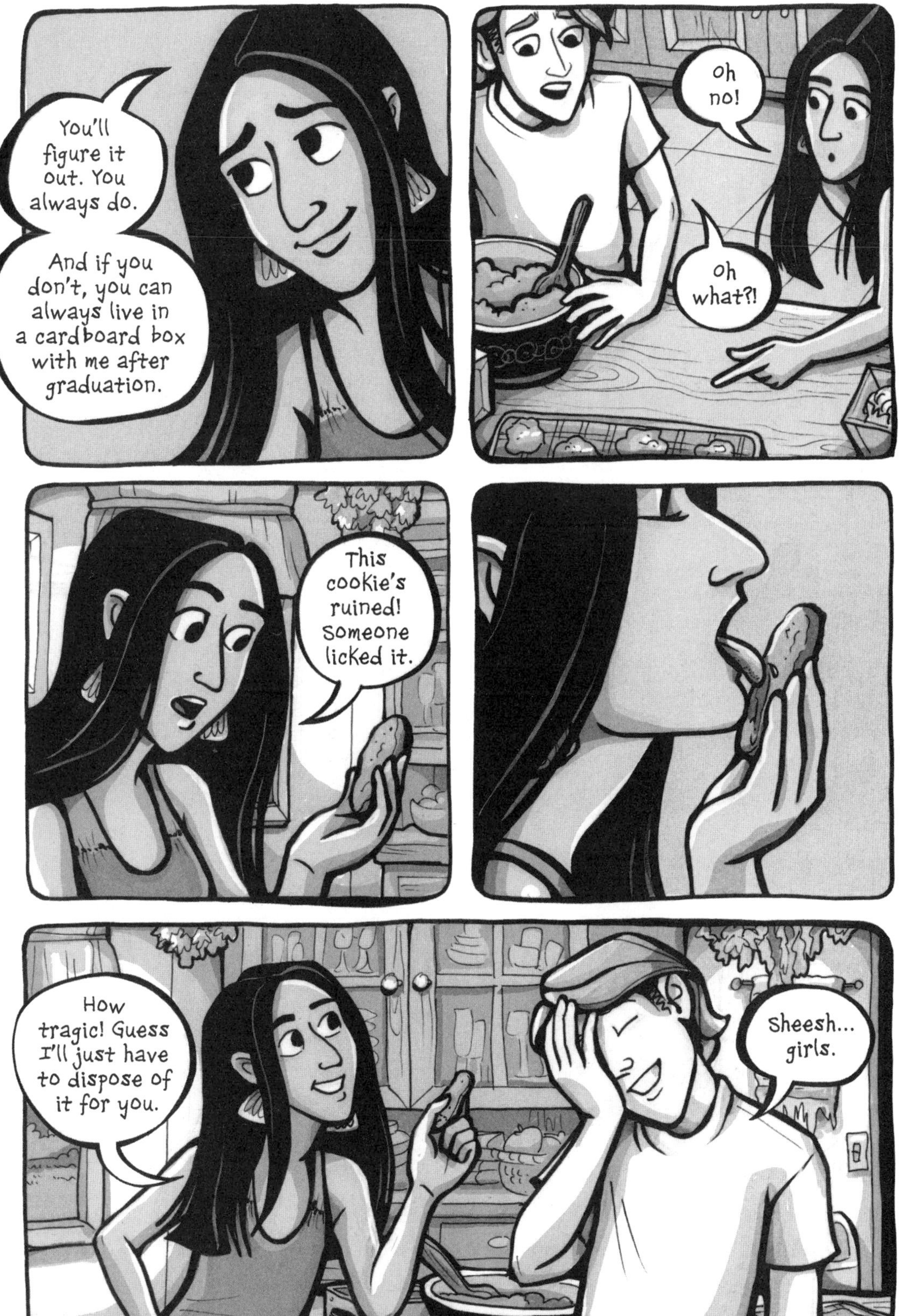
You'll figure it out. You always do.
And if you don't, you can always live in a cardboard box with me after graduation.
Oh no!
Oh what?!
This cookie's ruined! Someone licked it.
How tragic! Guess I'll just have to dispose of it for you.
Sheesh... girls.

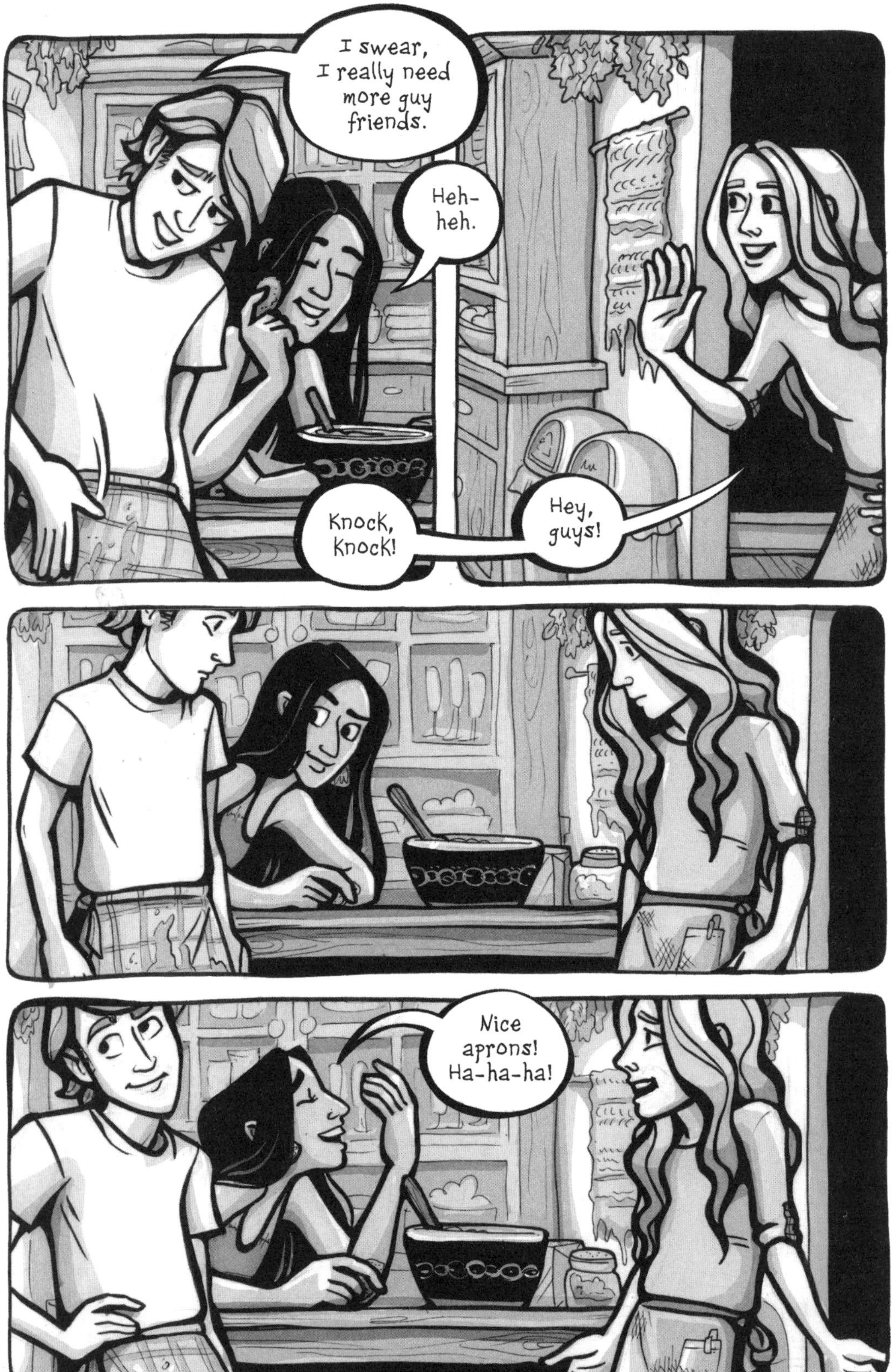
I swear, I really need more guy friends.
Heh-heh.
Knock, knock!
Hey, guys!
Nice aprons! Ha-ha-ha!

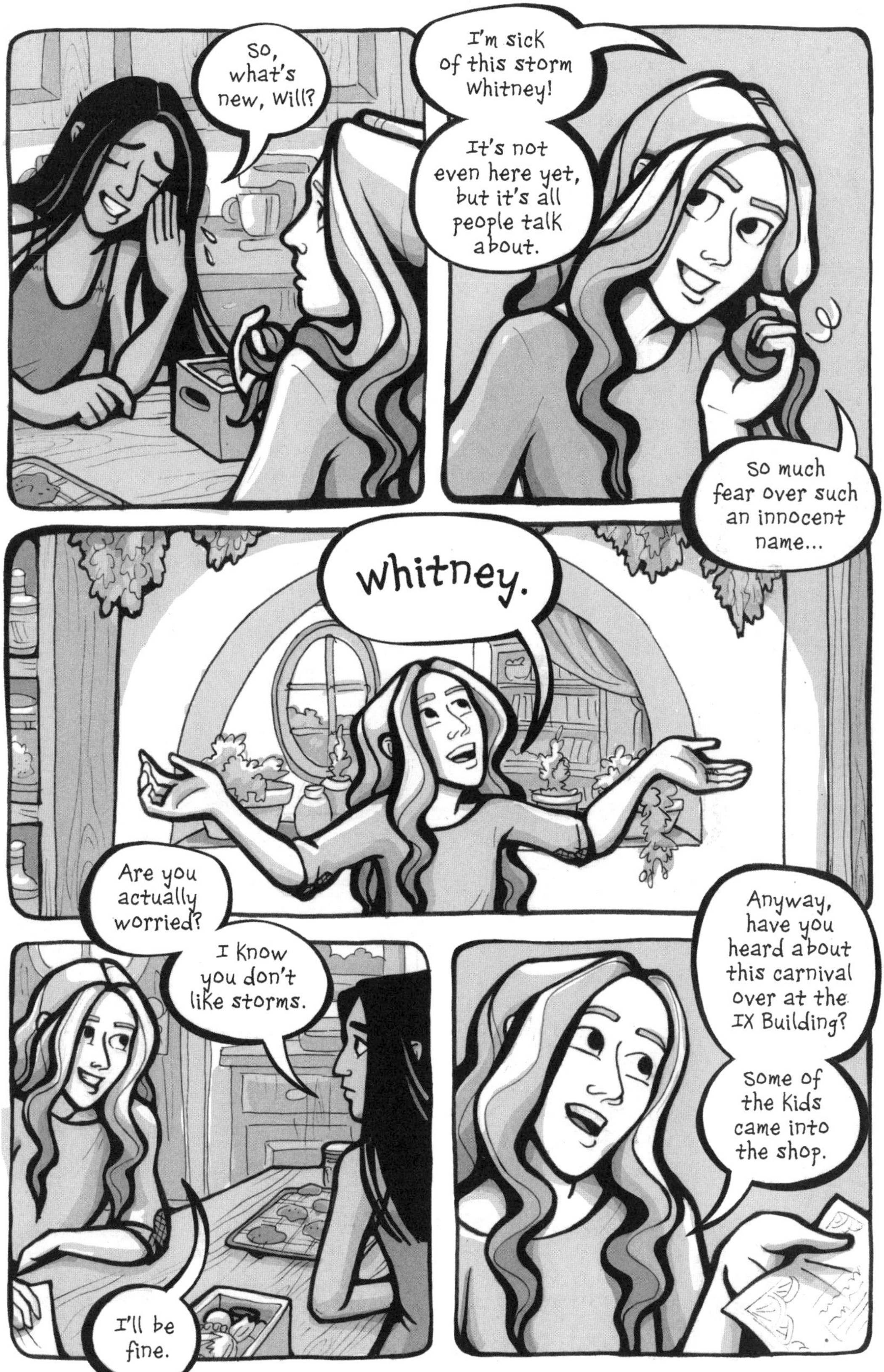
So, what's new, Will?
I'm sick of this storm Whitney!
It's not even here yet, but it's all people talk about.
So much fear over such an innocent name...
Whitney.
Are you actually worried?
I know you don't like storms.
I'll be fine.
Anyway, have you heard about this carnival over at the IX Building?
Some of the kids came into the shop.

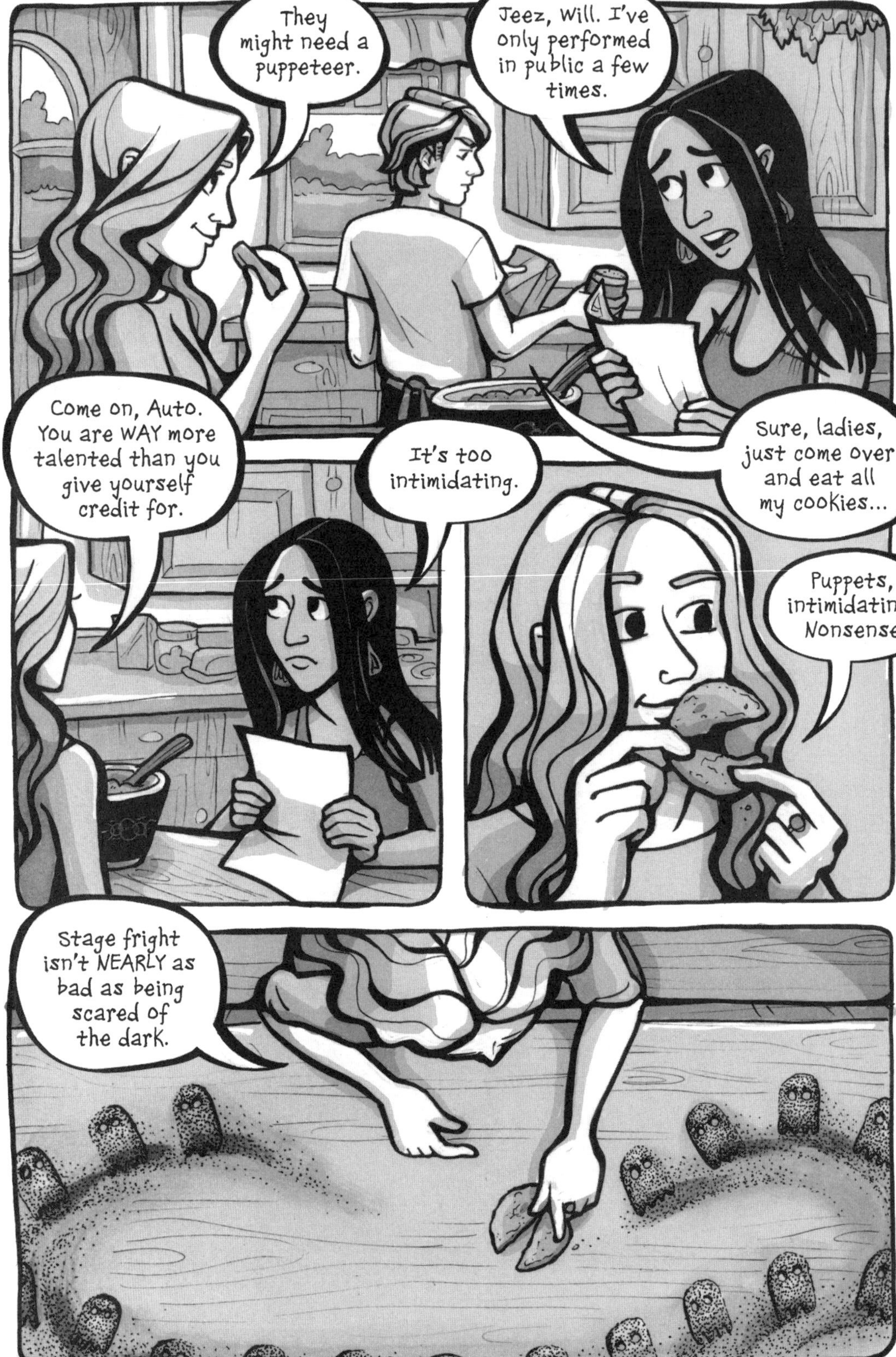
They might need a puppeteer.
Jeez, Will. I've only performed in public a few times.
Come on, Auto. You are WAY more talented than you give yourself credit for.
It's too intimidating.
Sure, ladies, just come over and eat all my cookies...
Puppets, intimidating? Nonsense!
Stage fright isn't NEARLY as bad as being scared of the dark.

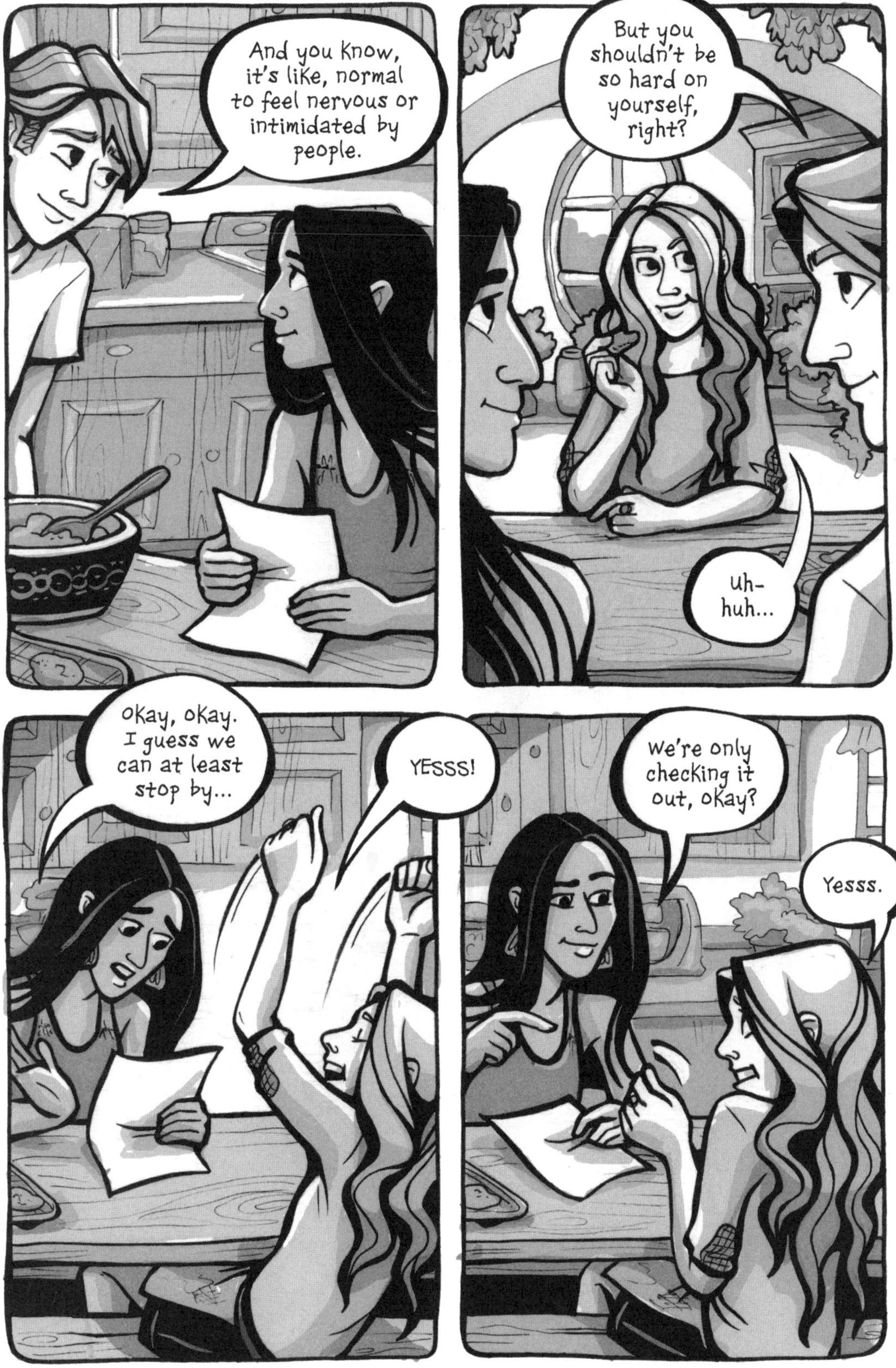
And you know, it's like, normal to feel nervous or intimidated by people.
But you shouldn't be so hard on yourself, right?
Uh-huh...
Okay, okay. I guess we can at least stop by...
YESSS!
We're only checking it out, okay?
Yesss.

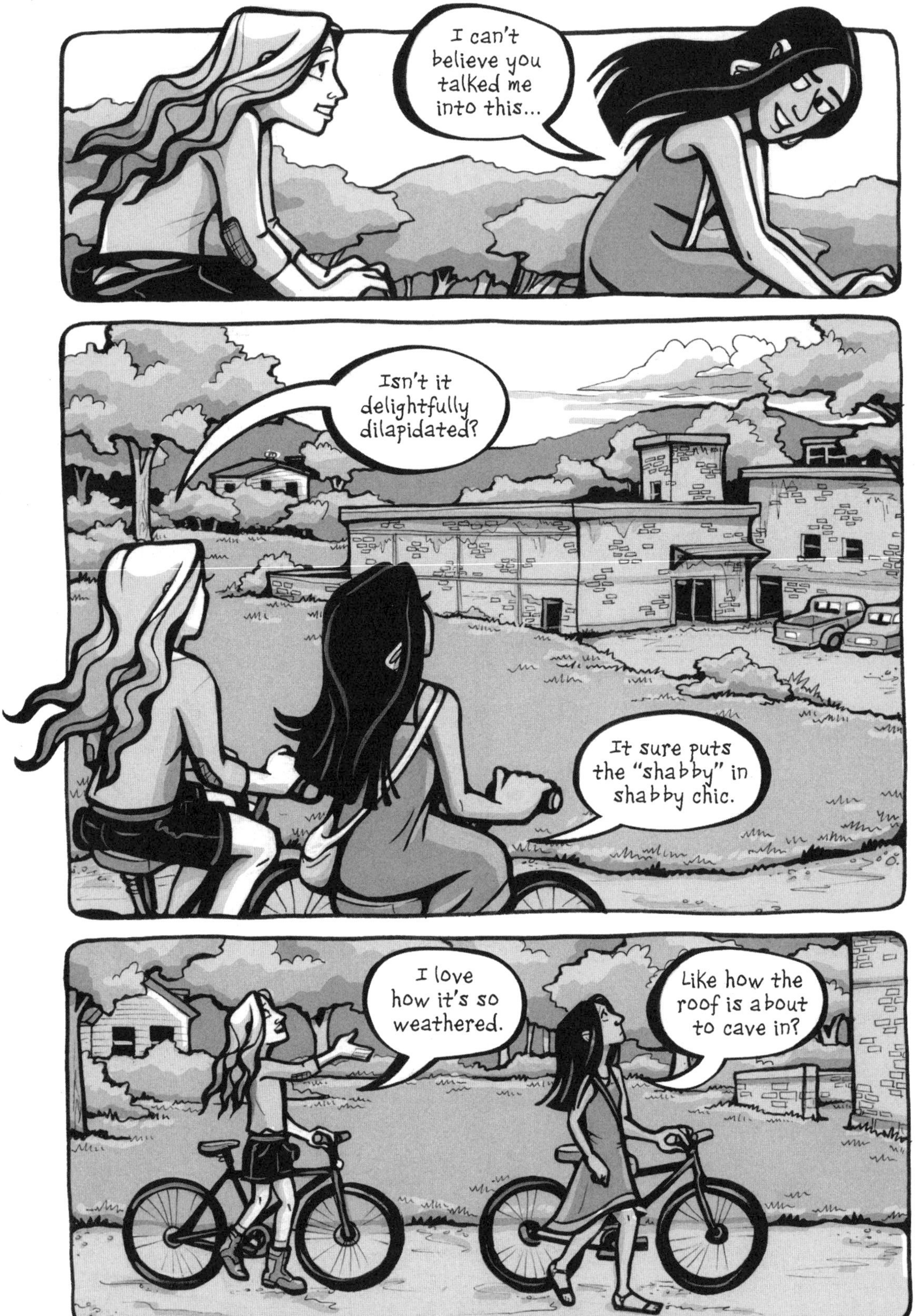
I can't believe you talked me into this...
Isn't it delightfully dilapidated?
It sure puts the "shabby" in shabby chic.
I love how it's so weathered.
Like how the roof is about to cave in?

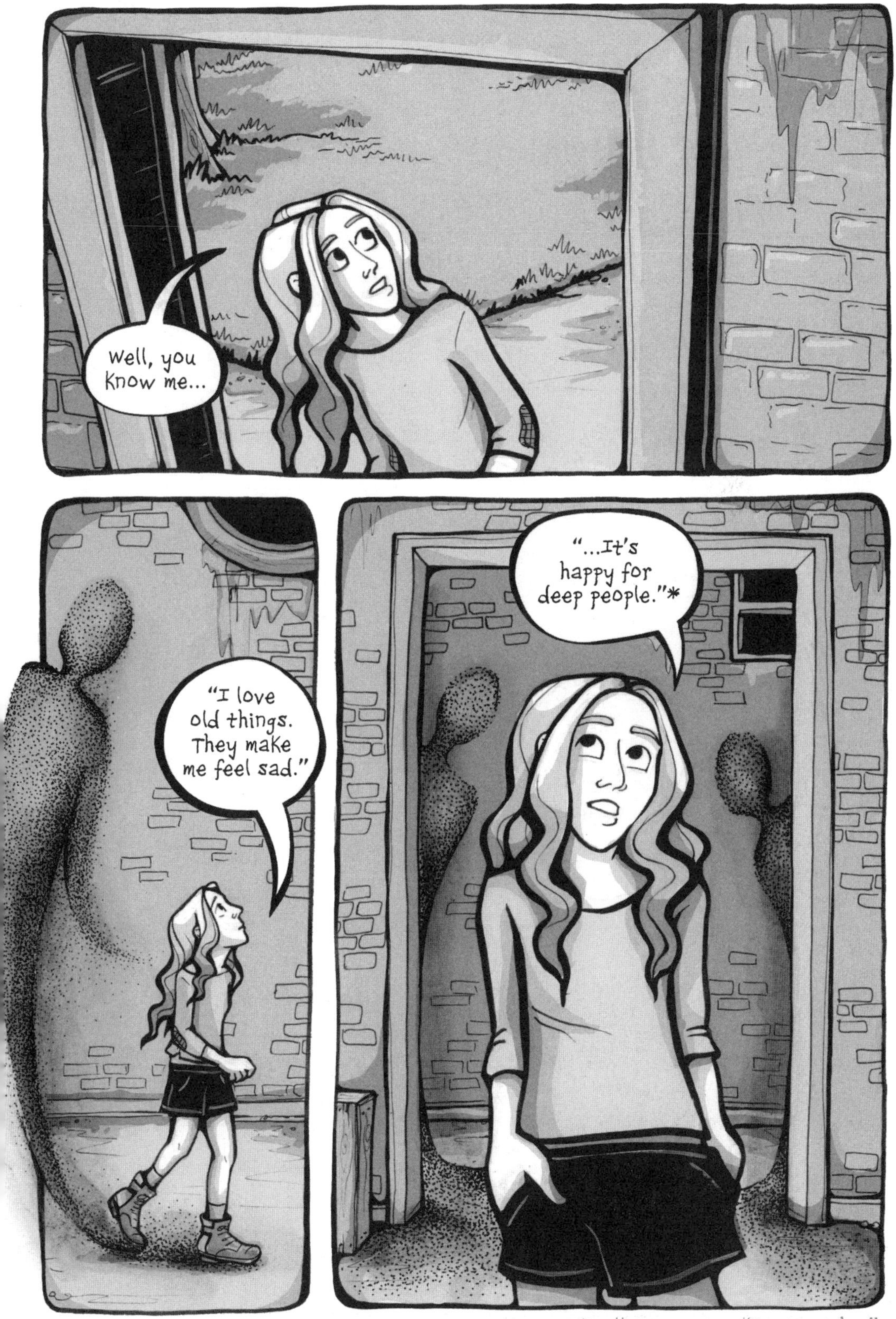
Well, you Know me...
"I love old things. They make me feel sad."
"...It's happy for deep people."*

*Sally Sparrow, "Doctor Who."

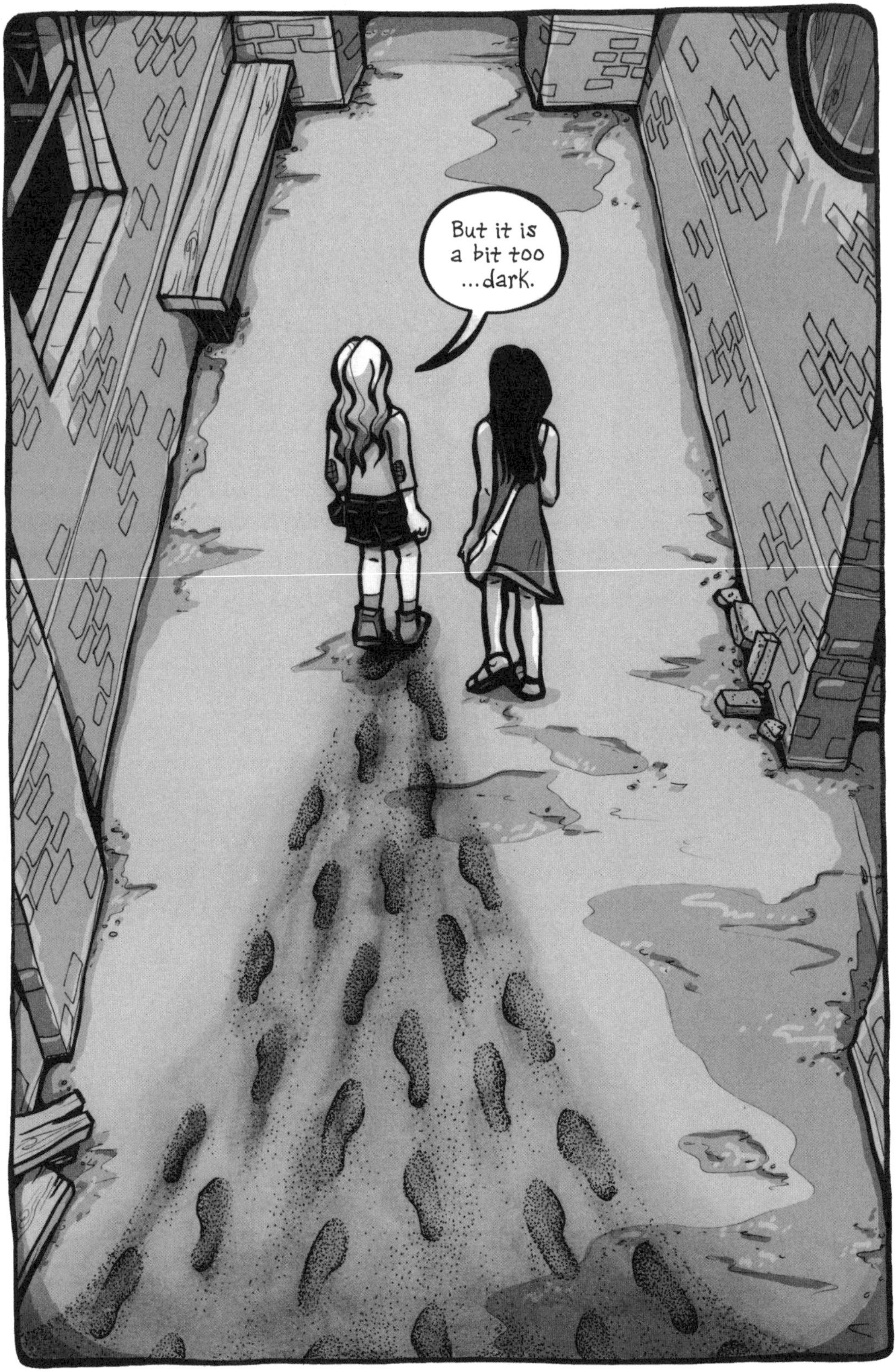
But it is a bit too ...dark.

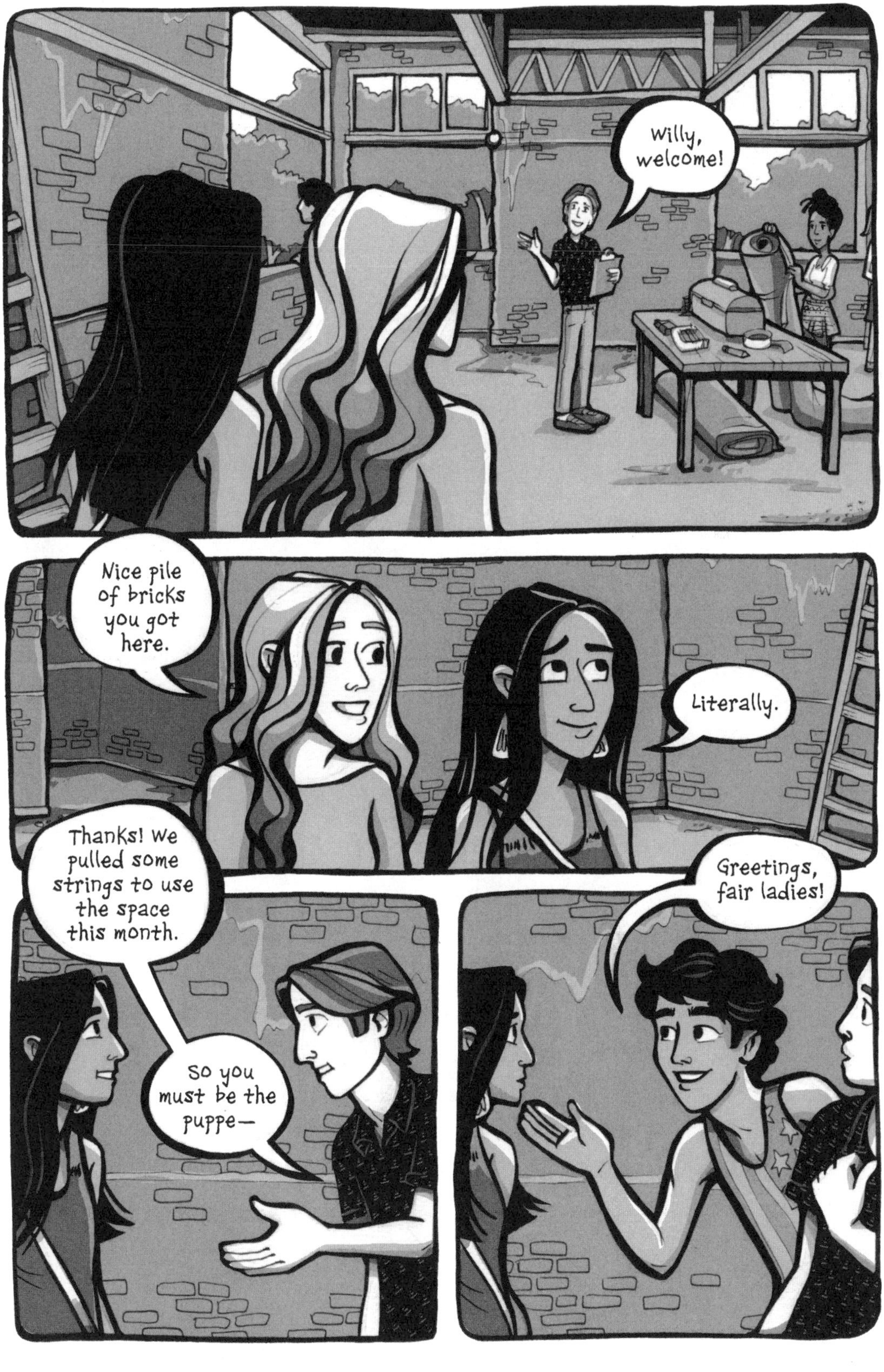
Willy, welcome!
Nice pile of bricks you got here.
Literally.
Thanks! We pulled some strings to use the space this month.
So you must be the puppe—
Greetings, fair ladies!

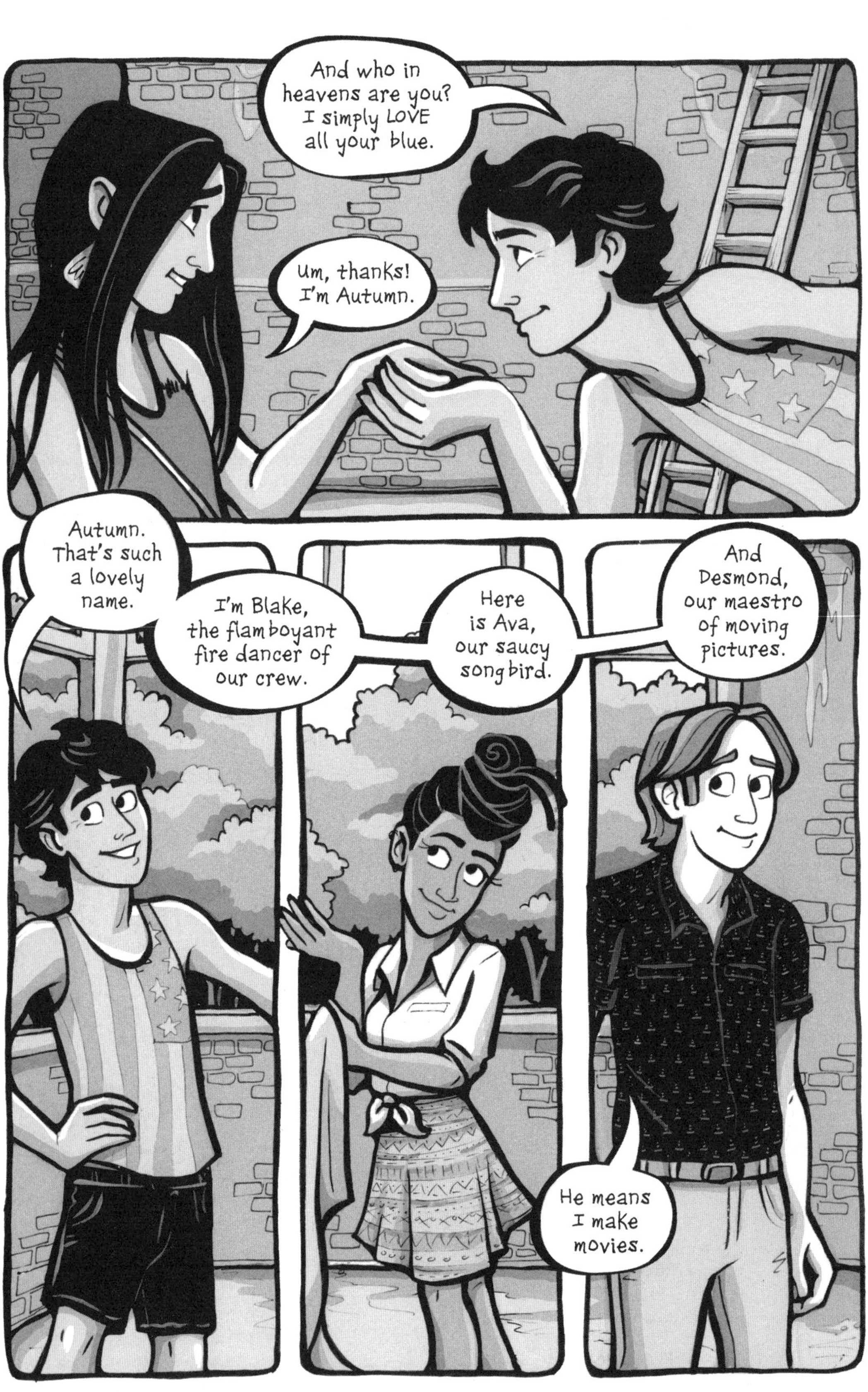
And who in heavens are you? I simply LOVE all your blue.
Um, thanks! I'm Autumn.
Autumn. That's such a lovely name.
I'm Blake, the flamboyant fire dancer of our crew.
Here is Ava, our saucy songbird.
And Desmond, our maestro of moving pictures.
He means I make movies.

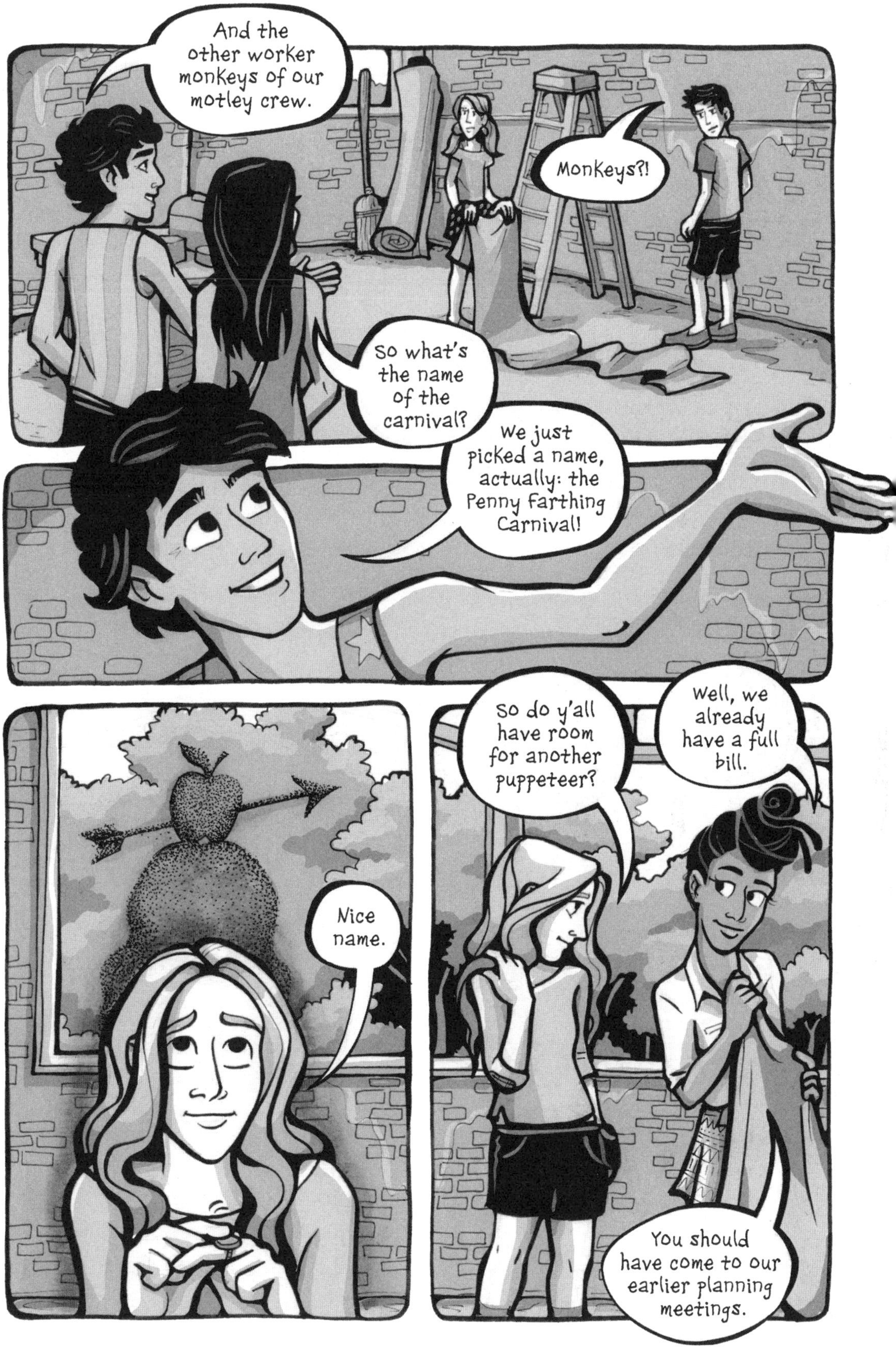
And the other worker monkeys of our motley crew.
Monkeys?!
So what's the name of the carnival?
We just picked a name, actually: the Penny Farthing Carnival!
Nice name.
So do y'all have room for another puppeteer?
Well, we already have a full bill.
You should have come to our earlier planning meetings.

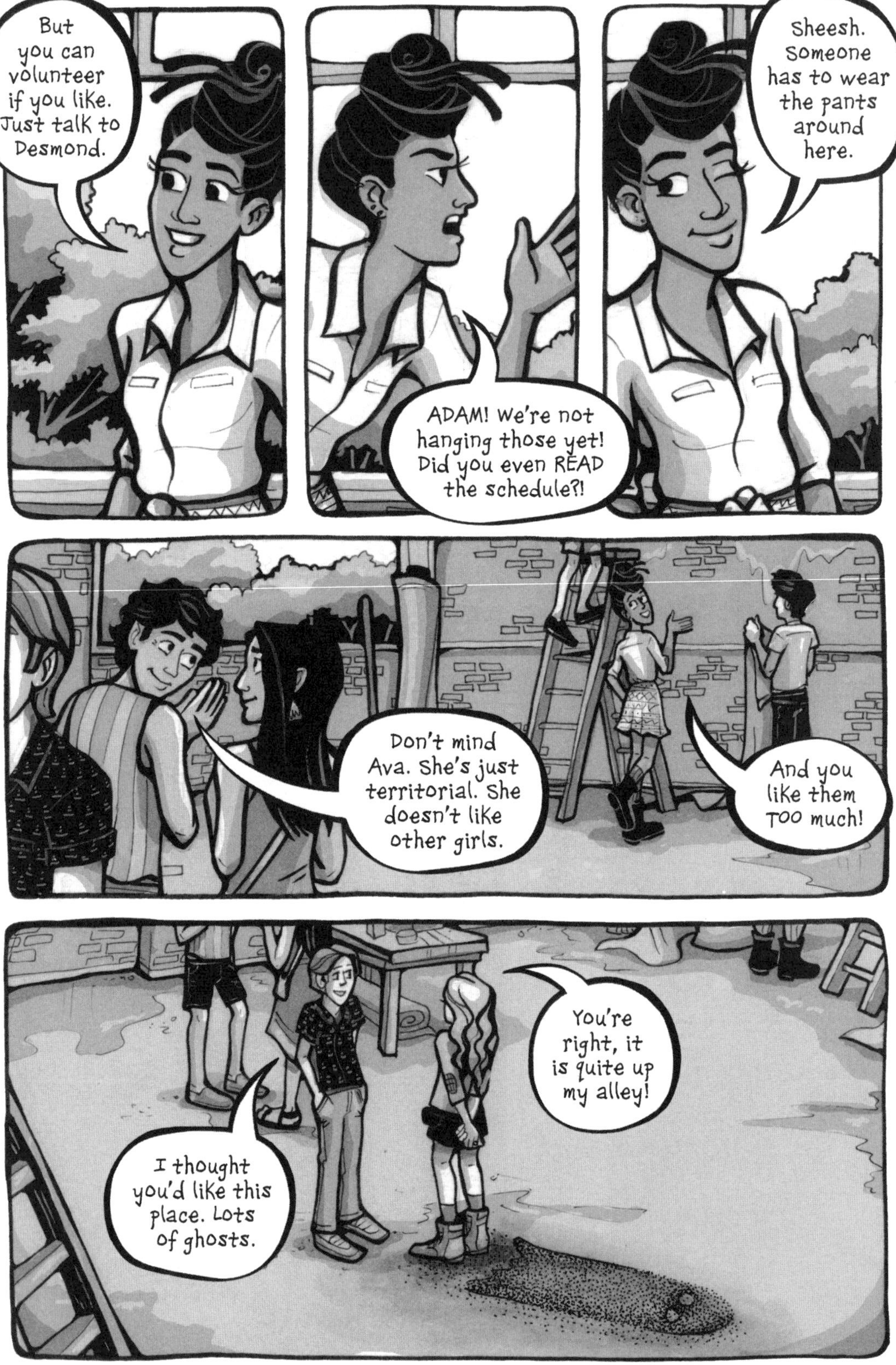

But you can volunteer if you like. Just talk to Desmond.
ADAM! We're not hanging those yet! Did you even READ the schedule?!
Sheesh. Someone has to wear the pants around here.
Don't mind Ava. She's just territorial. She doesn't like other girls.
And you like them TOO much!
I thought you'd like this place. Lots of ghosts.
You're right, it is quite up my alley!

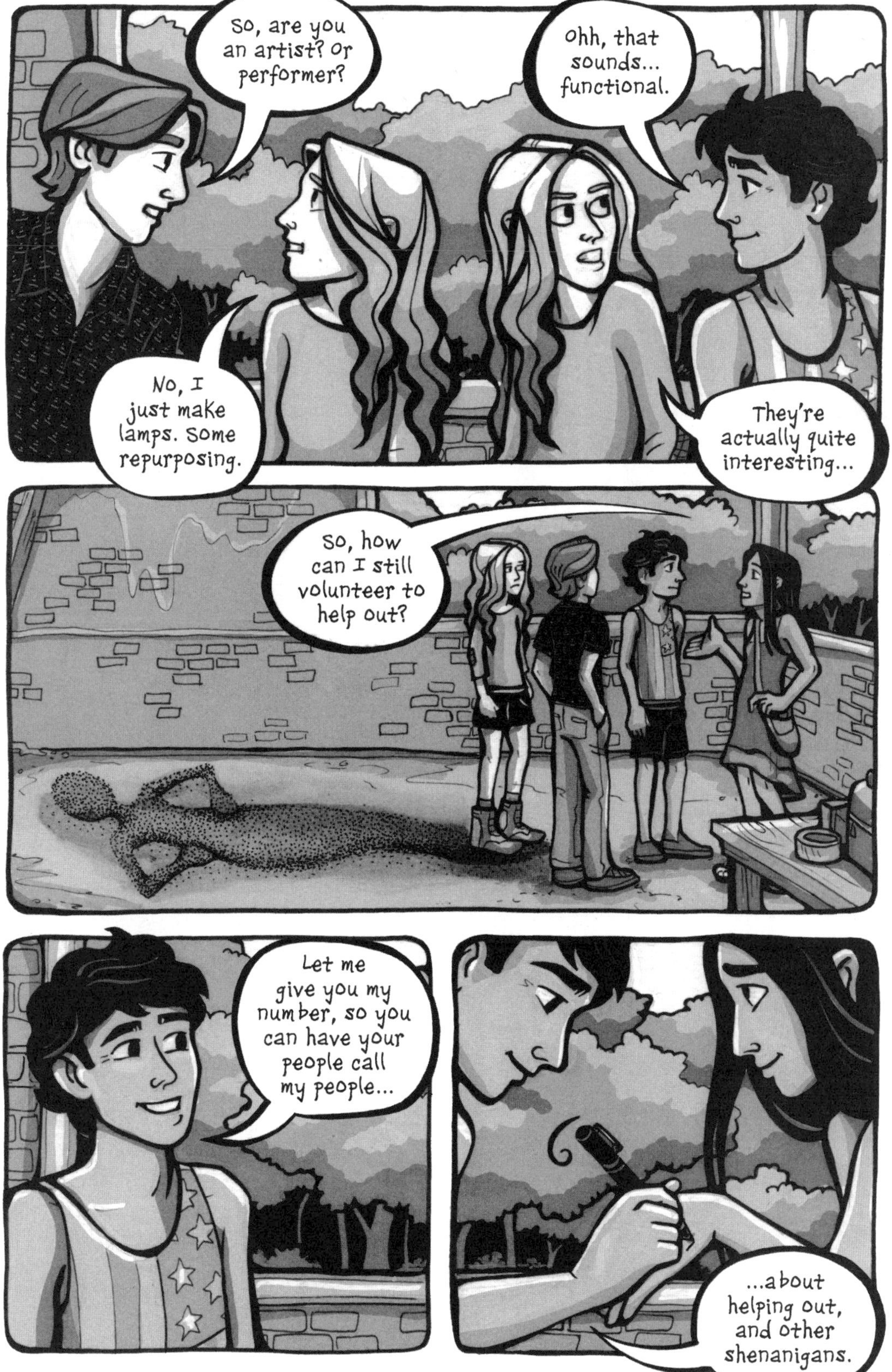
So, are you an artist? Or performer?
No, I just make lamps. Some repurposing.
Ohh, that sounds... functional.
They're actually quite interesting...
So, how can I still volunteer to help out?
Let me give you my number, so you can have your people call my people...
...about helping out, and other shenanigans.

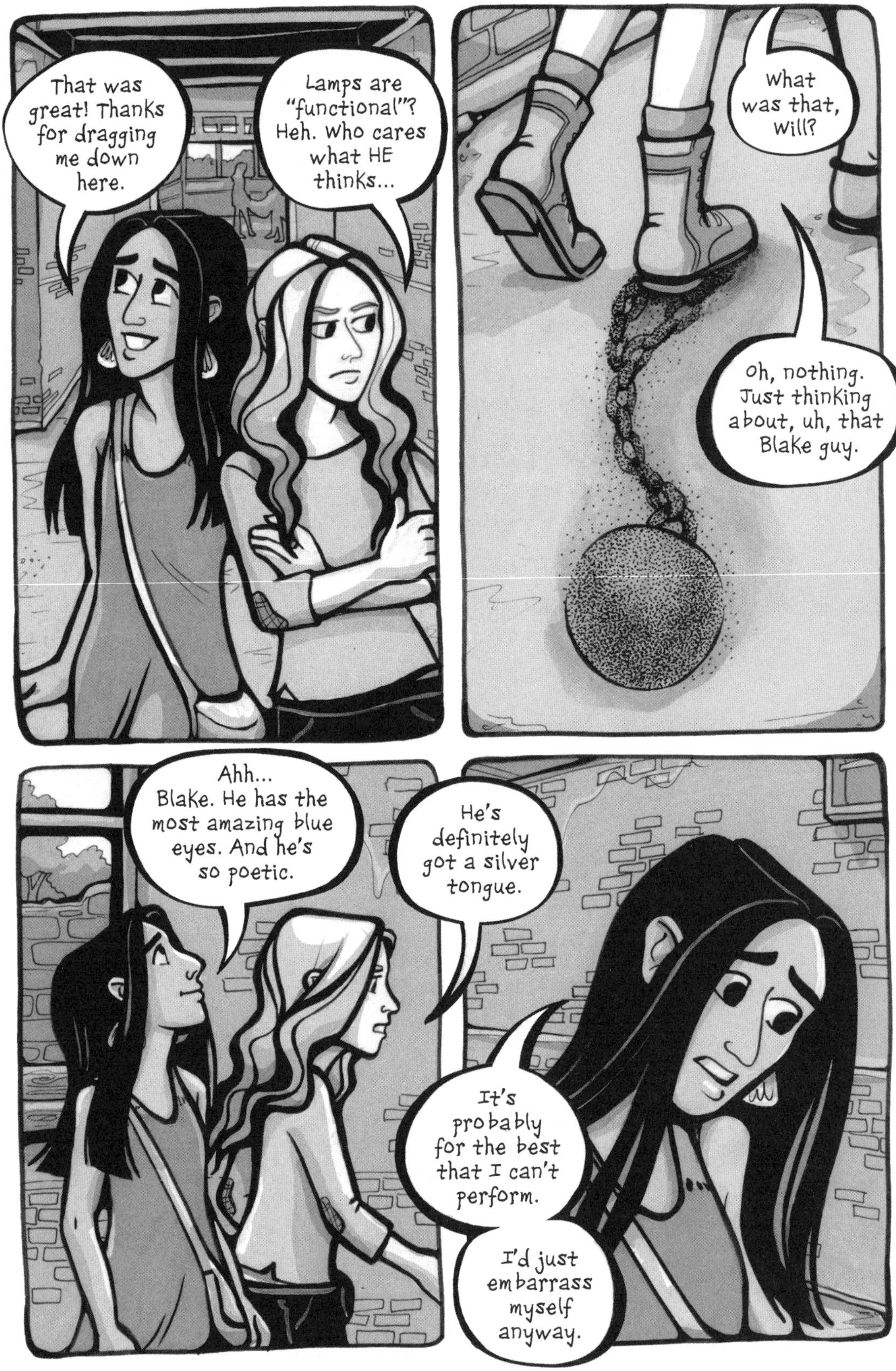
That was great! Thanks for dragging me down here.
Lamps are "functional"? Heh. Who cares what HE thinks...
What was that, Will?
Oh, nothing. Just thinking about, uh, that Blake guy.
Ahh... Blake. He has the most amazing blue eyes. And he's so poetic.
He's definitely got a silver tongue.
It's probably for the best that I can't perform.
I'd just embarrass myself anyway.

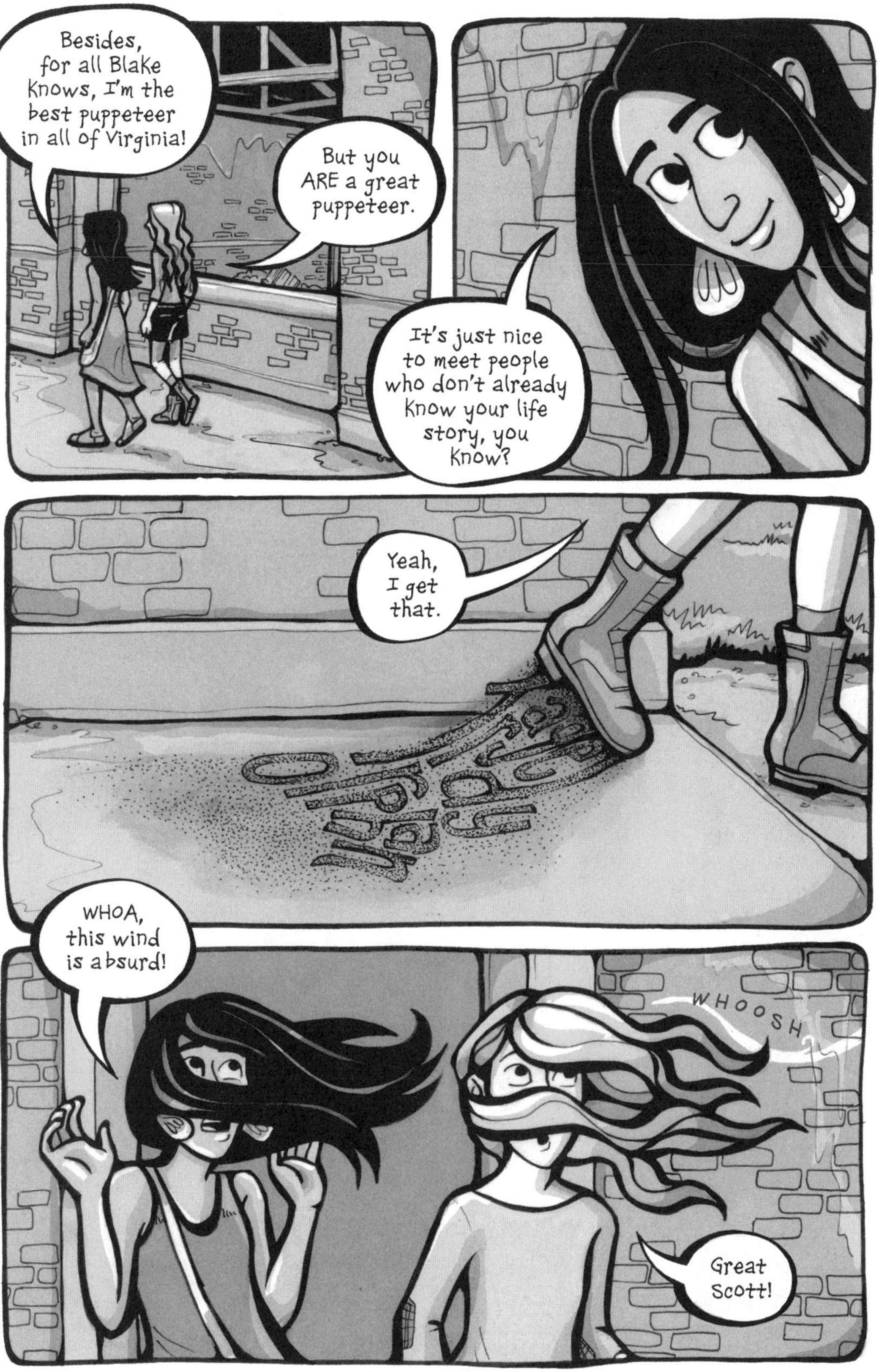
Besides, for all Blake Knows, I'm the best puppeteer in all of Virginia!
But you ARE a great puppeteer.
It's just nice to meet people who don't already know your life story, you know?
Yeah, I get that.
WHOA, this wind is absurd!
WHOOSH
Great Scott!

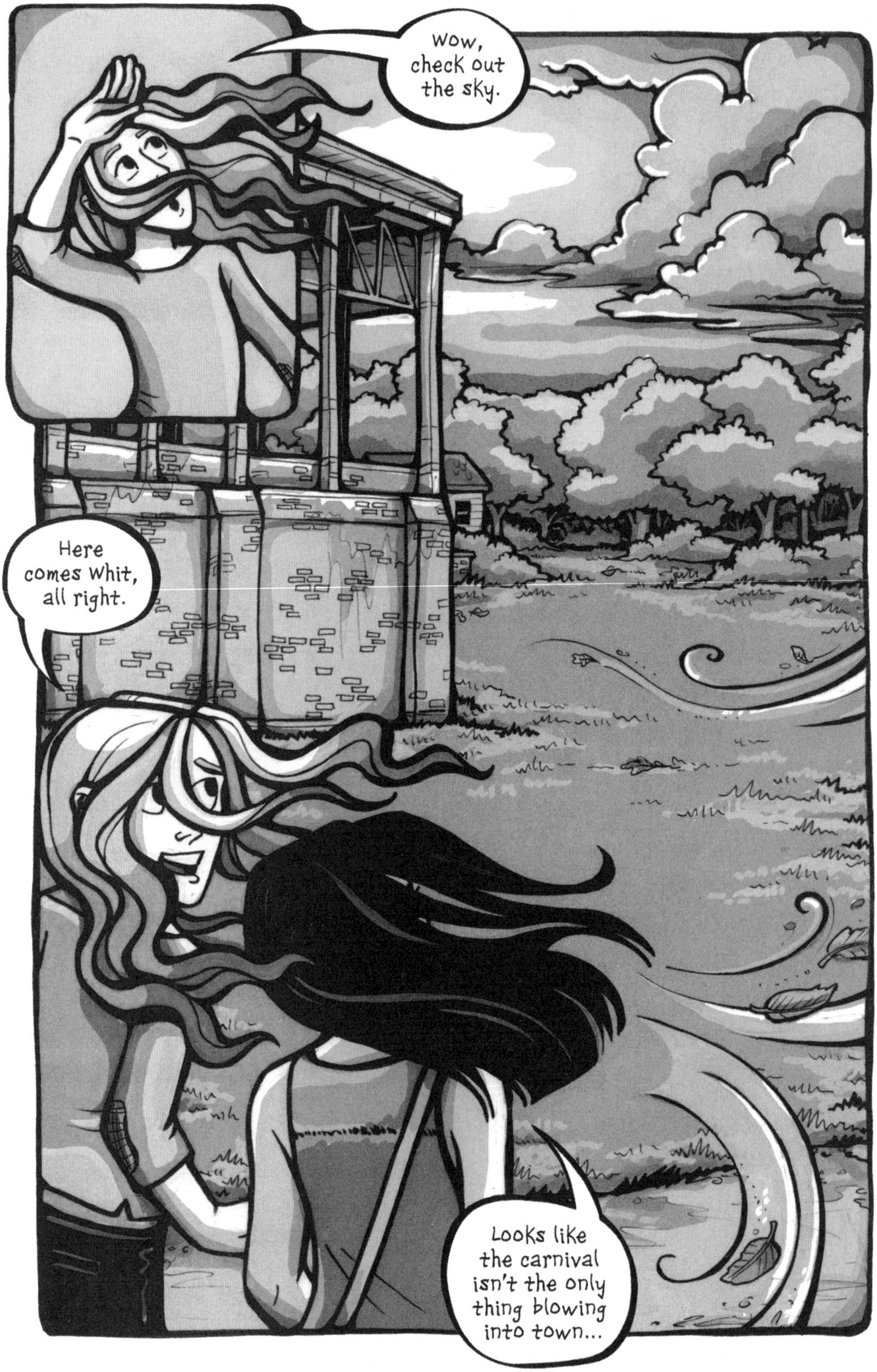
Wow,
check out
the sky.
Here
comes Whit,
all right.
Looks like
the carnival
isn't the only
thing blowing
into town...

OutWhitted

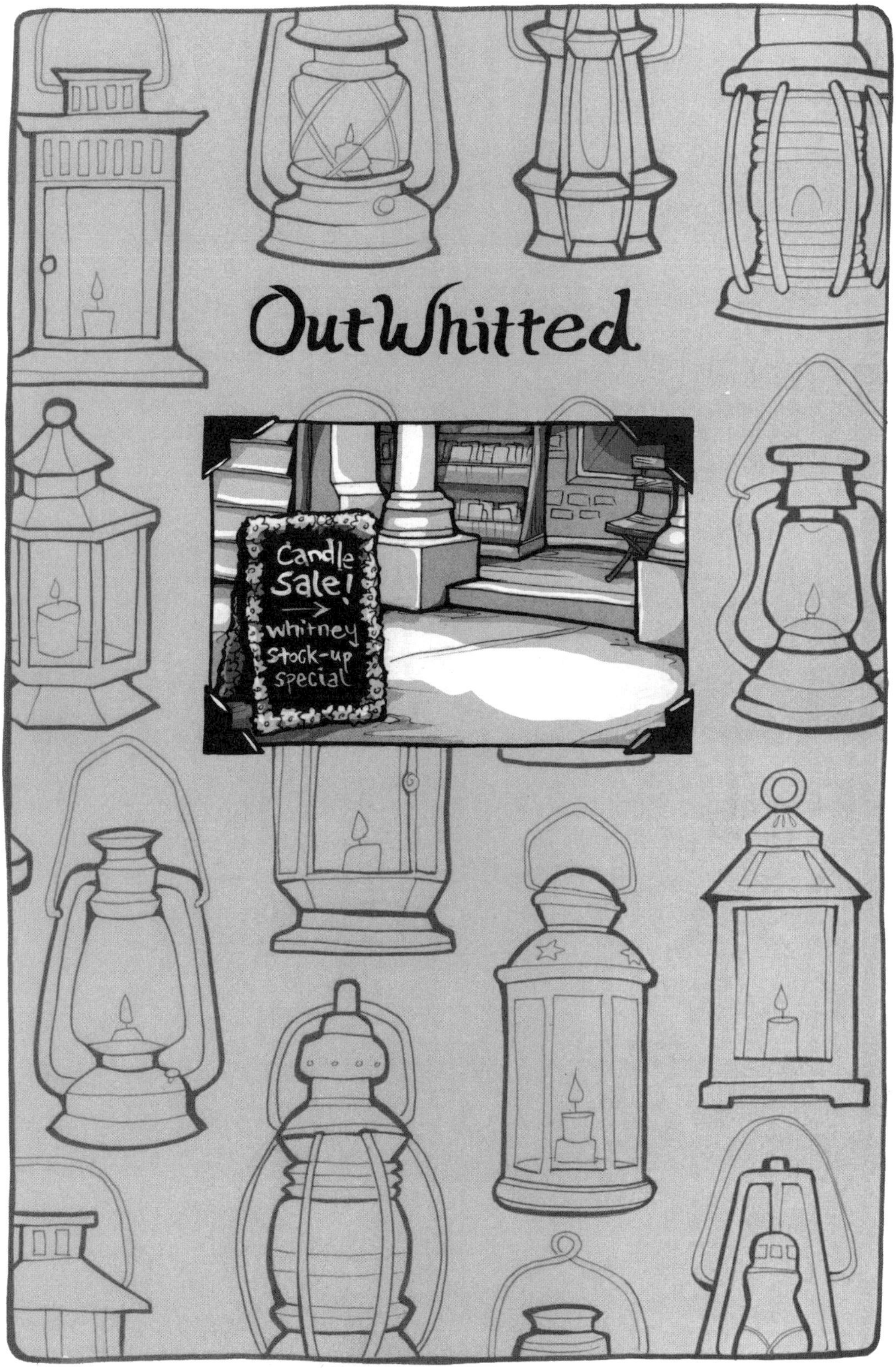
Candle Sale!
→
whitney Stock-up special

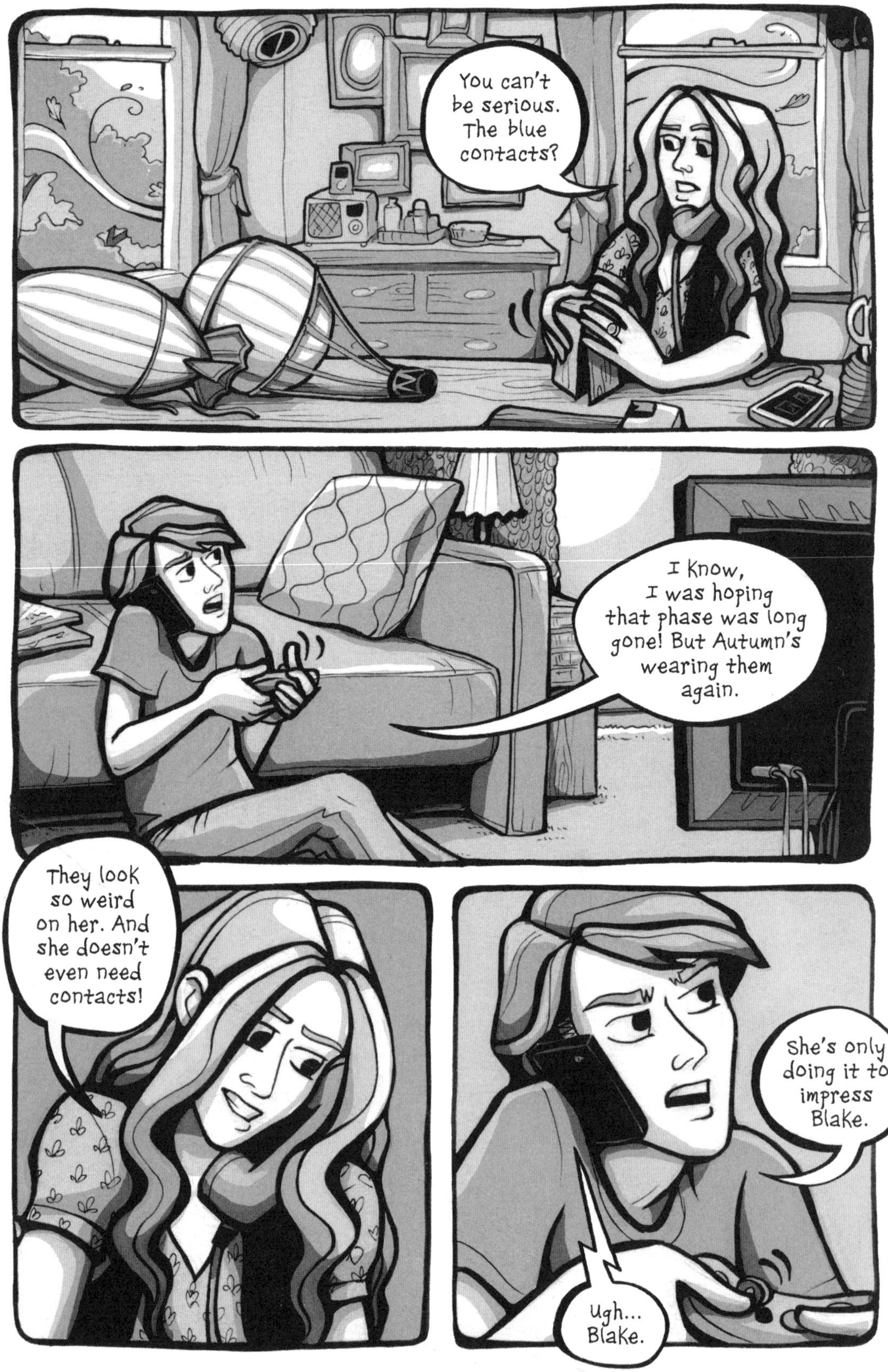
You can't be serious. The blue contacts?
I know, I was hoping that phase was long gone! But Autumn's wearing them again.
They look so weird on her. And she doesn't even need contacts!
She's only doing it to impress Blake.
Ugh... Blake.

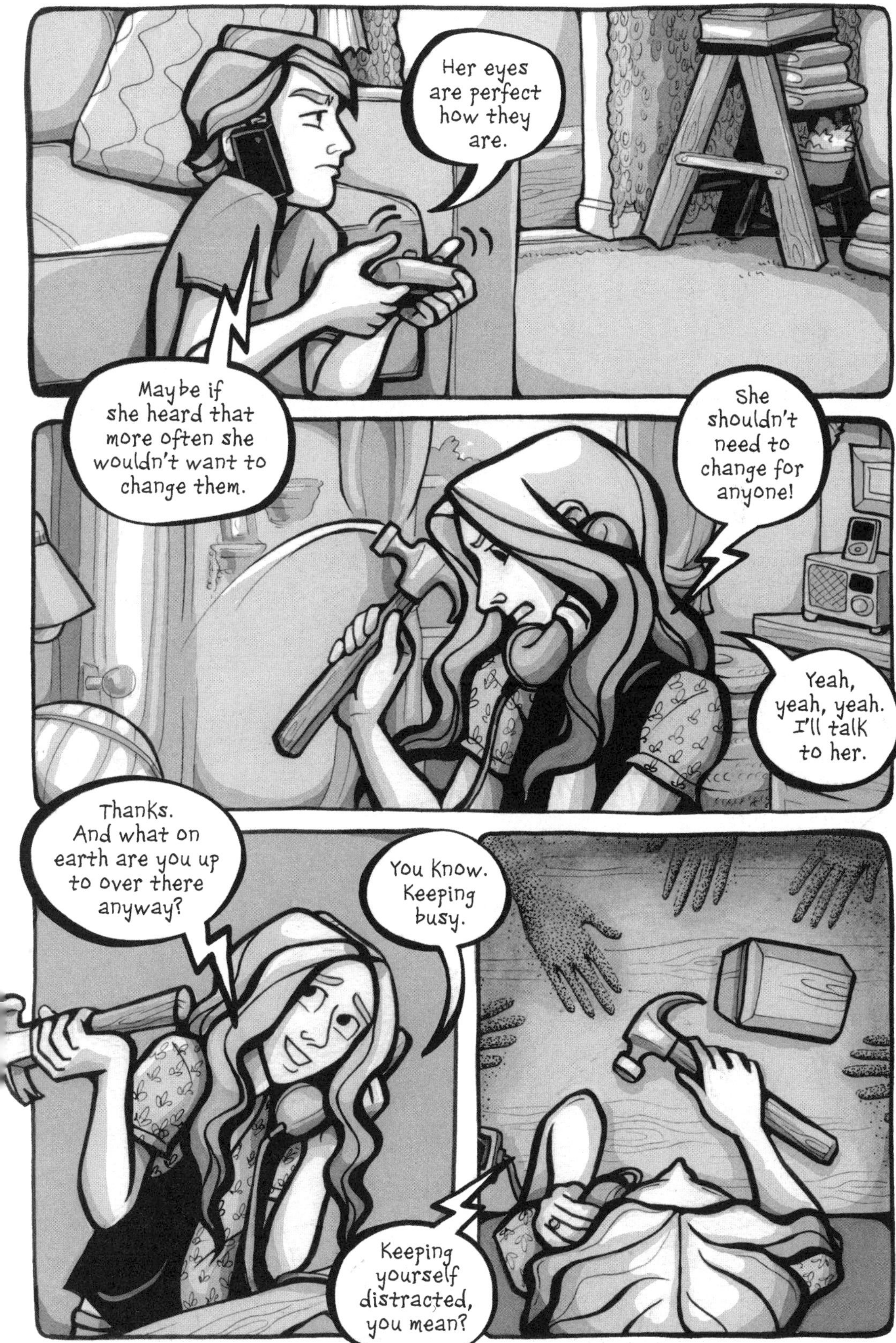
Her eyes are perfect how they are.
Maybe if she heard that more often she wouldn't want to change them.
She shouldn't need to change for anyone!
Yeah, yeah, yeah. I'll talk to her.
Thanks. And what on earth are you up to over there anyway?
You know. Keeping busy.
Keeping yourself distracted, you mean?

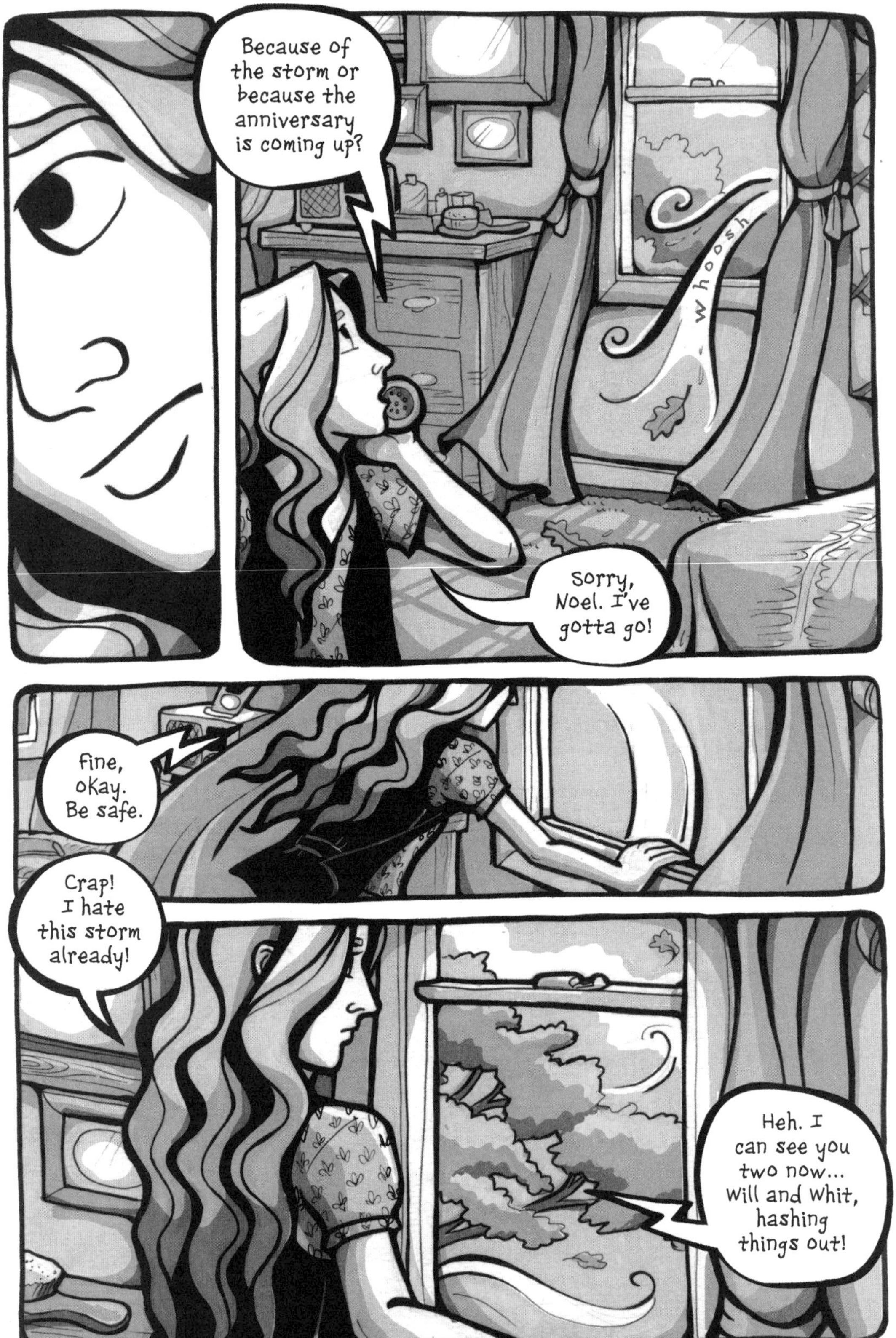
Because of the storm or because the anniversary is coming up?
whoosh
Sorry, Noel. I've gotta go!
fine, okay. Be safe.
Crap! I hate this storm already!
Heh. I can see you two now... Will and Whit, hashing things out!

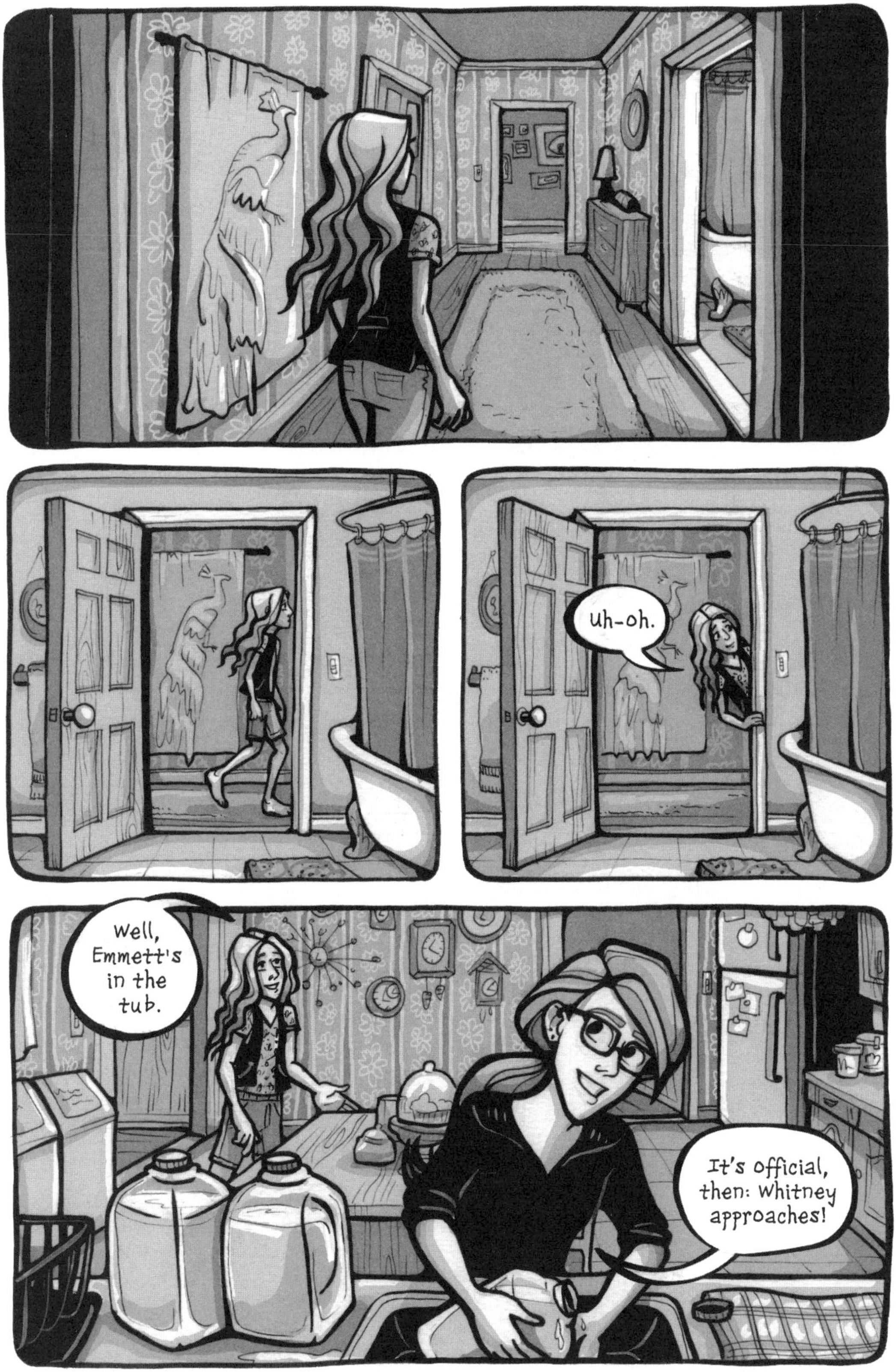
Uh-oh.
Well, Emmett's in the tub.
It's official, then: Whitney approaches!

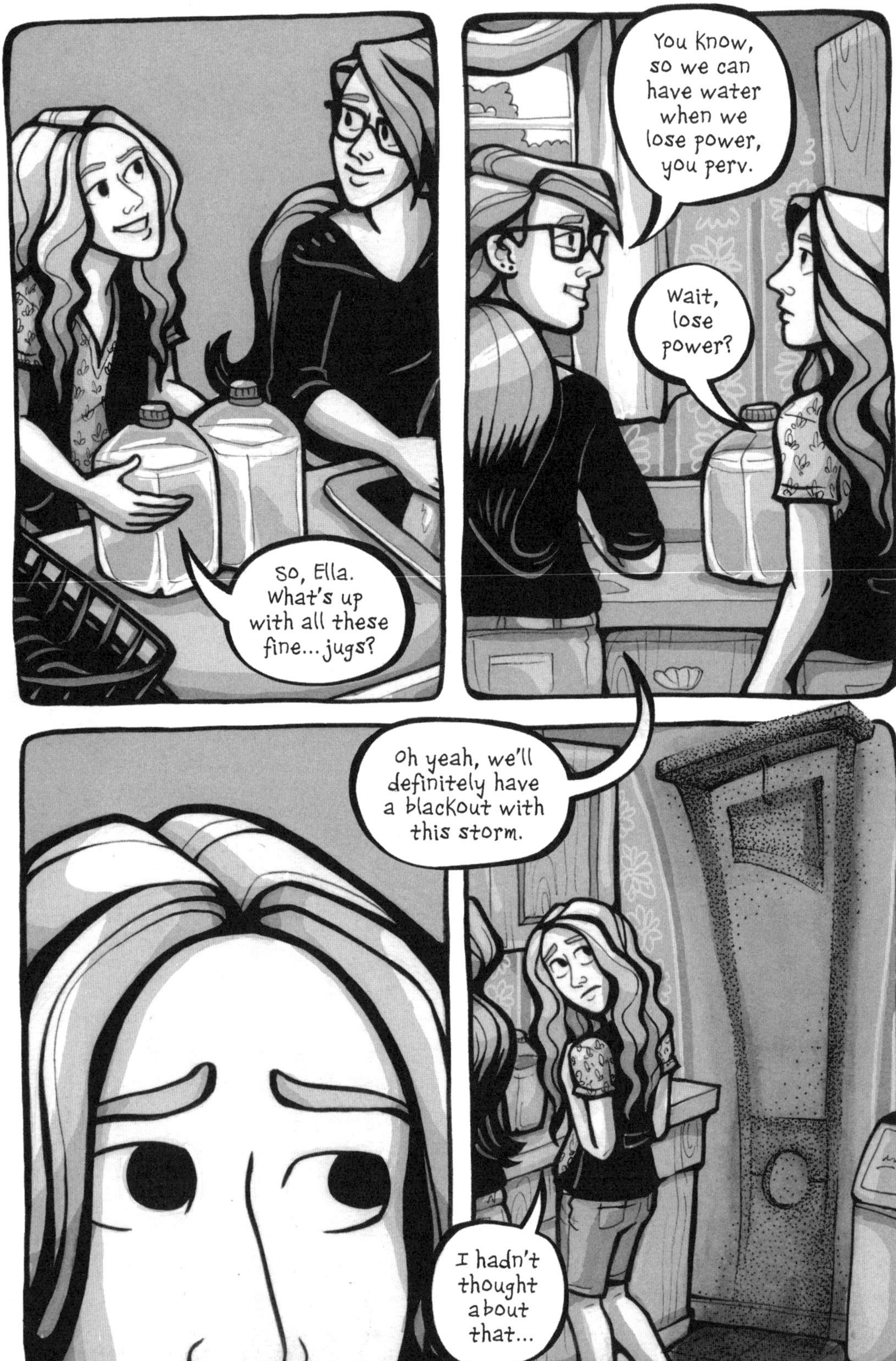
So, Ella. What's up with all these fine... jugs?
You know, so we can have water when we lose power, you perv.
Wait, lose power?
Oh yeah, we'll definitely have a blackout with this storm.
I hadn't thought about that...

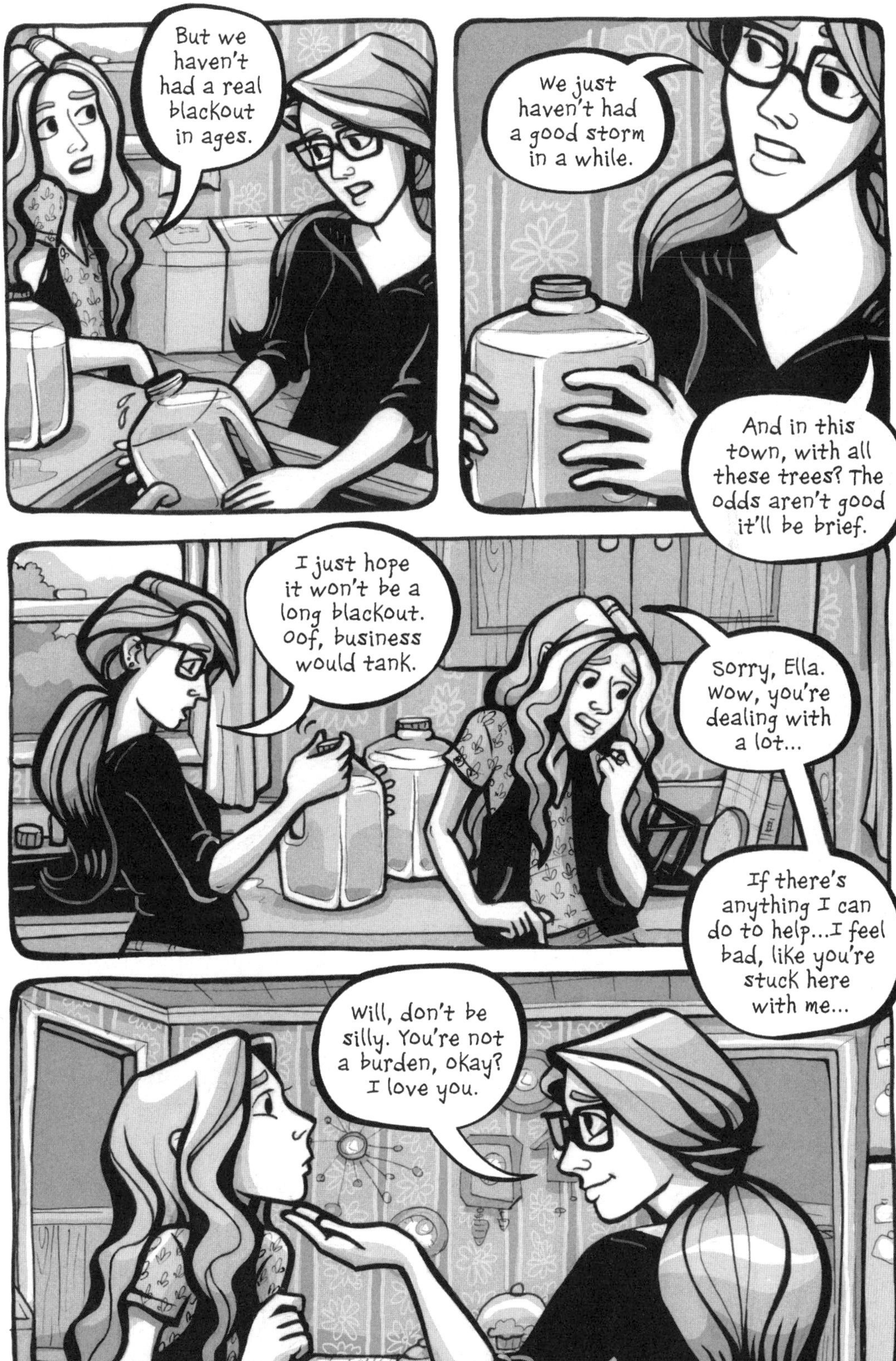
But we haven't had a real blackout in ages.
We just haven't had a good storm in a while.
And in this town, with all these trees? The odds aren't good it'll be brief.
I just hope it won't be a long blackout. Oof, business would tank.
Sorry, Ella. Wow, you're dealing with a lot...
If there's anything I can do to help...I feel bad, like you're stuck here with me...
Will, don't be silly. You're not a burden, okay? I love you.

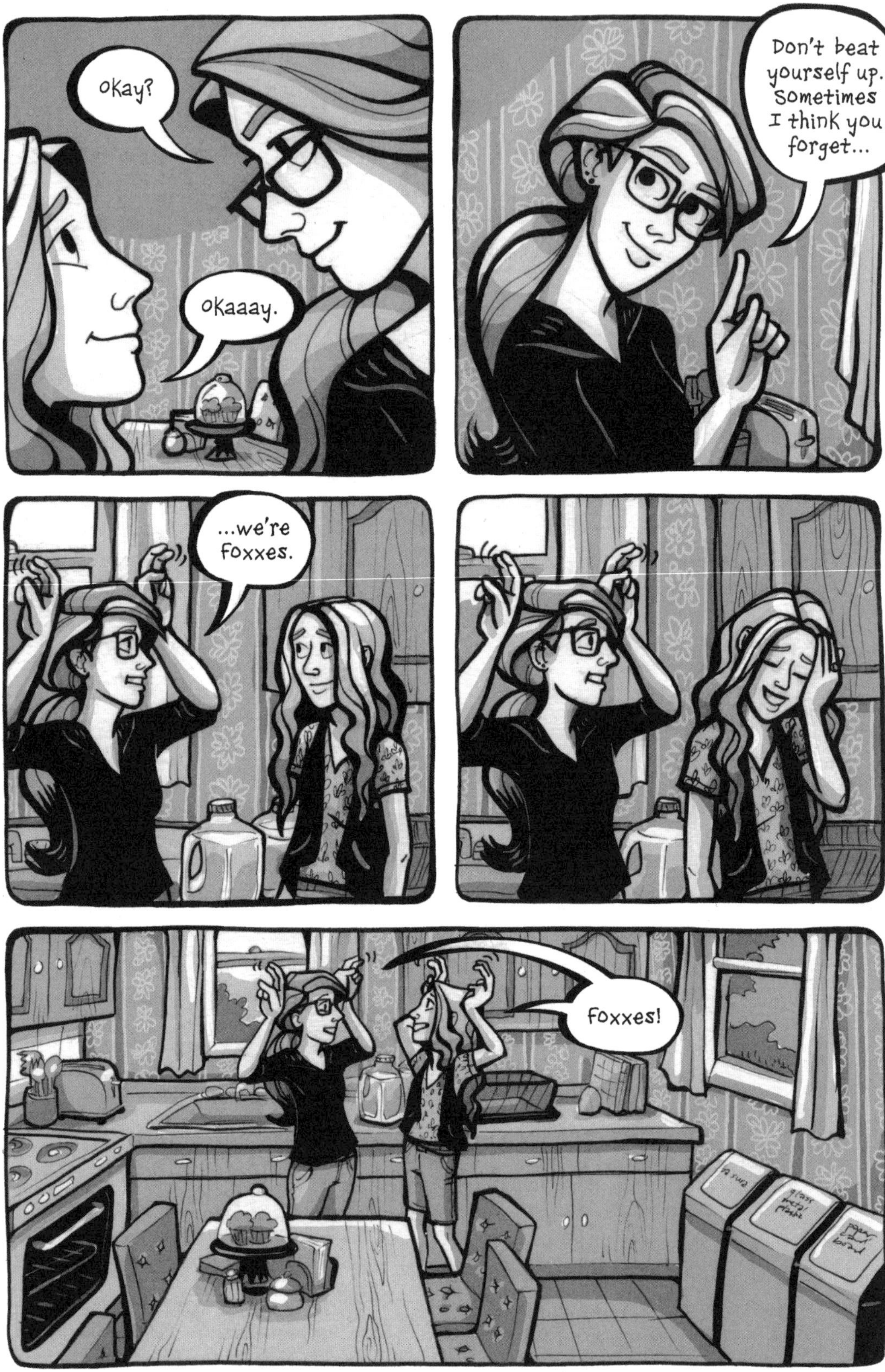

Okay?
Okaaay.
Don't beat yourself up. Sometimes I think you forget...
...we're foxxes.
Foxxes!

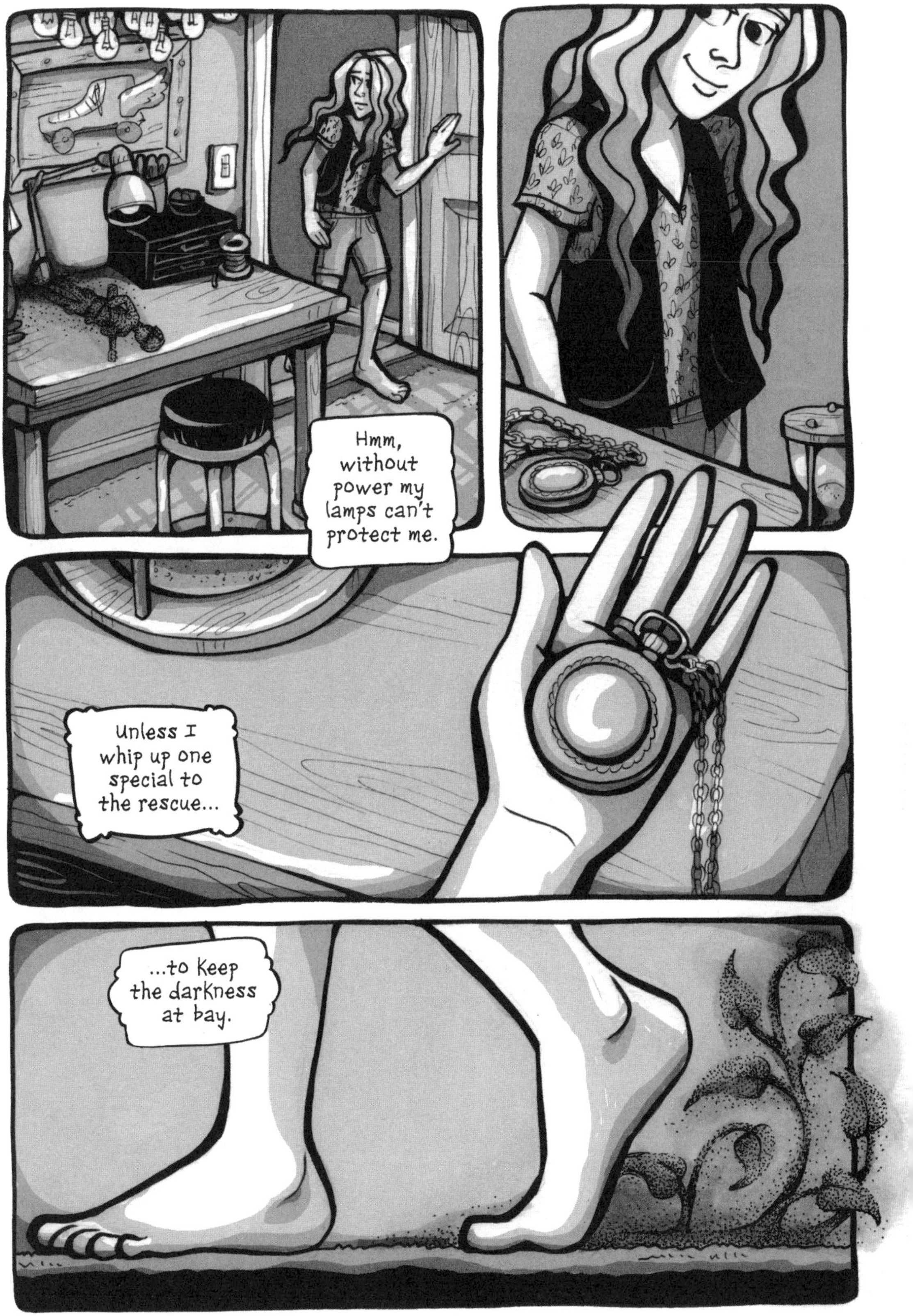
Hmm, without power my lamps can't protect me.
Unless I whip up one special to the rescue...
...to keep the darkness at bay.

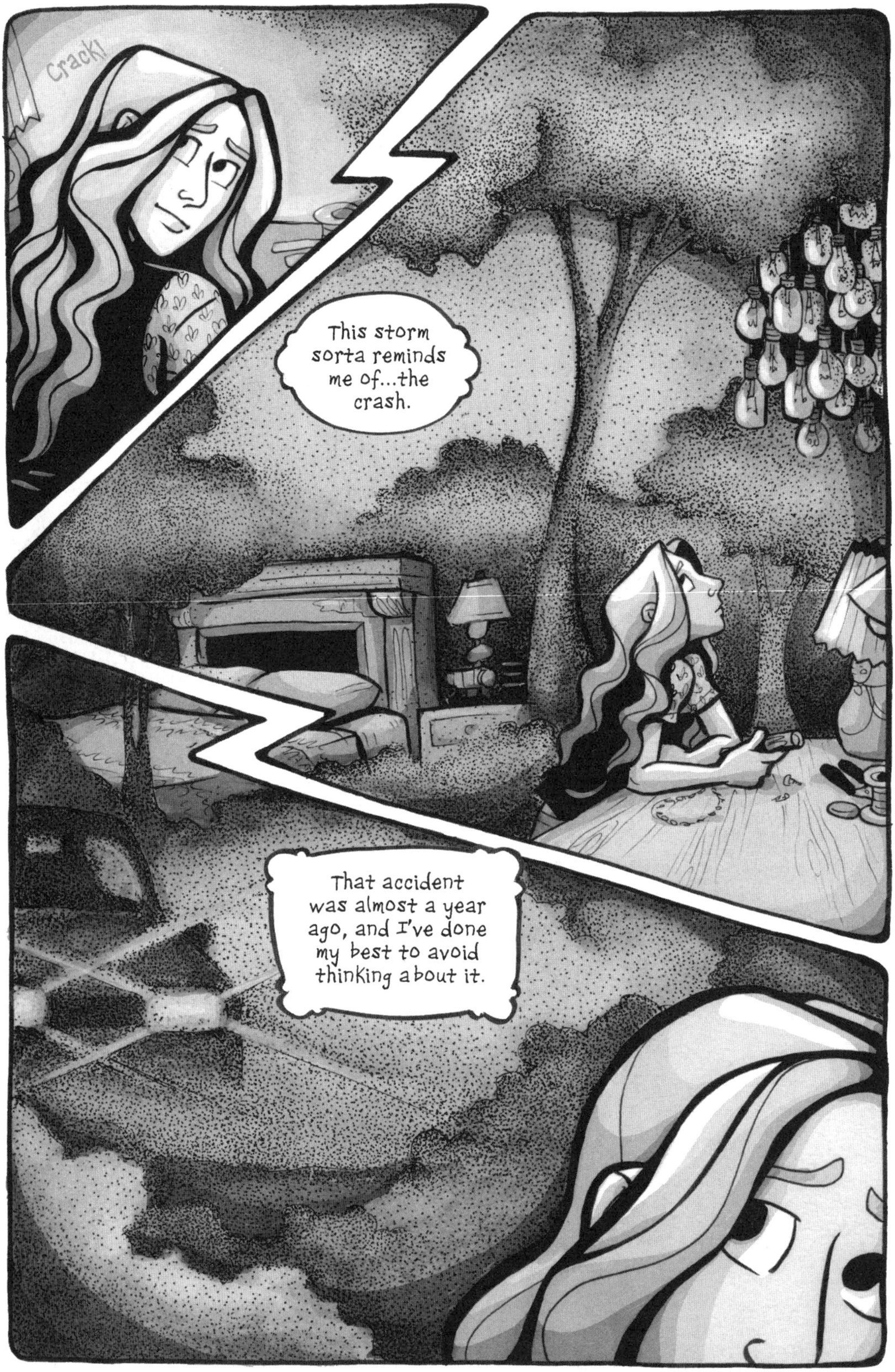
Crack!
This storm sorta reminds me of...the crash.
That accident was almost a year ago, and I've done my best to avoid thinking about it.

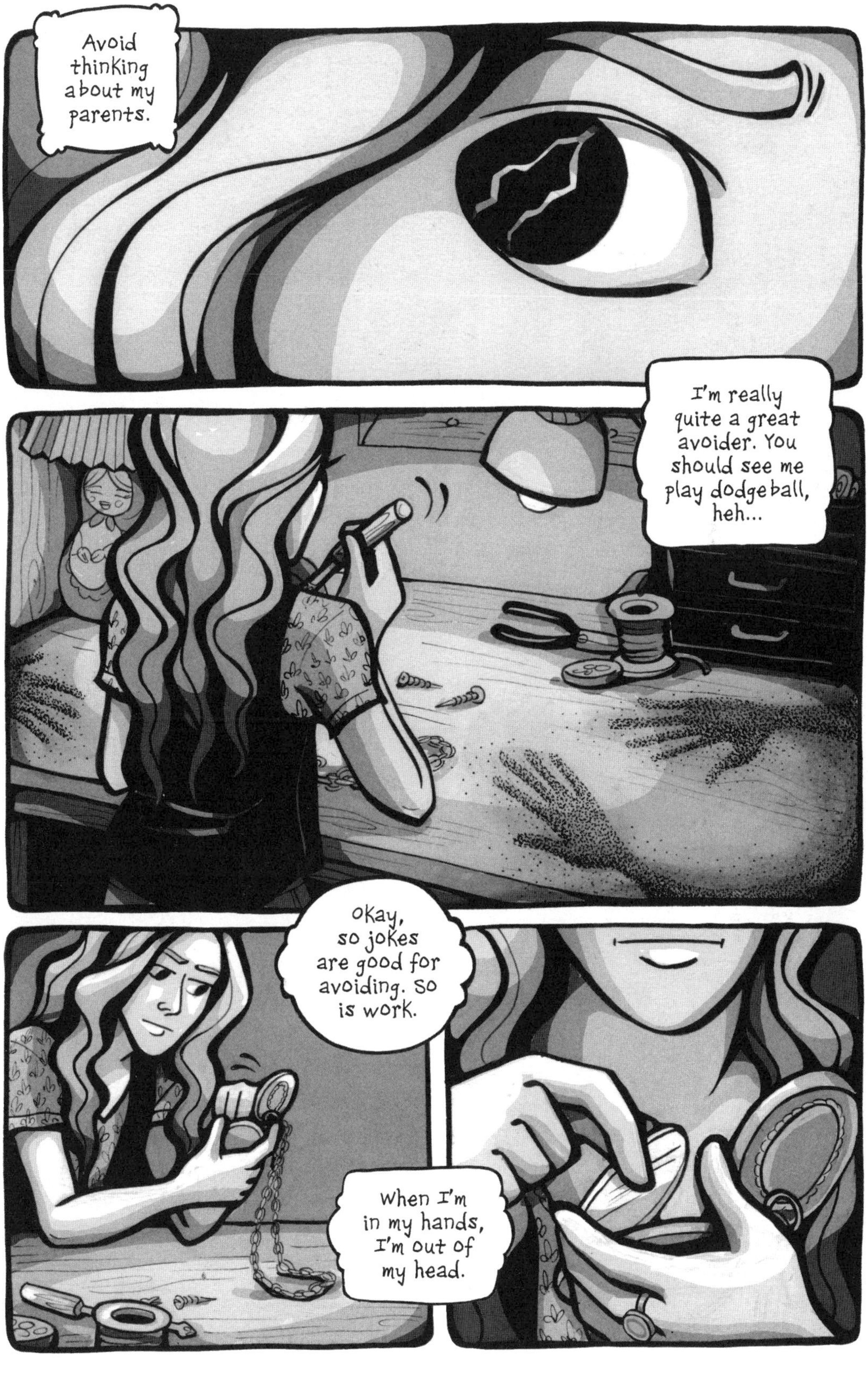
Avoid thinking about my parents.
I'm really quite a great avoider. You should see me play dodgeball, heh...
Okay, so jokes are good for avoiding. So is work.
When I'm in my hands, I'm out of my head.

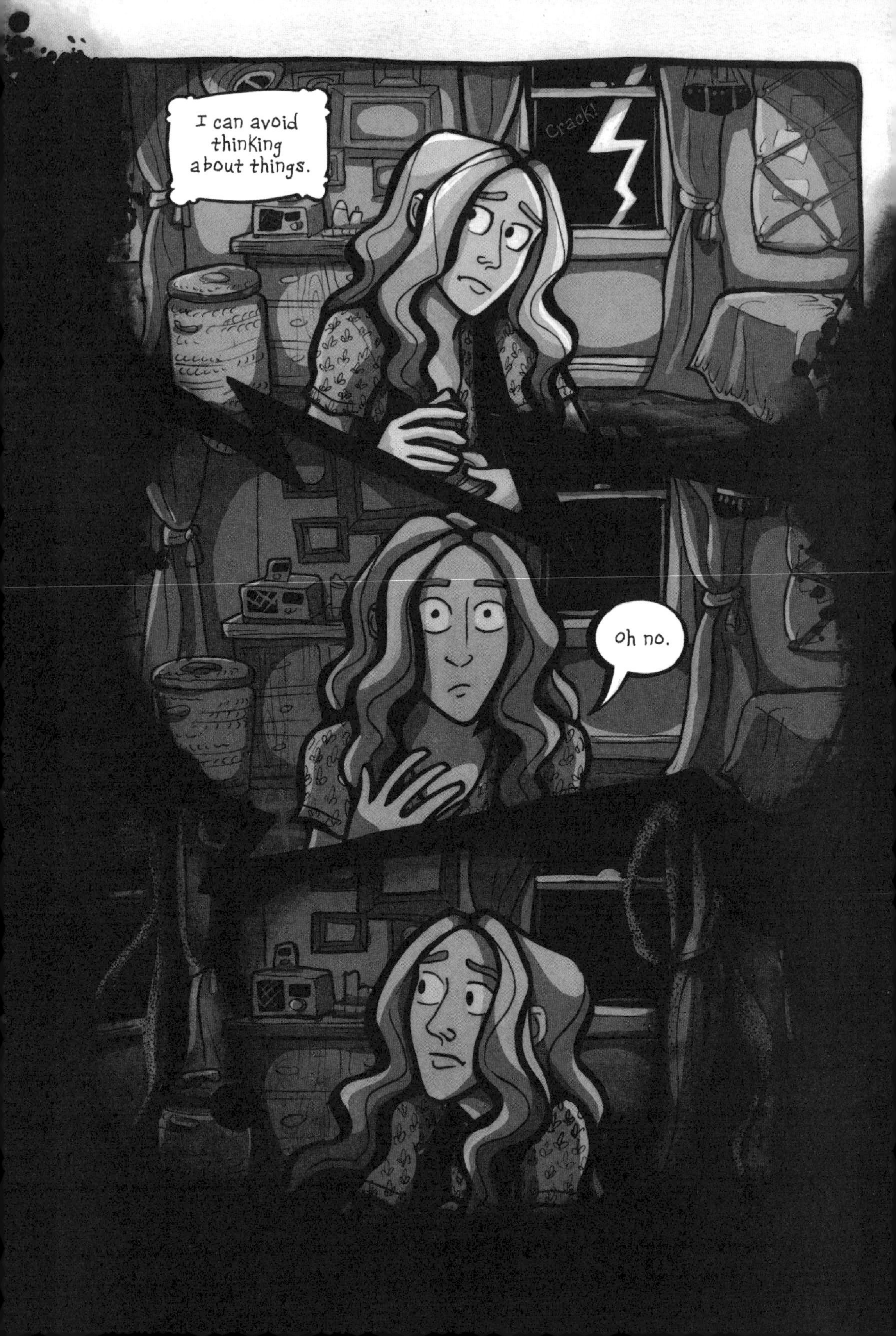
I can avoid thinking about things.
Crack!
oh no.

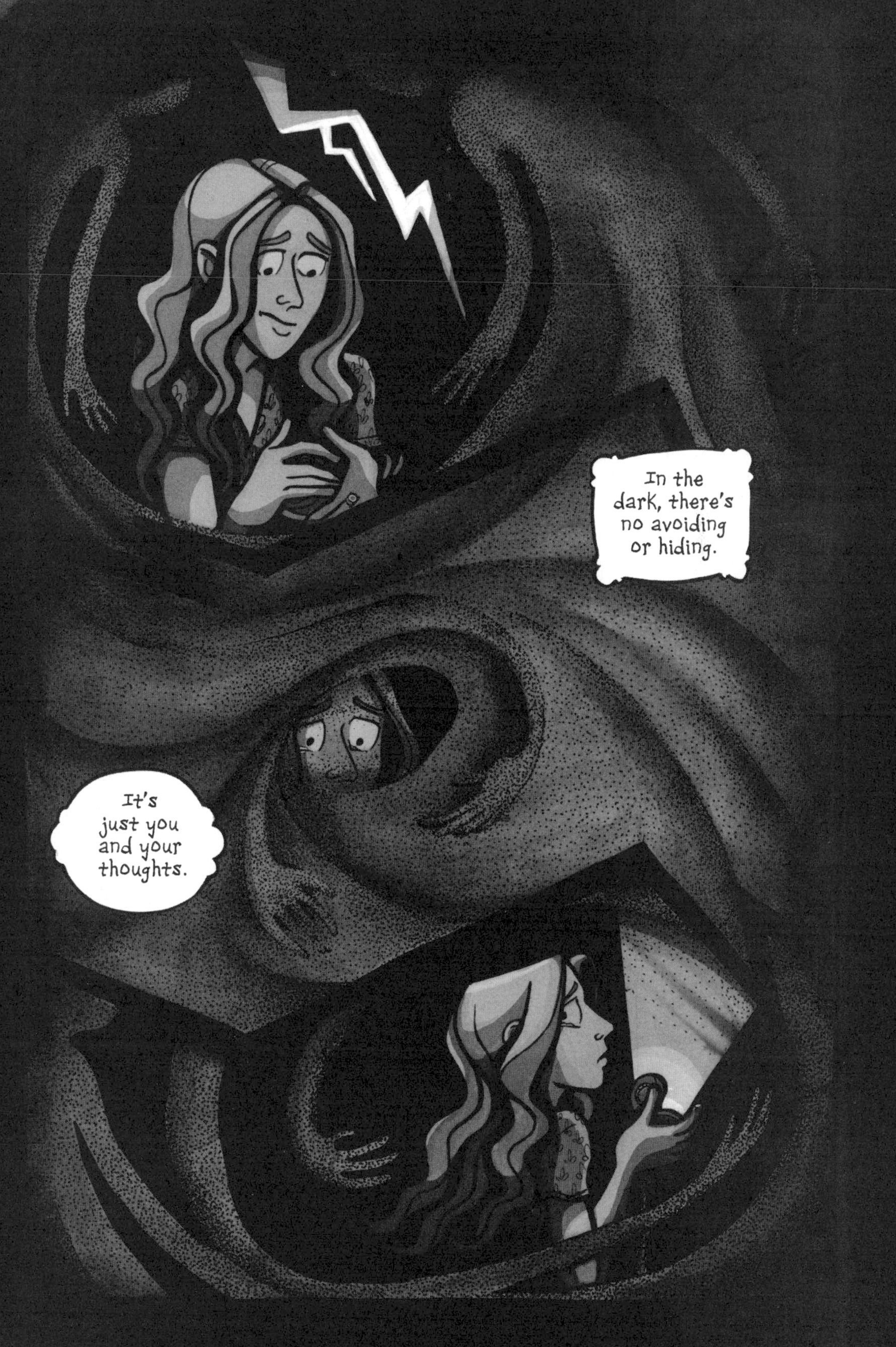
In the dark, there's no avoiding or hiding.
It's just you and your thoughts.

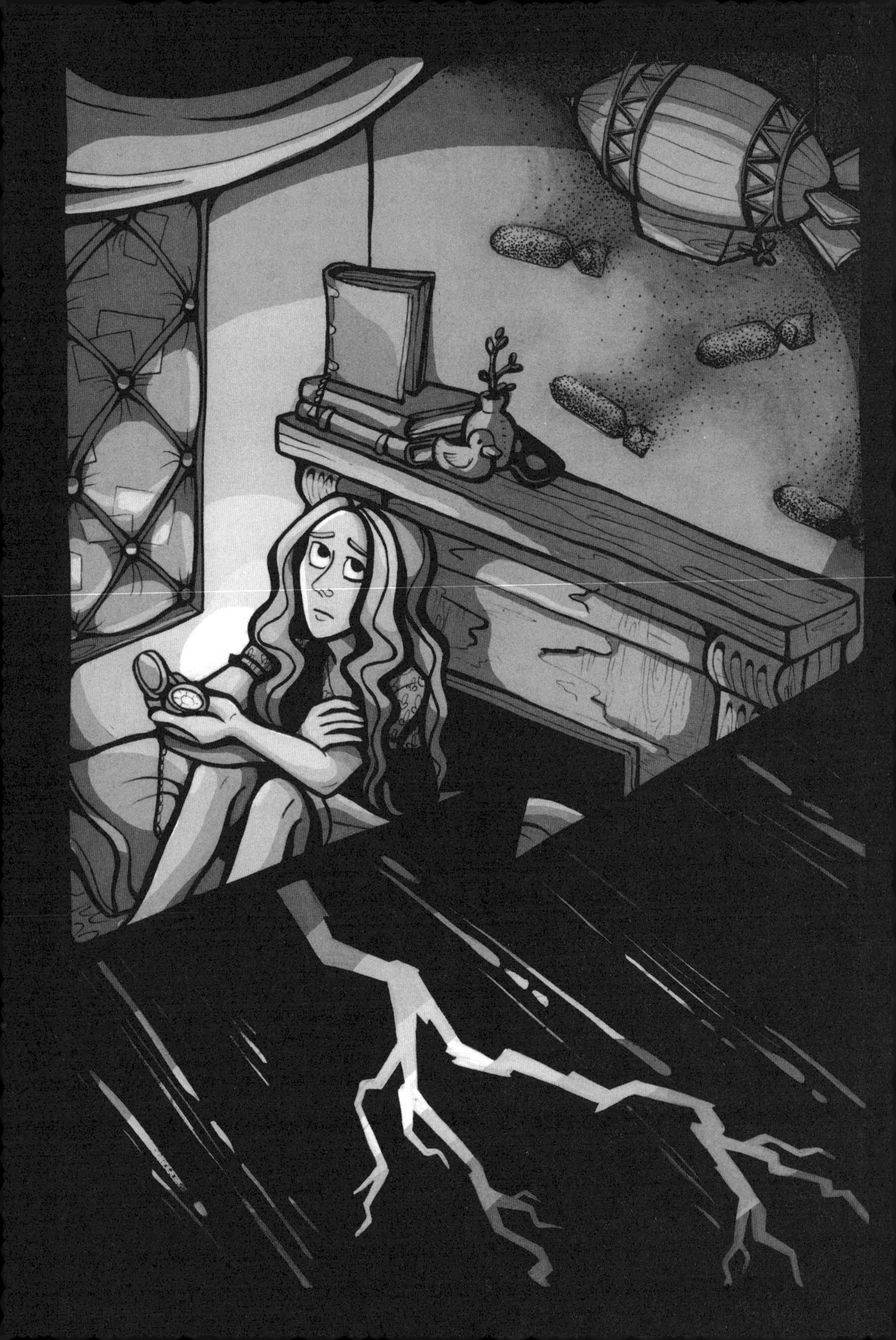

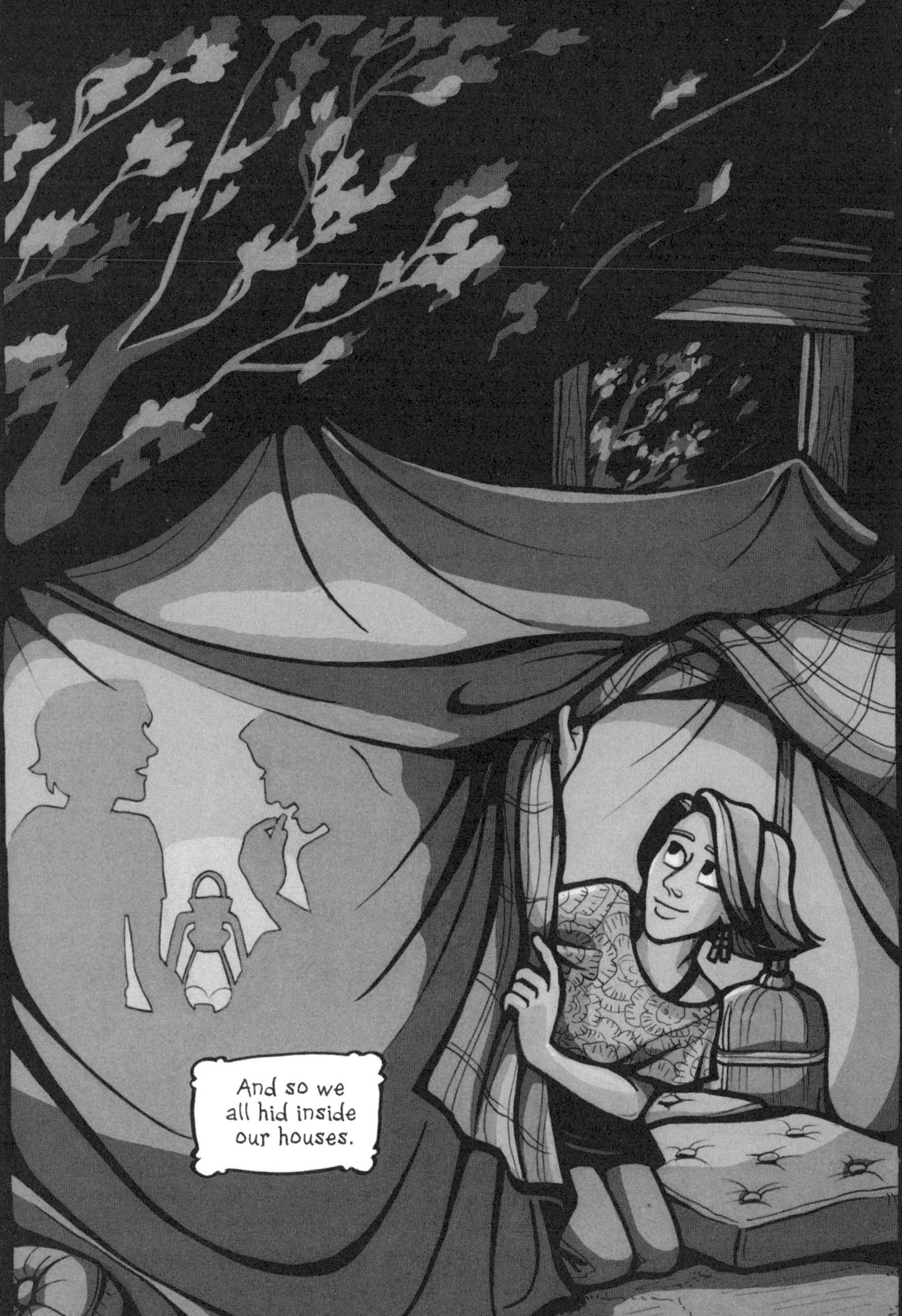
And so we all hid inside our houses.

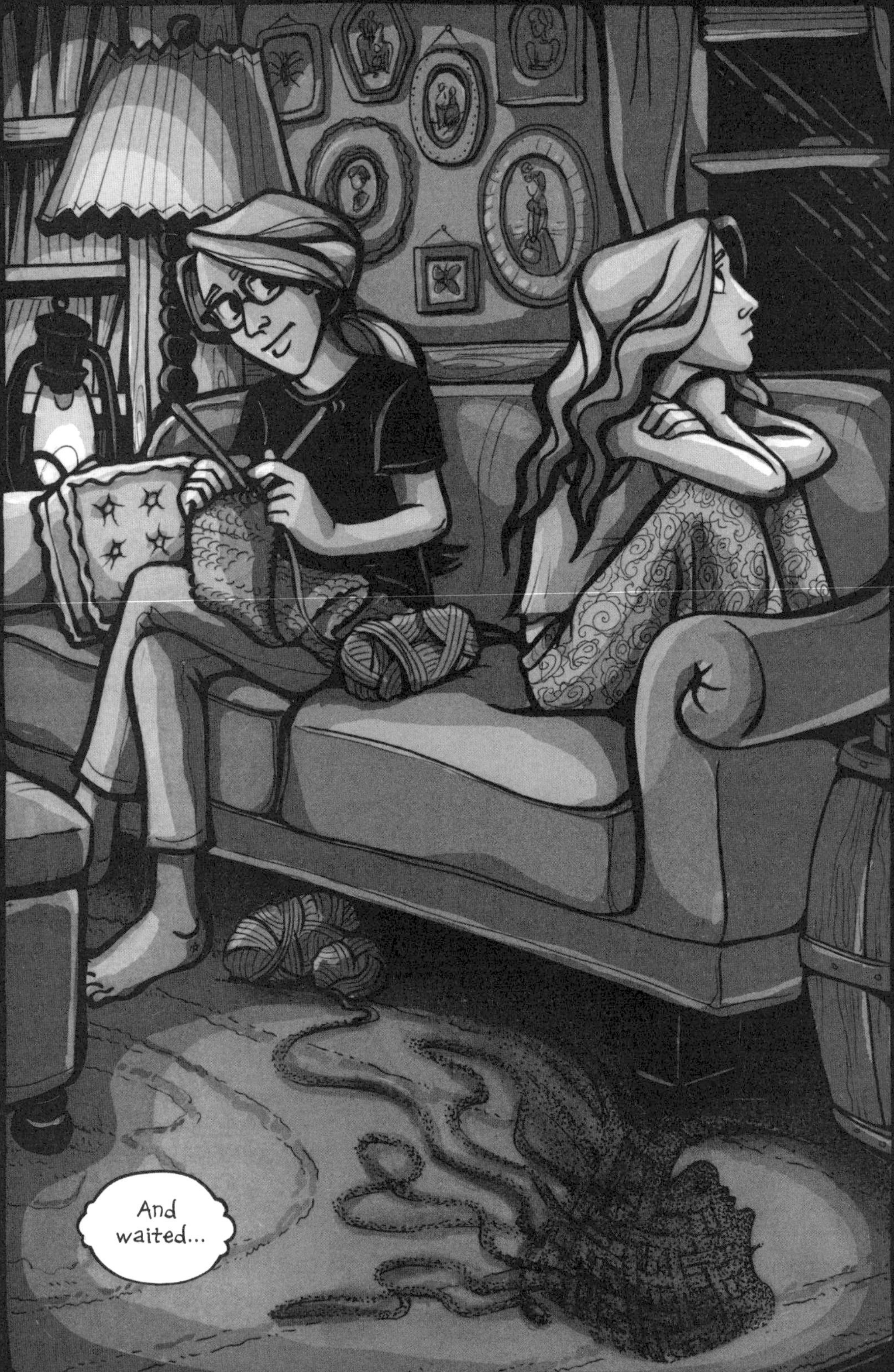
And waited...

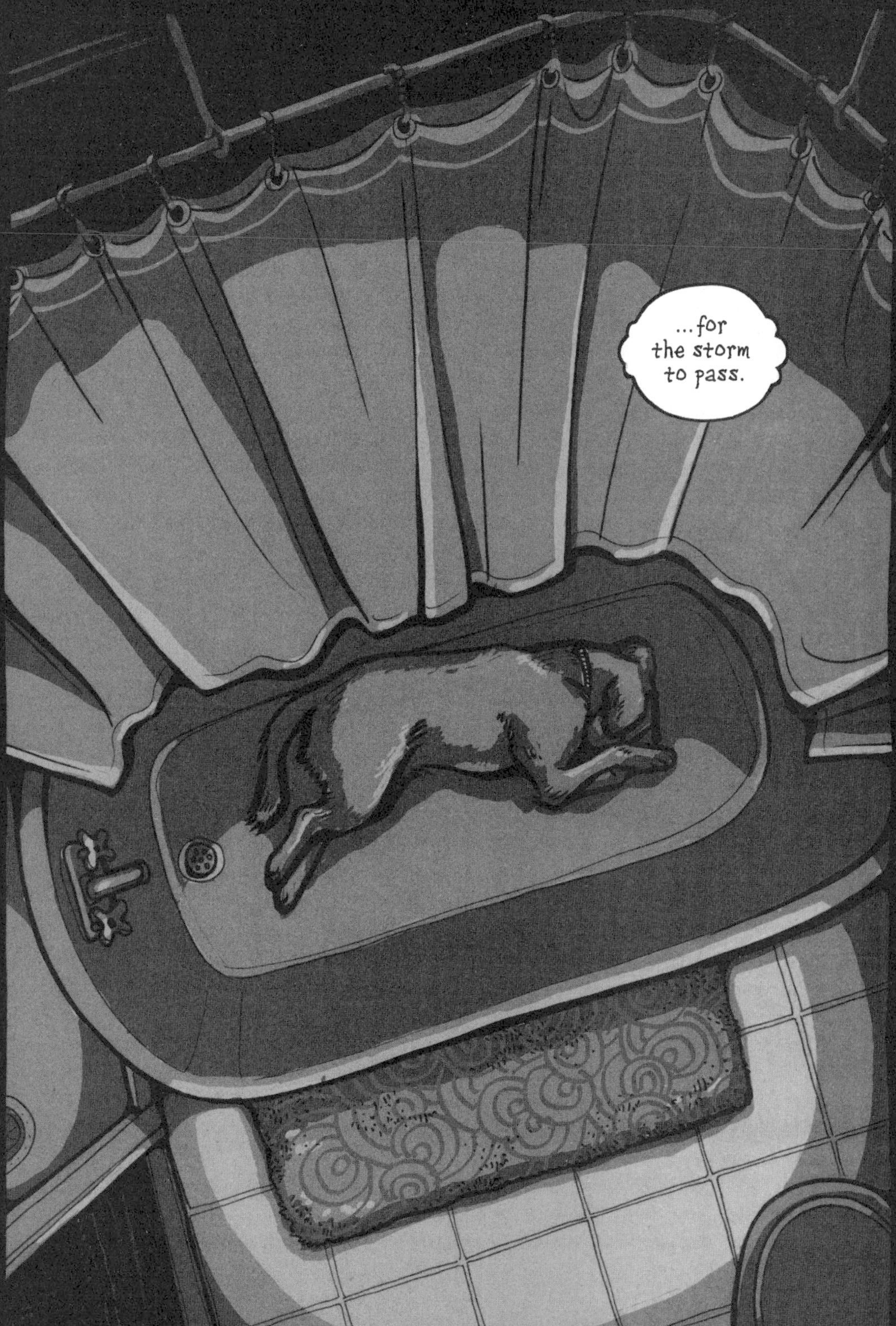
...for the storm to pass.

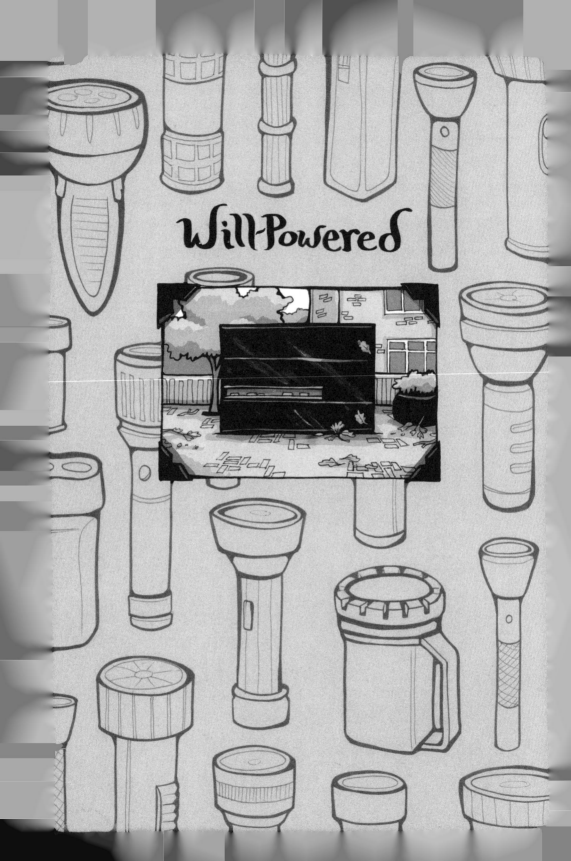

Will-Powered

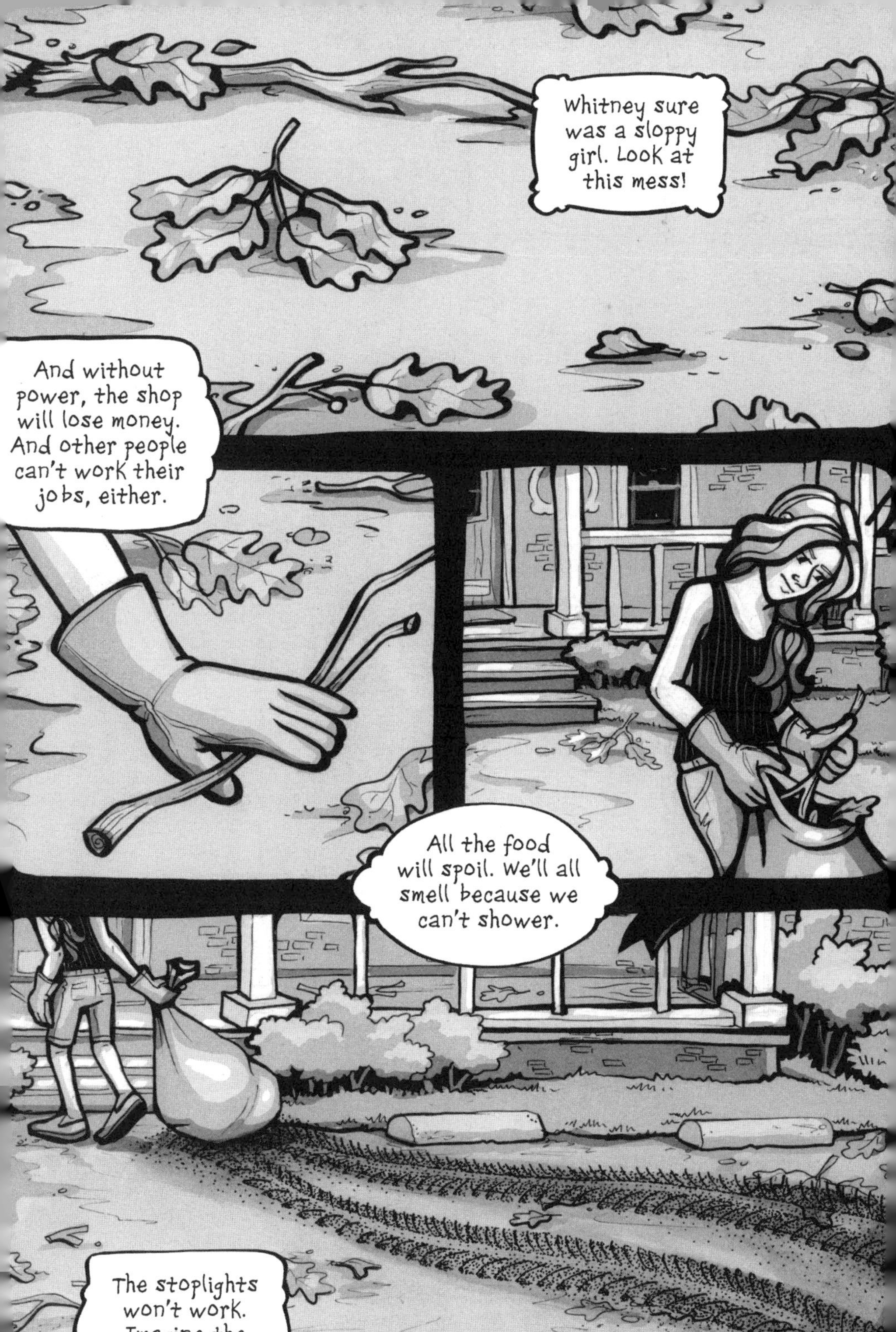
Whitney sure was a sloppy girl. Look at this mess!
And without power, the shop will lose money. And other people can't work their jobs, either.
All the food will spoil. We'll all smell because we can't shower.
The stoplights won't work. Imagine the accidents!

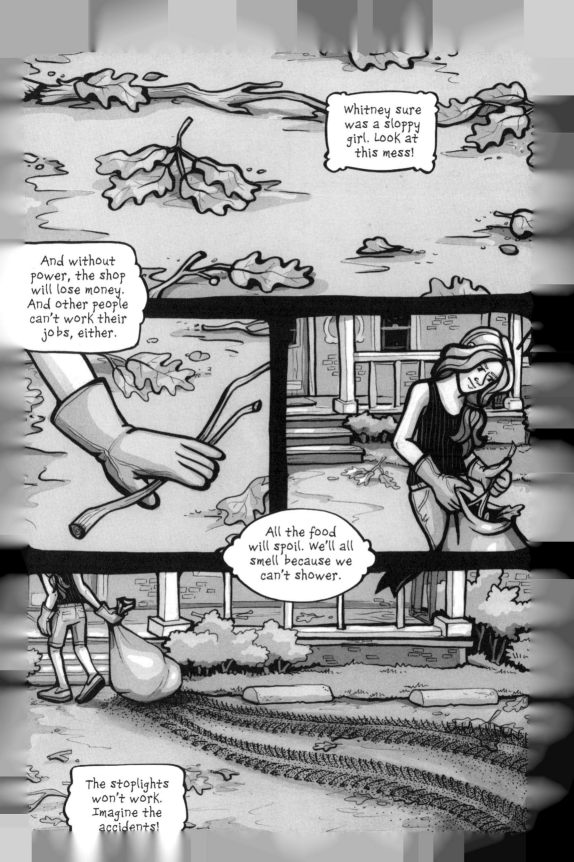

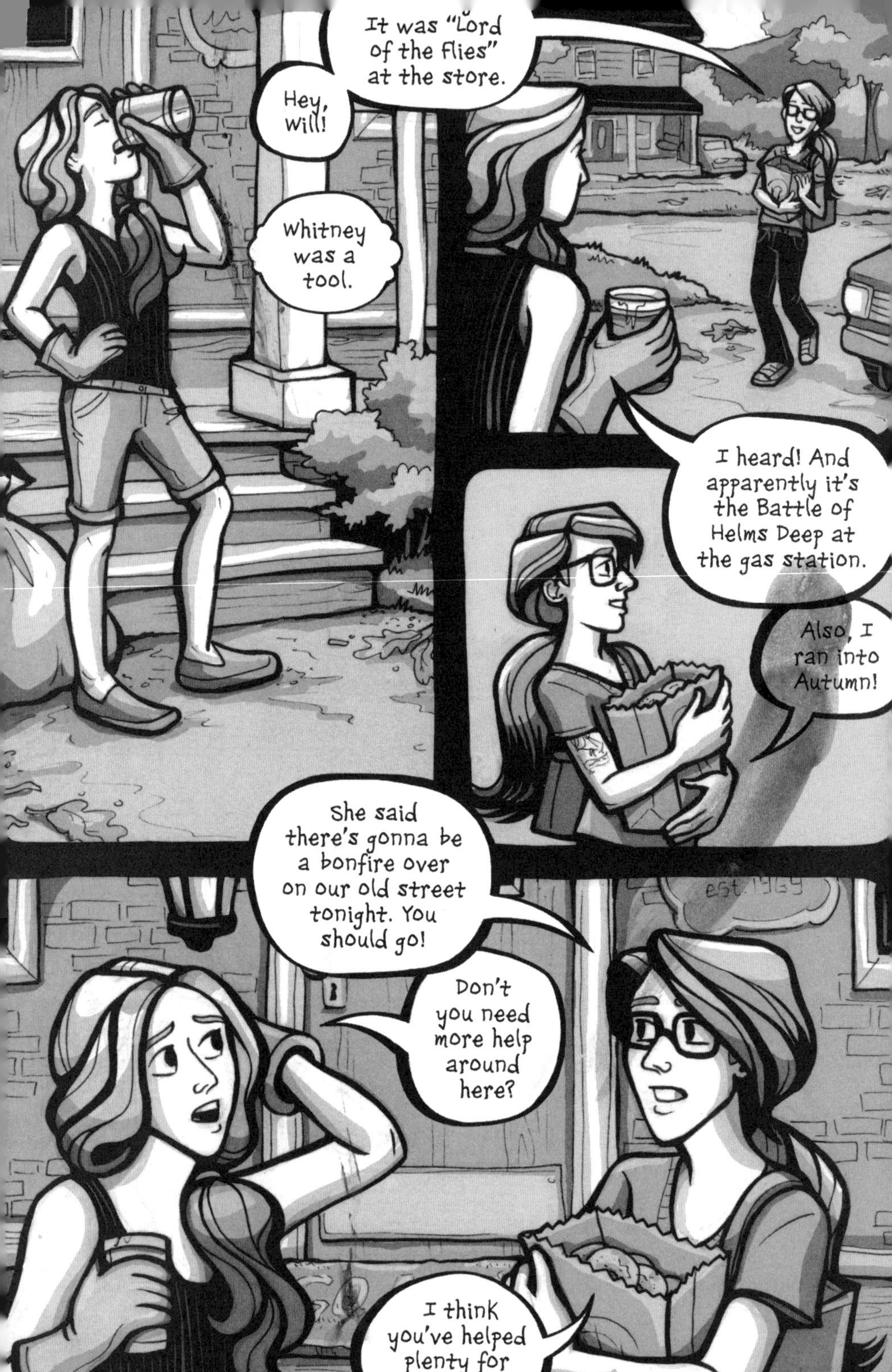
Hey, Will!
It was "Lord of the Flies" at the store.
Whitney was a tool.
I heard! And apparently it's the Battle of Helms Deep at the gas station.
Also, I ran into Autumn!
She said there's gonna be a bonfire over on our old street tonight. You should go!
Don't you need more help around here?
I think you've helped plenty for today.

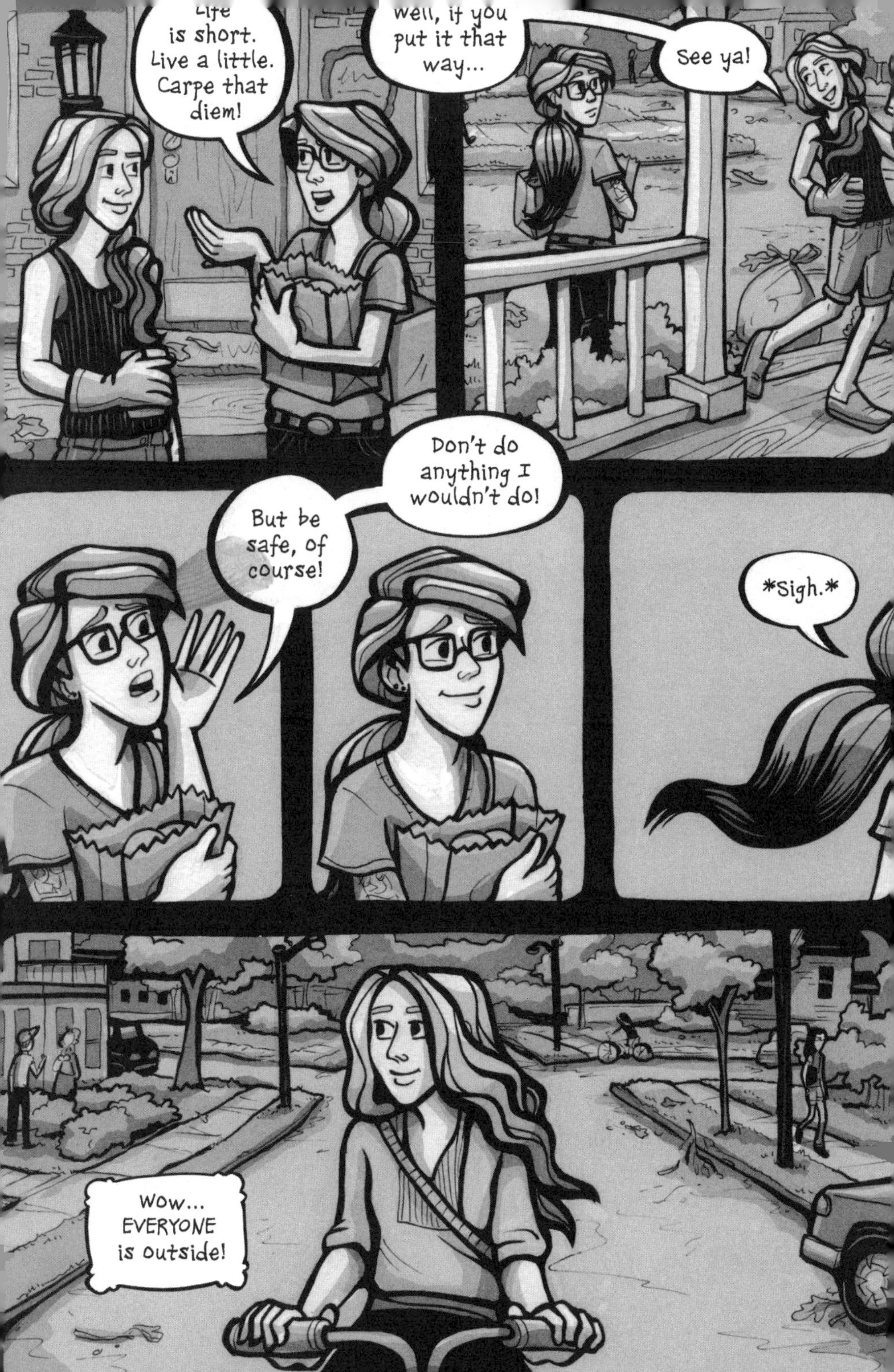
Life is short. Live a little. Carpe that diem!
Well, if you put it that way...
See ya!
But be safe, of course!
Don't do anything I wouldn't do!
Sigh.
Wow... EVERYONE is outside!

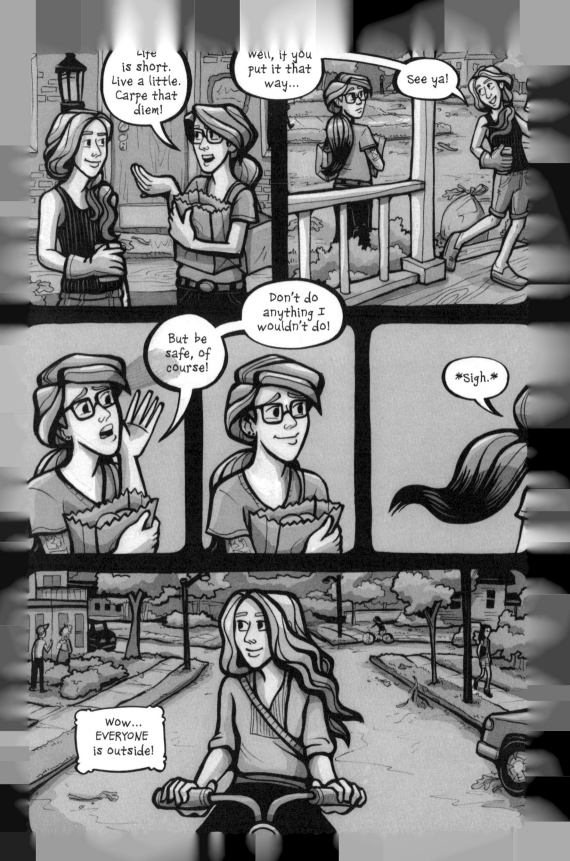

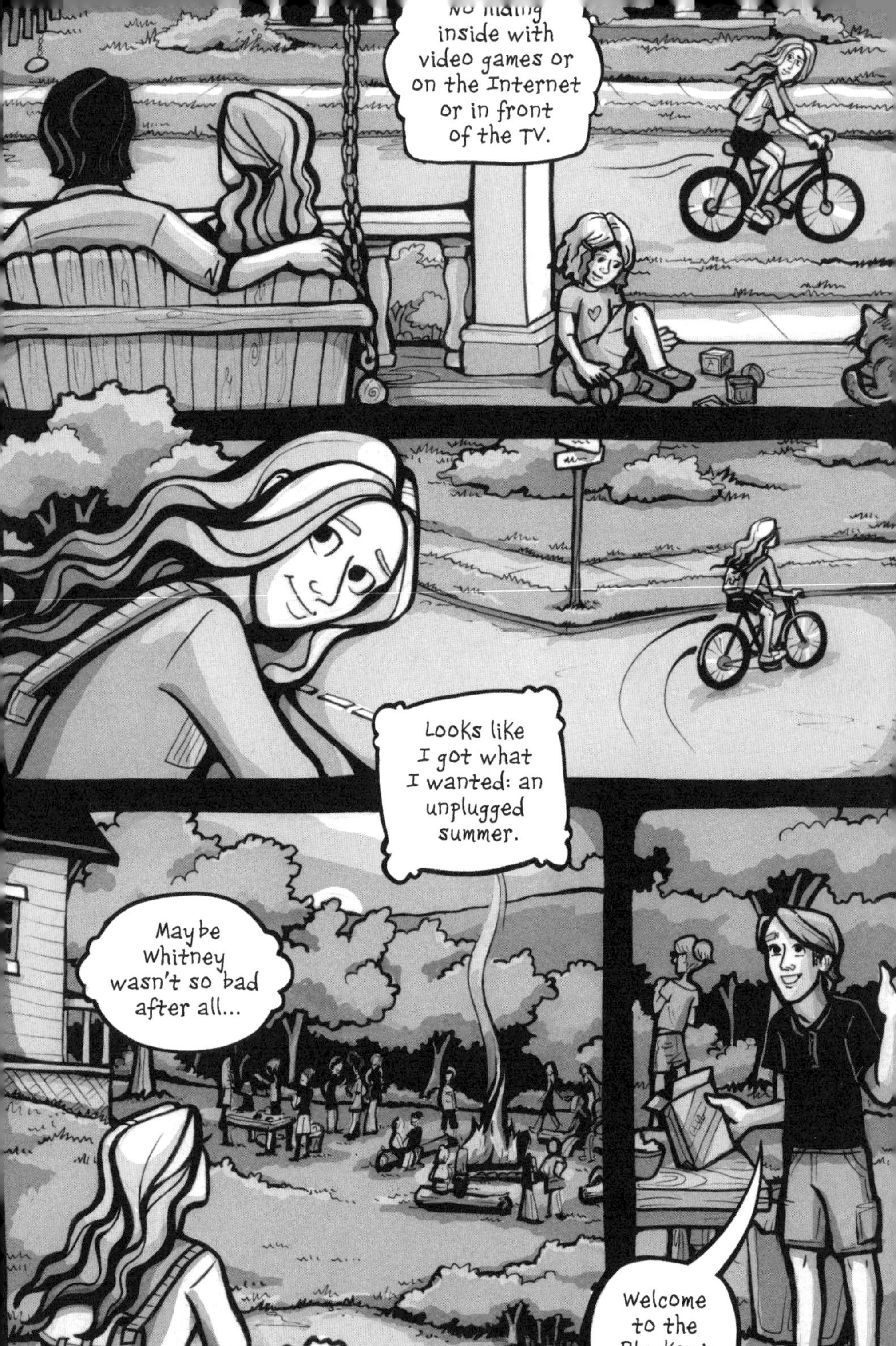
inside with video games or on the Internet or in front of the TV.
Looks like I got what I wanted: an unplugged summer.
Maybe Whitney wasn't so bad after all...
Welcome to the BlackOut Bonfire!

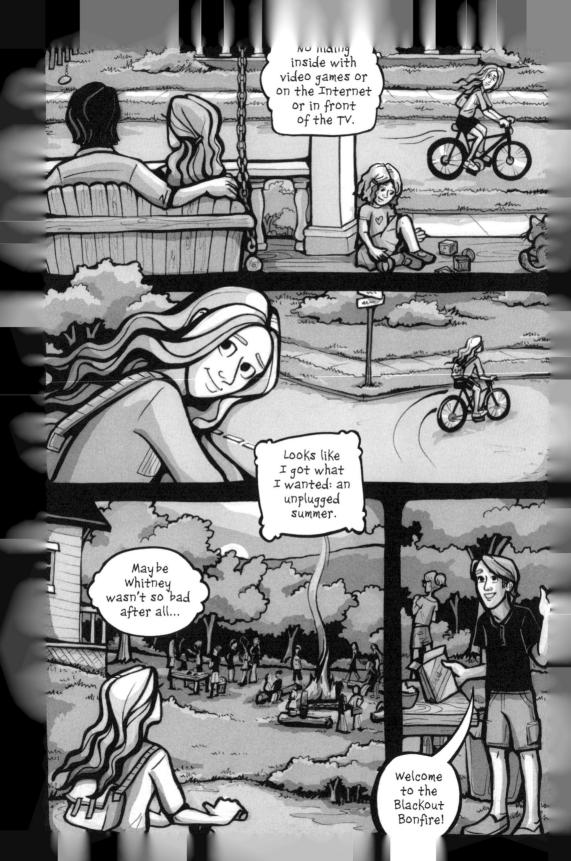

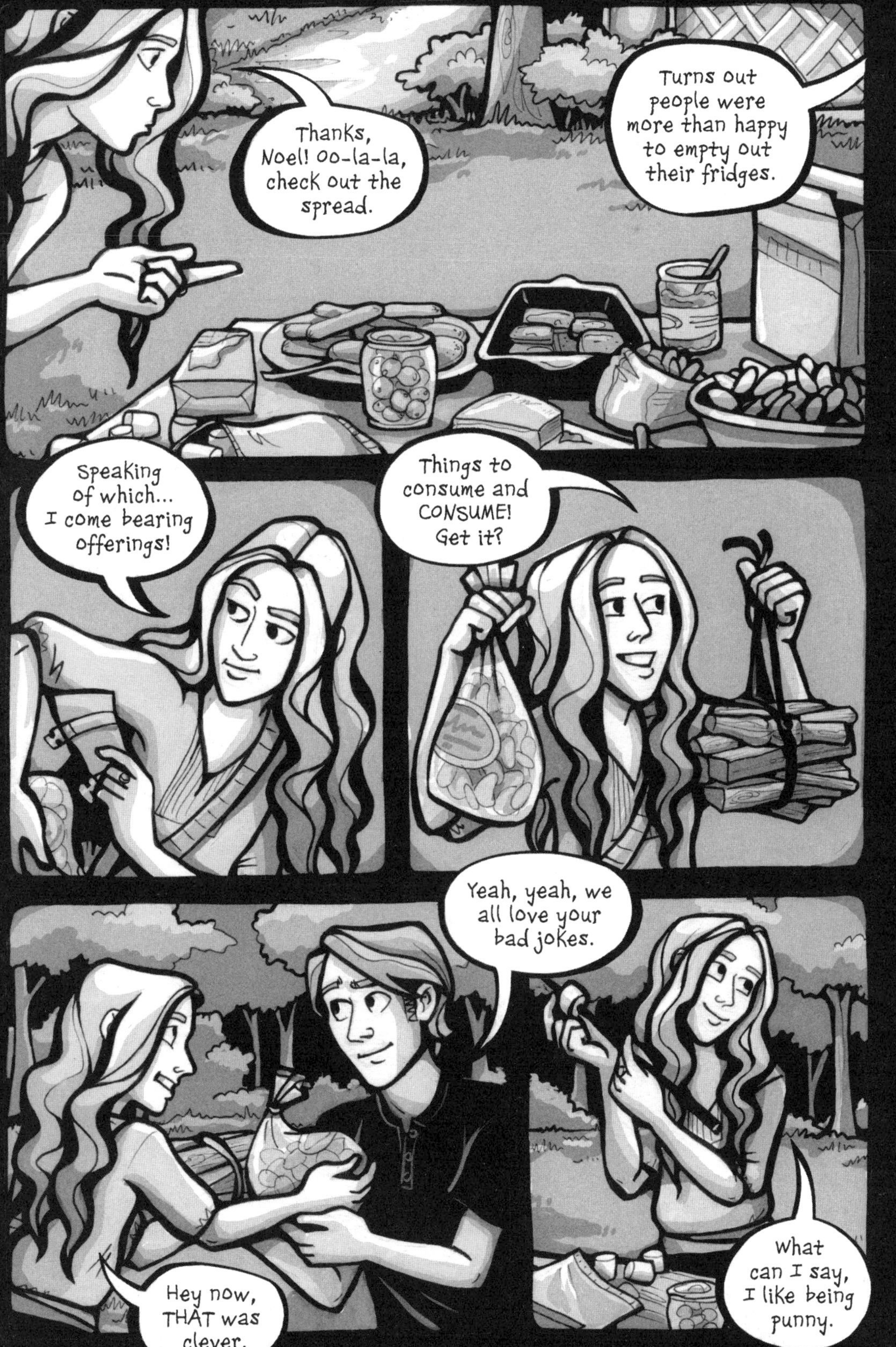
Thanks, Noel! Oo-la-la, check out the spread.
Turns out people were more than happy to empty out their fridges.
Speaking of which... I come bearing offerings!
Things to consume and CONSUME! Get it?
Yeah, yeah, we all love your bad jokes.
Hey now, THAT was clever.
What can I say, I like being punny.

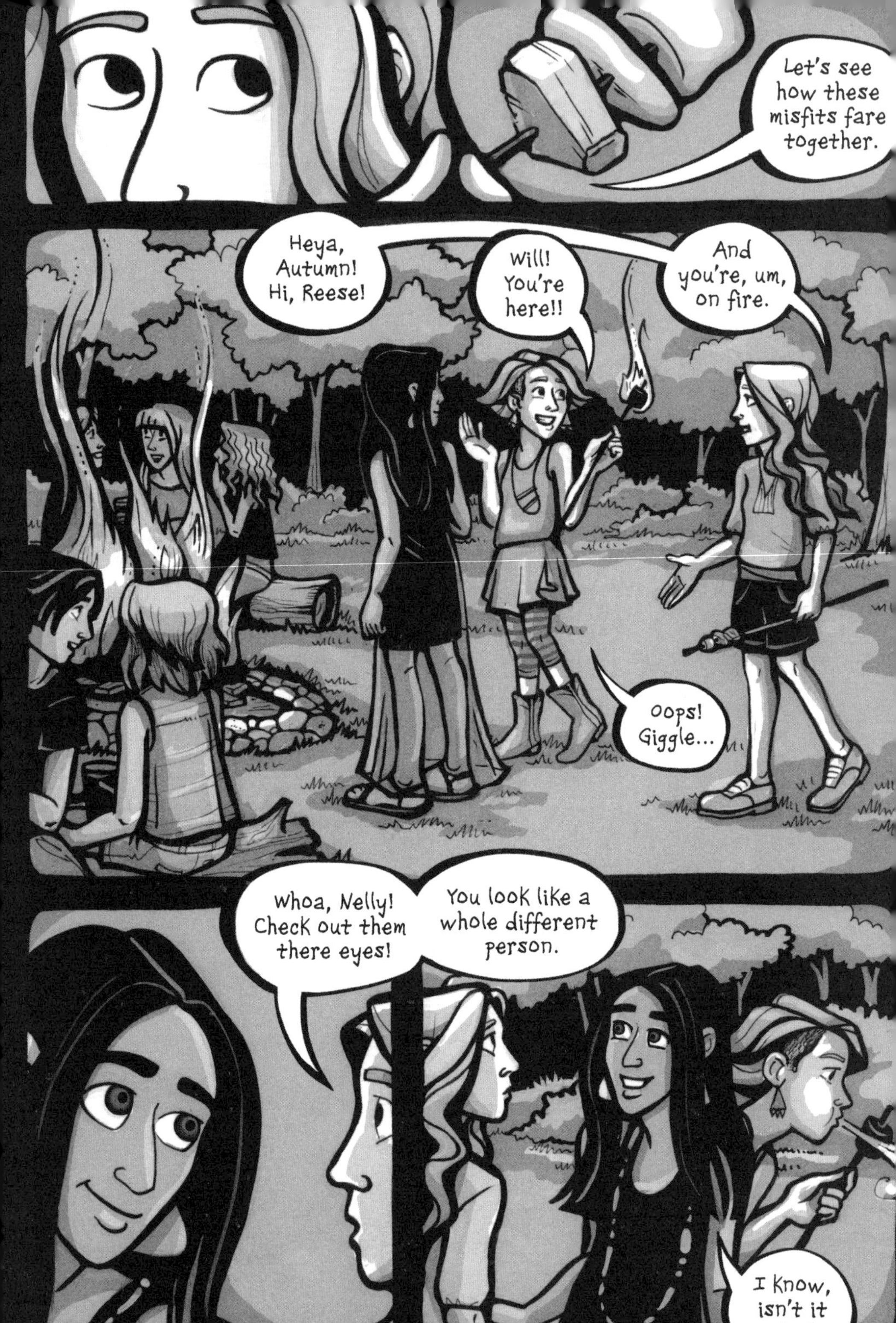
Let's see how these misfits fare together.
Heya, Autumn! Hi, Reese!
Will! You're here!!
And you're, um, on fire.
Oops! Giggle...
Whoa, Nelly! Check out them there eyes!
You look like a whole different person.
I know, isn't it fun?

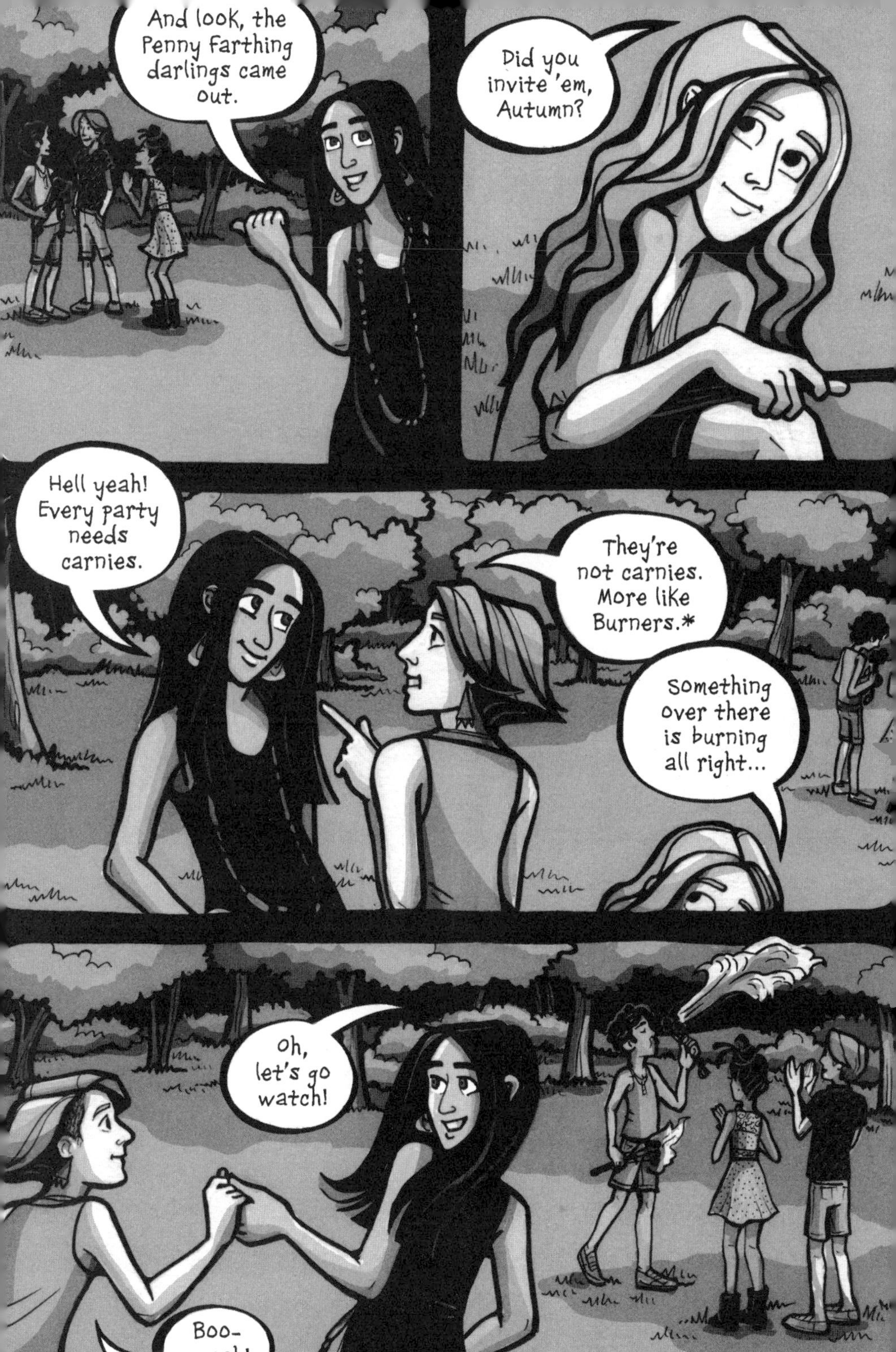
And look, the Penny farthing darlings came out.
Did you invite 'em, Autumn?
Hell yeah! Every party needs carnies.
They're not carnies. More like Burners.*
Something over there is burning all right...
Oh, let's go watch!
Boo-yeah!

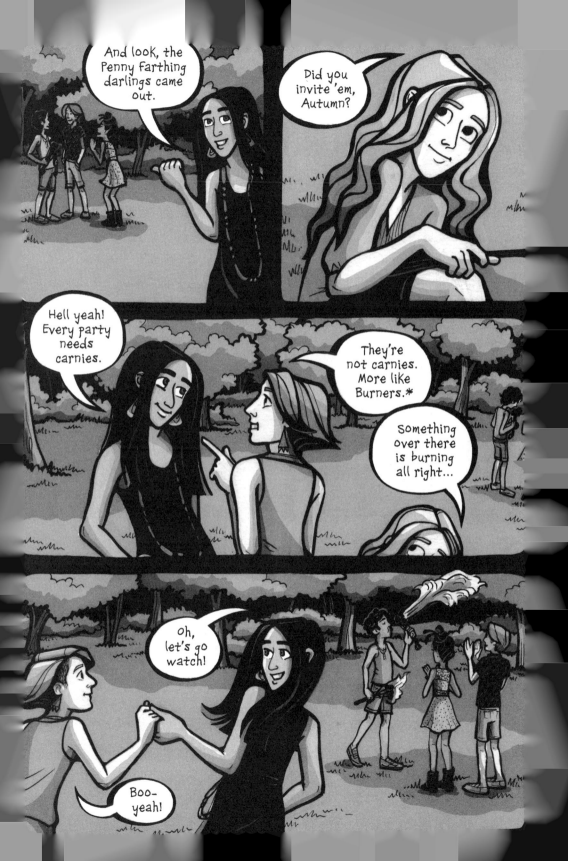

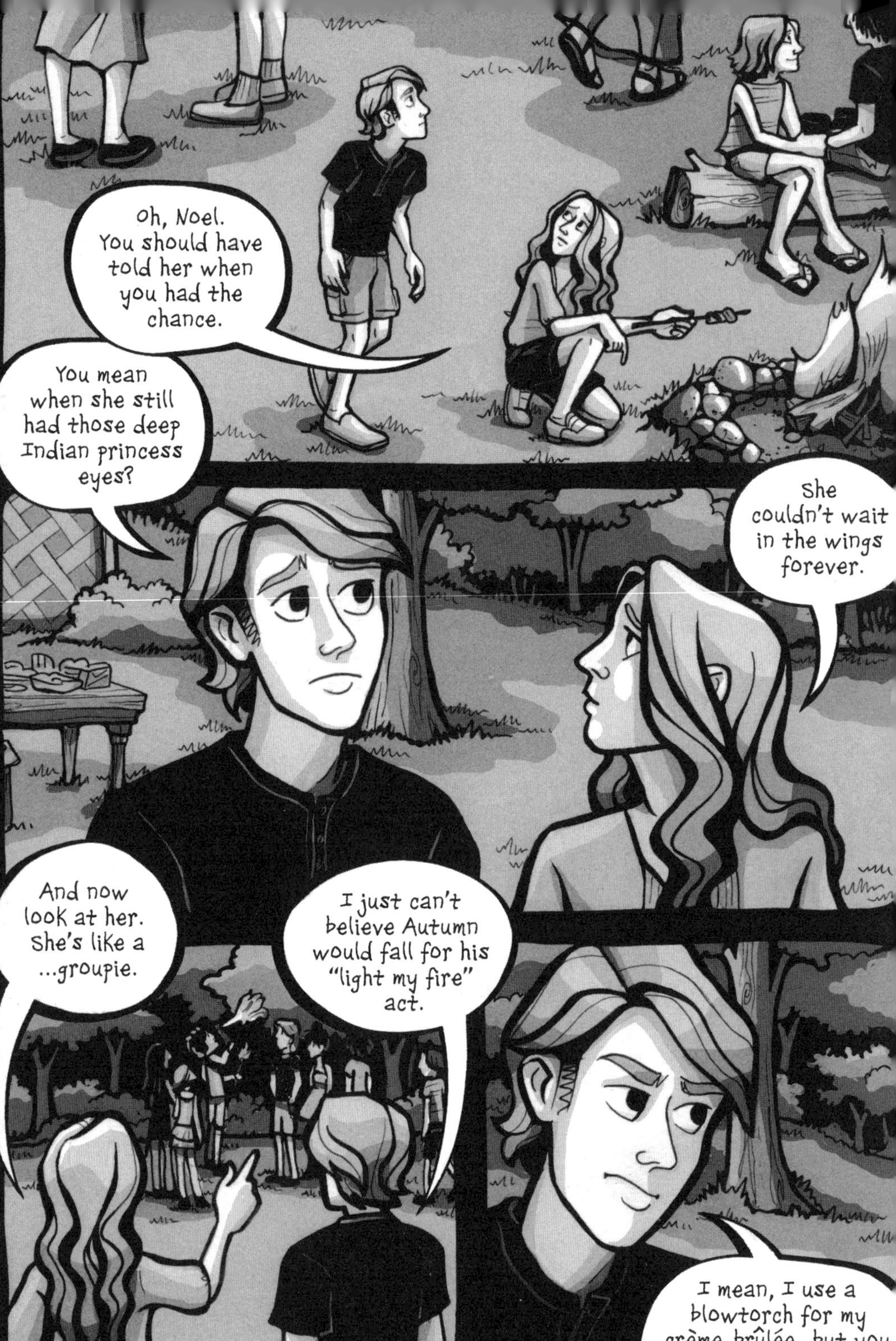

Oh, Noel. You should have told her when you had the chance.
You mean when she still had those deep Indian princess eyes?
She couldn't wait in the wings forever.
And now look at her. She's like a ...groupie.
I just can't believe Autumn would fall for his "light my fire" act.
I mean, I use a blowtorch for my crème brûlée, but you don't see ME showing off about it!

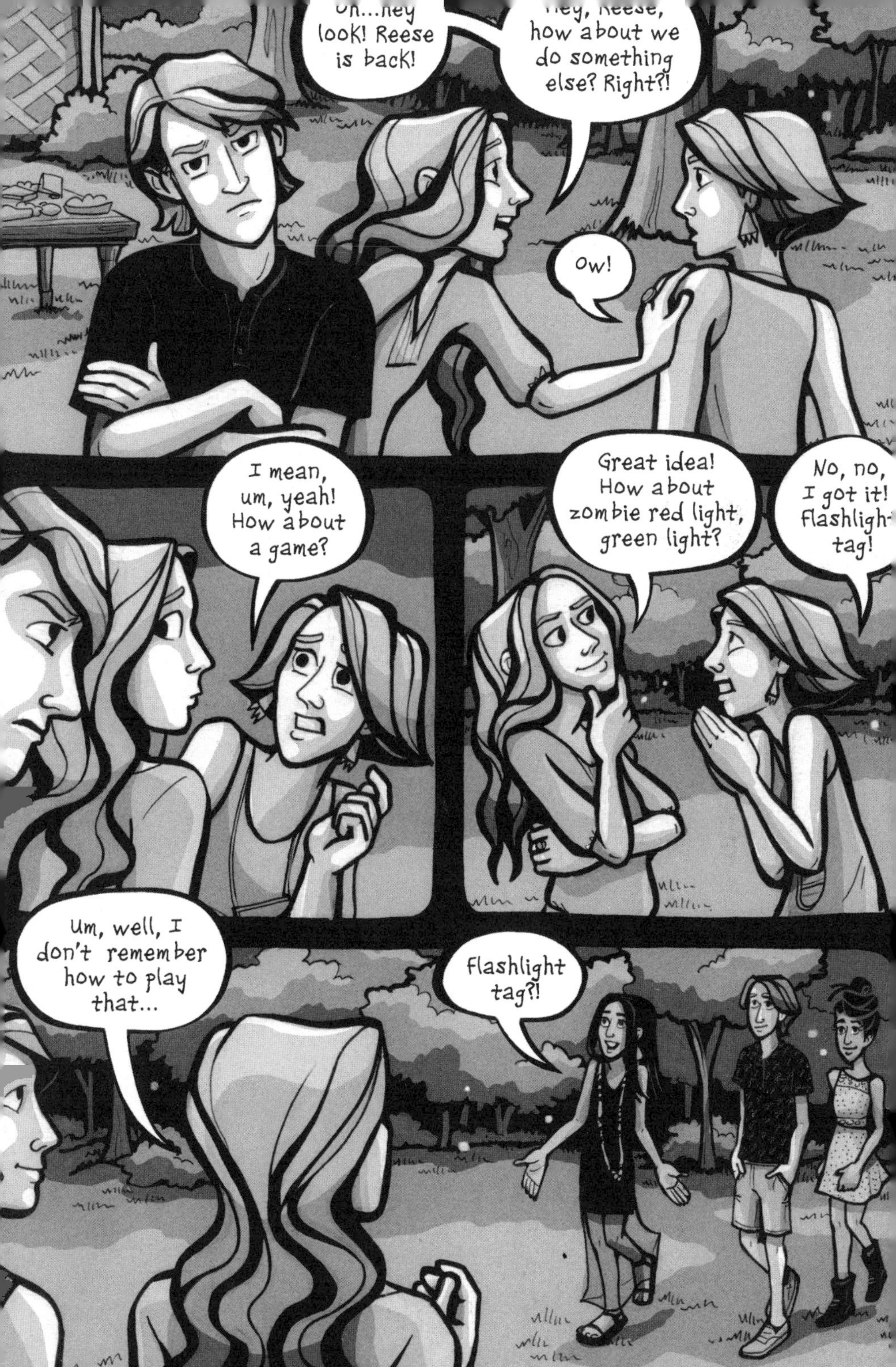
look! Reese is back!
how about we do something else? Right?!
Ow!
I mean, um, yeah! How about a game?
Great idea! How about zombie red light, green light?
No, no, I got it! Flashligh tag!
Um, well, I don't remember how to play that...
Flashlight tag?!

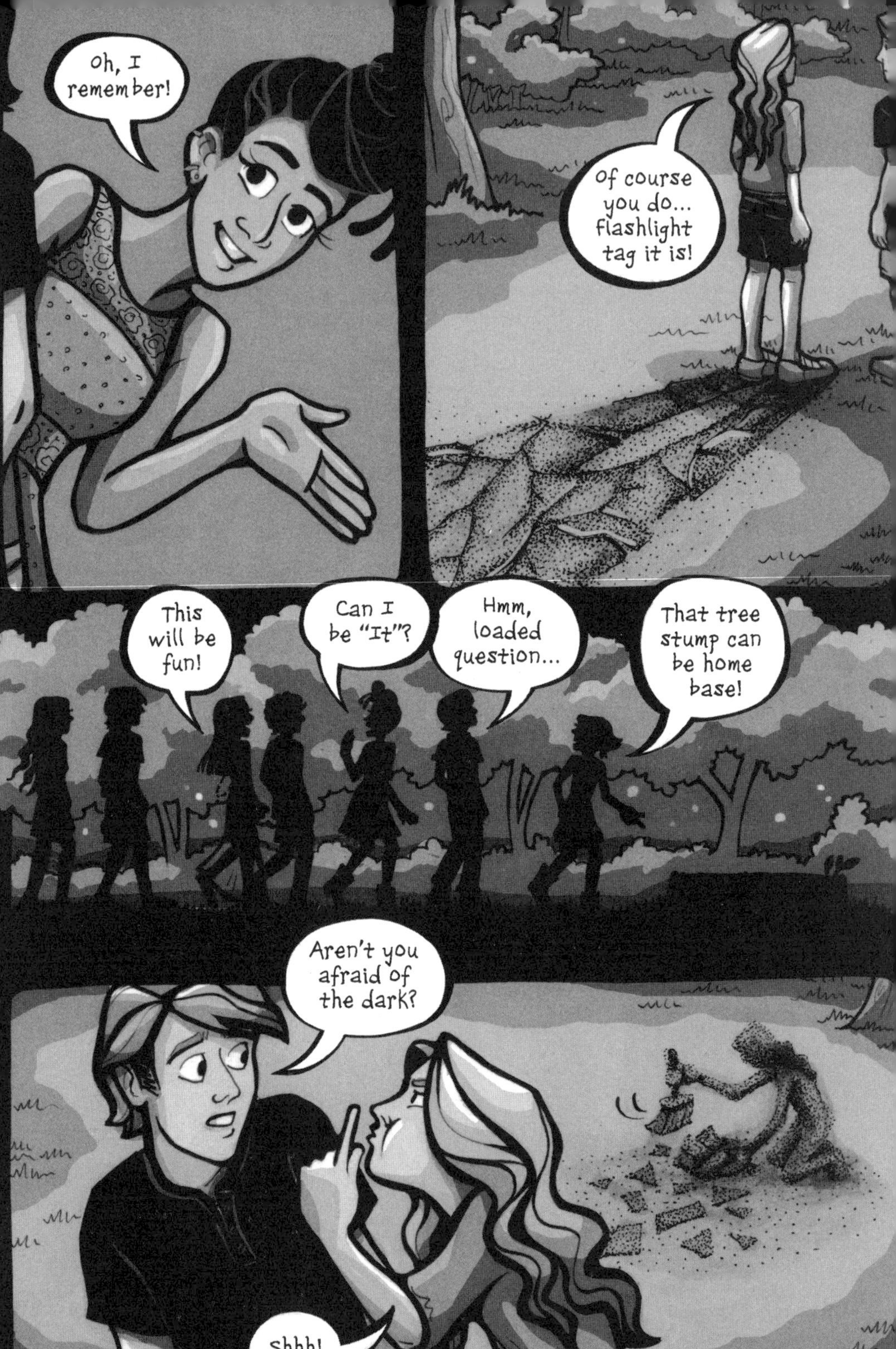
Oh, I remember!
Of course you do... flashlight tag it is!
This will be fun!
Can I be "It"?
Hmm, loaded question...
That tree stump can be home base!
Aren't you afraid of the dark?
Shhh!

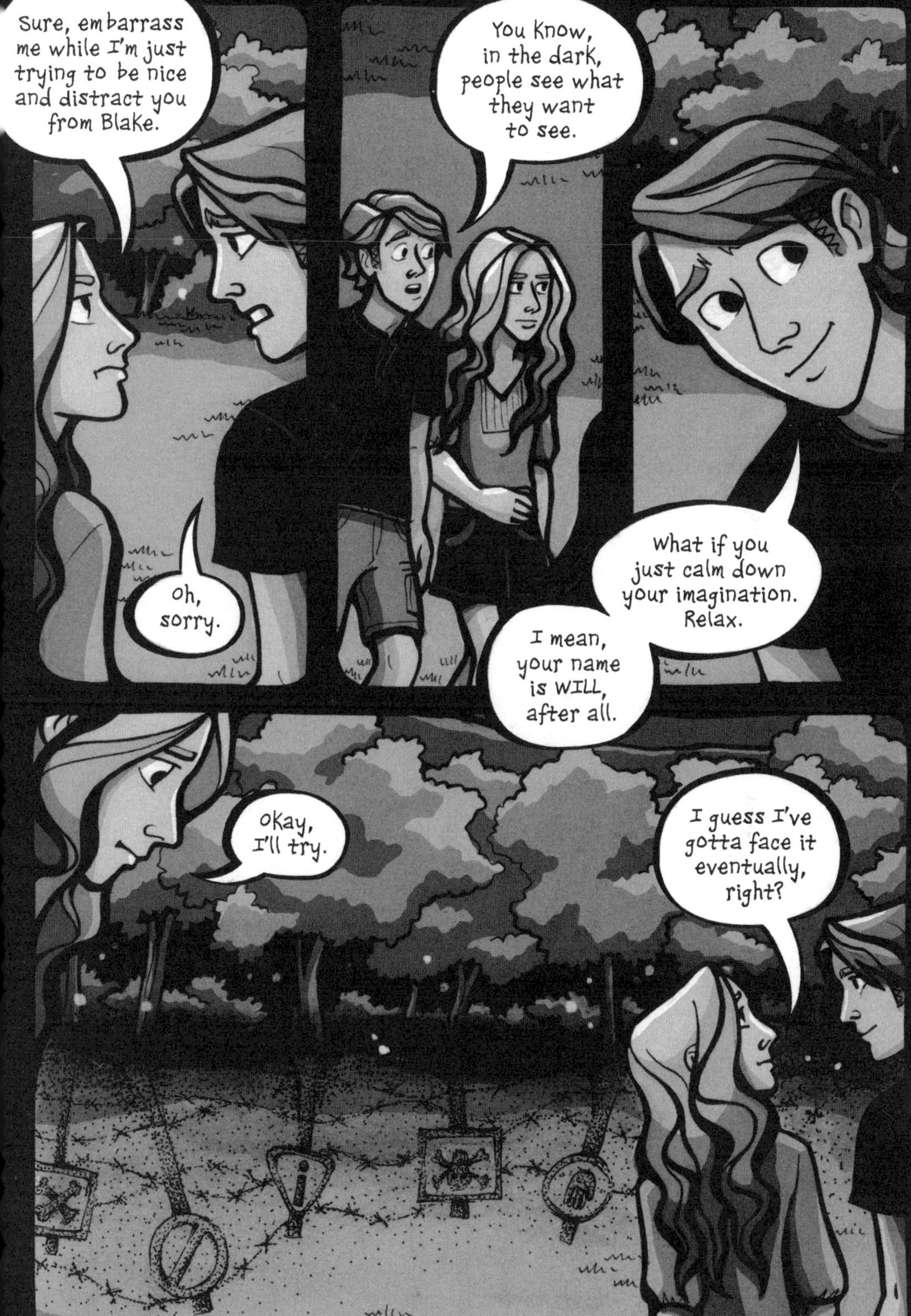
Sure, embarrass me while I'm just trying to be nice and distract you from Blake.
Oh, sorry.
You know, in the dark, people see what they want to see.
What if you just calm down your imagination. Relax.
I mean, your name is WILL, after all.
Okay, I'll try.
I guess I've gotta face it eventually, right?

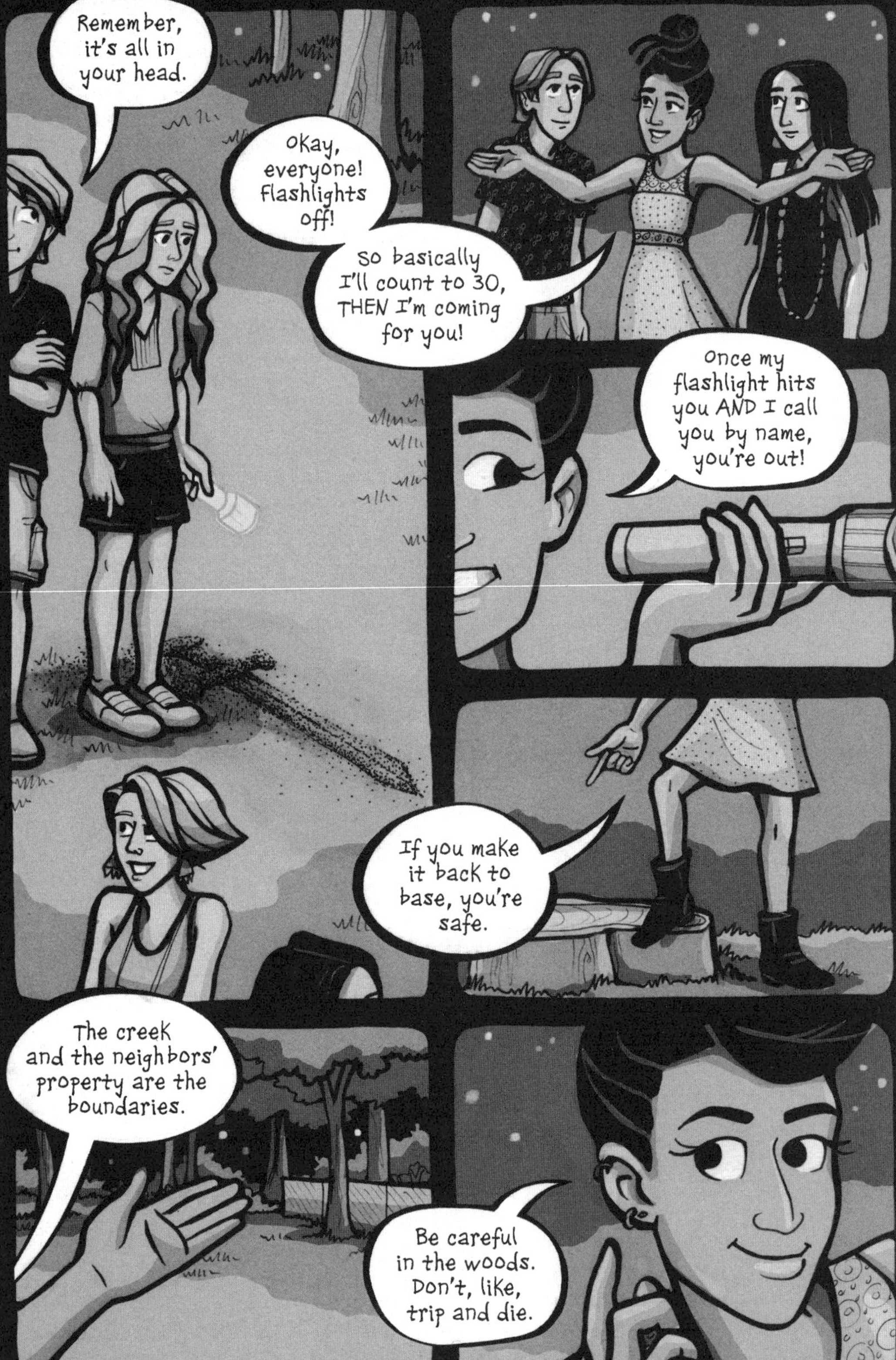
Remember, it's all in your head.
Okay, everyone! Flashlights off!
So basically I'll count to 30, THEN I'm coming for you!
Once my flashlight hits you AND I call you by name, you're out!
If you make it back to base, you're safe.
The creek and the neighbors' property are the boundaries.
Be careful in the woods. Don't, like, trip and die.

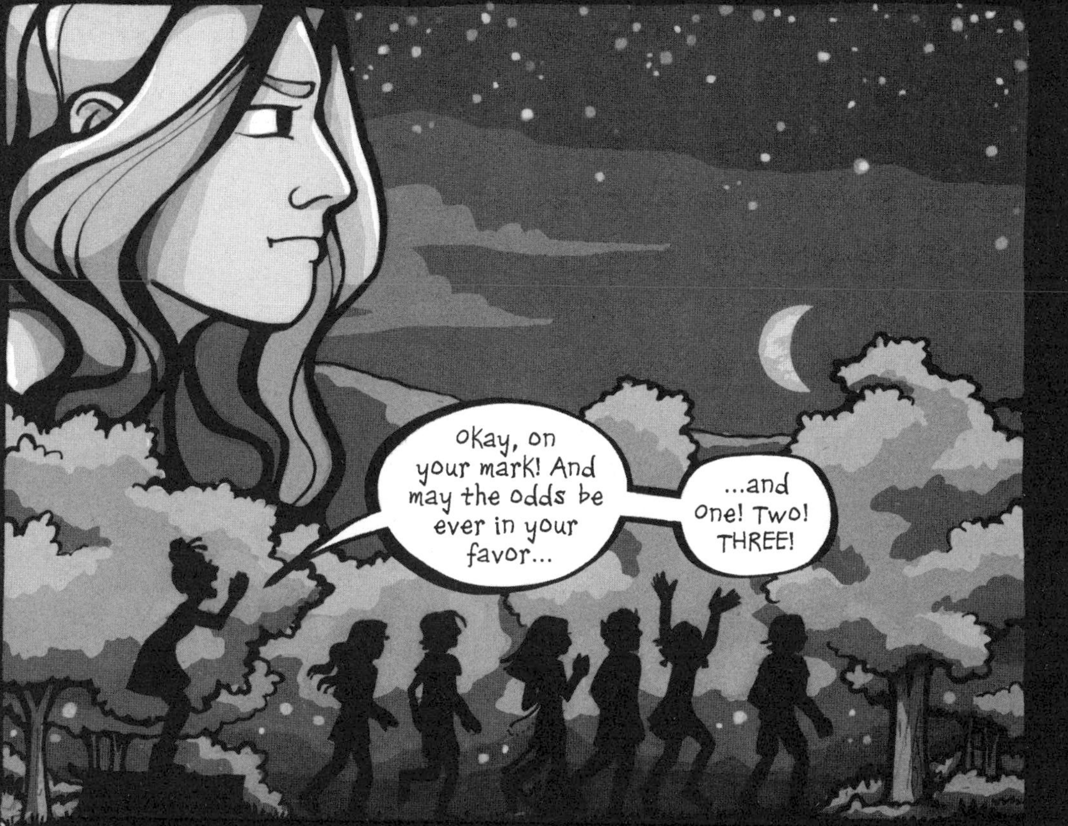
Okay, on your mark! And may the odds be ever in your favor...
...and one! Two! THREE!
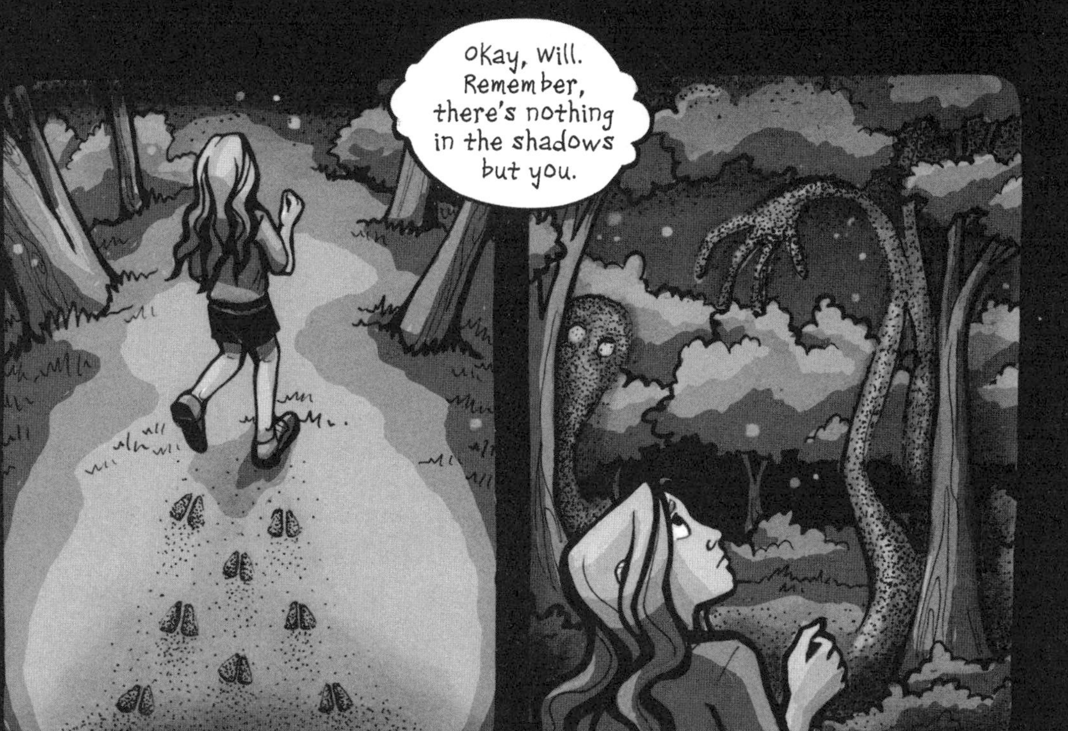
Okay, Will. Remember, there's nothing in the shadows but you.

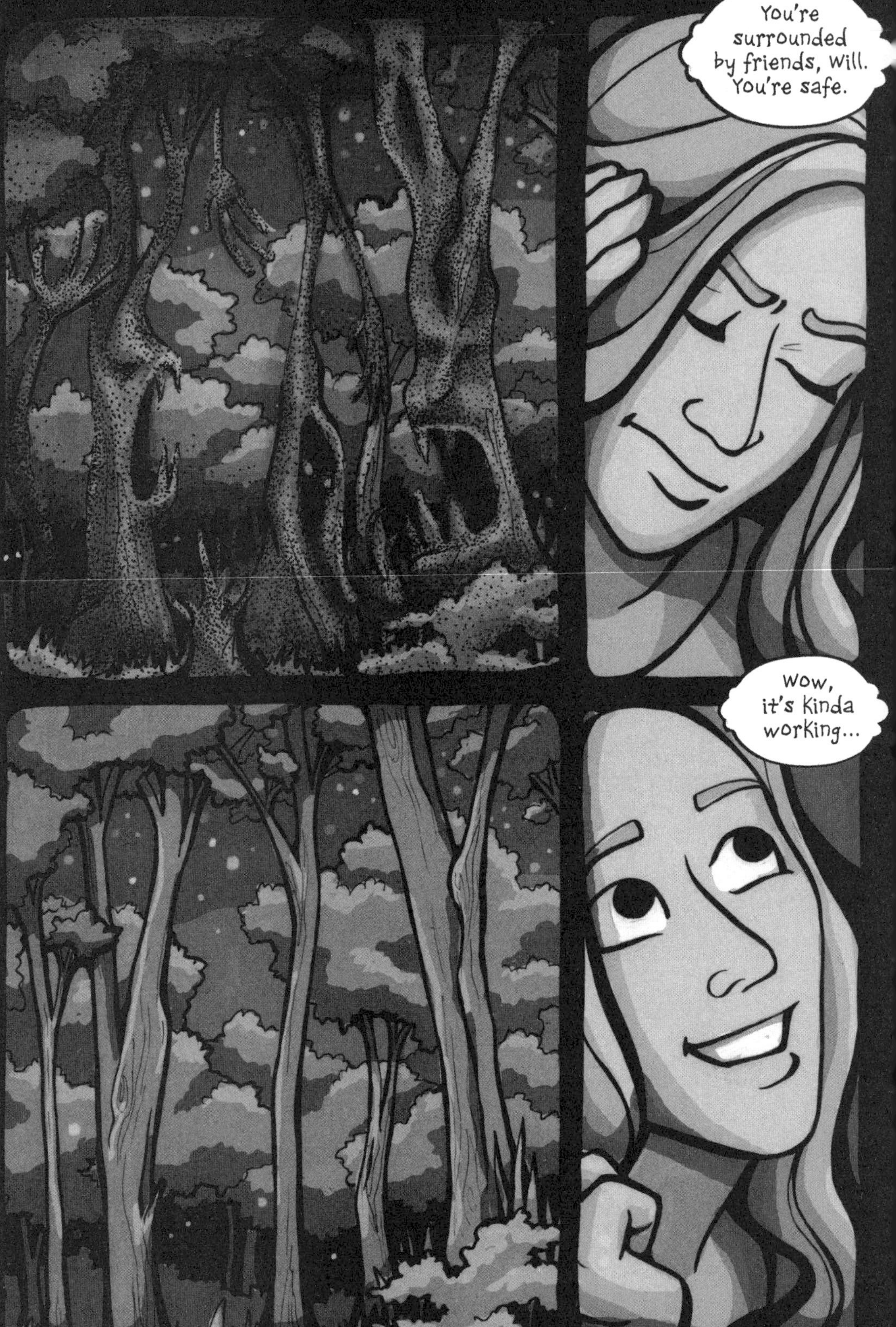

You're surrounded by friends, Will. You're safe.
Wow, it's kinda working...

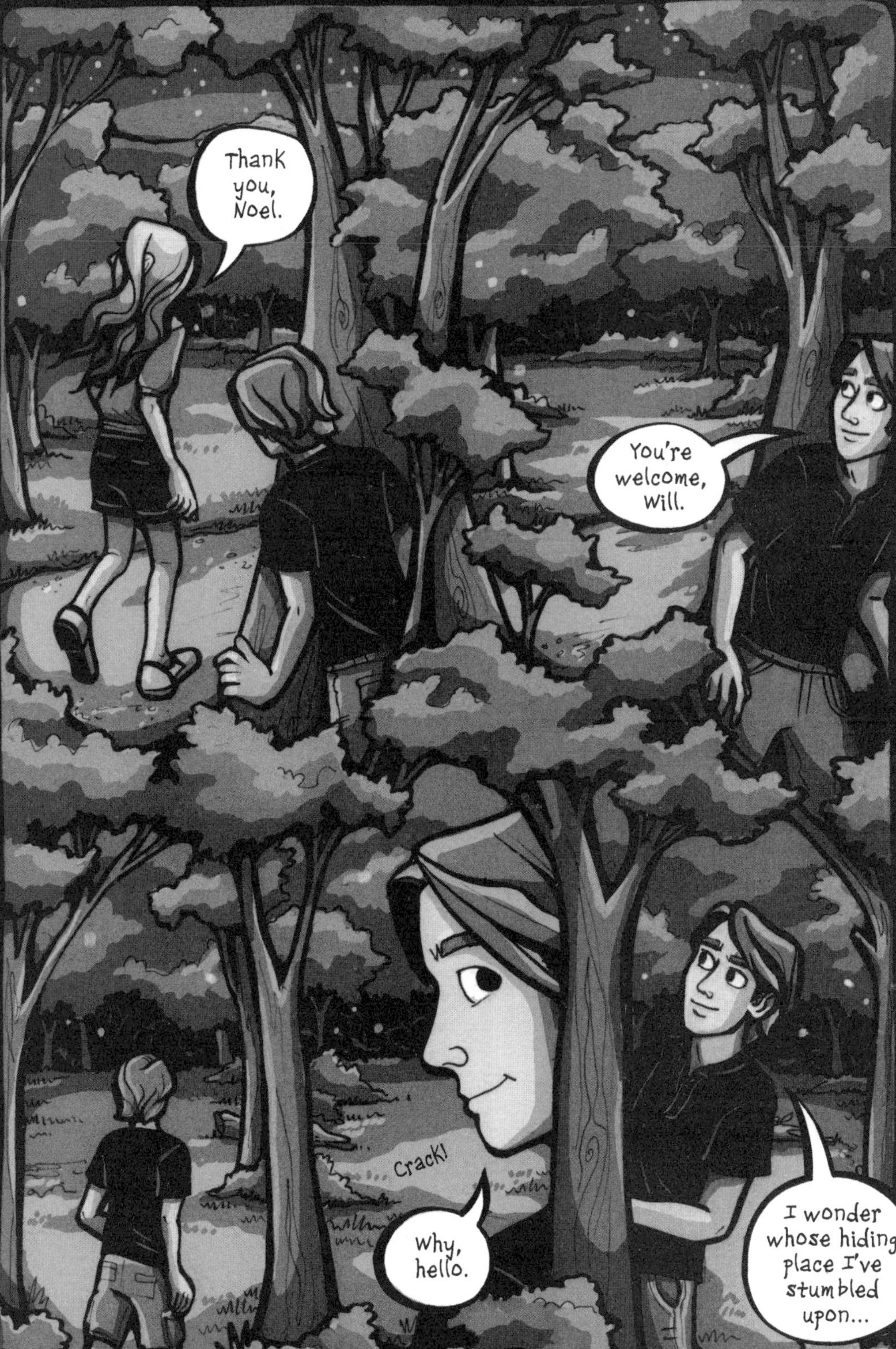
Thank you, Noel.
You're welcome, Will.
Crack!
Why, hello.
I wonder whose hiding place I've stumbled upon...

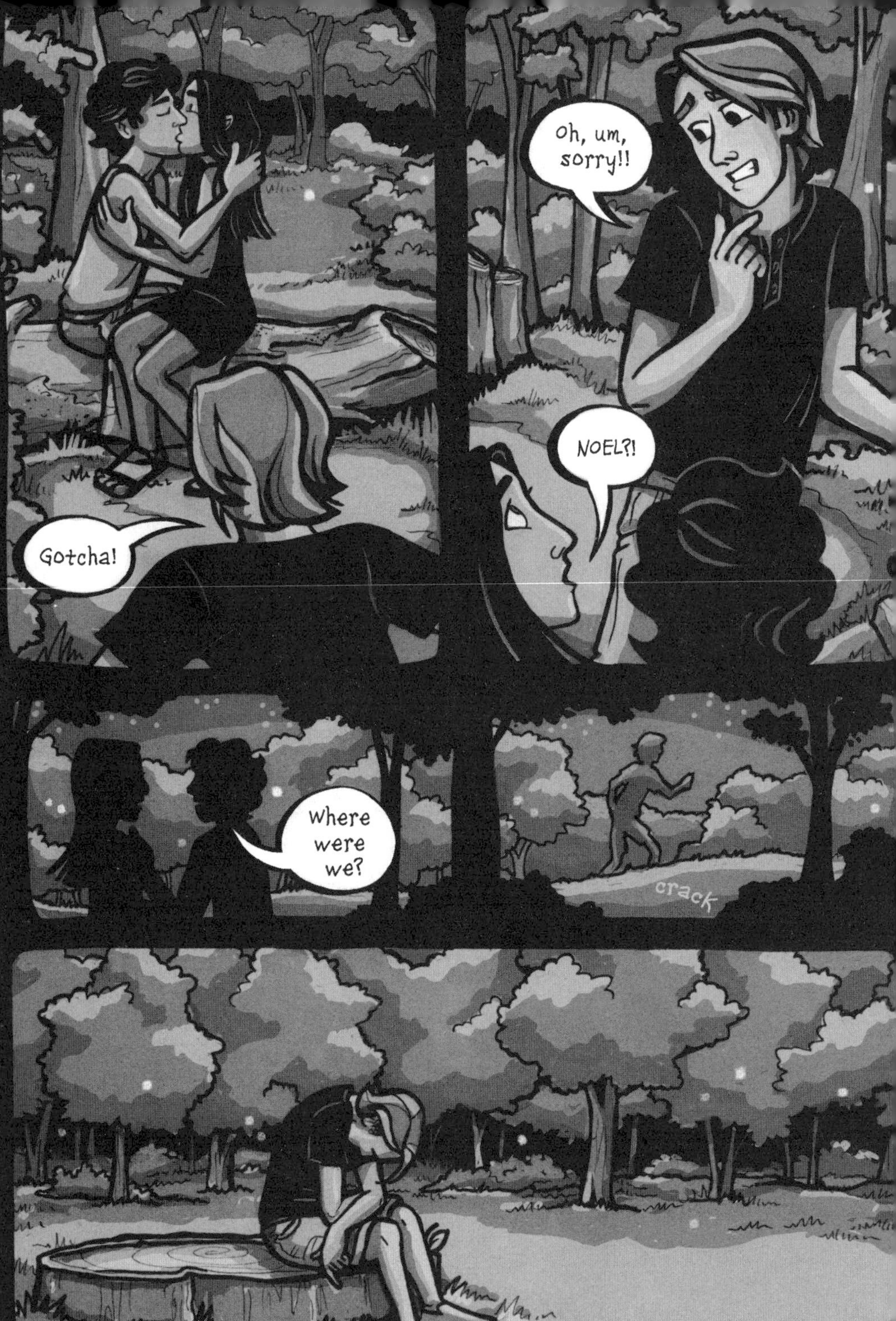
Gotcha!
Oh, um, sorry!!
NOEL?!
Where were we?
crack

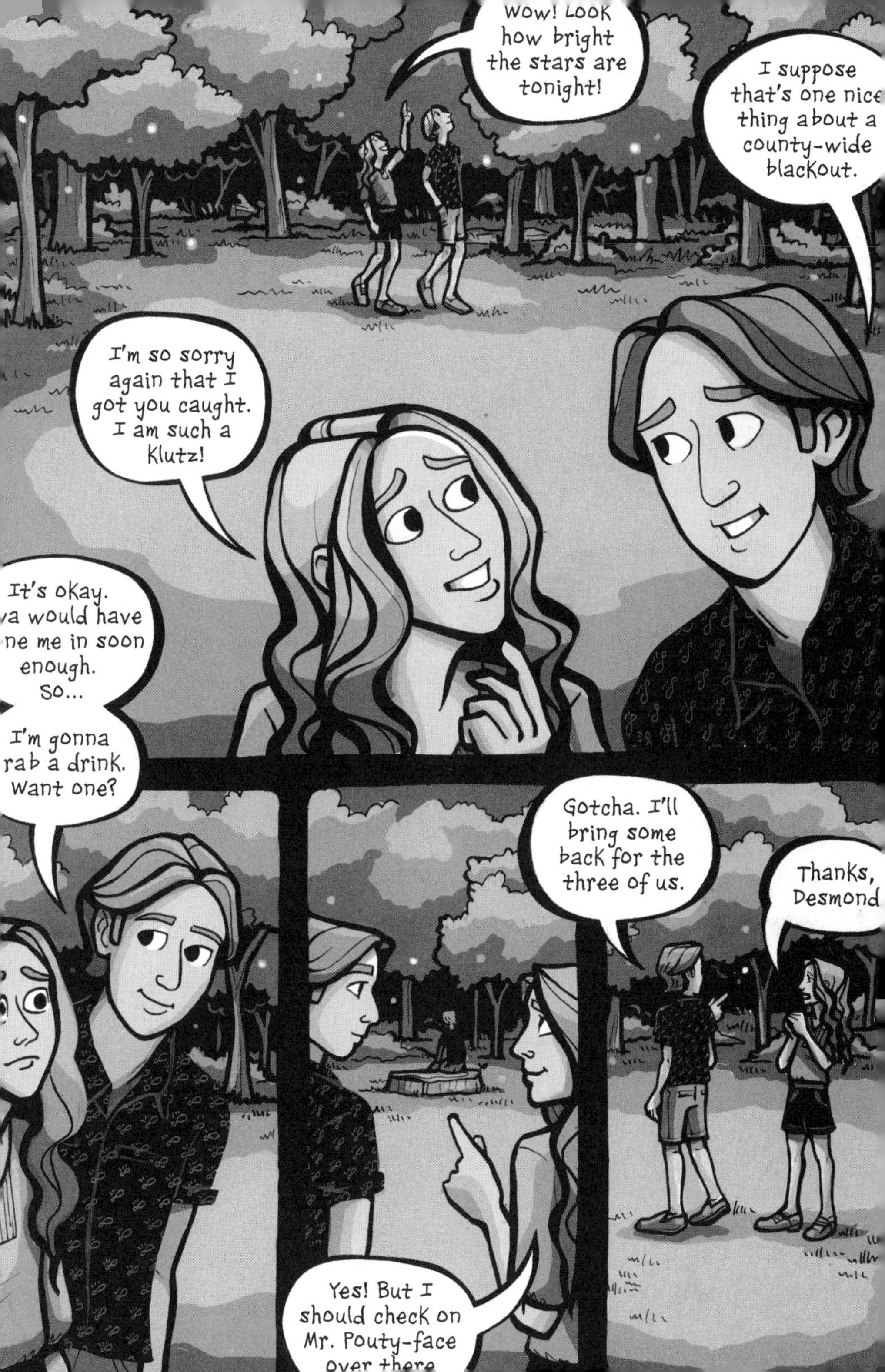
WOW! LOOK how bright the stars are tonight!
I suppose that's one nice thing about a county-wide blackout.
I'm so sorry again that I got you caught. I am such a Klutz!
It's okay. va would have ne me in soon enough. So...
I'm gonna rab a drink. Want one?
Yes! But I should check on Mr. Pouty-face
Gotcha. I'll bring some back for the three of us.
Thanks, Desmond

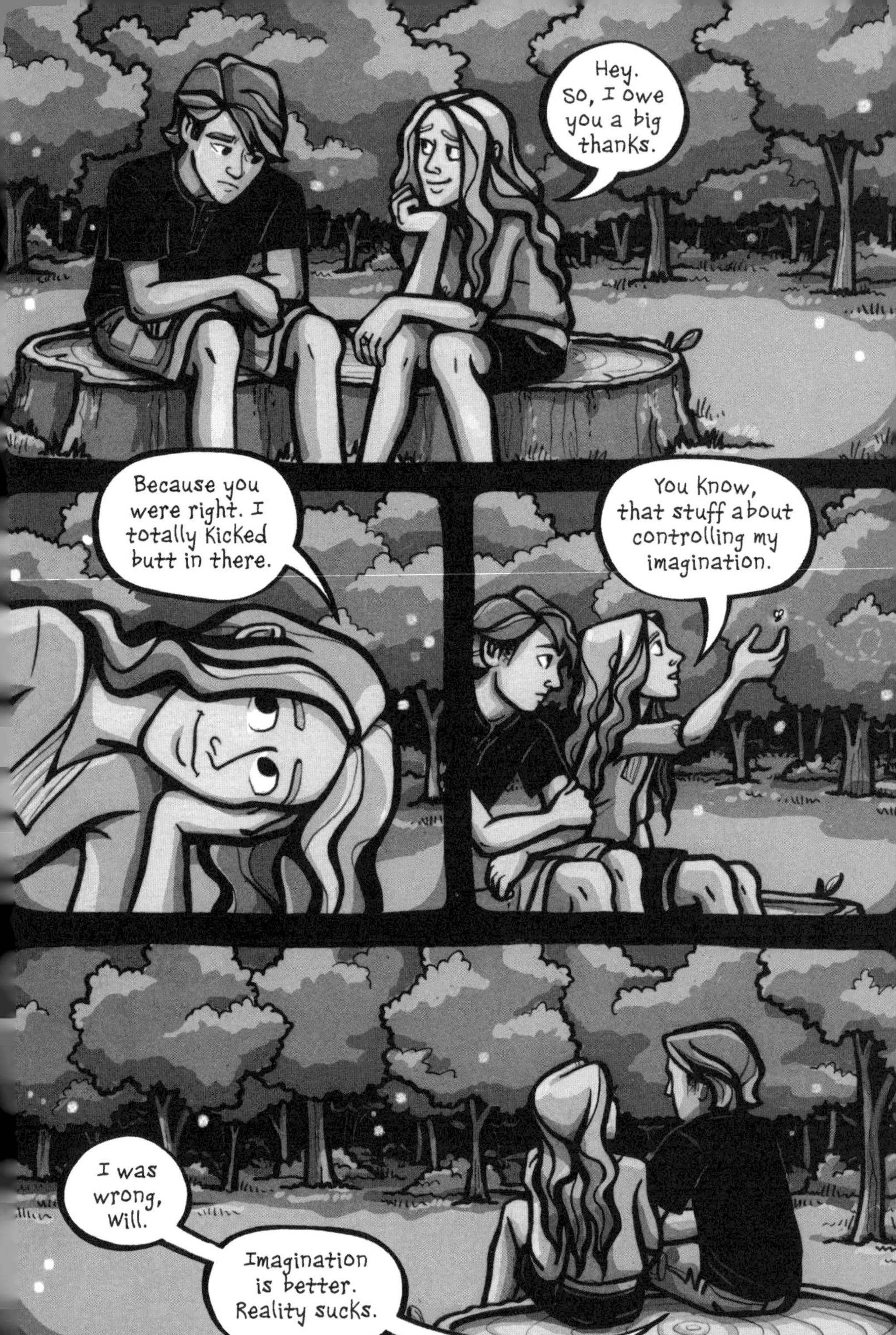
Hey. So, I owe you a big thanks.
Because you were right. I totally kicked butt in there.
You know, that stuff about controlling my imagination.
I was wrong, Will.
Imagination is better. Reality sucks.

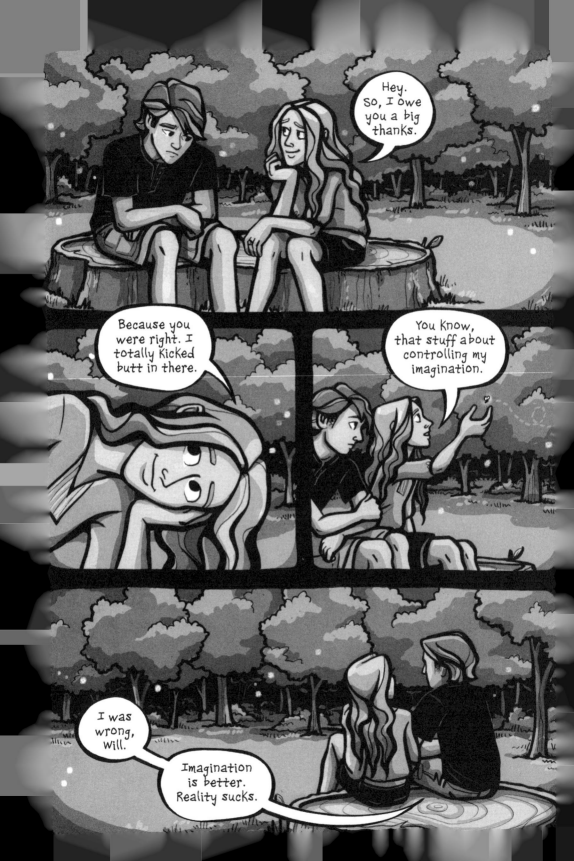

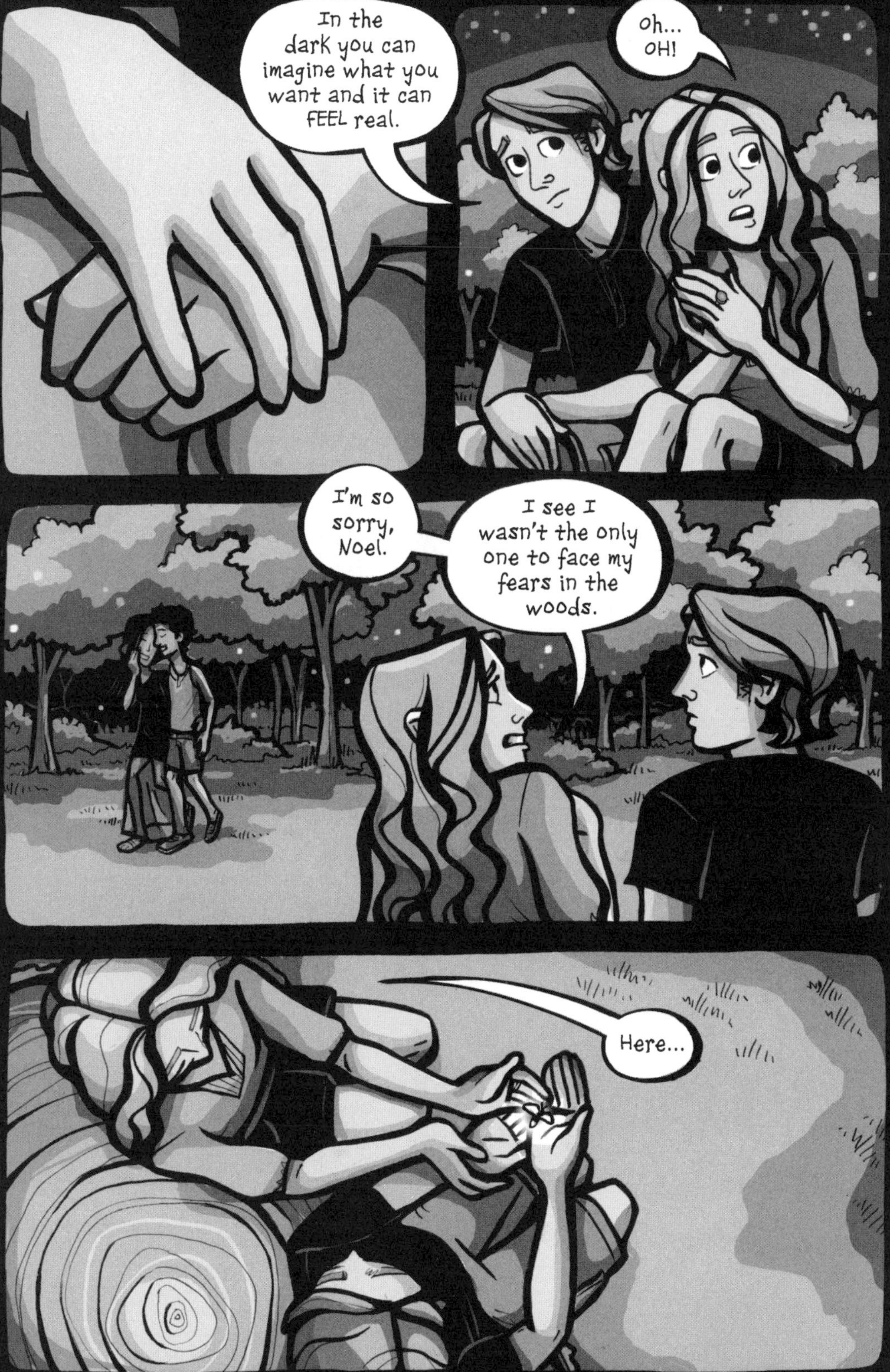
In the dark you can imagine what you want and it can FEEL real.
Oh... OH!
I'm so sorry, Noel.
I see I wasn't the only one to face my fears in the woods.
Here...

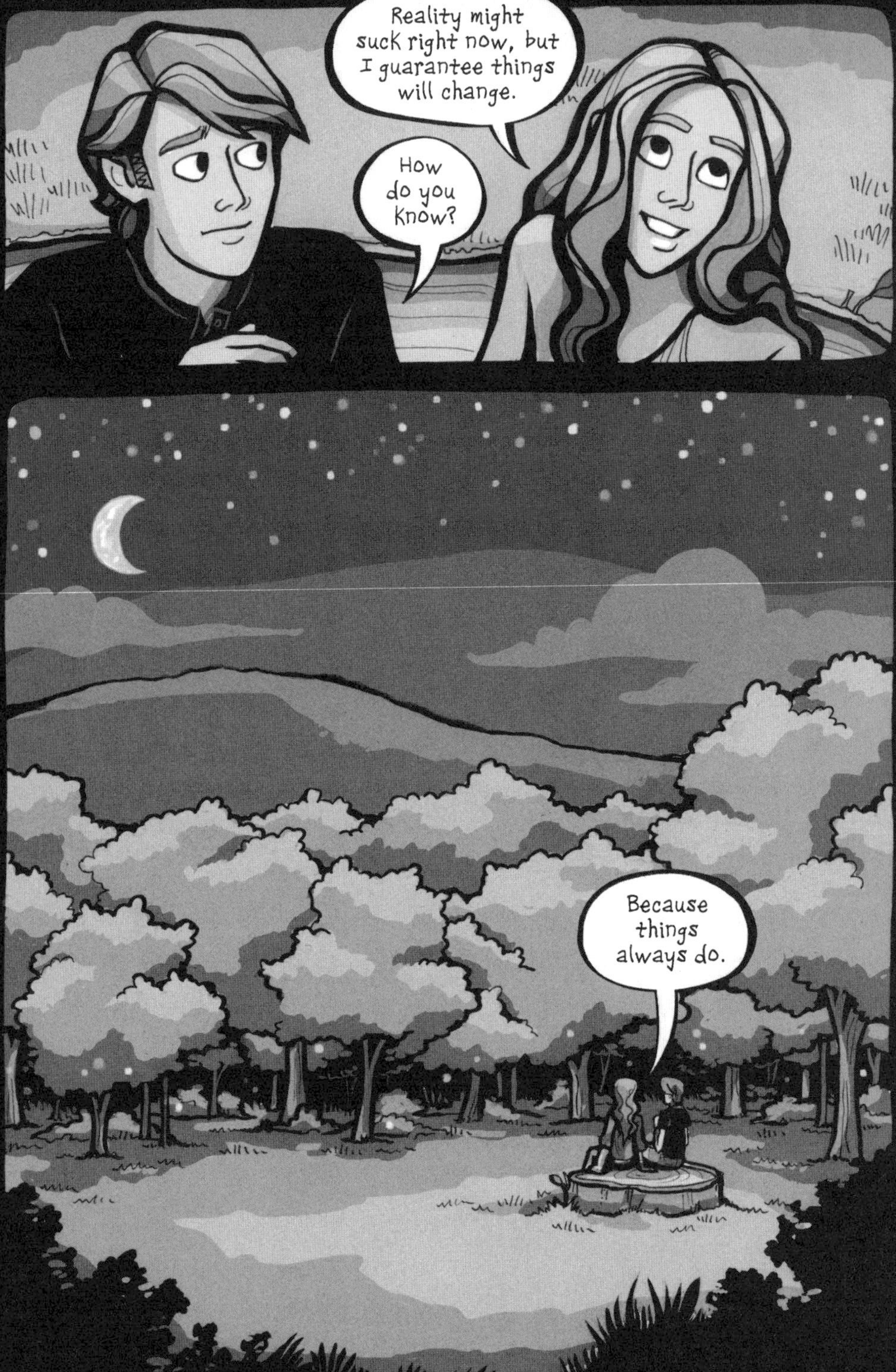
Reality might suck right now, but I guarantee things will change.
How do you know?
Because things always do.

The Dark Side

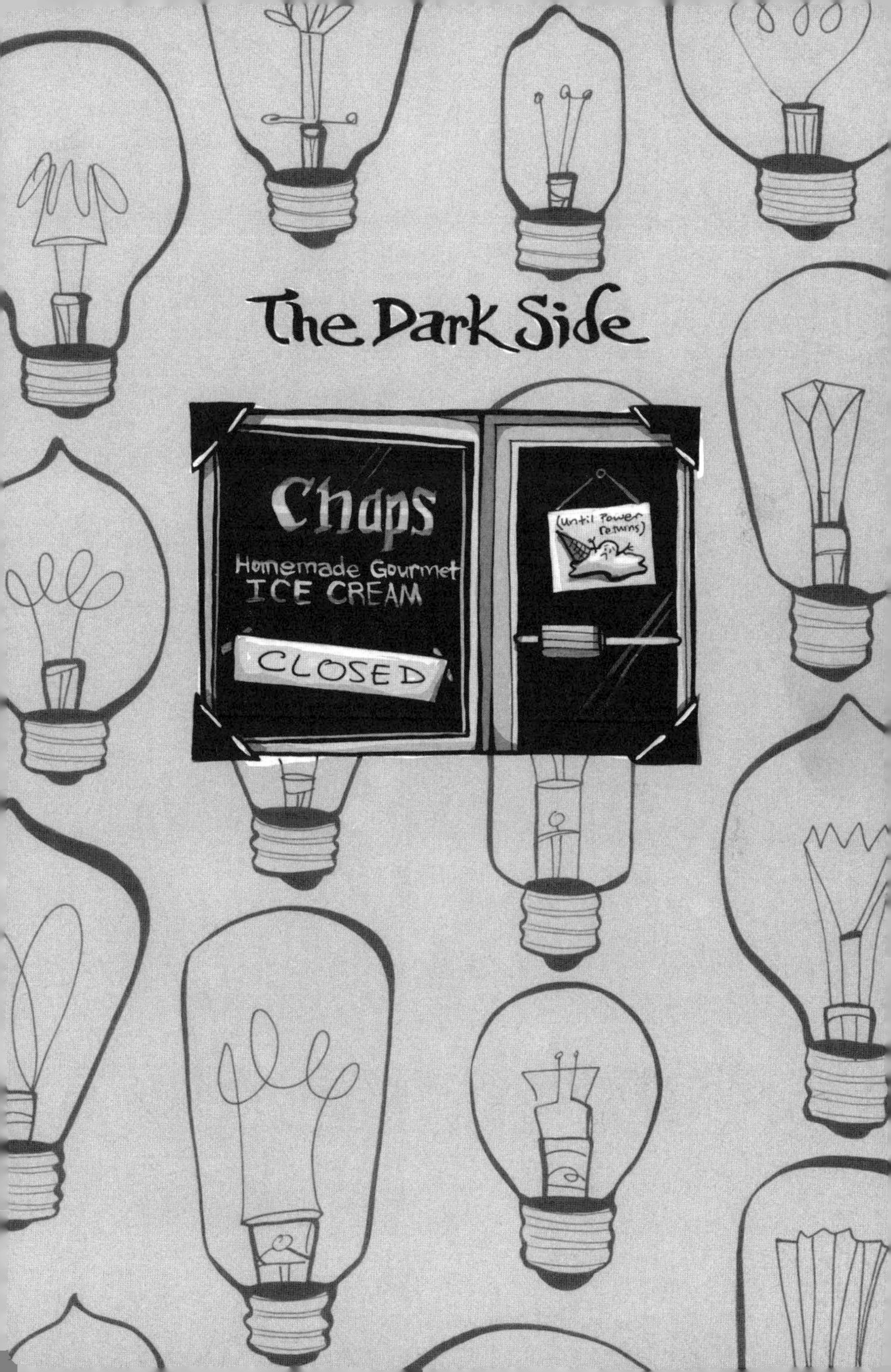
Chaps
Homemade Gourmet
ICE CREAM
CLOSED
(until Power returns)

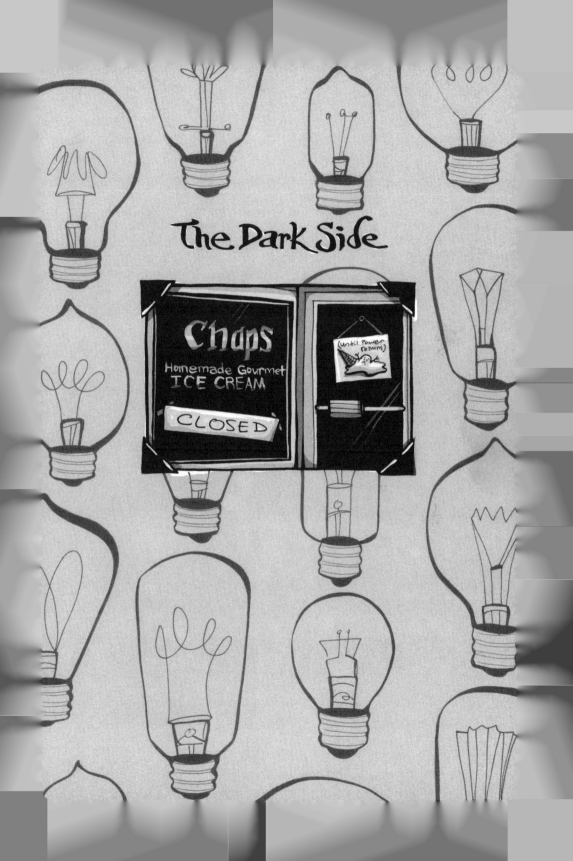

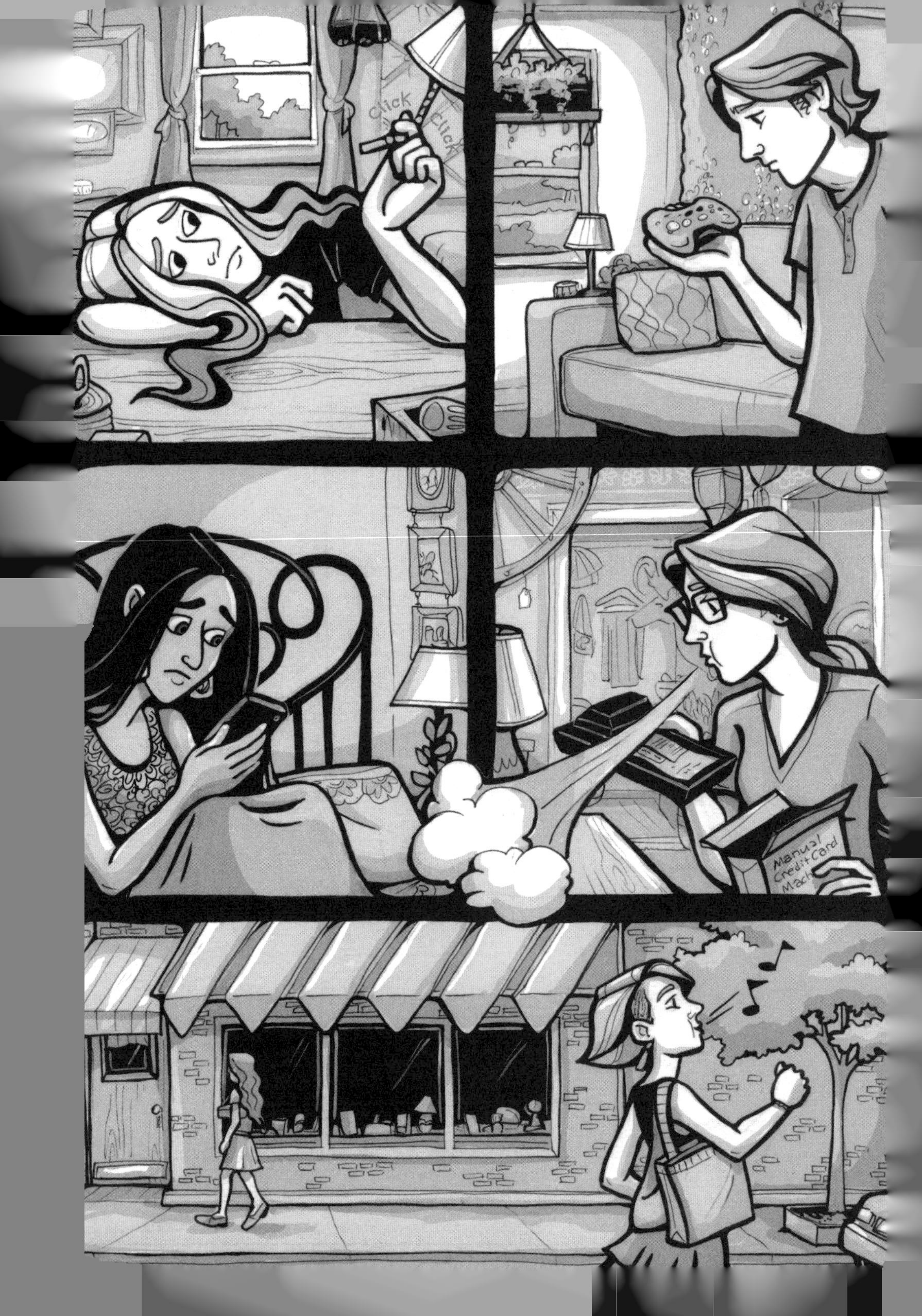
Click
Click
Manual
Credit Card
Mach

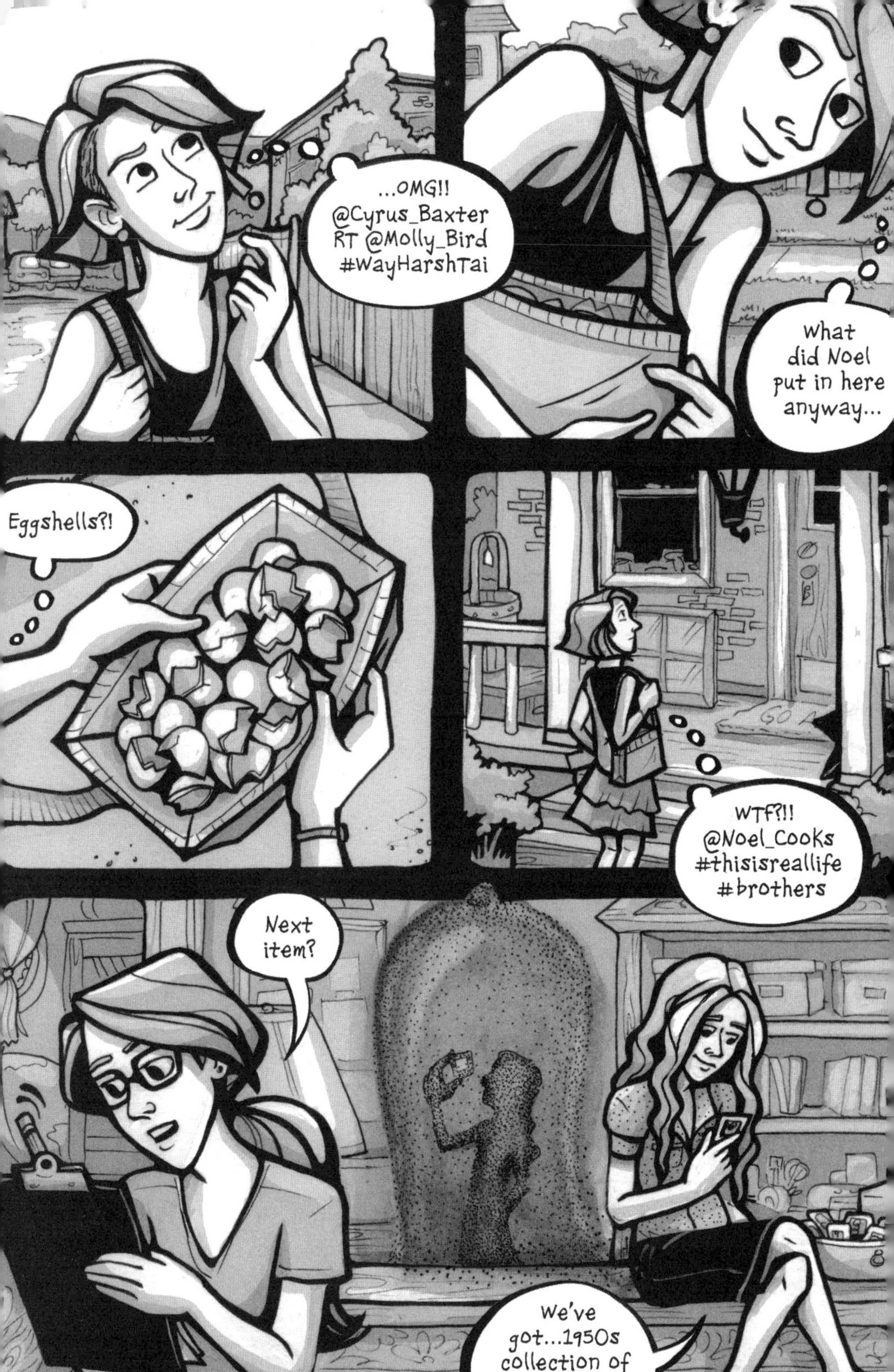

...OMG!!
@Cyrus_Baxter
RT @Molly_Bird
#WayHarshTai
What did Noel put in here anyway...
Eggshells?!
WTF?!!
@Noel_Cooks
#thisisreallife
#brothers
Next item?
We've got...1950s collection of

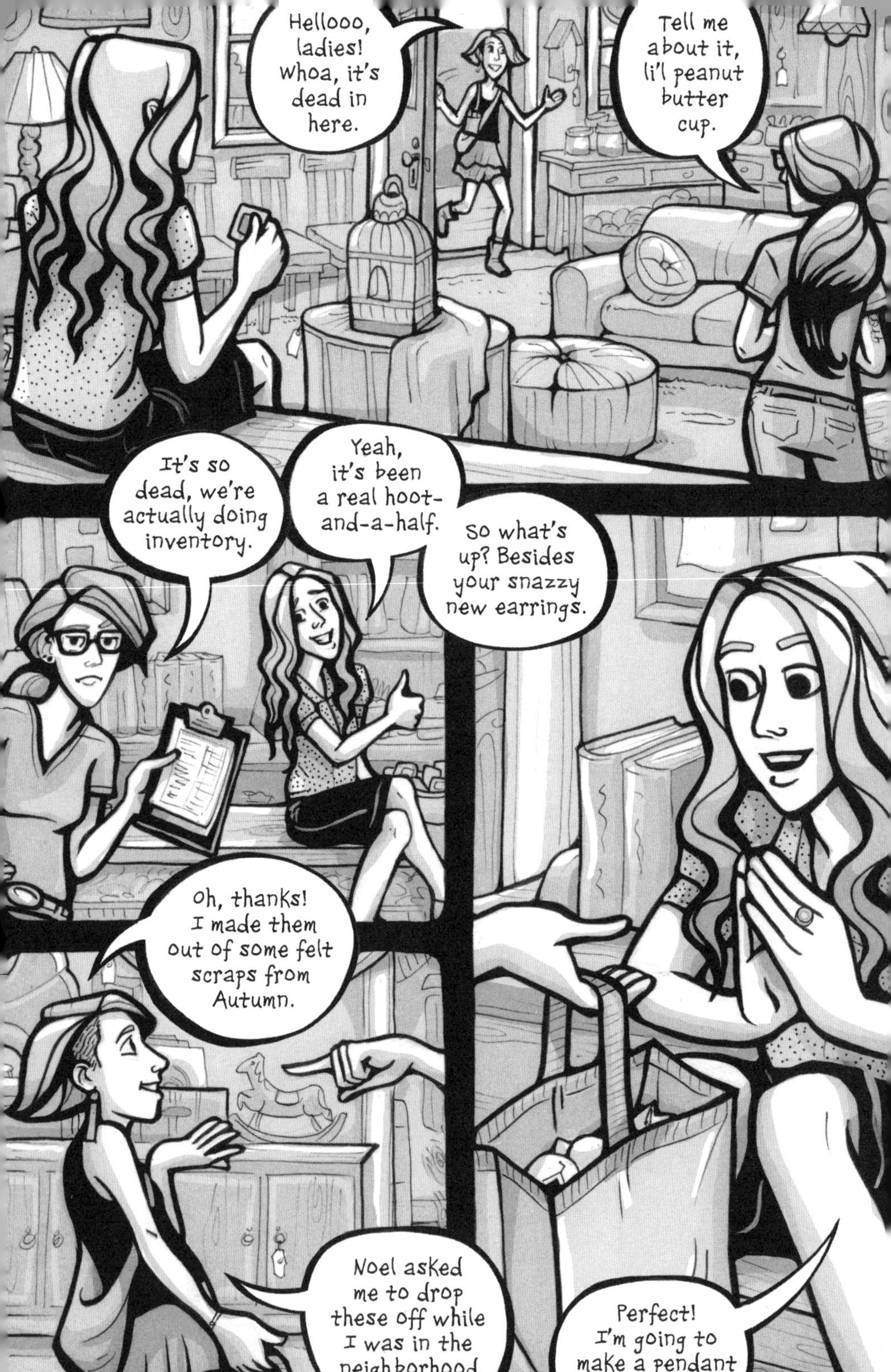

Hellooo, ladies! Whoa, it's dead in here.
Tell me about it, li'l peanut butter cup.
It's so dead, we're actually doing inventory.
Yeah, it's been a real hoot-and-a-half.
So what's up? Besides your snazzy new earrings.
Oh, thanks! I made them out of some felt scraps from Autumn.
Noel asked me to drop these off while I was in the neighborhood.
Perfect! I'm going to make a pendant

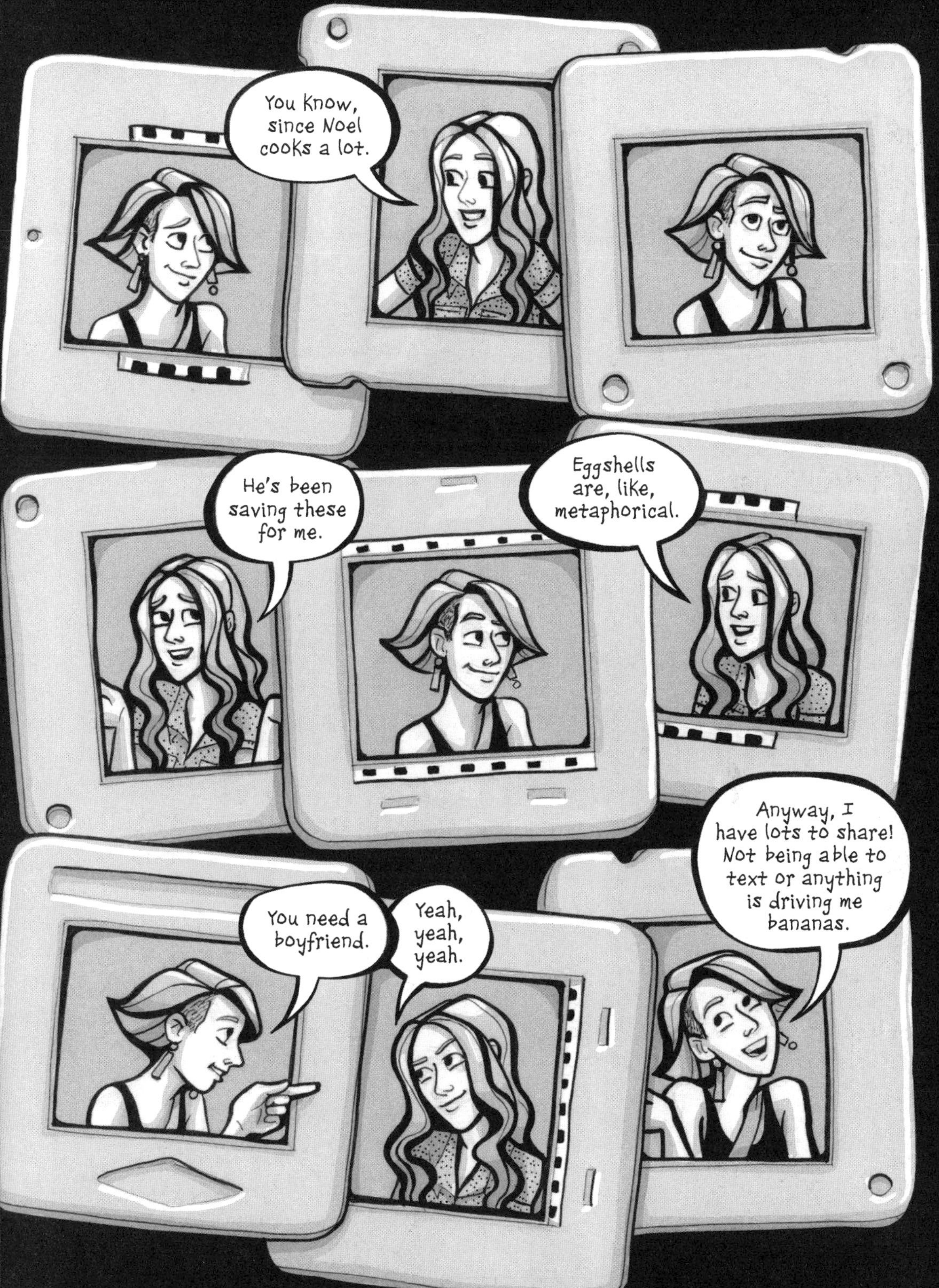

You Know, since Noel cooks a lot.
He's been saving these for me.
Eggshells are, like, metaphorical.
You need a boyfriend.
Yeah, yeah, yeah.
Anyway, I have lots to share! Not being able to text or anything is driving me bananas.

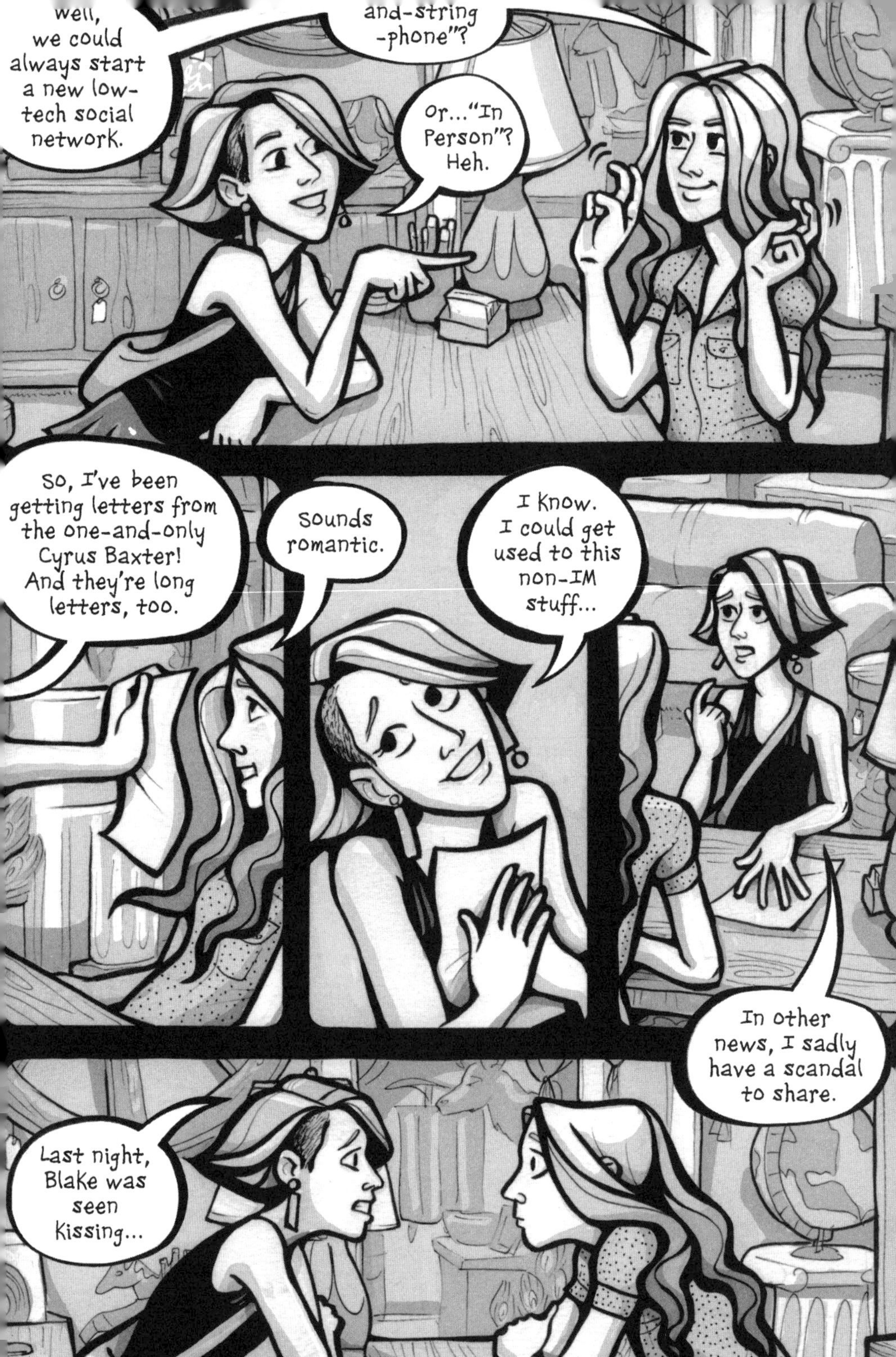
well, we could always start a new low-tech social network.
and-string -phone"?
Or..."In Person"? Heh.
So, I've been getting letters from the one-and-only Cyrus Baxter! And they're long letters, too.
Sounds romantic.
I know. I could get used to this non-IM stuff...
In other news, I sadly have a scandal to share.
Last night, Blake was seen kissing...

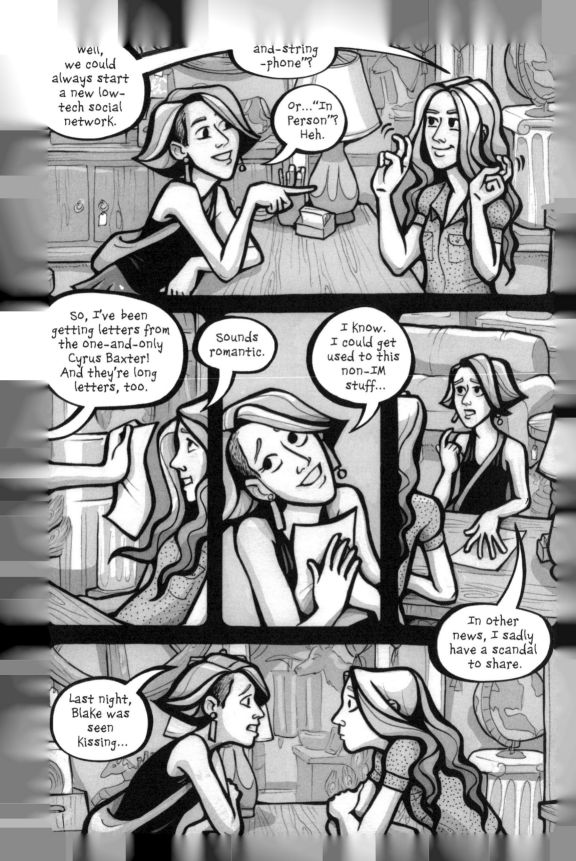

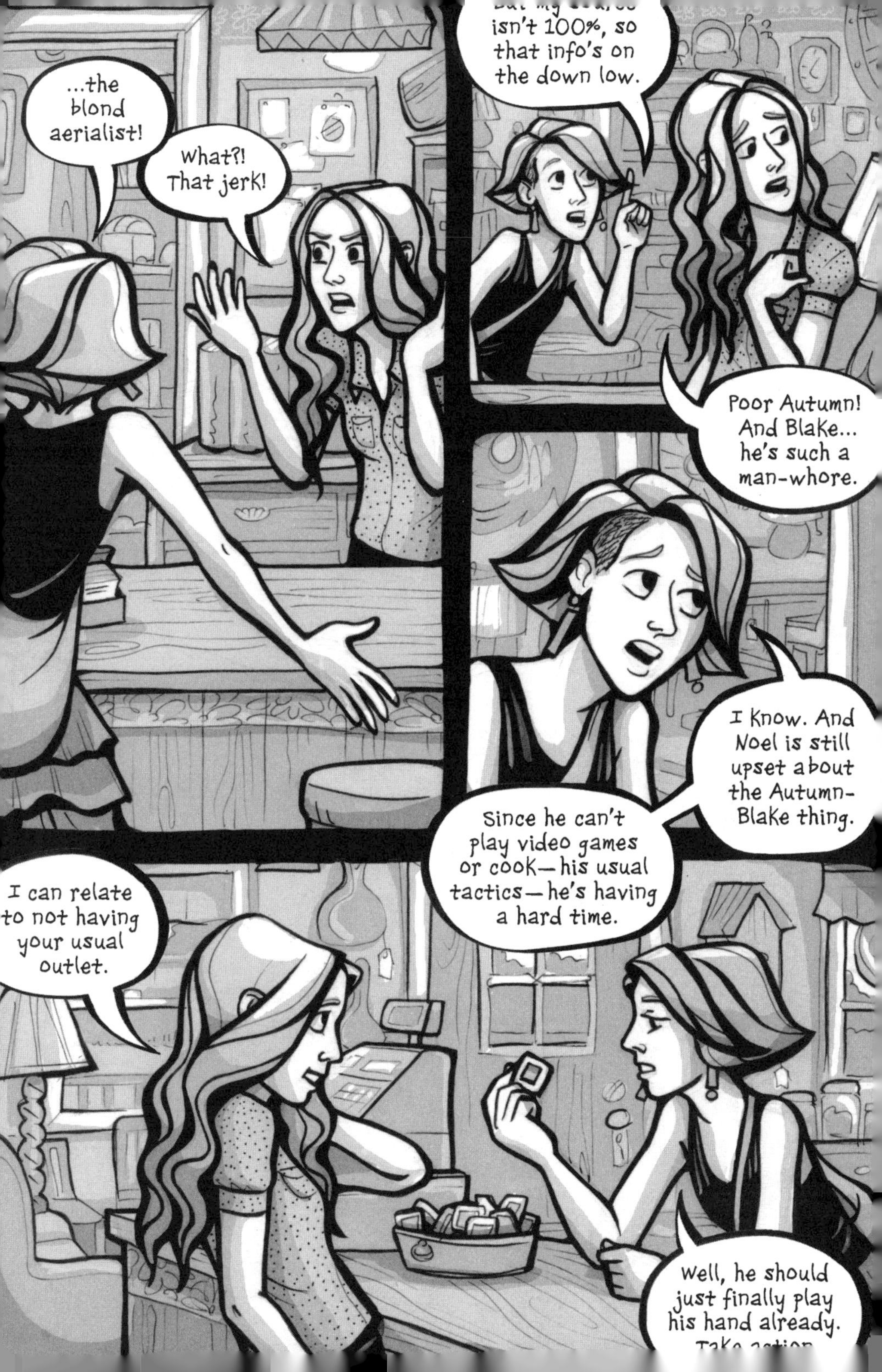
...the blond aerialist!
What?! That jerk!
isn't 100%, so that info's on the down low.
Poor Autumn! And Blake... he's such a man-whore.
I know. And Noel is still upset about the Autumn-Blake thing.
Since he can't play video games or cook—his usual tactics—he's having a hard time.
I can relate to not having your usual outlet.
Well, he should just finally play his hand already.

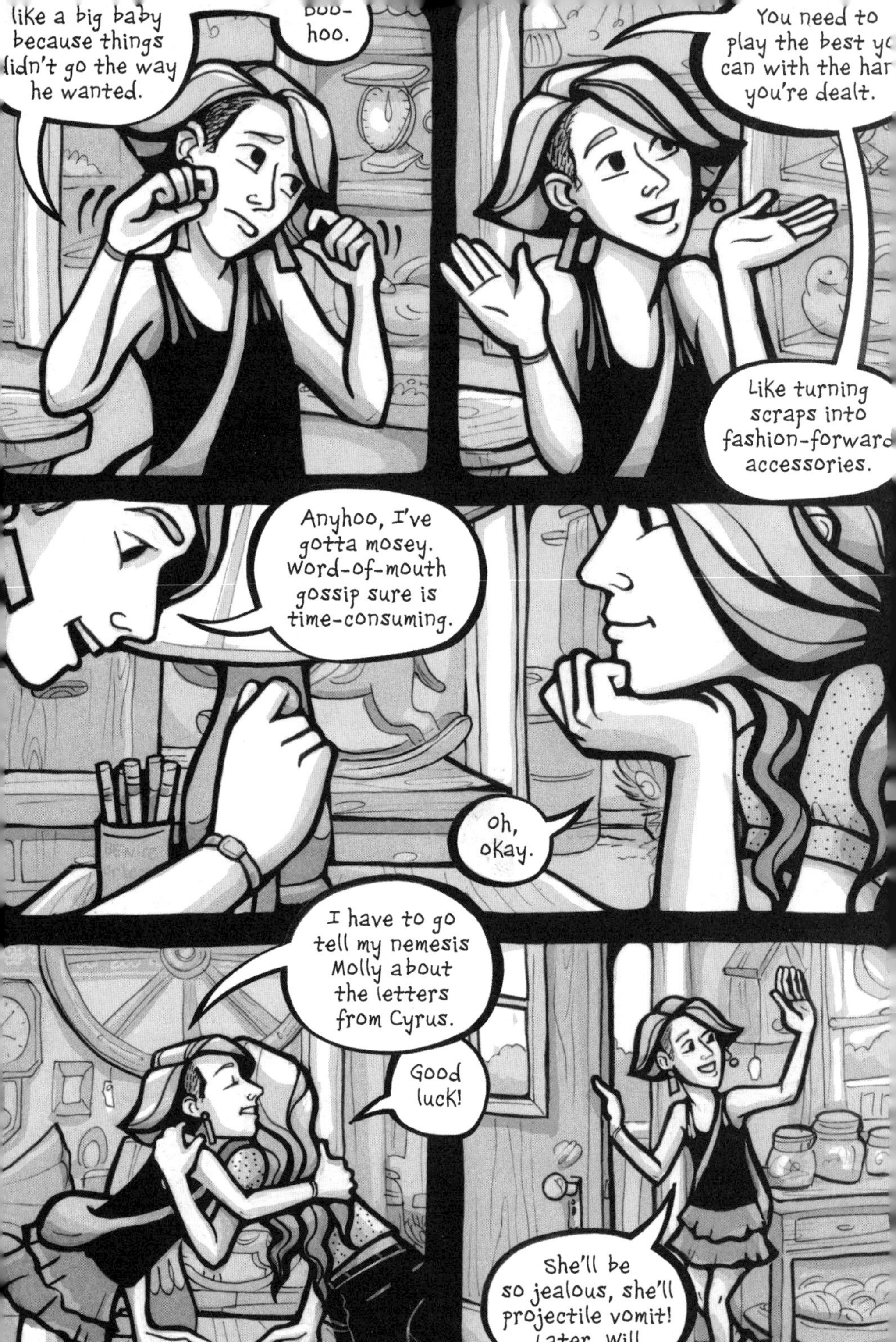
like a big baby because things didn't go the way he wanted.
Boo-hoo.
You need to play the best you can with the hand you're dealt.
Like turning scraps into fashion-forward accessories.
Anyhoo, I've gotta mosey. Word-of-mouth gossip sure is time-consuming.
Oh, okay.
I have to go tell my nemesis Molly about the letters from Cyrus.
Good luck!
She'll be so jealous, she'll projectile vomit! Later, Will.

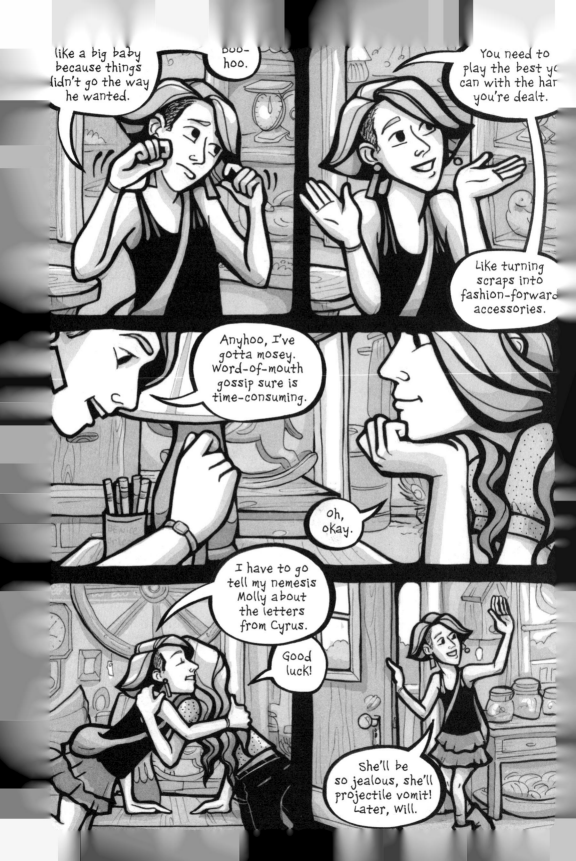

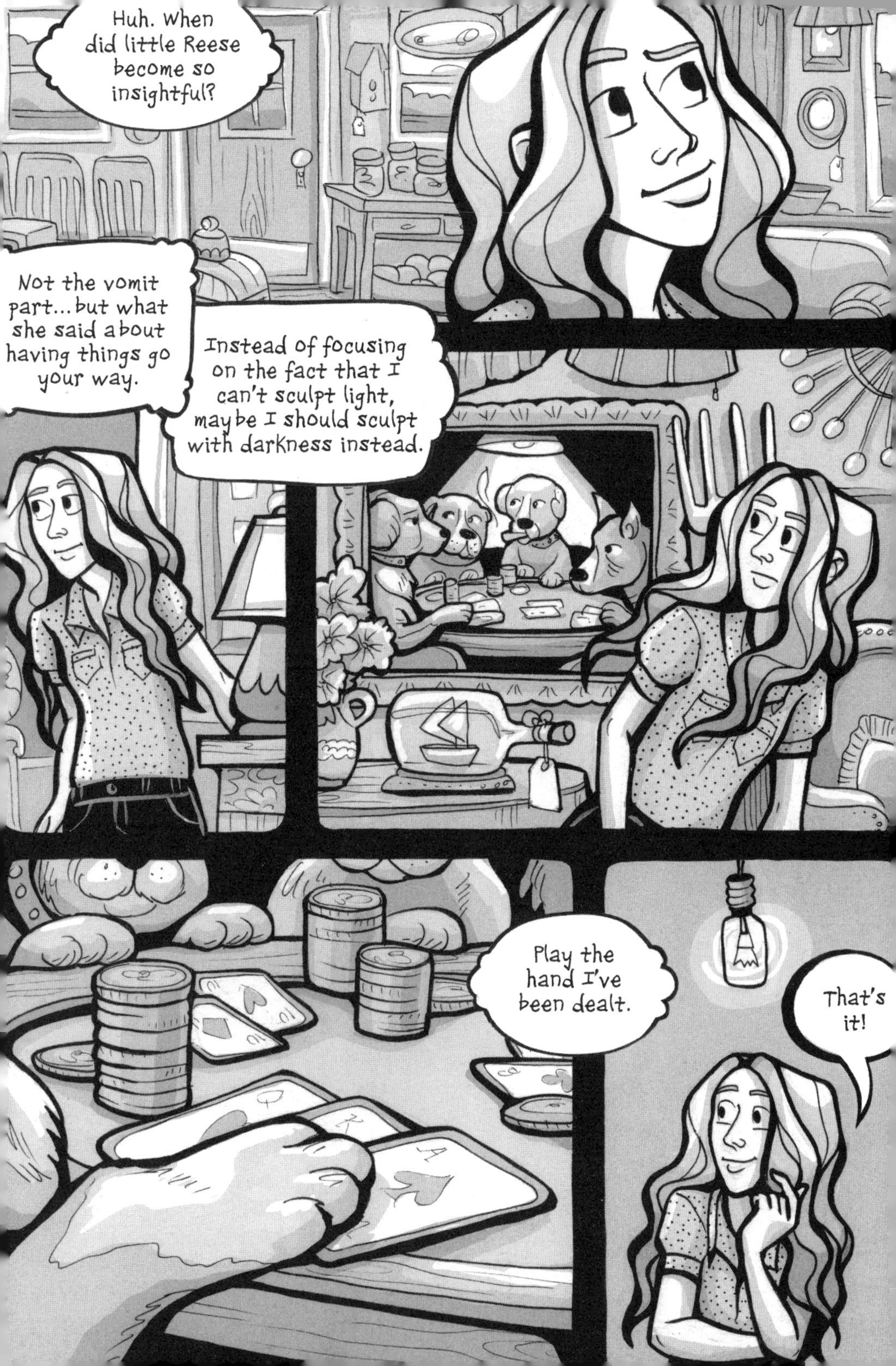
Huh. When did little Reese become so insightful?
Not the vomit part...but what she said about having things go your way.
Instead of focusing on the fact that I can't sculpt light, maybe I should sculpt with darkness instead.
Play the hand I've been dealt.
That's it!

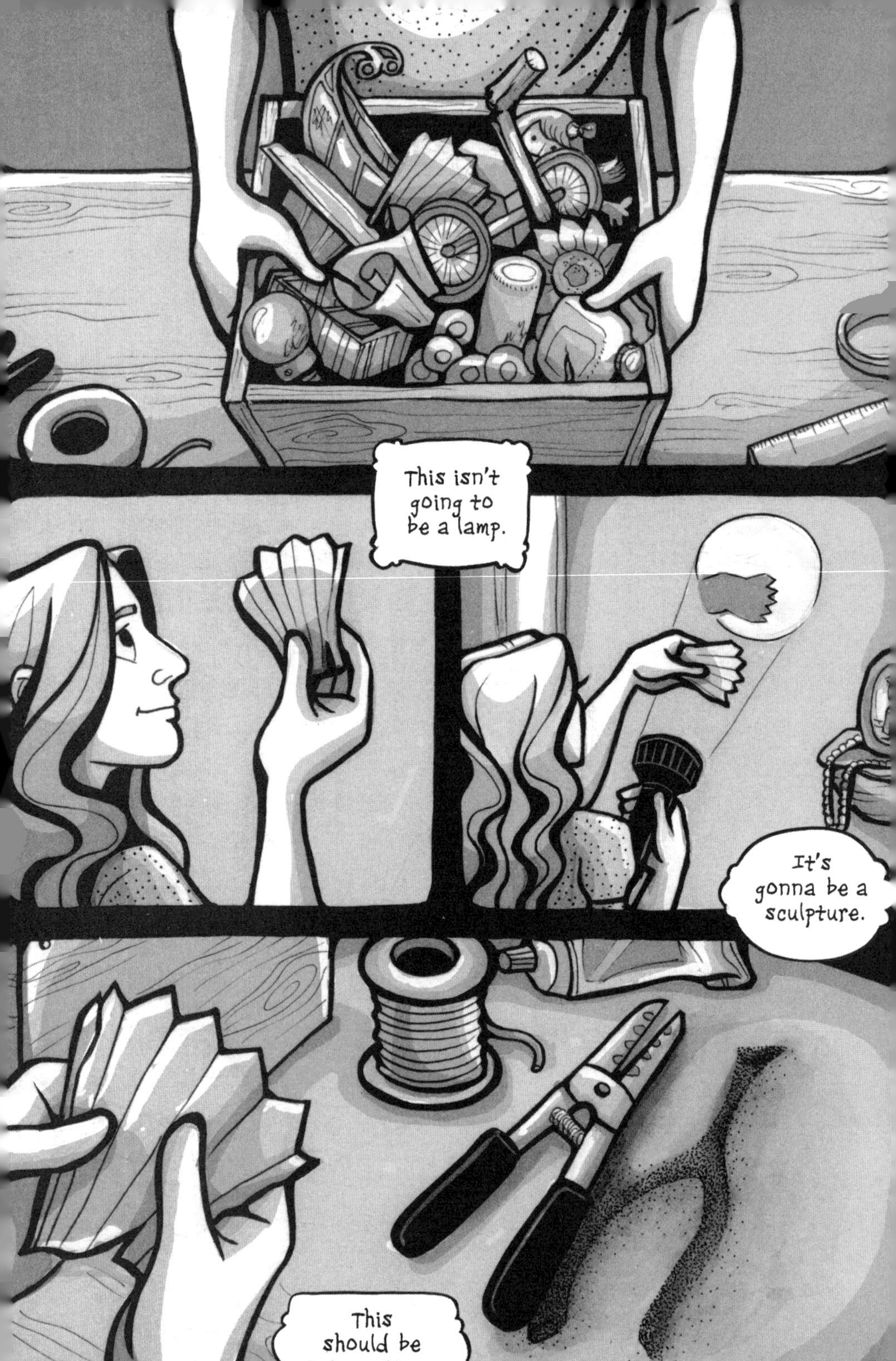
This isn't going to be a lamp.
It's gonna be a sculpture.
This should be

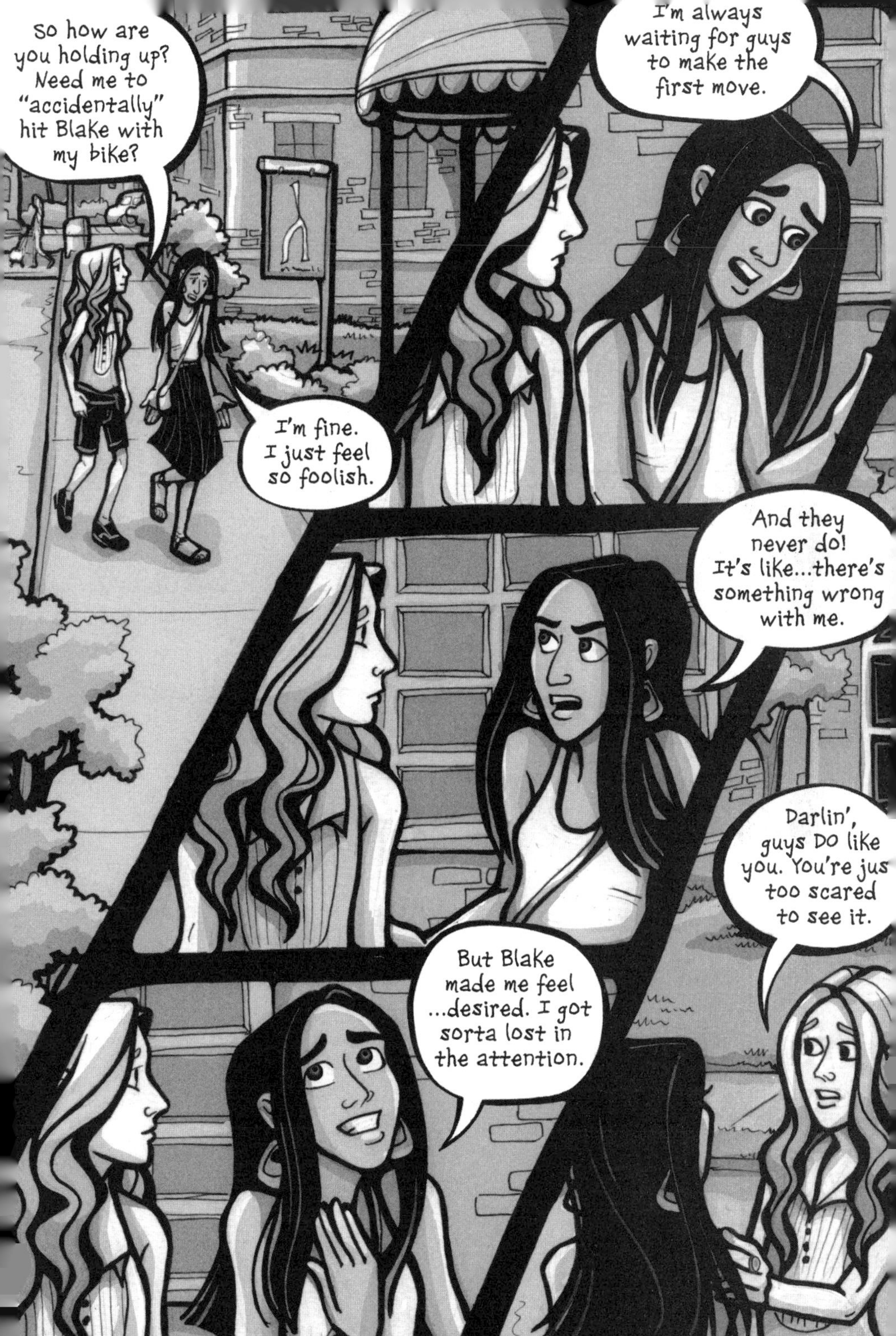
So how are you holding up? Need me to "accidentally" hit Blake with my bike?
I'm fine. I just feel so foolish.
I'm always waiting for guys to make the first move.
And they never do! It's like...there's something wrong with me.
But Blake made me feel ...desired. I got sorta lost in the attention.
Darlin', guys DO like you. You're jus too scared to see it.

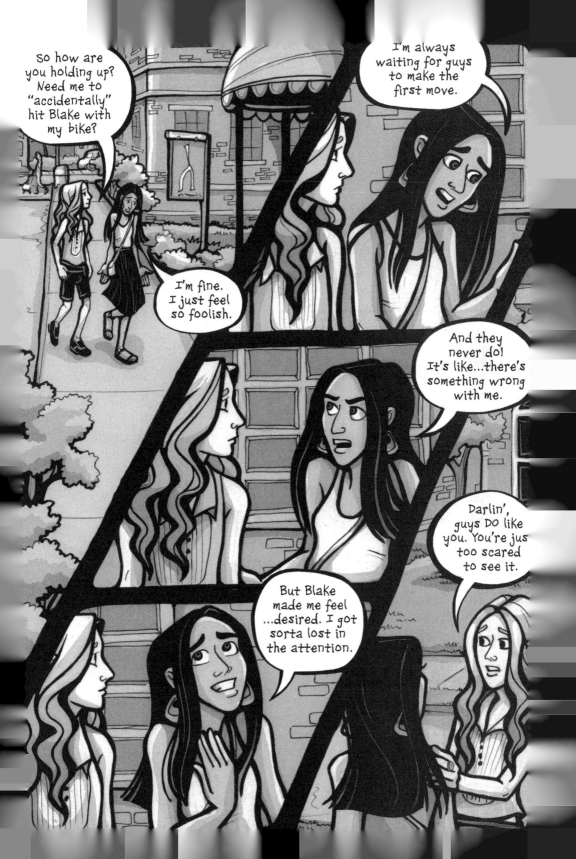

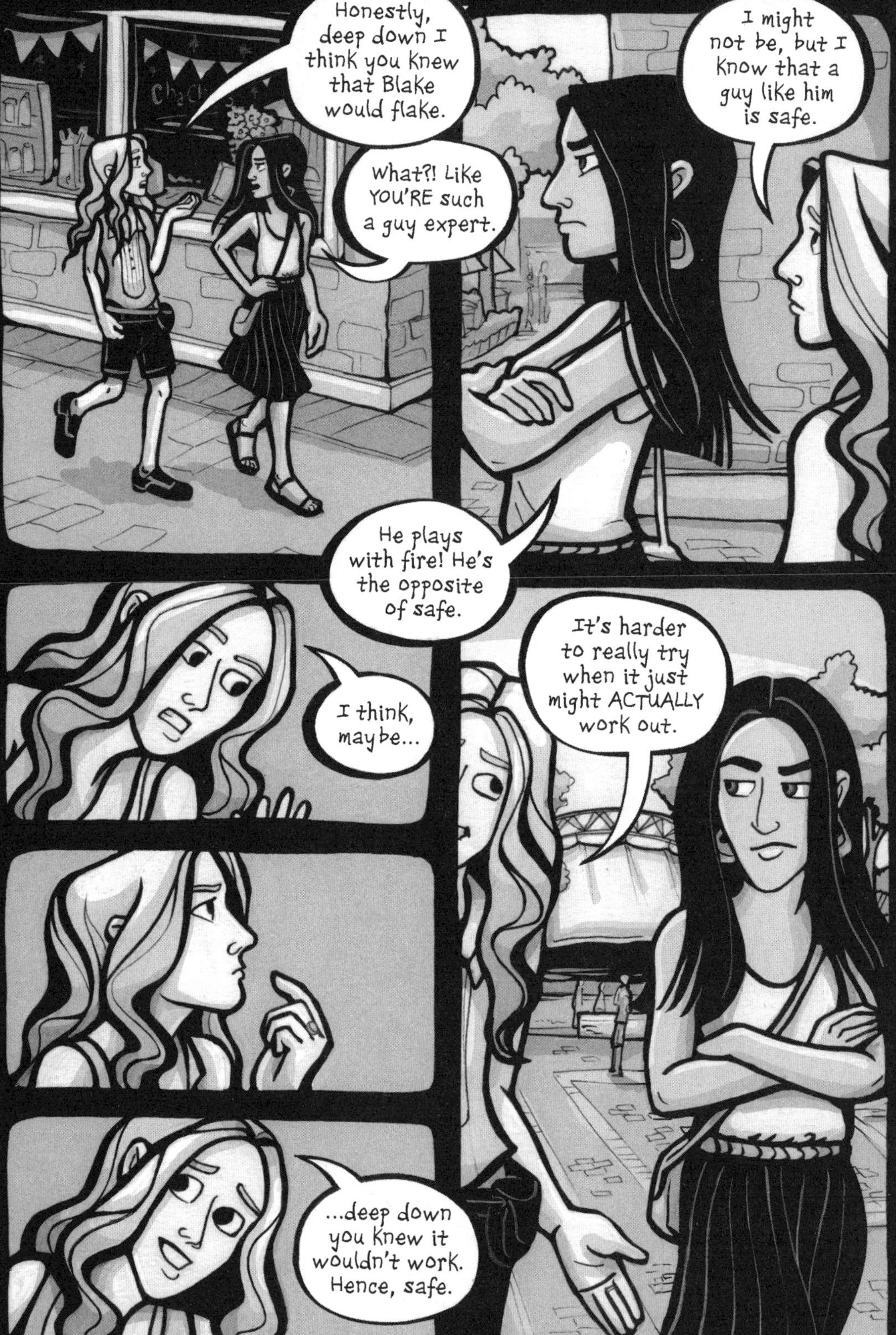
Honestly, deep down I think you knew that Blake would flake.
What?! Like YOU'RE such a guy expert.
I might not be, but I know that a guy like him is safe.
He plays with fire! He's the opposite of safe.
I think, maybe...
...deep down you knew it wouldn't work. Hence, safe.
It's harder to really try when it just might ACTUALLY work out.

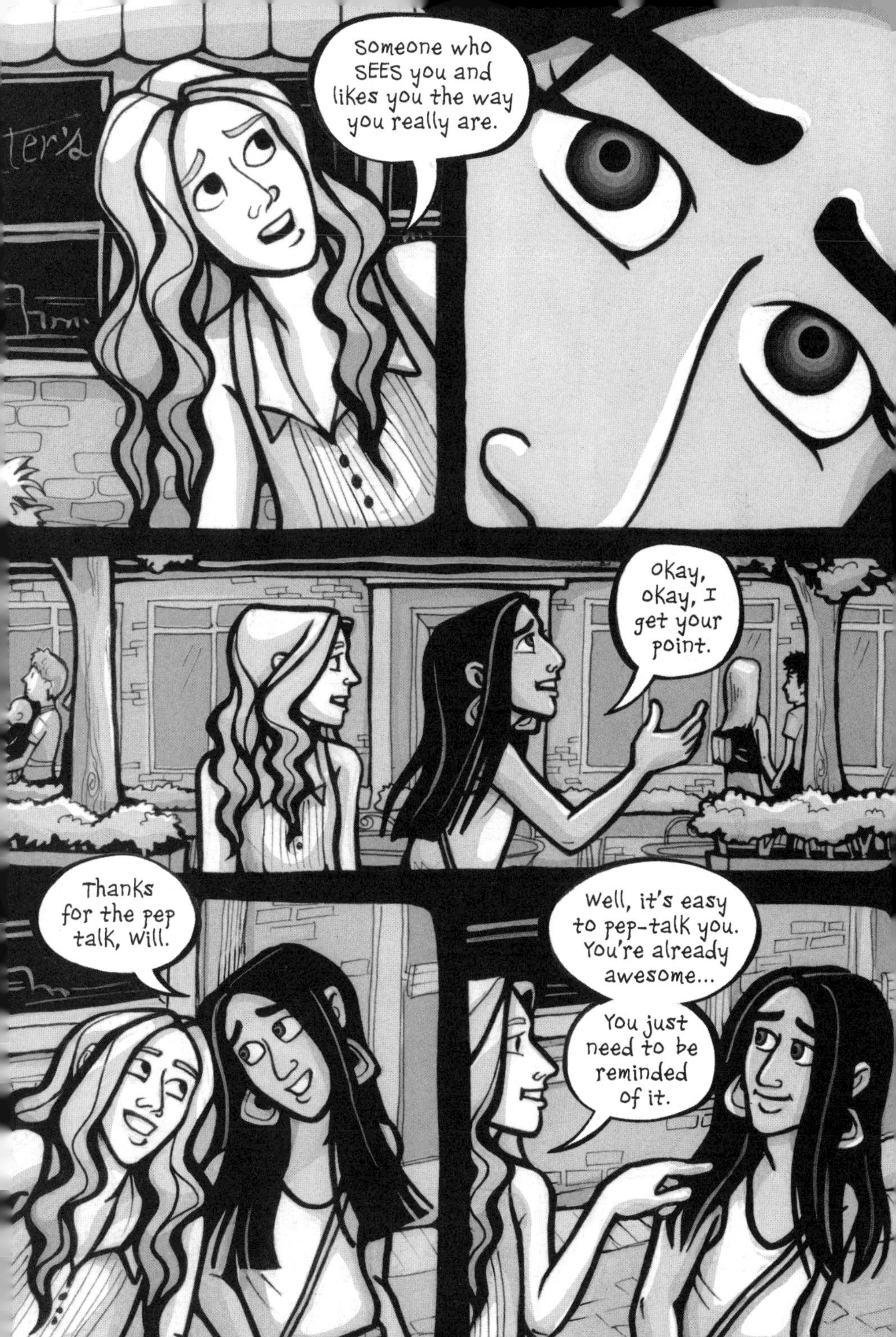

Someone who SEES you and likes you the way you really are.
Okay, okay, I get your point.
Thanks for the pep talk, Will.
Well, it's easy to pep-talk you. You're already awesome...
You just need to be reminded of it.

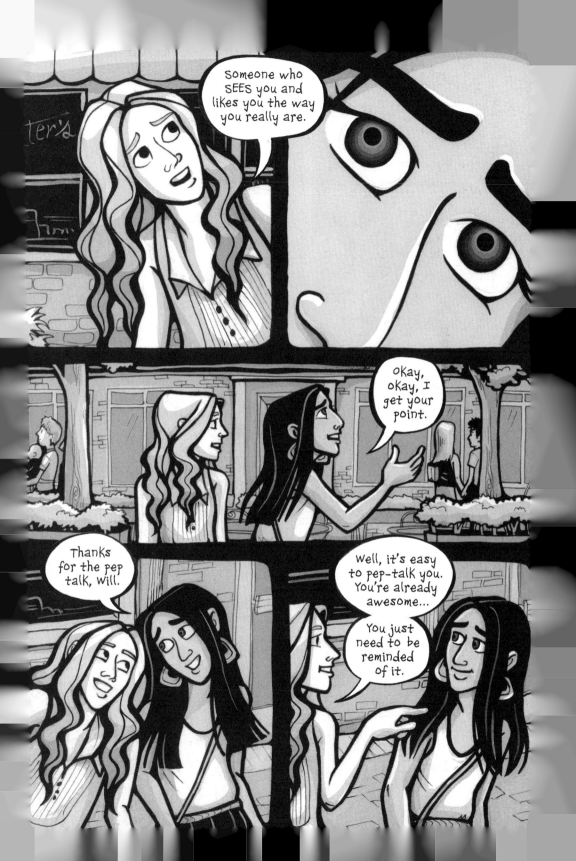

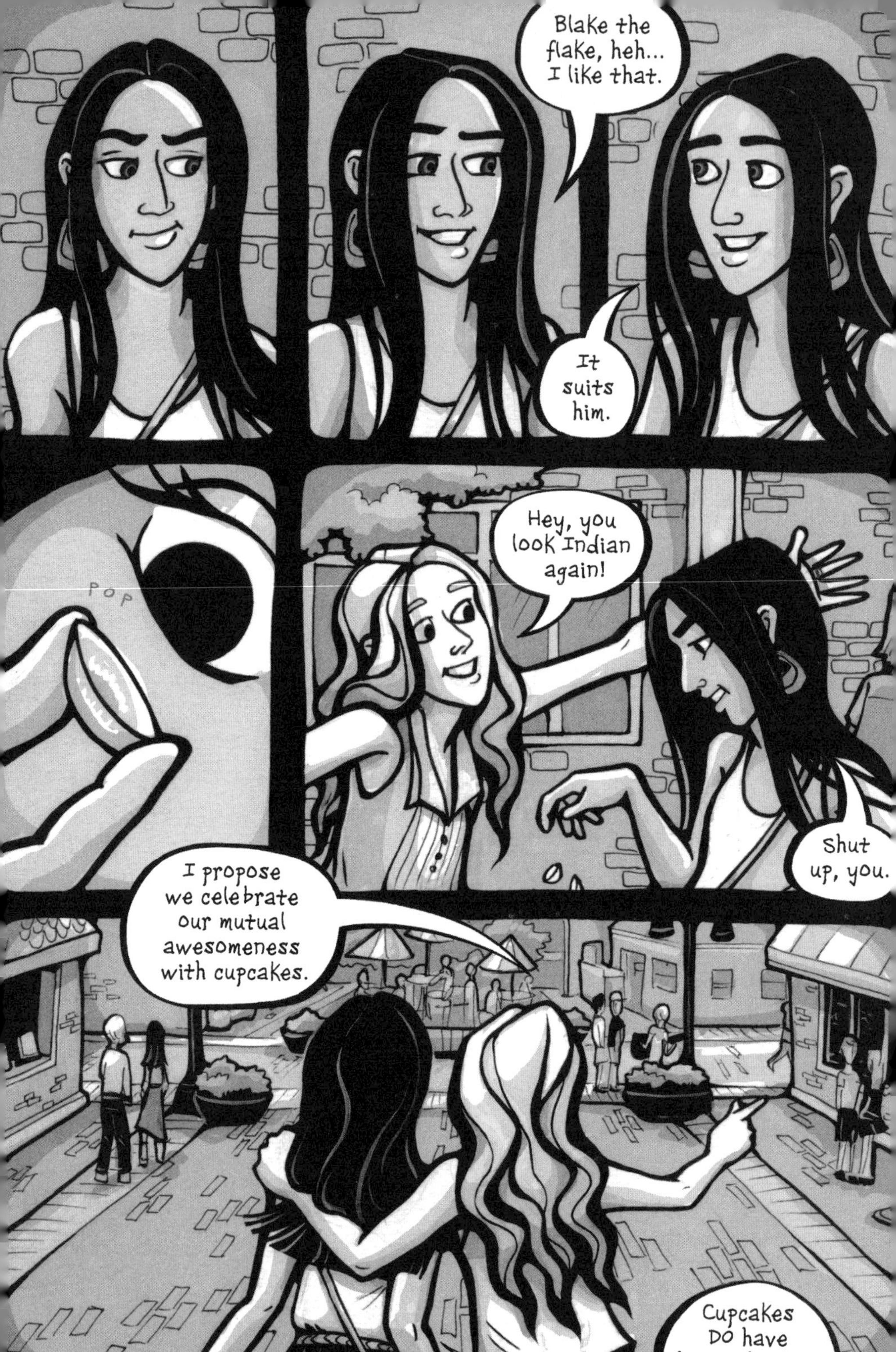
Blake the flake, heh... I like that.
It suits him.
POP
Hey, you look Indian again!
Shut up, you.
I propose we celebrate our mutual awesomeness with cupcakes.
Cupcakes DO have heart-healing

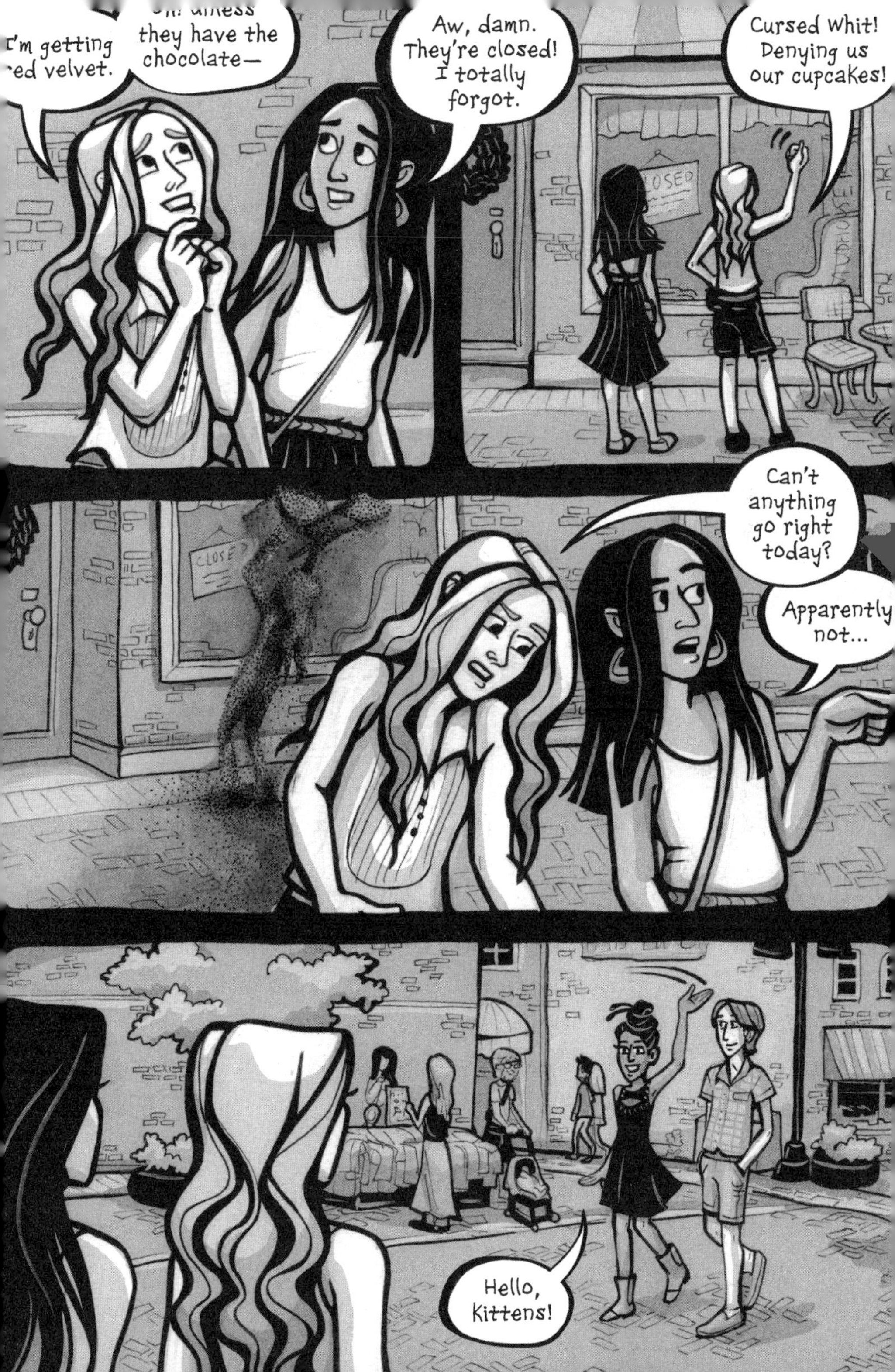
I'm getting
ed velvet.
they have the chocolate—
Aw, damn. They're closed! I totally forgot.
Cursed Whit! Denying us our cupcakes!
CLOSED
Can't anything go right today?
Apparently not...
CLOSE
Hello, Kittens!

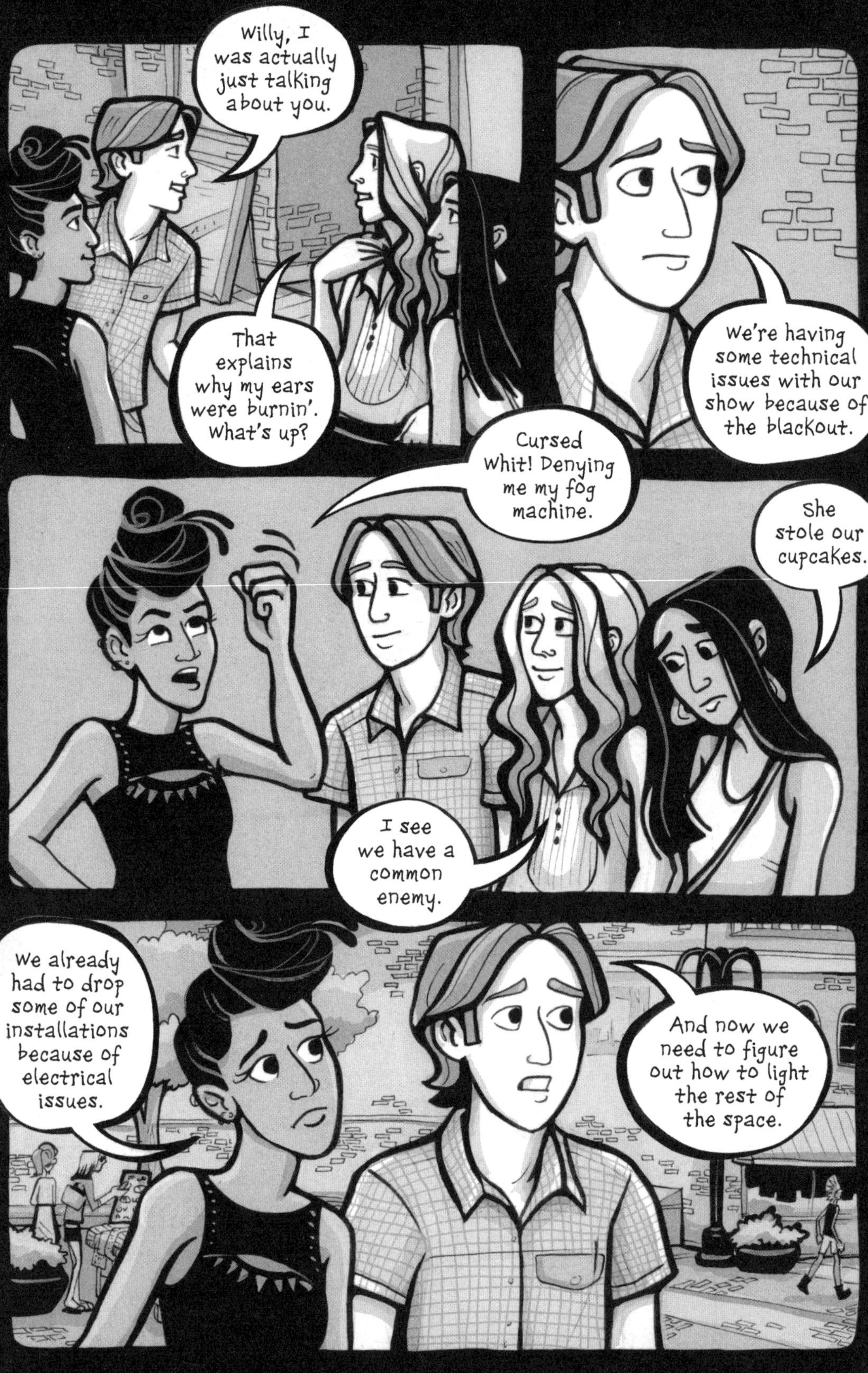
Willy, I was actually just talking about you.
That explains why my ears were burnin'. What's up?
We're having some technical issues with our show because of the blackout.
Cursed Whit! Denying me my fog machine.
She stole our cupcakes.
I see we have a common enemy.
We already had to drop some of our installations because of electrical issues.
And now we need to figure out how to light the rest of the space.

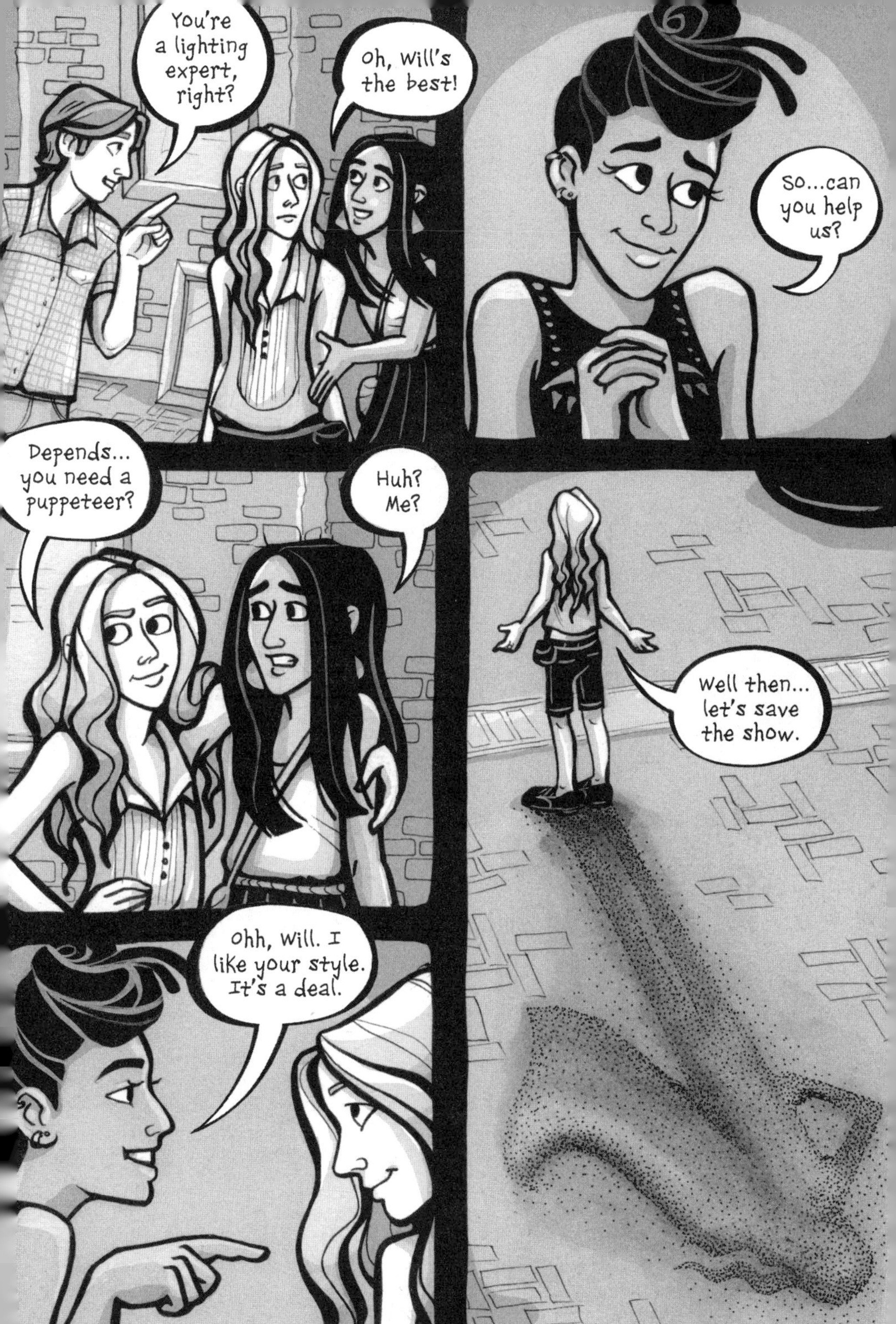
You're a lighting expert, right?
Oh, Will's the best!
So...can you help us?
Depends... you need a puppeteer?
Huh? Me?
Ohh, Will. I like your style. It's a deal.
Well then... let's save the show.

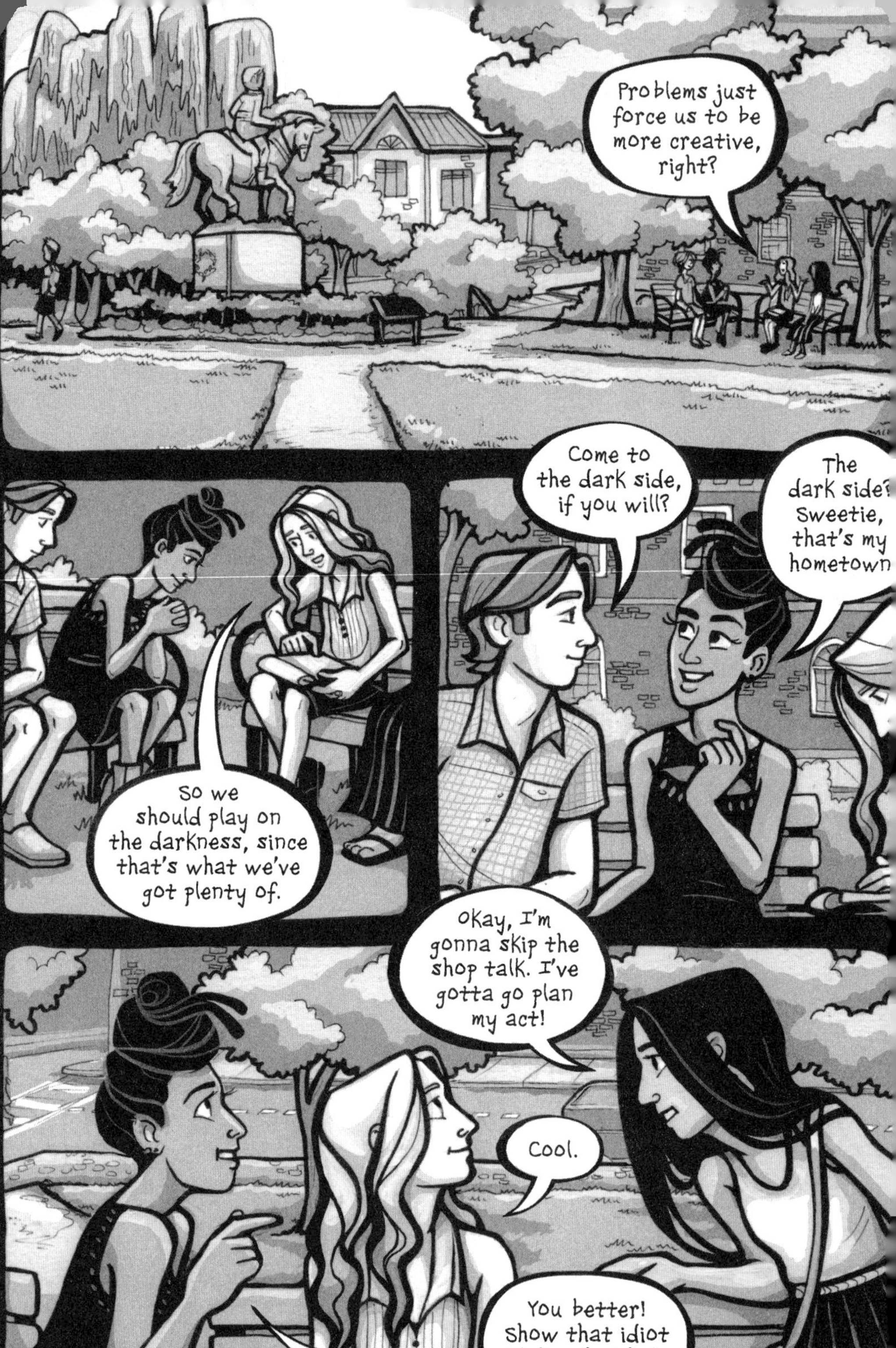
Problems just force us to be more creative, right?
So we should play on the darkness, since that's what we've got plenty of.
Come to the dark side, if you will?
The dark side? Sweetie, that's my hometown
Okay, I'm gonna skip the shop talk. I've gotta go plan my act!
Cool.
You better! Show that idiot Blake what he's

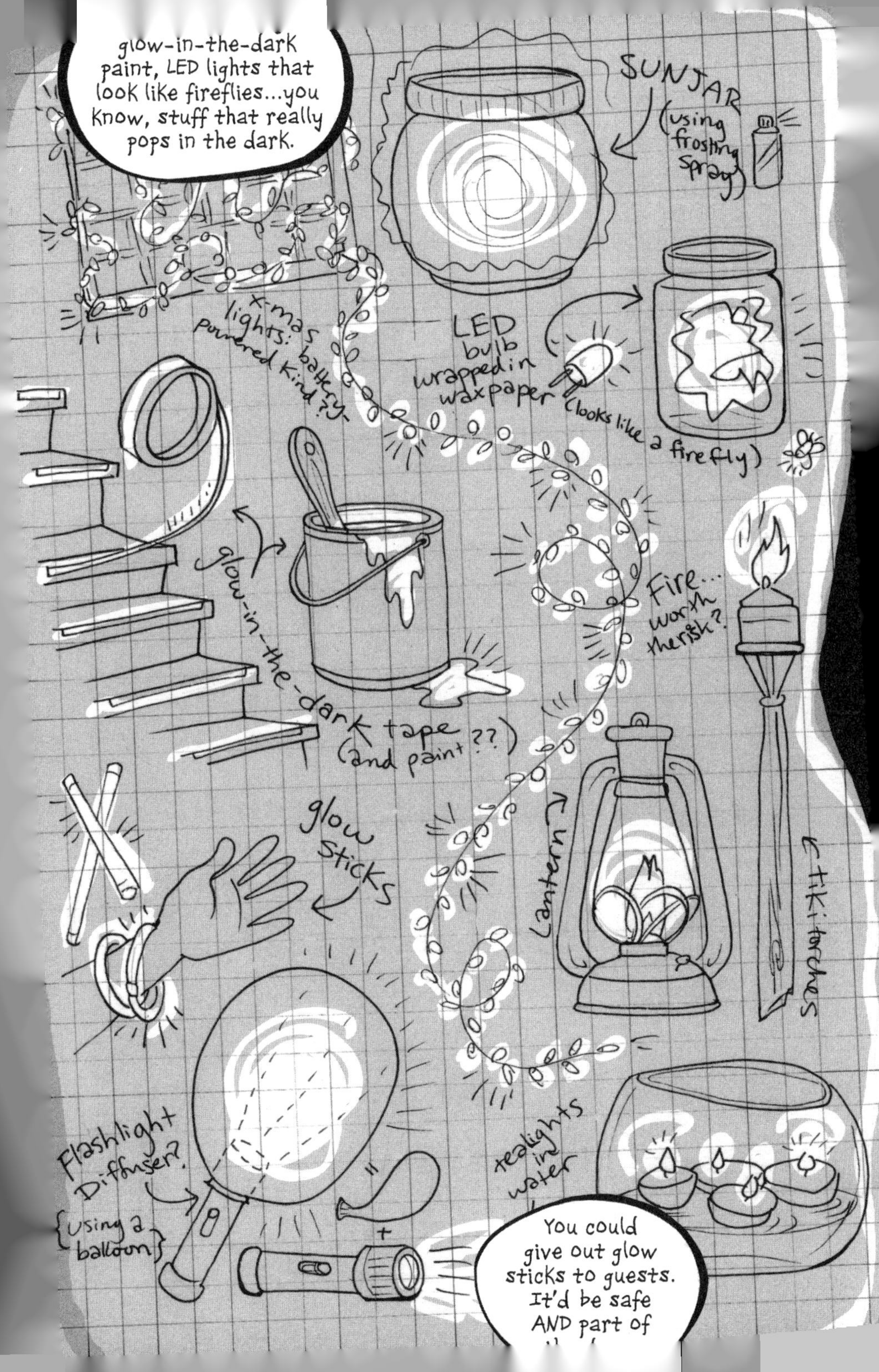

glow-in-the-dark paint, LED lights that look like fireflies...you know, stuff that really pops in the dark.
SUNJAR (using frosting spray)
x-mas lights: battery powered kind??
LED bulb wrapped in wax paper (looks like a firefly)
glow-in-the-dark tape (and paint??)
Fire... worth the risk?
glow sticks
Lantern
tiki torches
Flashlight Diffuser? {Using a balloon}
tealights in water
You could give out glow sticks to guests. It'd be safe AND part of

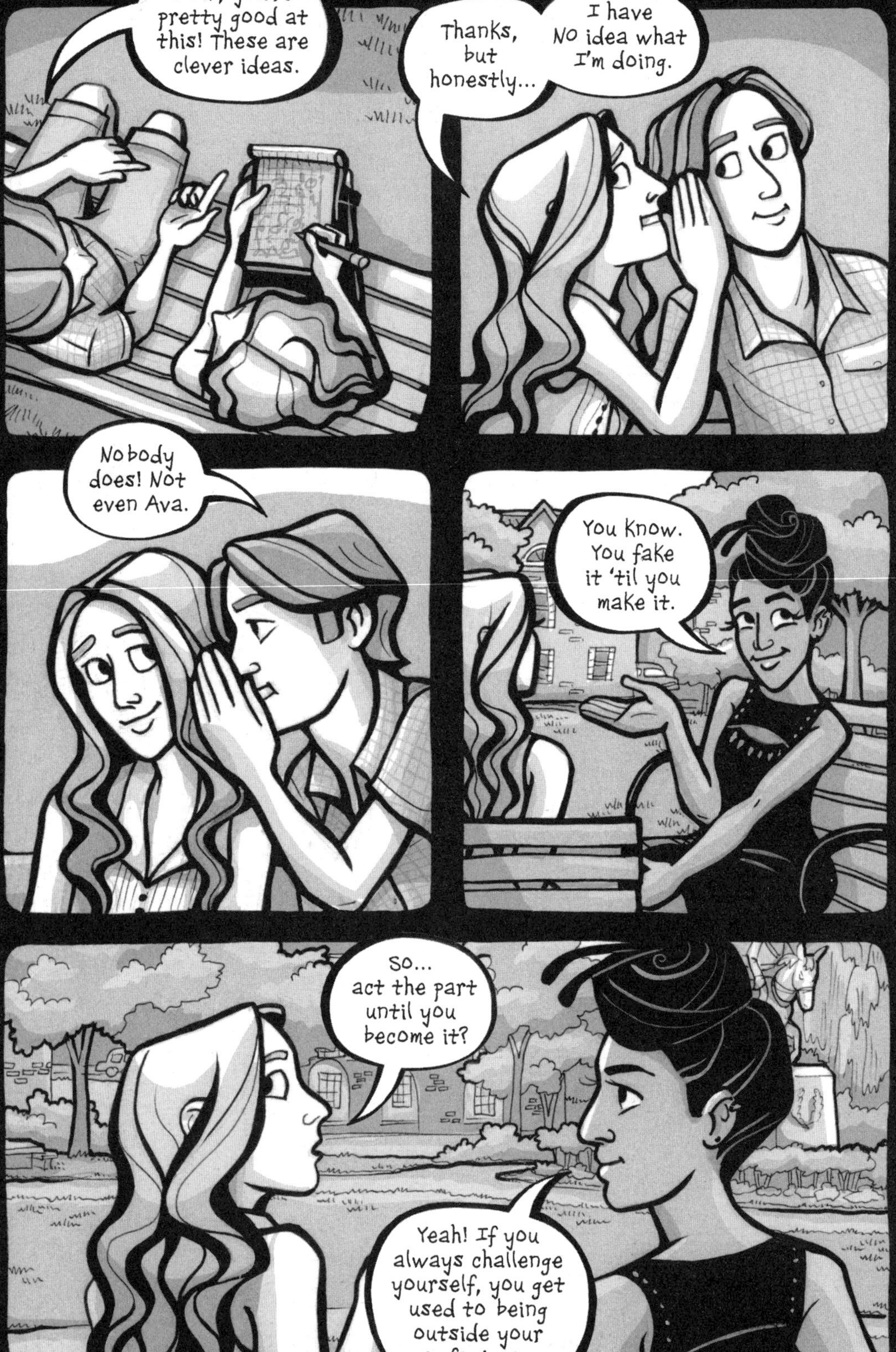
Wow, you're pretty good at this! These are clever ideas.
Thanks, but honestly...
I have NO idea what I'm doing.
Nobody does! Not even Ava.
You know. You fake it 'til you make it.
So... act the part until you become it?
Yeah! If you always challenge yourself, you get used to being outside your comfort zone.

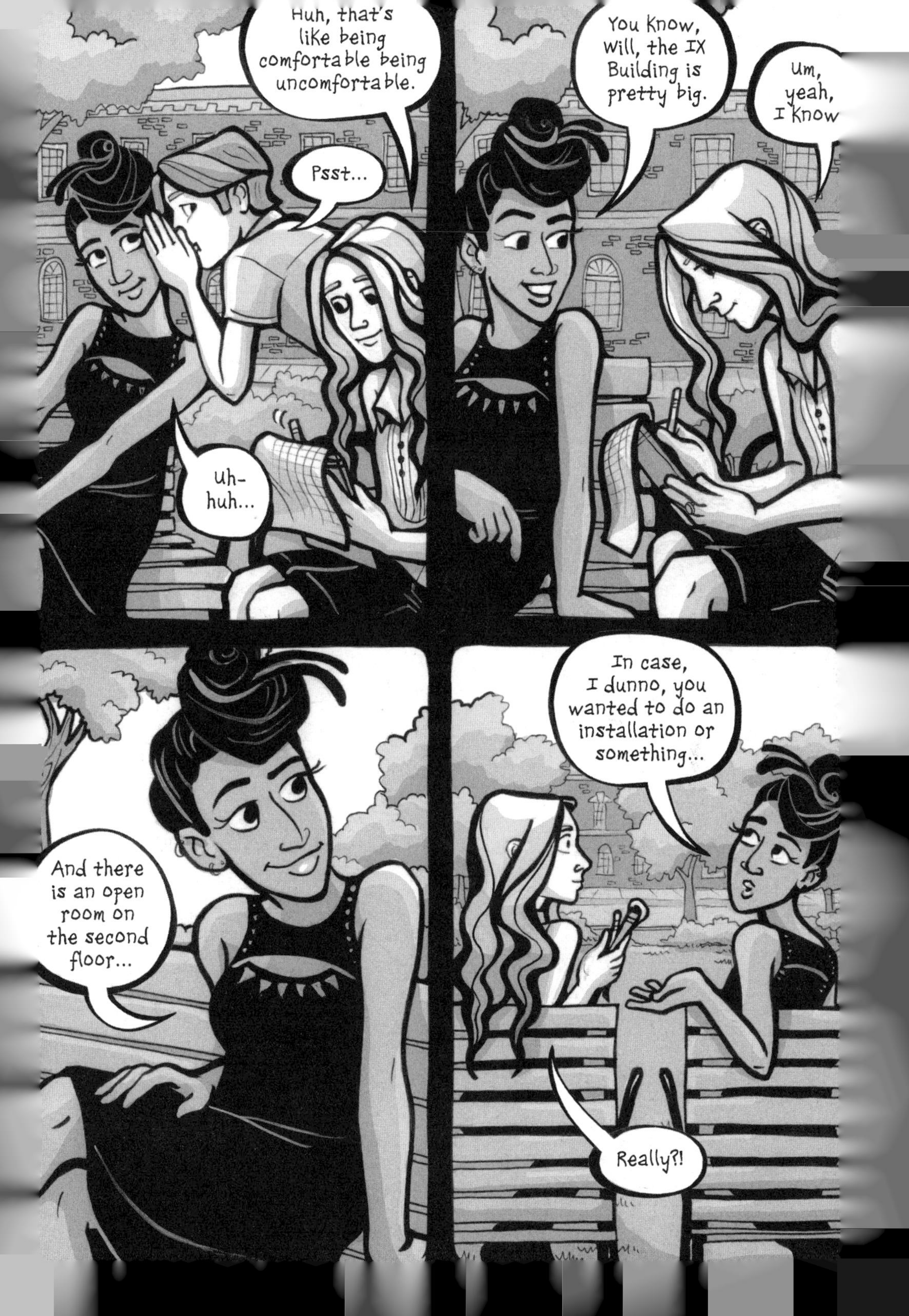
Huh, that's like being comfortable being uncomfortable.
Psst...
Uh-huh...
You know, Will, the IX Building is pretty big.
Um, yeah, I know
And there is an open room on the second floor...
In case, I dunno, you wanted to do an installation or something...
Really?!

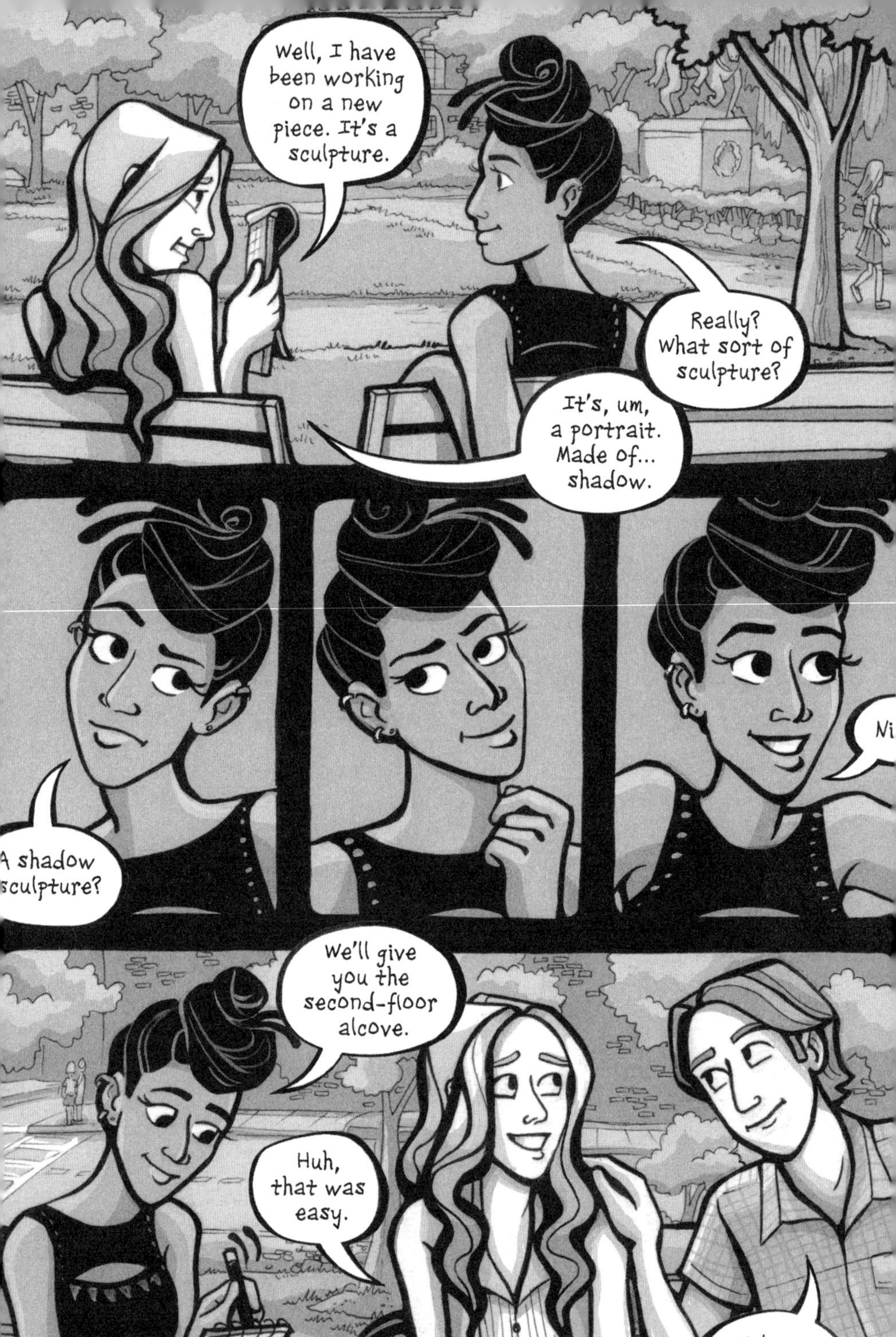
Well, I have been working on a new piece. It's a sculpture.
Really? What sort of sculpture?
It's, um, a portrait. Made of... shadow.
A shadow sculpture?
Ni
We'll give you the second-floor alcove.
Huh, that was easy.
Welcome to the show, comrade.

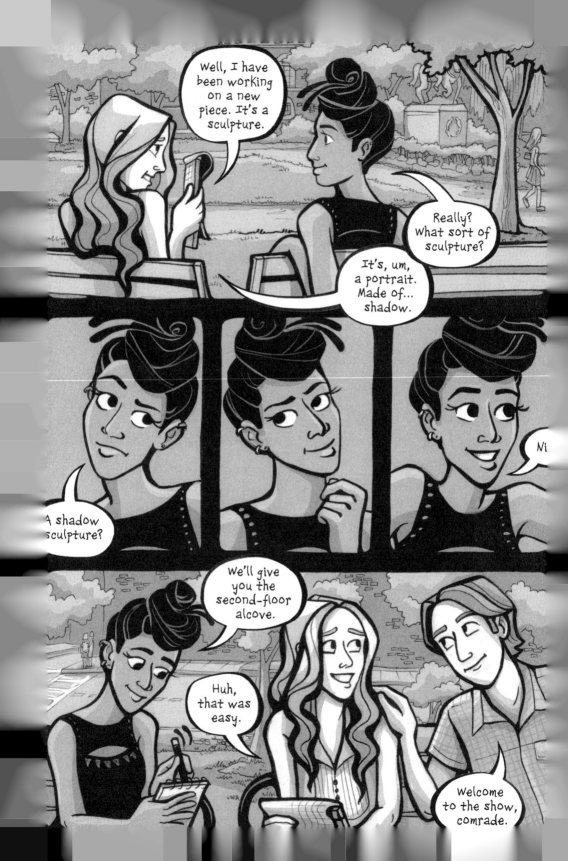

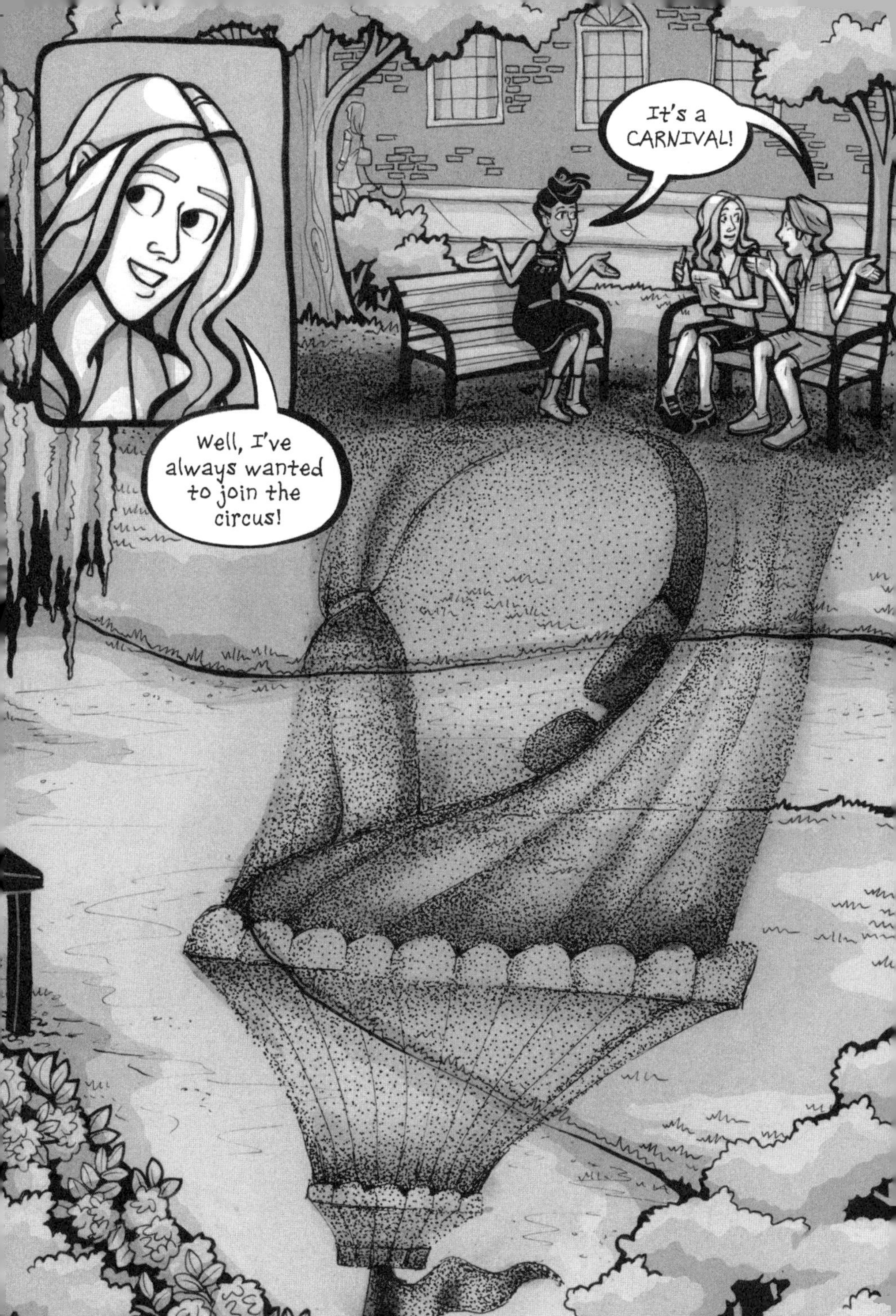
Well, I've always wanted to join the circus!
It's a CARNIVAL!

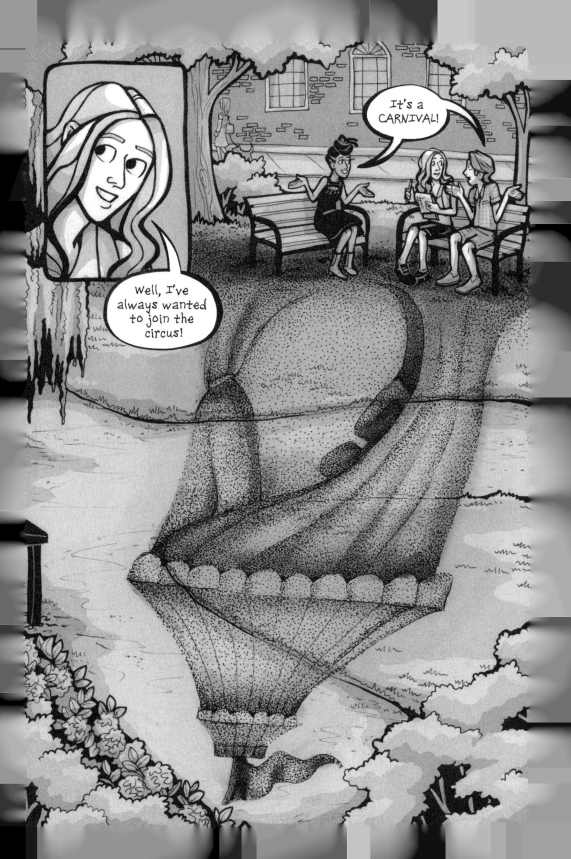

Shadowboxing

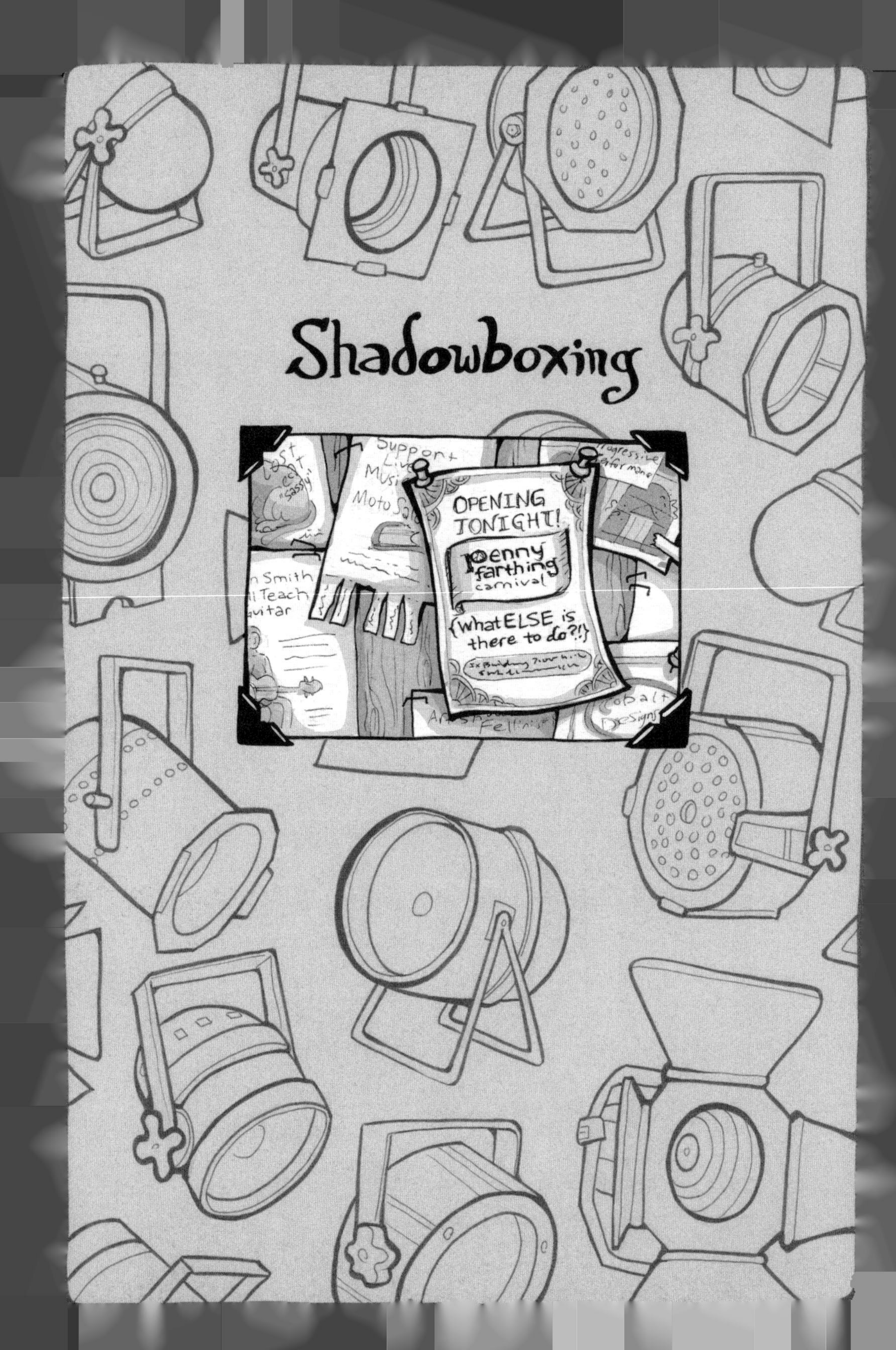
OPENING TONIGHT!
penny farthing carnival
{What ELSE is there to do?!}

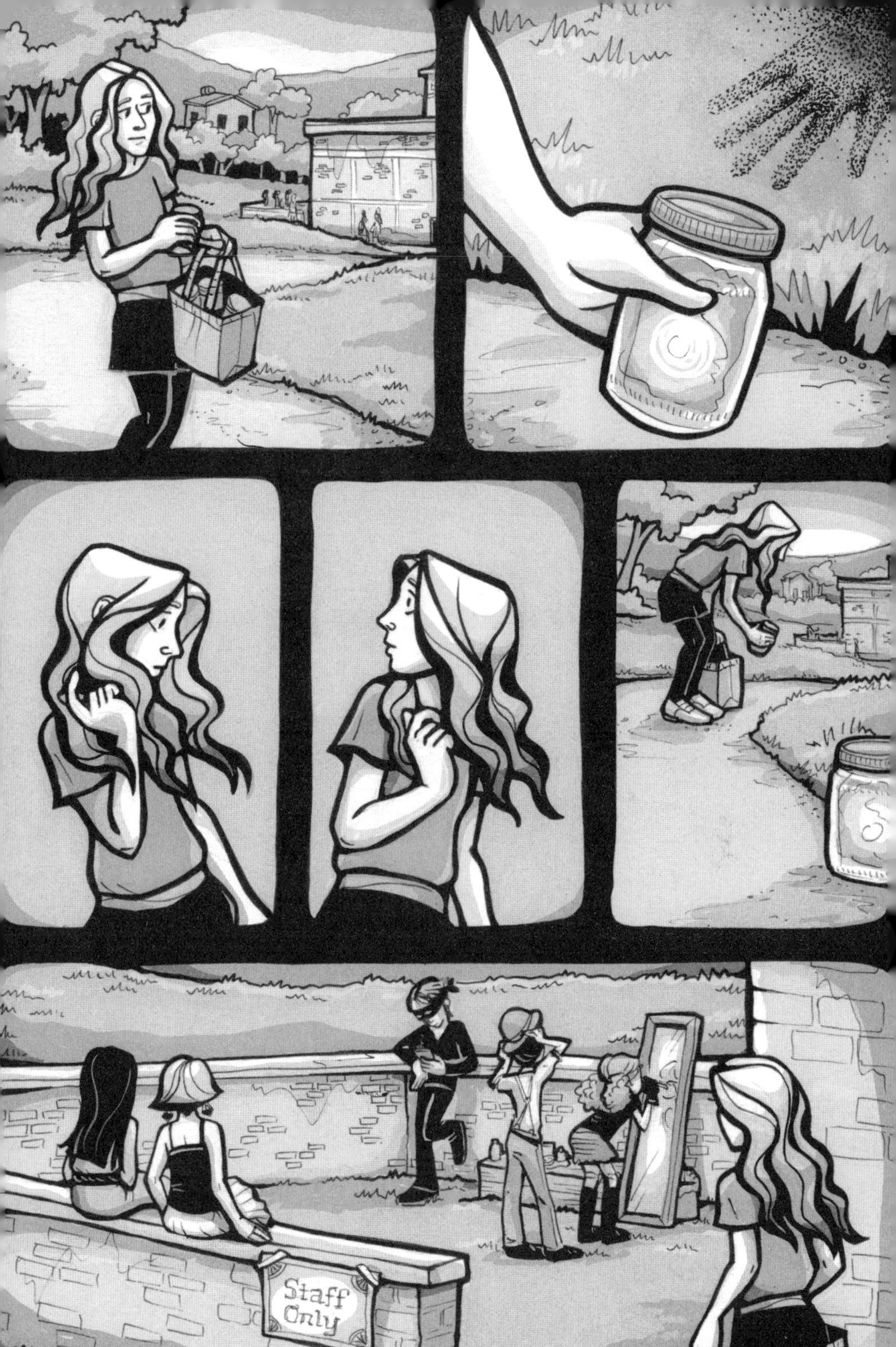
Staff
Only

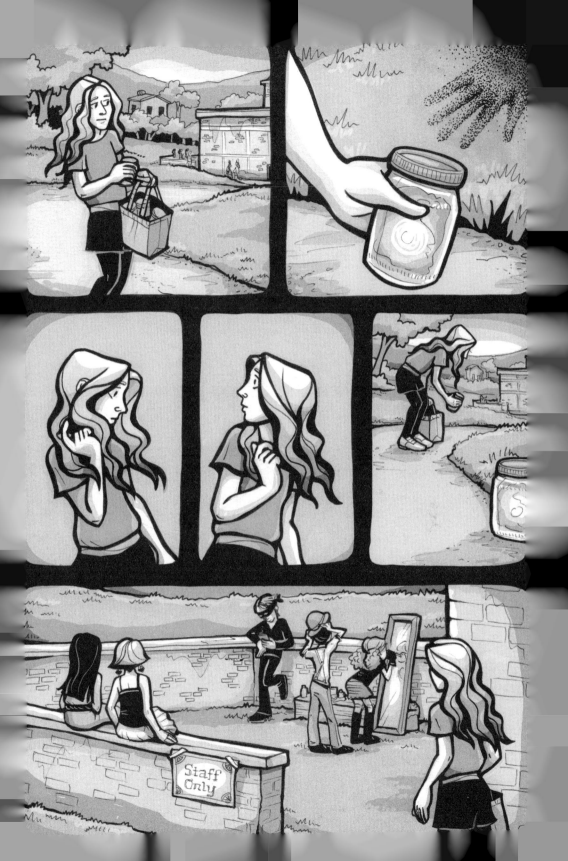

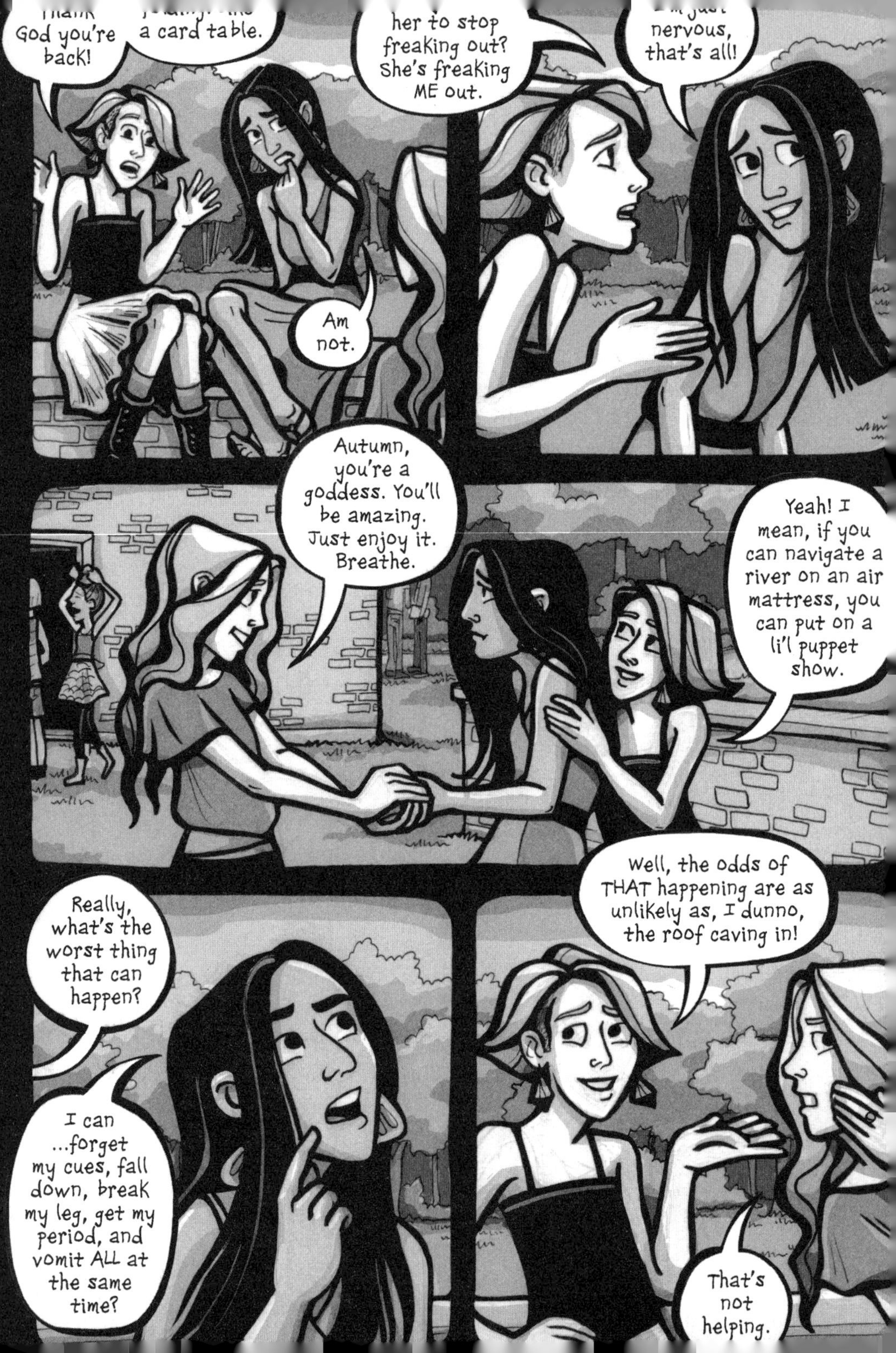
God you're back!
a card table.
her to stop freaking out? She's freaking ME out.
Am not.
nervous, that's all!
Autumn, you're a goddess. You'll be amazing. Just enjoy it. Breathe.
Yeah! I mean, if you can navigate a river on an air mattress, you can put on a li'l puppet show.
Really, what's the worst thing that can happen?
I can ...forget my cues, fall down, break my leg, get my period, and vomit ALL at the same time?
Well, the odds of THAT happening are as unlikely as, I dunno, the roof caving in!
That's not helping.

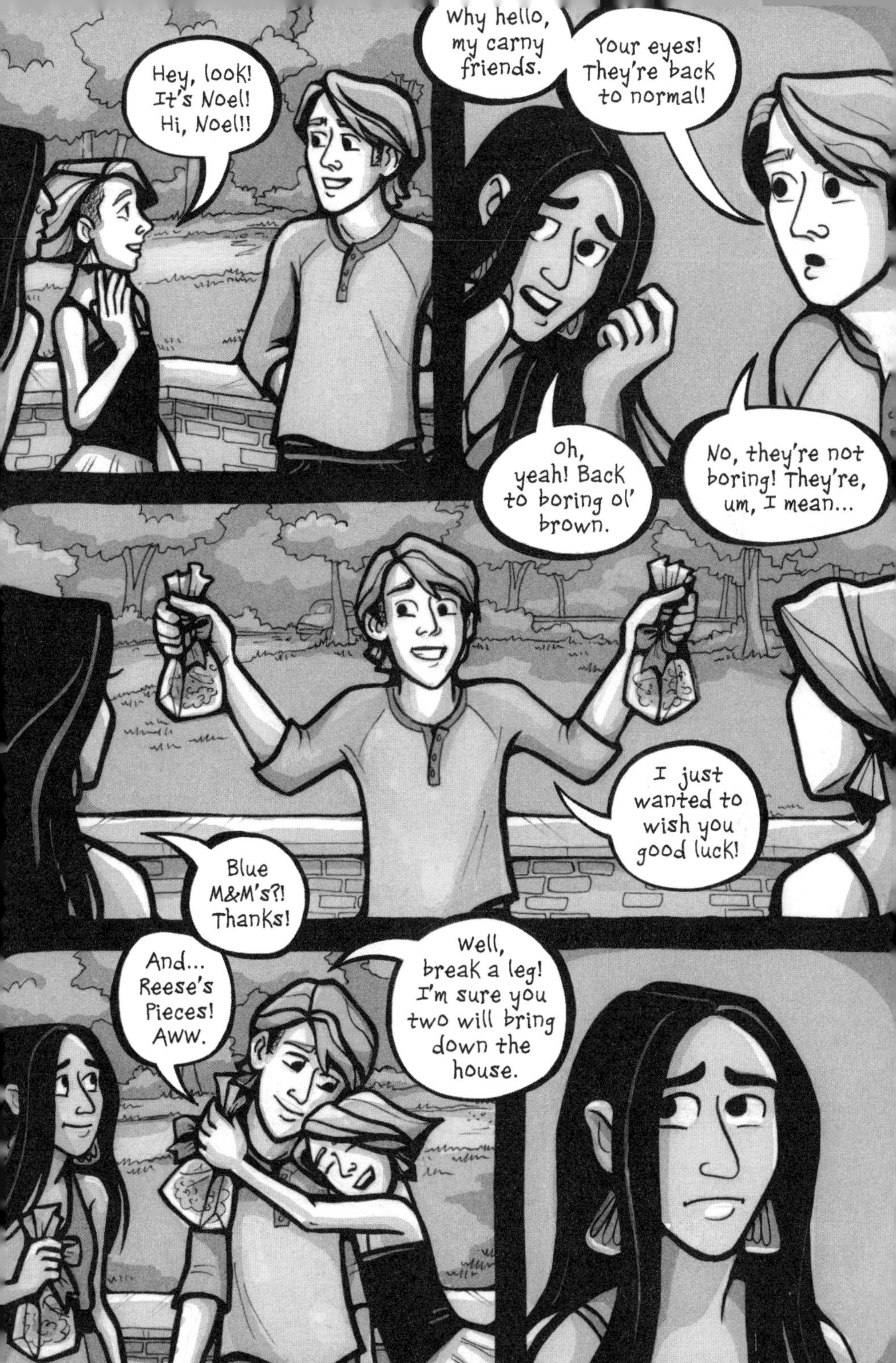
Hey, look! It's Noel! Hi, Noel!!
Why hello, my carny friends.
Your eyes! They're back to normal!
Oh, yeah! Back to boring ol' brown.
No, they're not boring! They're, um, I mean...
I just wanted to wish you good luck!
Blue M&M's?! Thanks!
And... Reese's Pieces! AWW.
Well, break a leg! I'm sure you two will bring down the house.

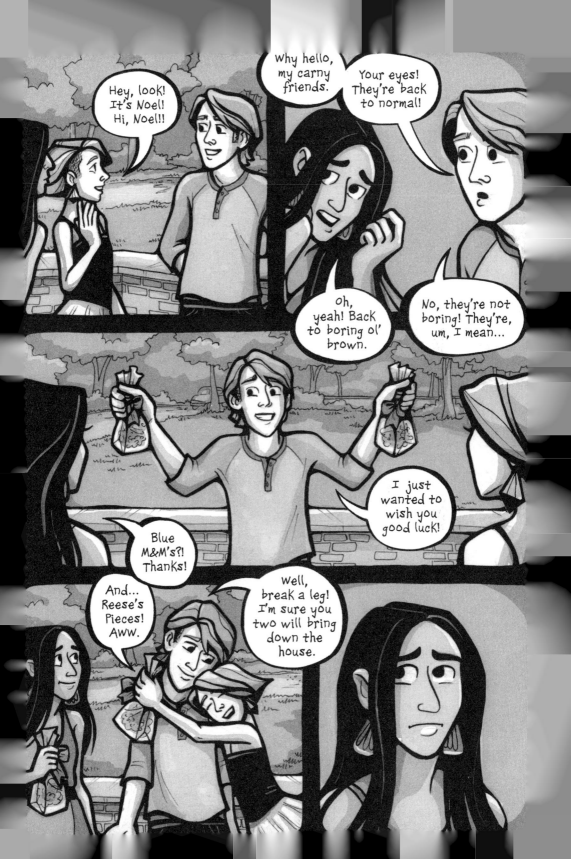

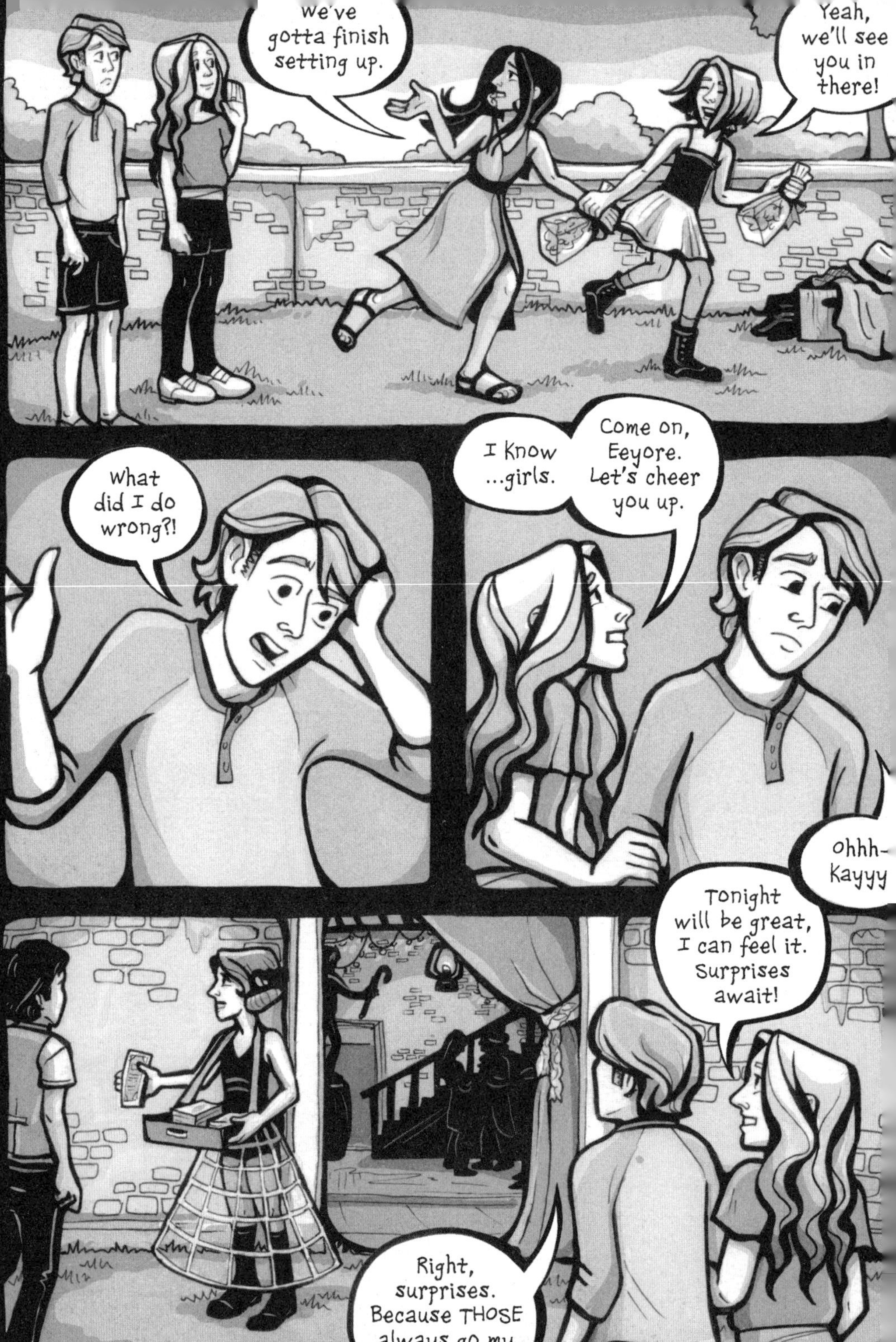
we've gotta finish setting up.
Yeah, we'll see you in there!
What did I do wrong?!
I know ...girls.
Come on, Eeyore. Let's cheer you up.
Ohhh-Kayyy
Tonight will be great, I can feel it. Surprises await!
Right, surprises. Because THOSE always go my way...

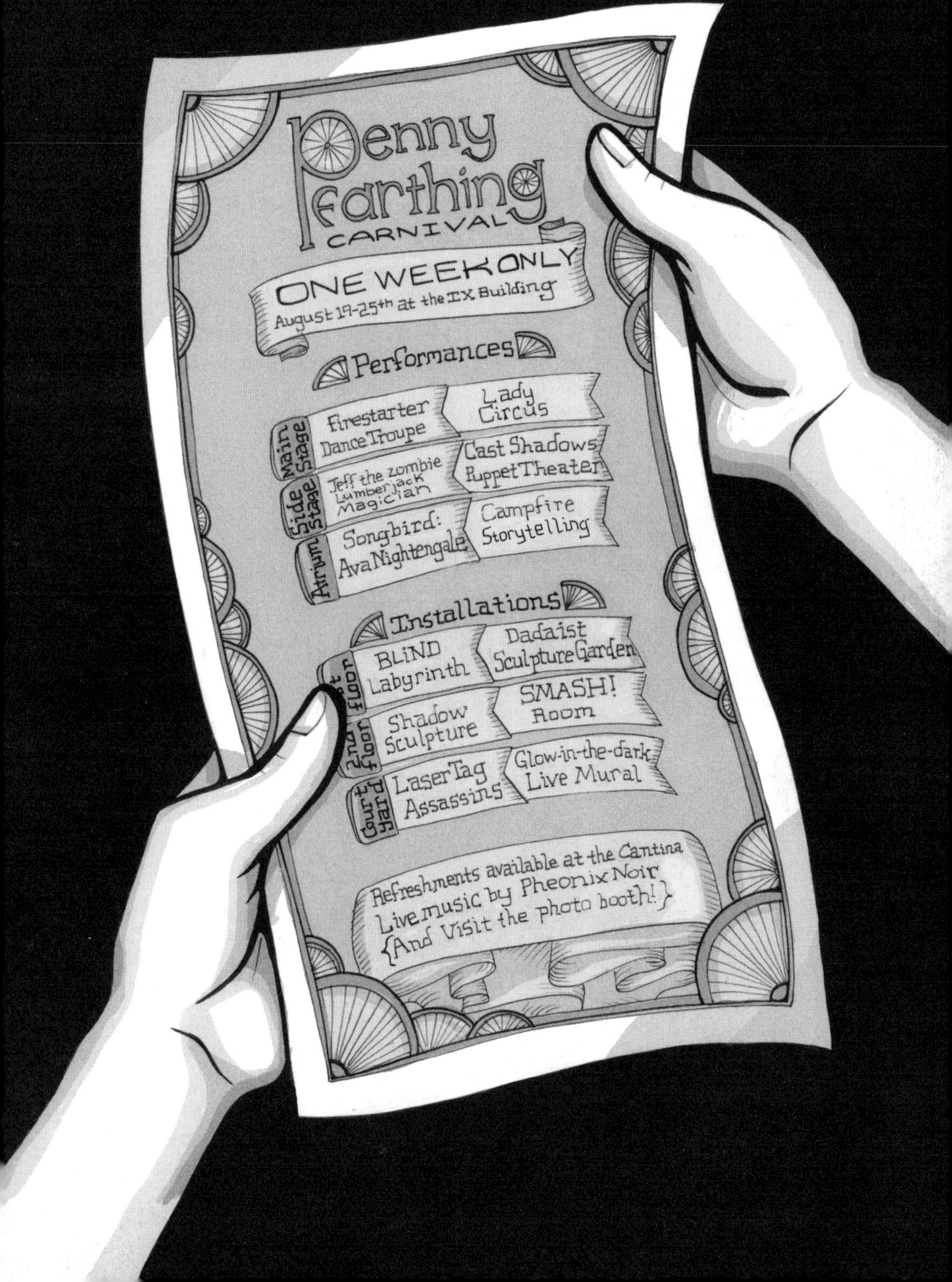
Penny Farthing Carnival
ONE WEEK ONLY
August 19-25th at the IX Building
Performances
Main Stage
Firestarter Dance Troupe
Lady Circus
Side Stage
Jeff the zombie Lumberjack Magician
Cast Shadows Puppet Theater
Atrium
Songbird: Ava Nightengale
Campfire Storytelling
Installations
1st floor
BLIND Labyrinth
Dadaist Sculpture Garden
2nd floor
Shadow Sculpture
SMASH! Room
Court Yard
Laser Tag Assassins
Glow-in-the-dark Live Mural
Refreshments available at the Cantina
Live music by Pheonix Noir
{And Visit the photo booth!}

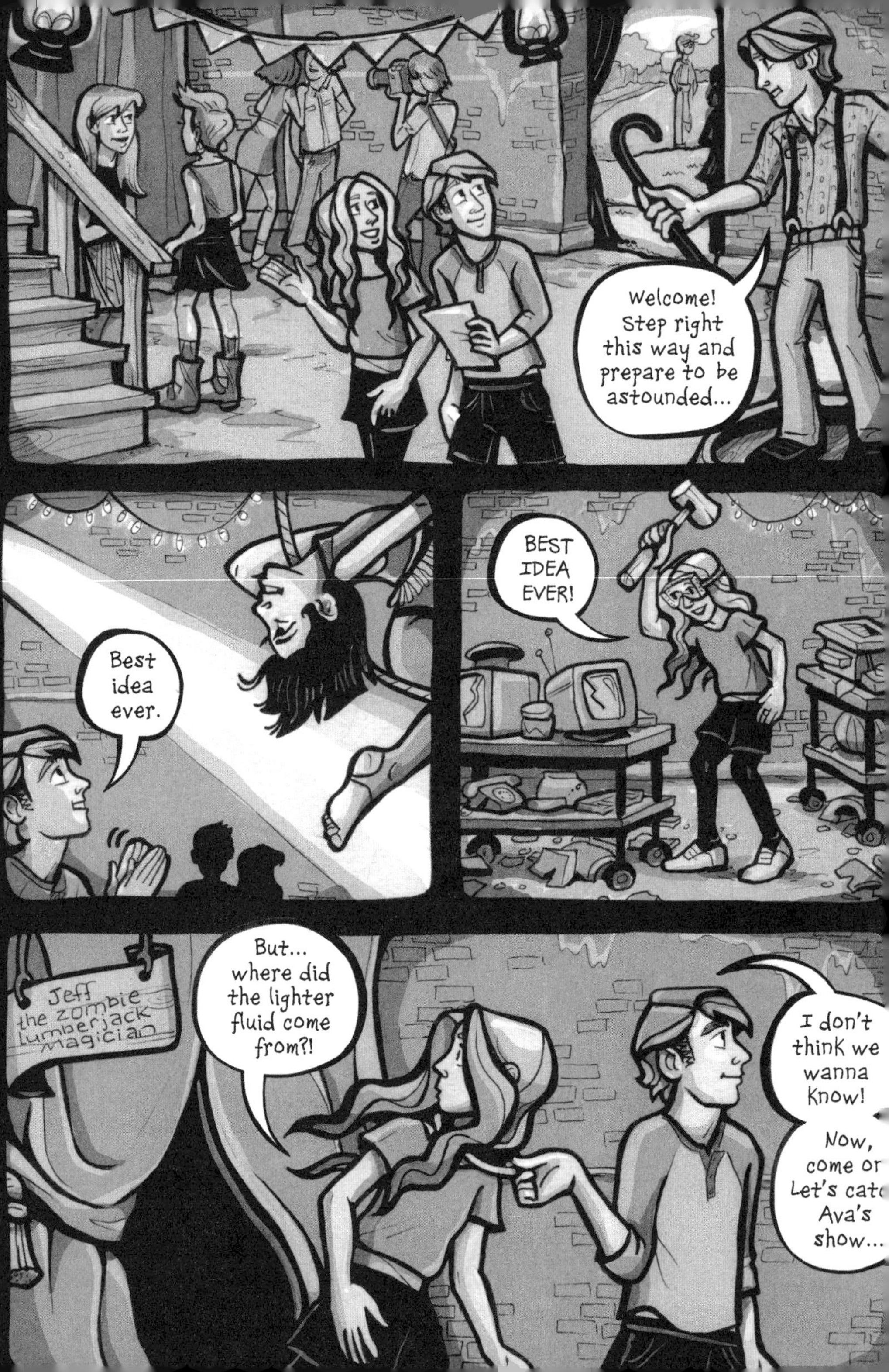
Welcome! Step right this way and prepare to be astounded...
Best idea ever.
BEST IDEA EVER!
Jeff the zombie lumberjack magician
But... where did the lighter fluid come from?!
I don't think we wanna know!
Now, come or
Let's catc
Ava's show...

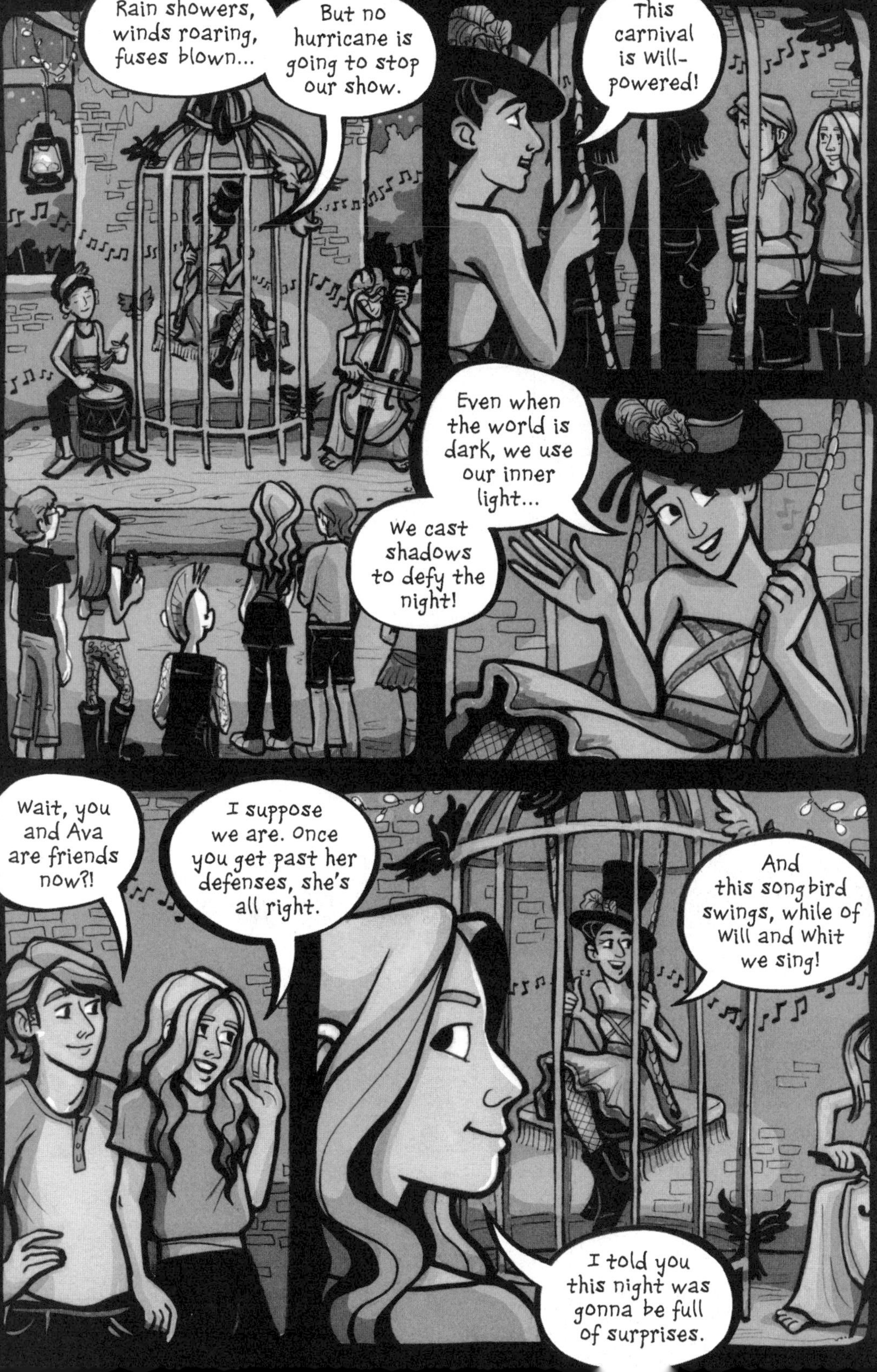
Rain showers, winds roaring, fuses blown...
But no hurricane is going to stop our show.
This carnival is Will-powered!
Even when the world is dark, we use our inner light...
We cast shadows to defy the night!
Wait, you and Ava are friends now?!
I suppose we are. Once you get past her defenses, she's all right.
And this songbird swings, while of Will and Whit we sing!
I told you this night was gonna be full of surprises.

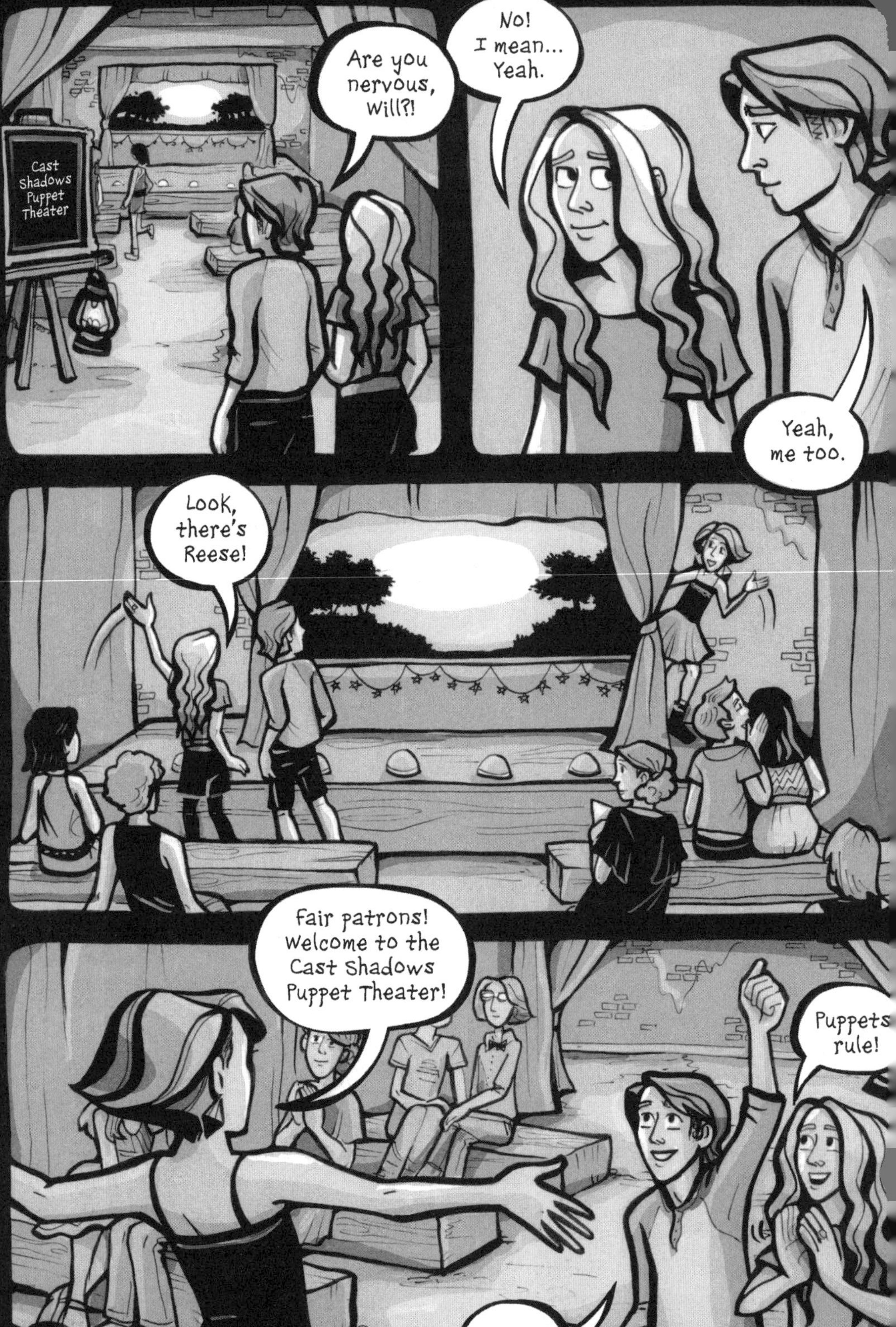
Cast Shadows Puppet Theater
Are you nervous, Will?!
No! I mean... Yeah.
Yeah, me too.
Look, there's Reese!
Fair patrons! Welcome to the Cast Shadows Puppet Theater!
Puppets rule!
Whoop-whoop!

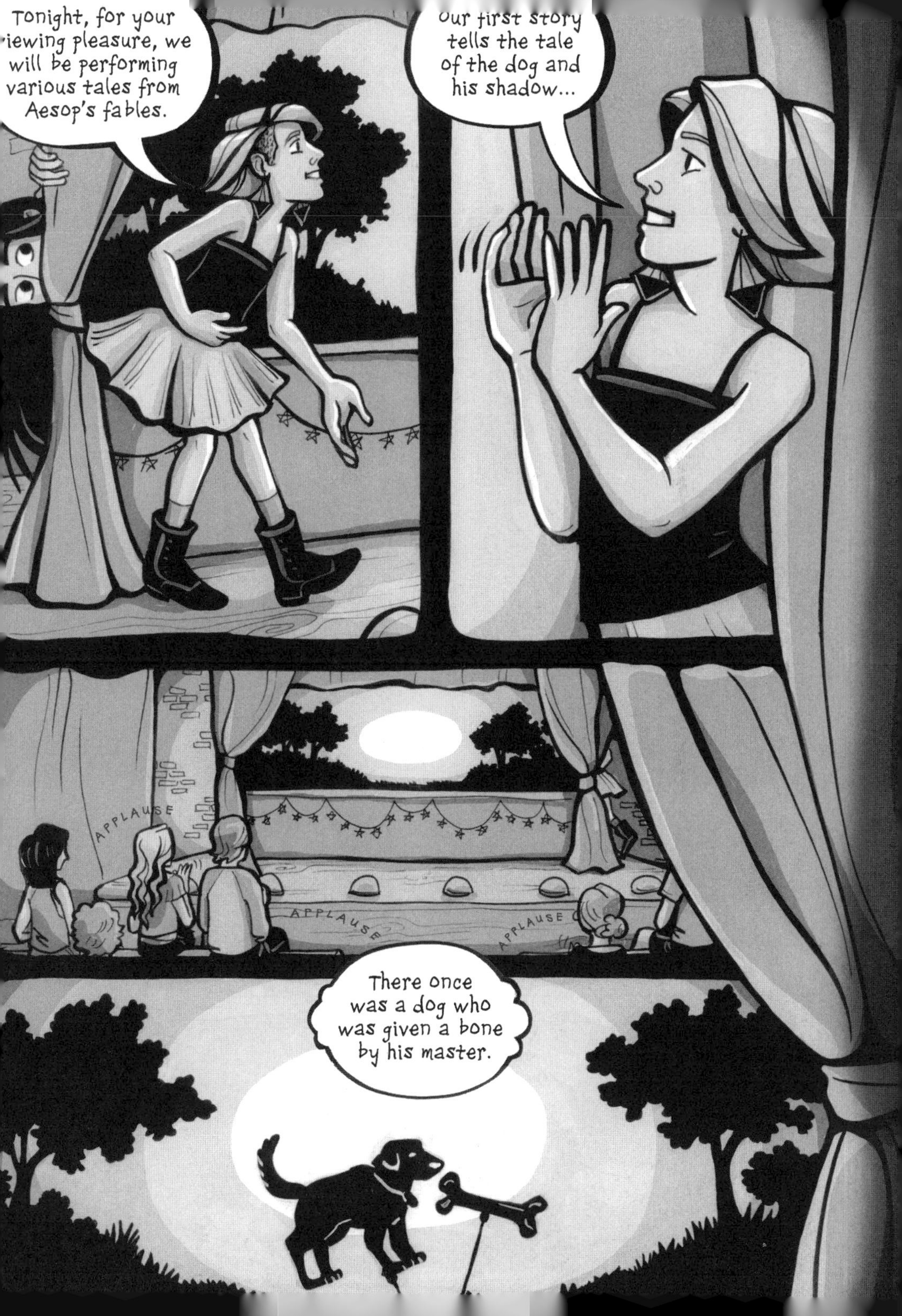
Tonight, for your viewing pleasure, we will be performing various tales from Aesop's fables.
Our first story tells the tale of the dog and his shadow...
APPLAUSE
APPLAUSE
APPLAUSE
There once was a dog who was given a bone by his master.

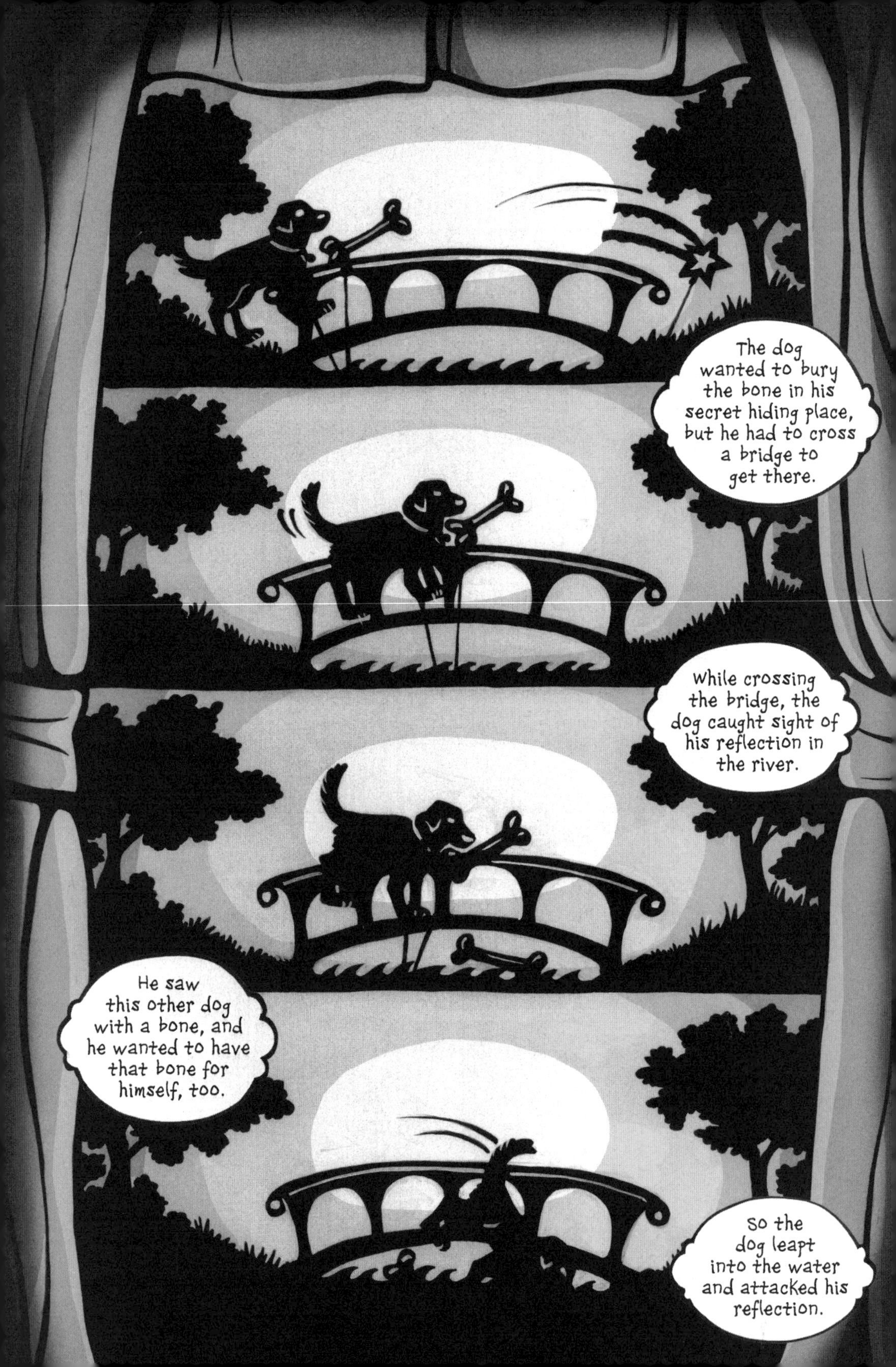
The dog wanted to bury the bone in his secret hiding place, but he had to cross a bridge to get there.
While crossing the bridge, the dog caught sight of his reflection in the river.
He saw this other dog with a bone, and he wanted to have that bone for himself, too.
So the dog leapt into the water and attacked his reflection.

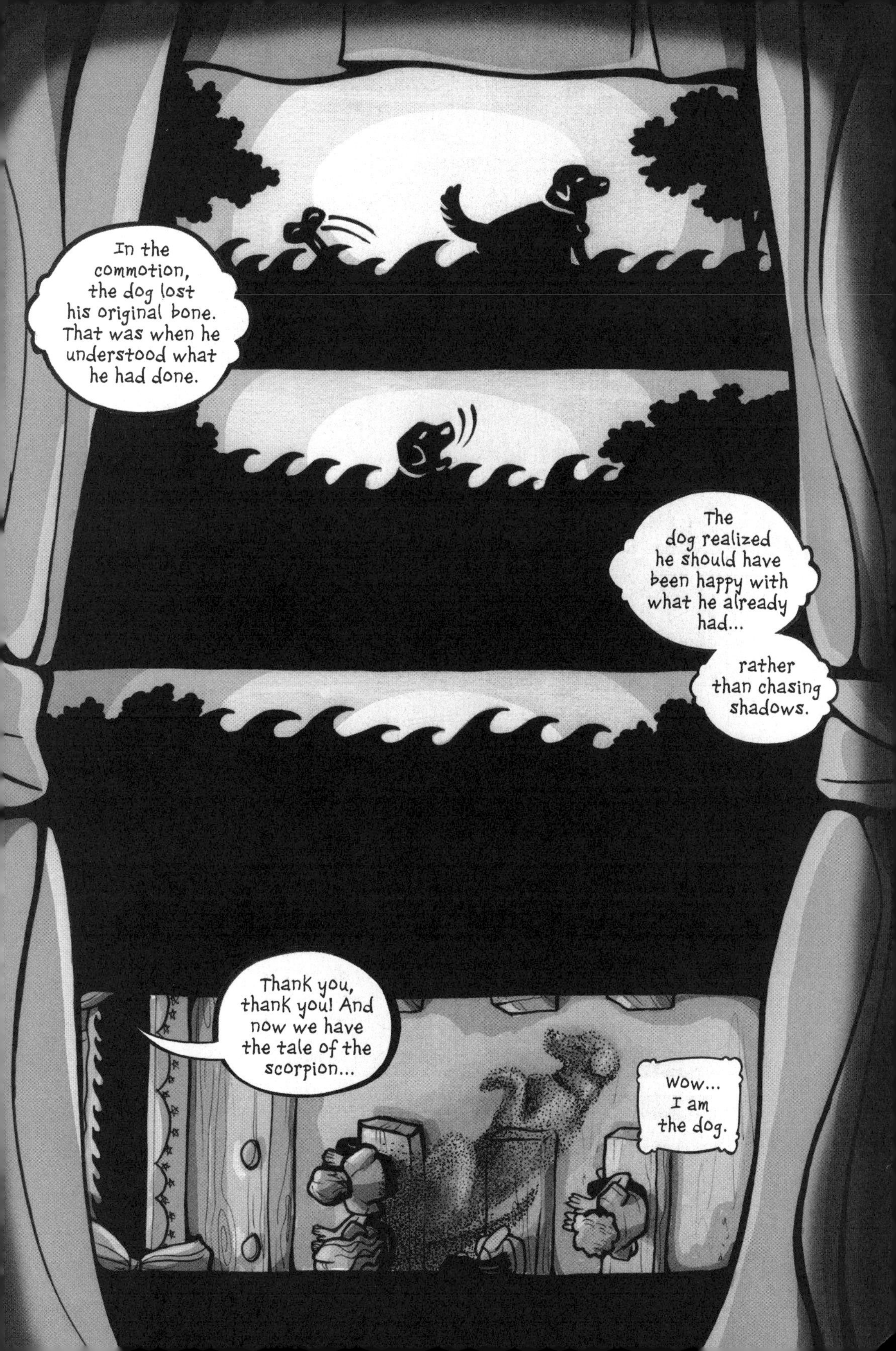
In the commotion, the dog lost his original bone. That was when he understood what he had done.
The dog realized he should have been happy with what he already had...
rather than chasing shadows.
Thank you, thank you! And now we have the tale of the scorpion...
Wow... I am the dog.

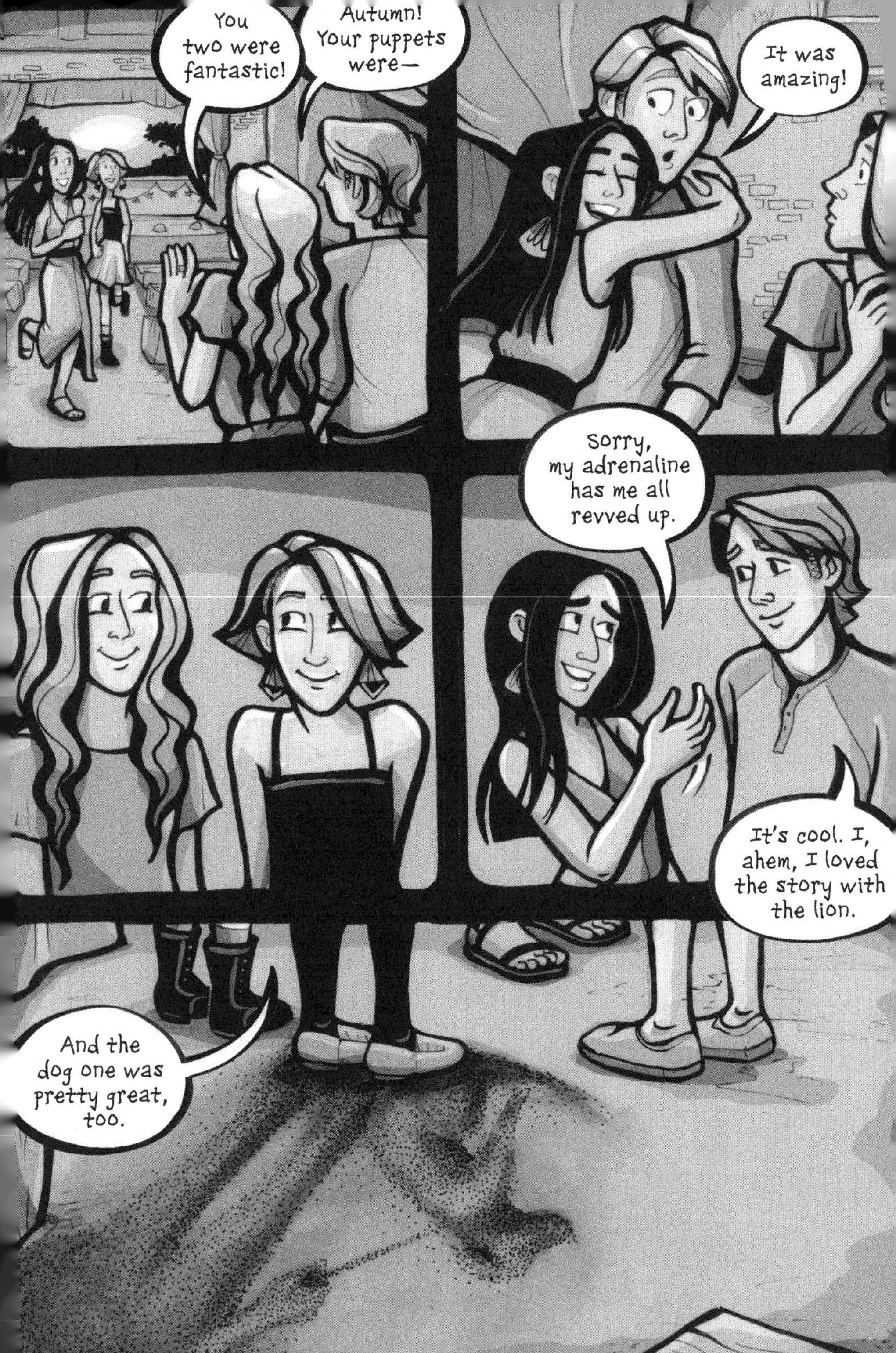
You two were fantastic!
Autumn! Your puppets were—
It was amazing!
Sorry, my adrenaline has me all revved up.
It's cool. I, ahem, I loved the story with the lion.
And the dog one was pretty great, too.

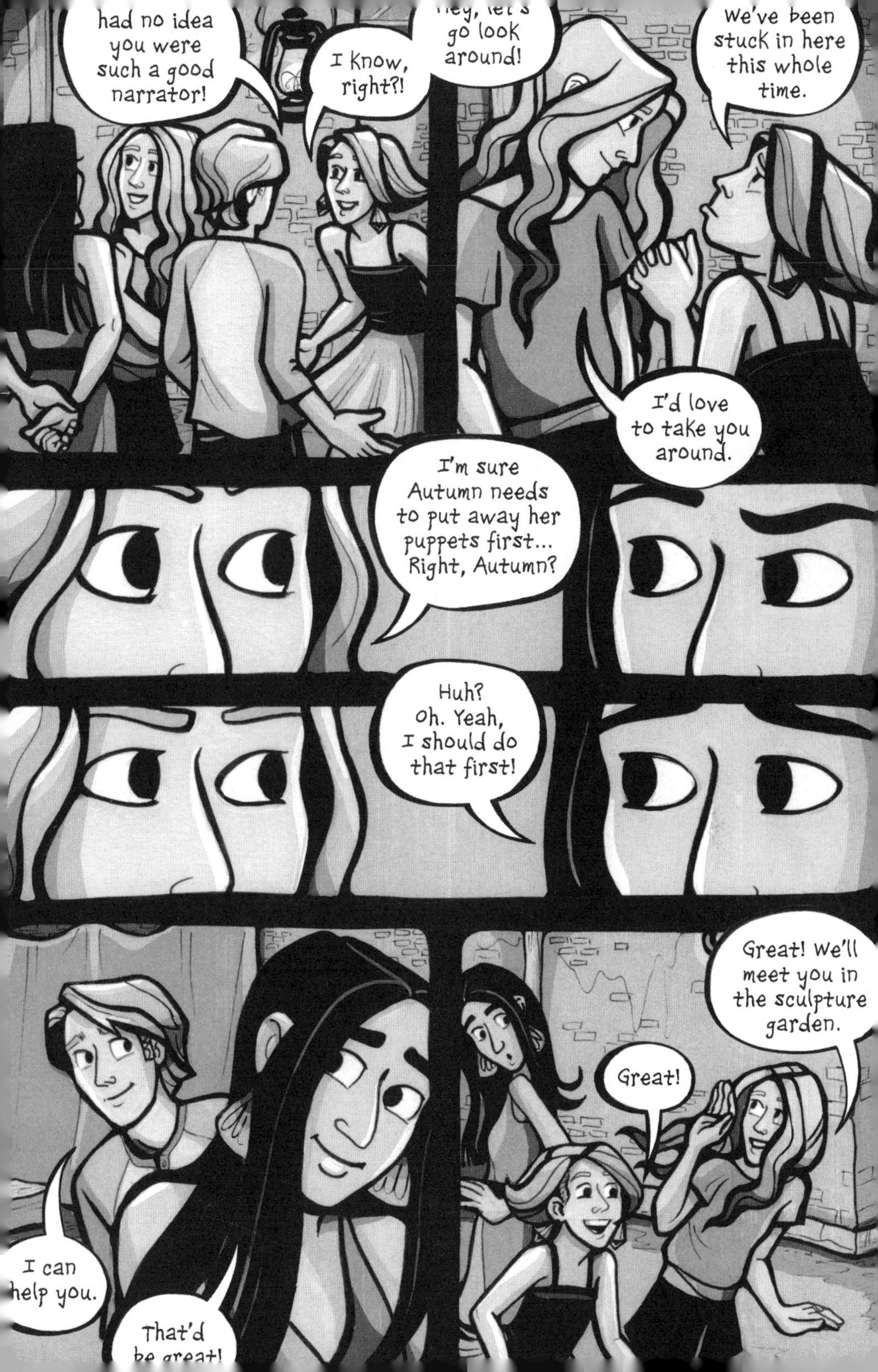
had no idea you were such a good narrator!
I know, right?!
hey, let's go look around!
We've been stuck in here this whole time.
I'd love to take you around.
I'm sure Autumn needs to put away her puppets first... Right, Autumn?
Huh? Oh. Yeah, I should do that first!
I can help you.
That'd be great!
Great! We'll meet you in the sculpture garden.
Great!

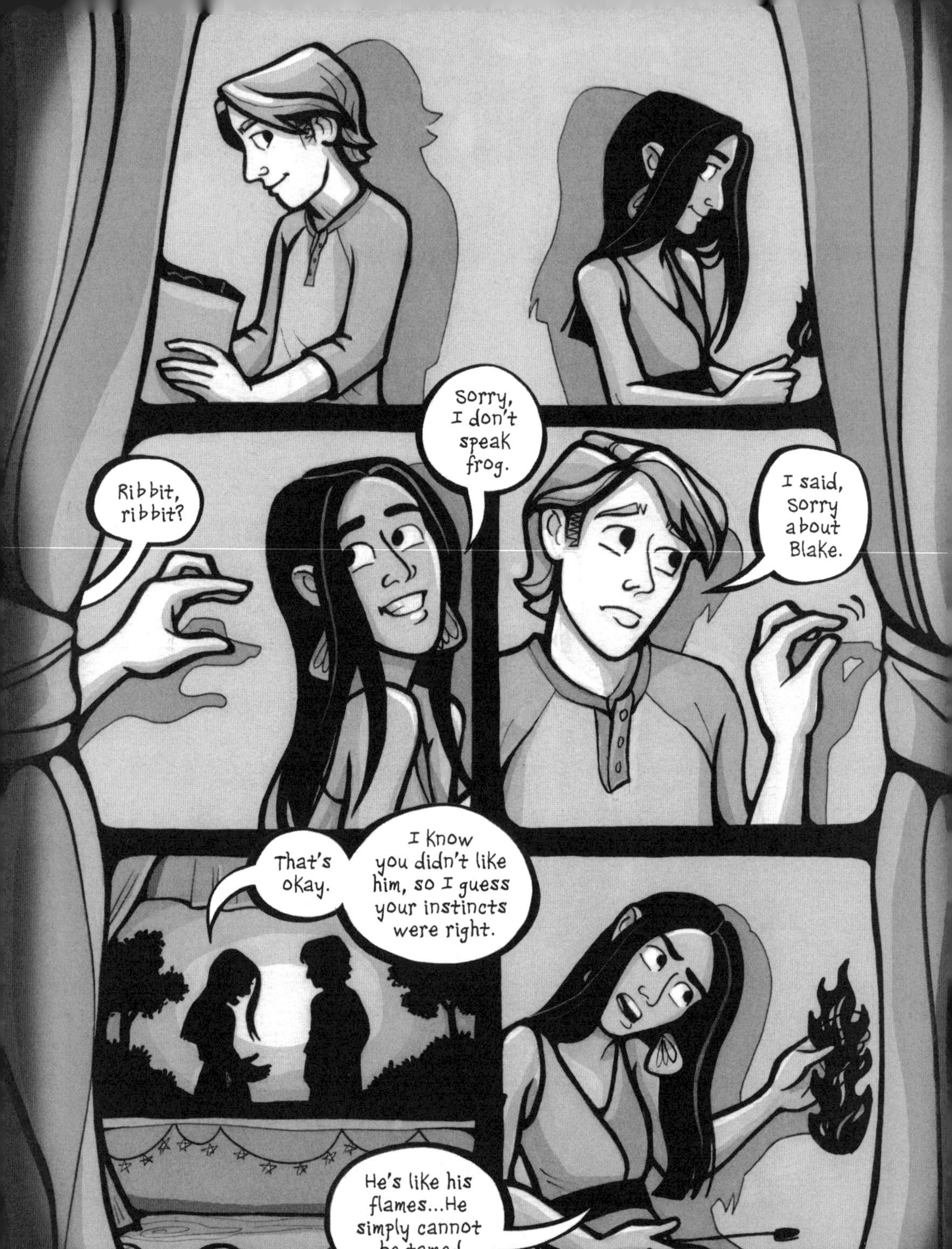
Sorry, I don't speak frog.
Ribbit, ribbit?
I said, sorry about Blake.
That's okay.
I know you didn't like him, so I guess your instincts were right.
He's like his flames...He simply cannot be tamed.

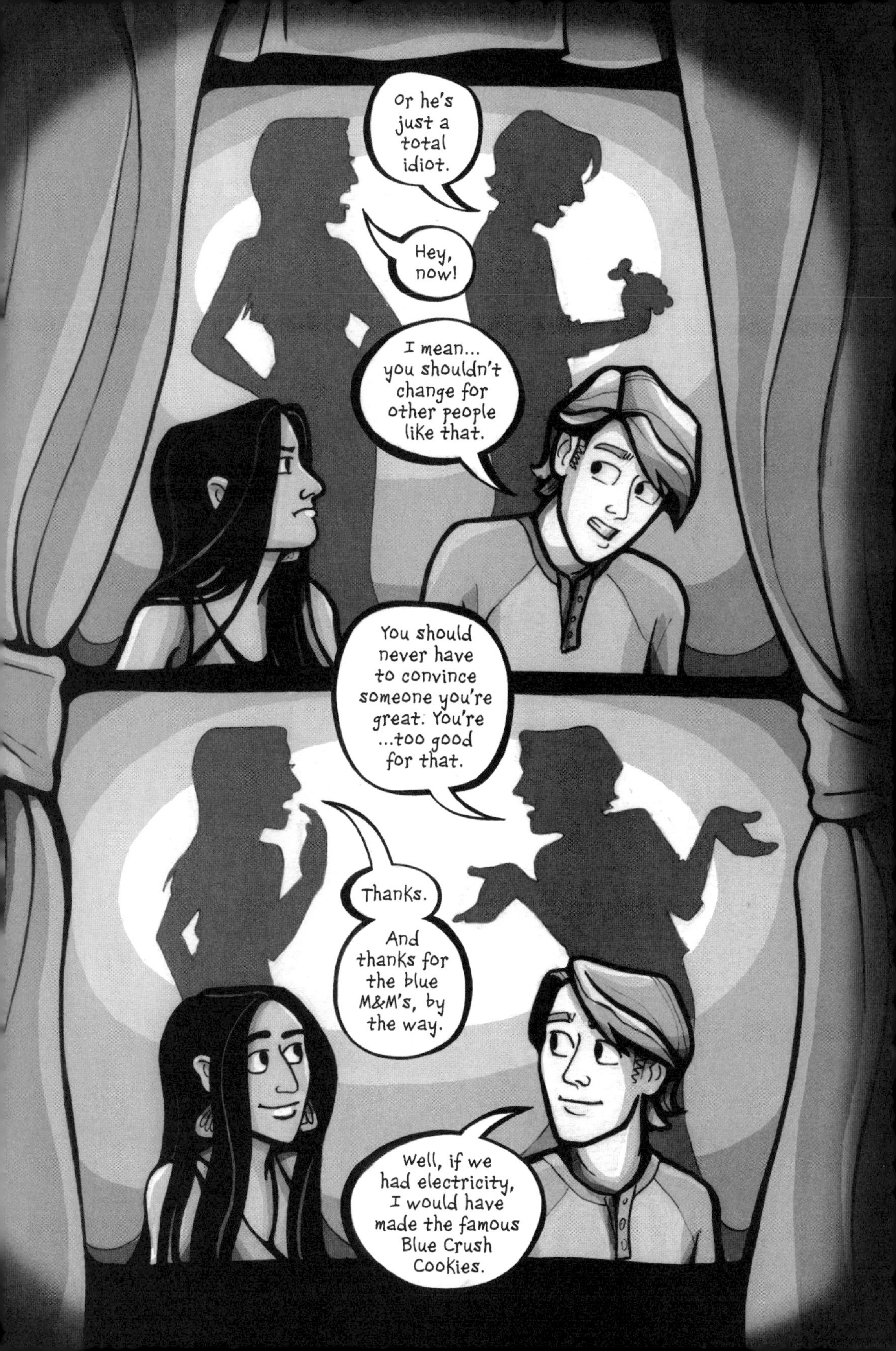
Or he's just a total idiot.
Hey, now!
I mean... you shouldn't change for other people like that.
You should never have to convince someone you're great. You're ...too good for that.
Thanks.
And thanks for the blue M&M's, by the way.
Well, if we had electricity, I would have made the famous Blue Crush Cookies.

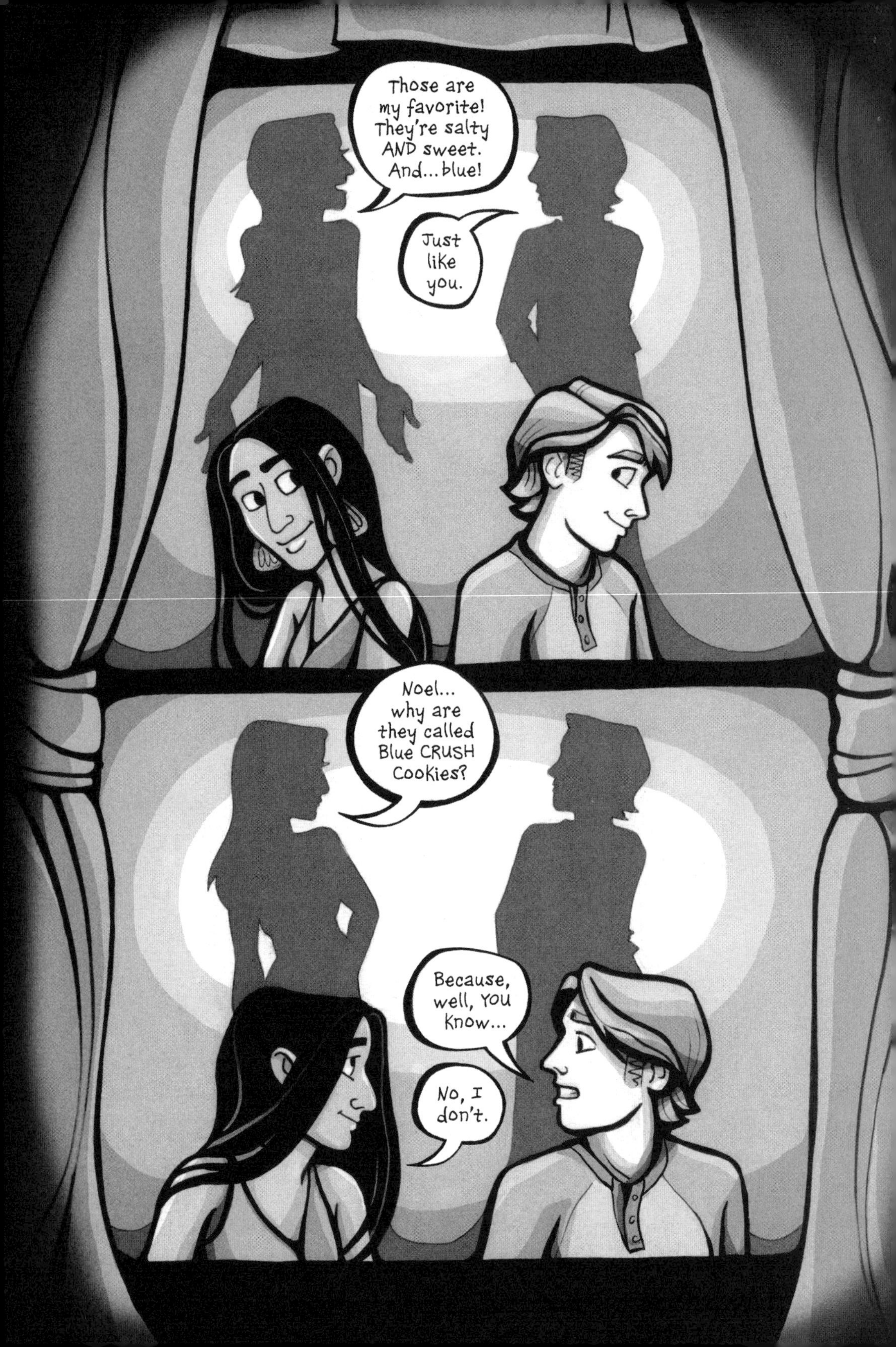
Those are my favorite! They're salty AND sweet. And... blue!
Just like you.
Noel... why are they called Blue CRUSH Cookies?
Because, well, YOU know...
No, I don't.

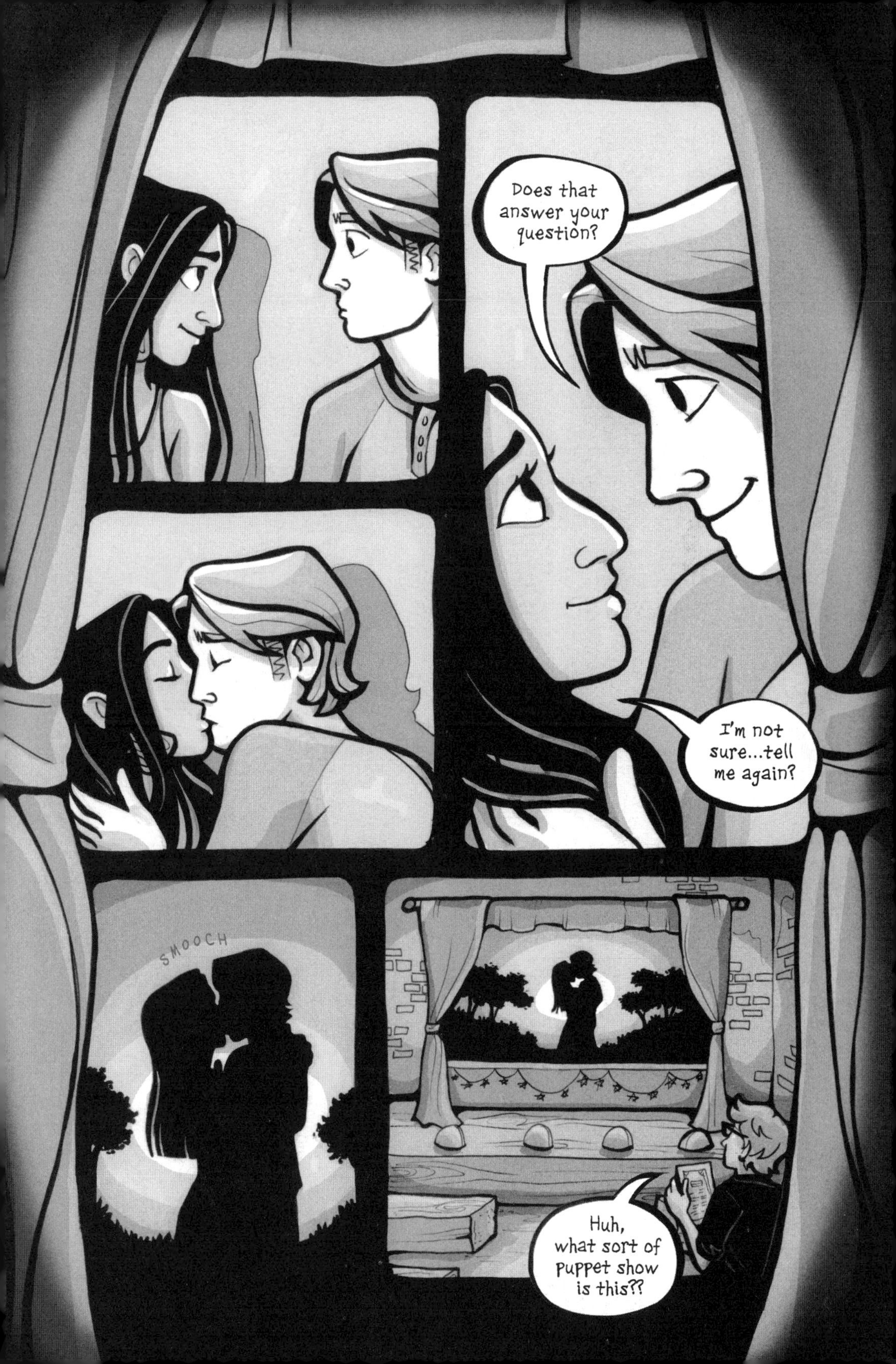
Does that answer your question?
I'm not sure...tell me again?
SMOOCH
Huh, what sort of puppet show is this??

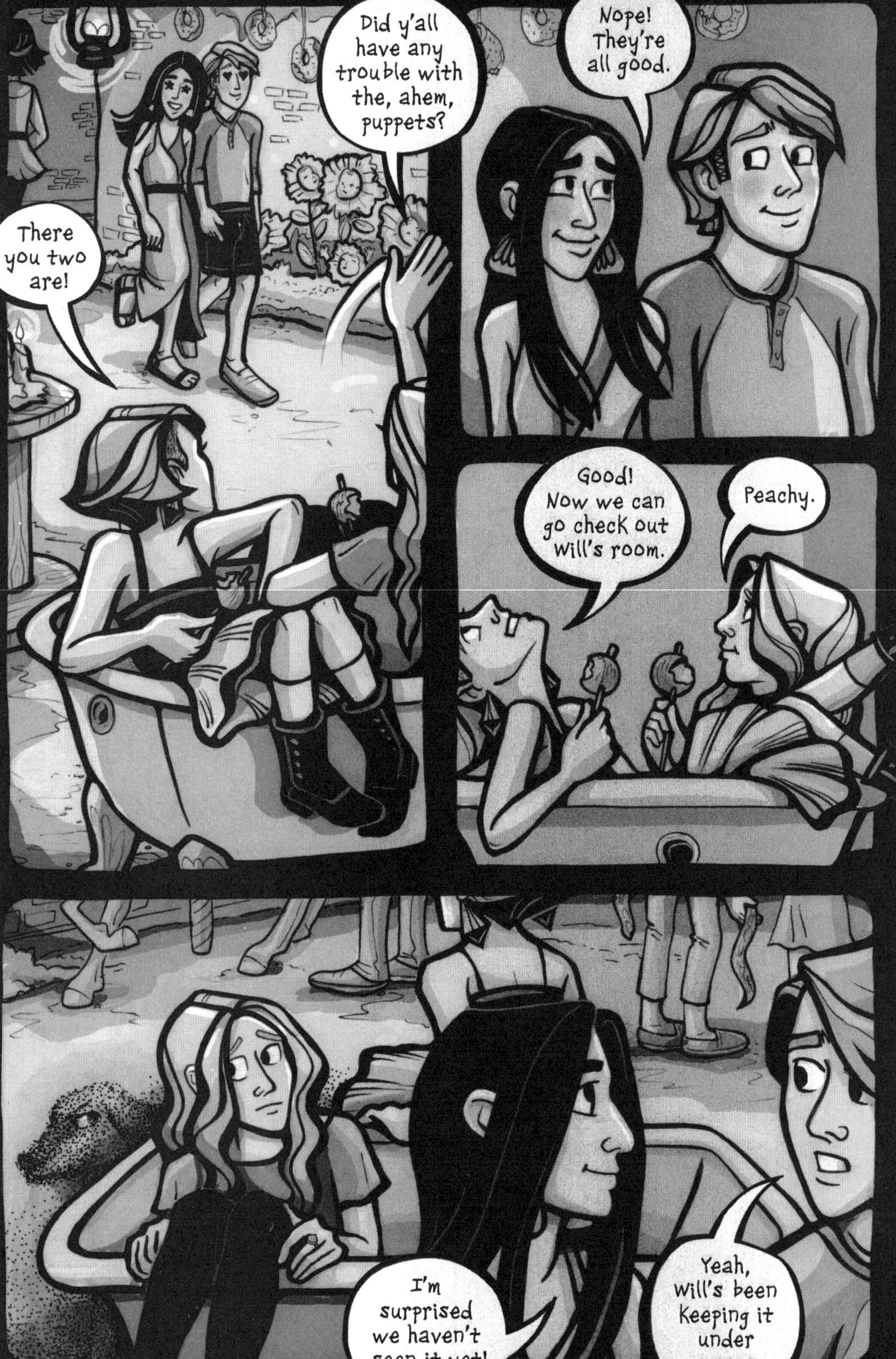
There you two are!
Did y'all have any trouble with the, ahem, puppets?
Nope! They're all good.
Good! Now we can go check out Will's room.
Peachy.
I'm surprised we haven't seen it yet!
Yeah, Will's been keeping it under wraps.

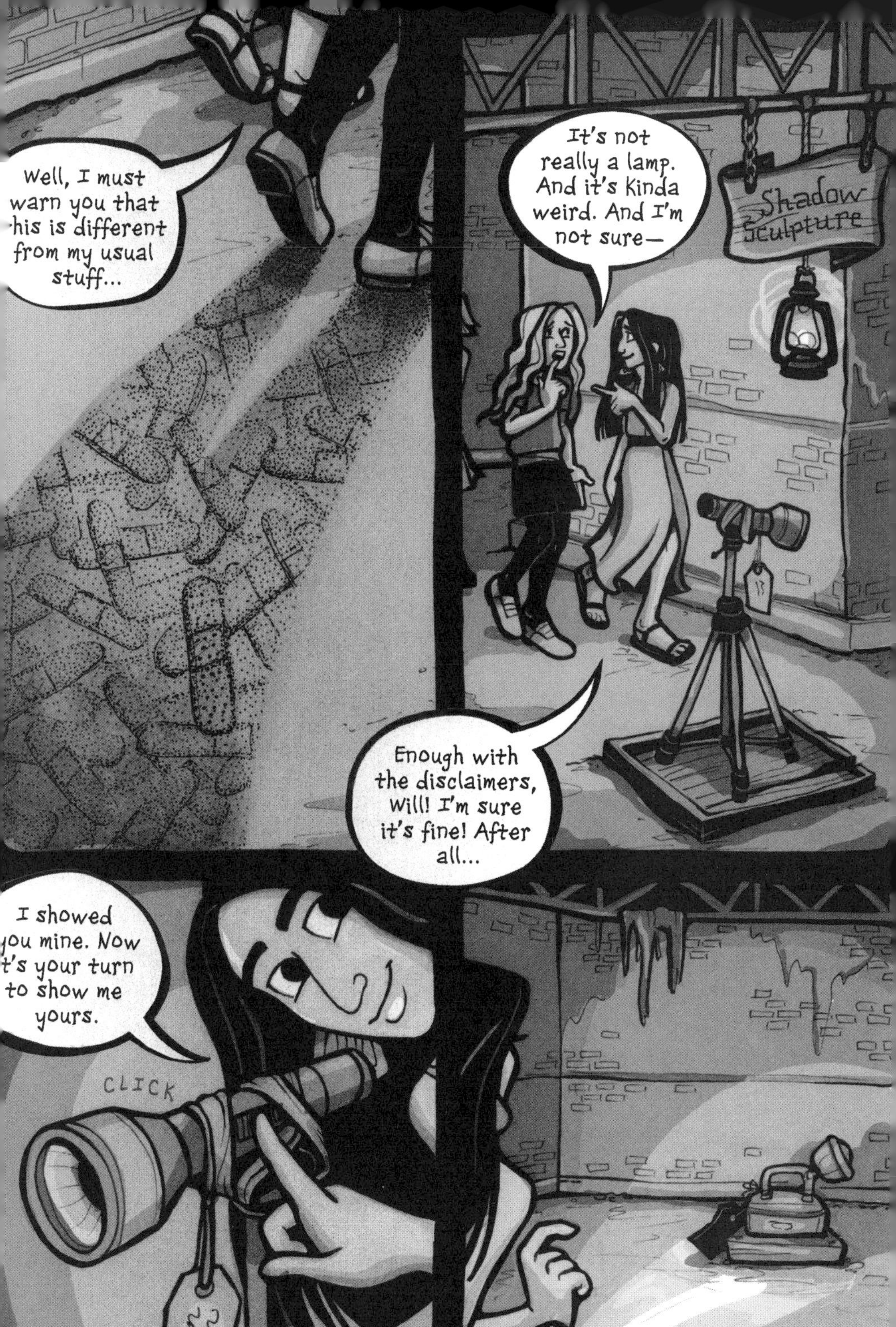

Well, I must warn you that his is different from my usual stuff...
It's not really a lamp. And it's Kinda weird. And I'm not sure—
Shadow Sculpture
Enough with the disclaimers, Will! I'm sure it's fine! After all...
I showed you mine. Now it's your turn to show me yours.
CLICK

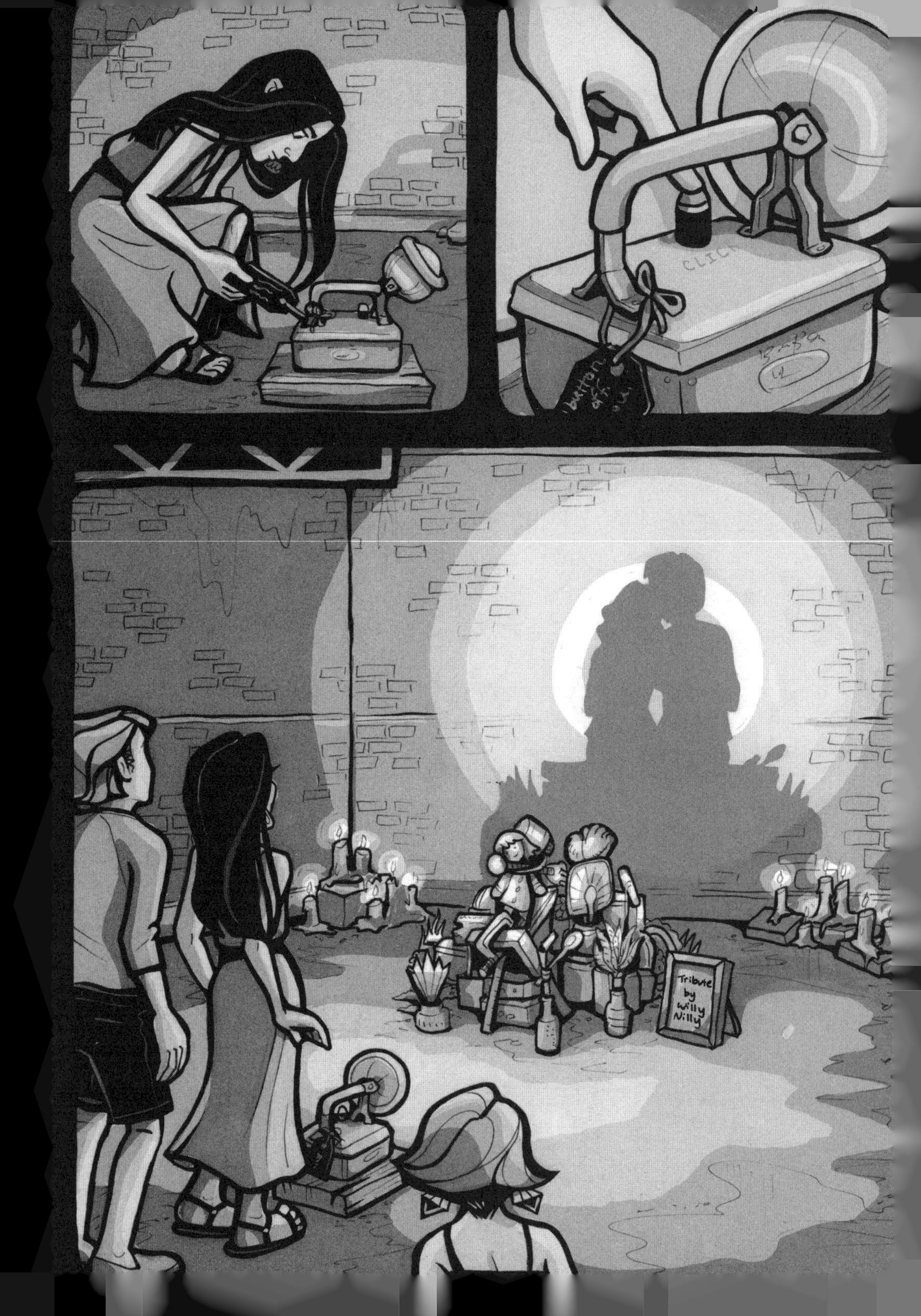
Tribute by Willy Nilly

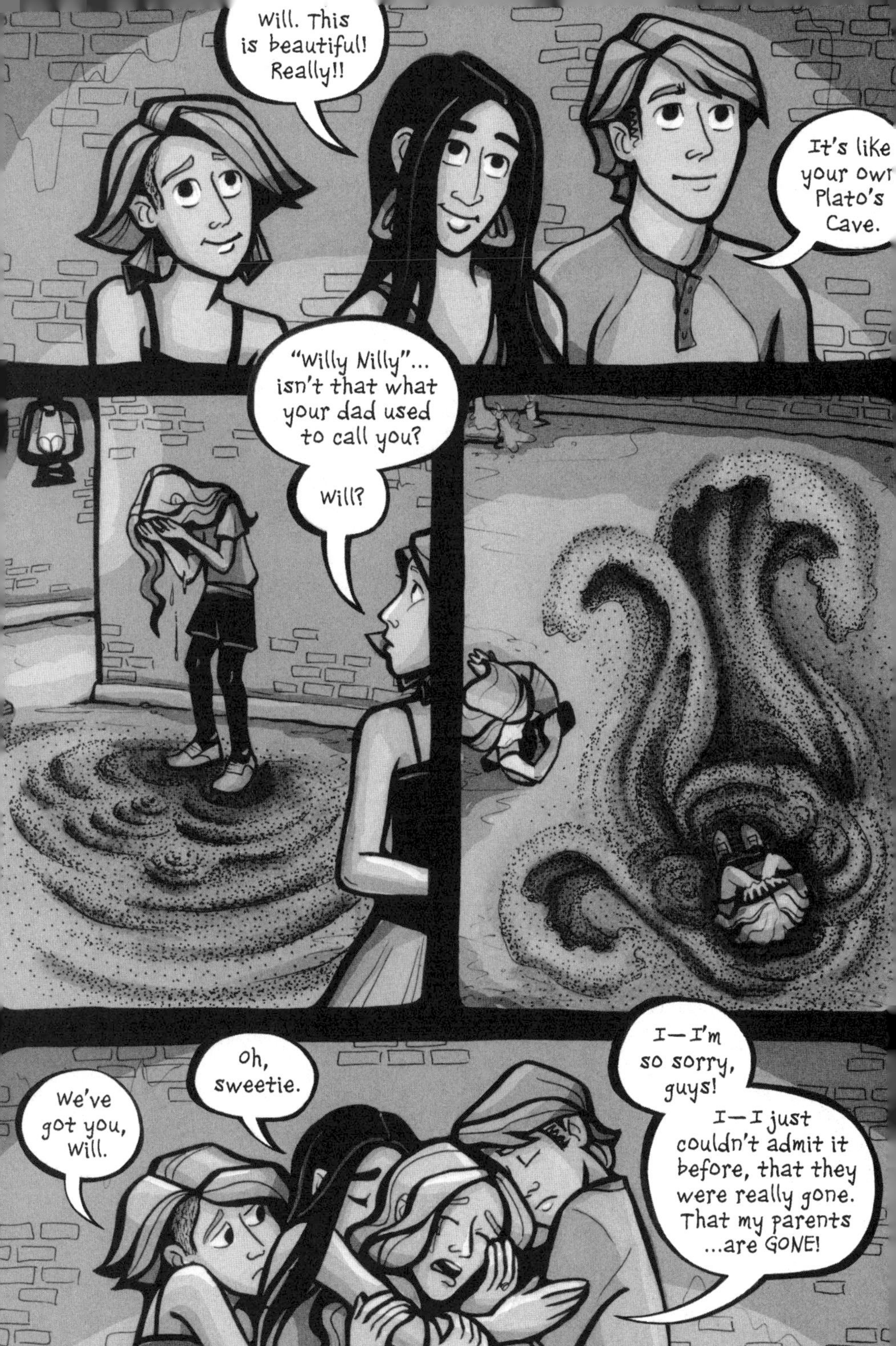
Will. This is beautiful! Really!!
It's like your own Plato's Cave.
"Willy Nilly"... isn't that what your dad used to call you?
Will?
We've got you, Will.
Oh, sweetie.
I—I'm so sorry, guys!
I—I just couldn't admit it before, that they were really gone. That my parents ...are GONE!

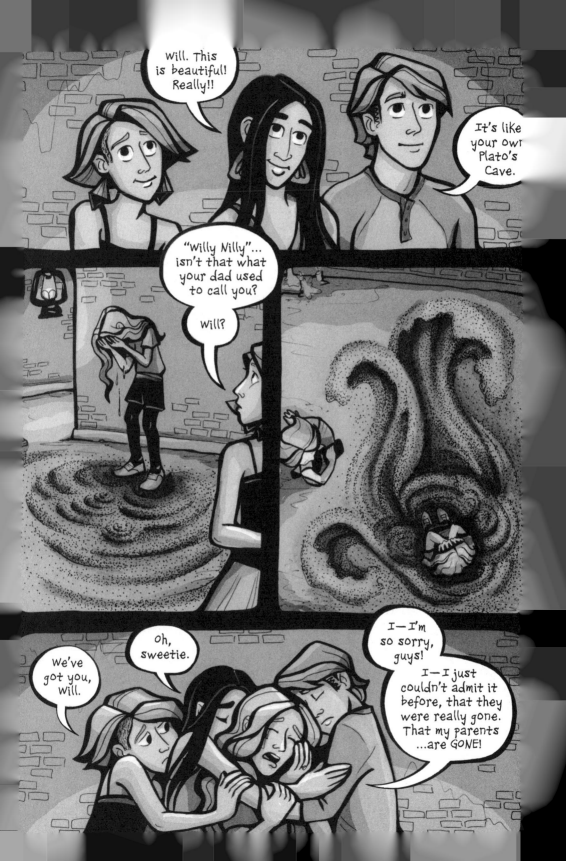

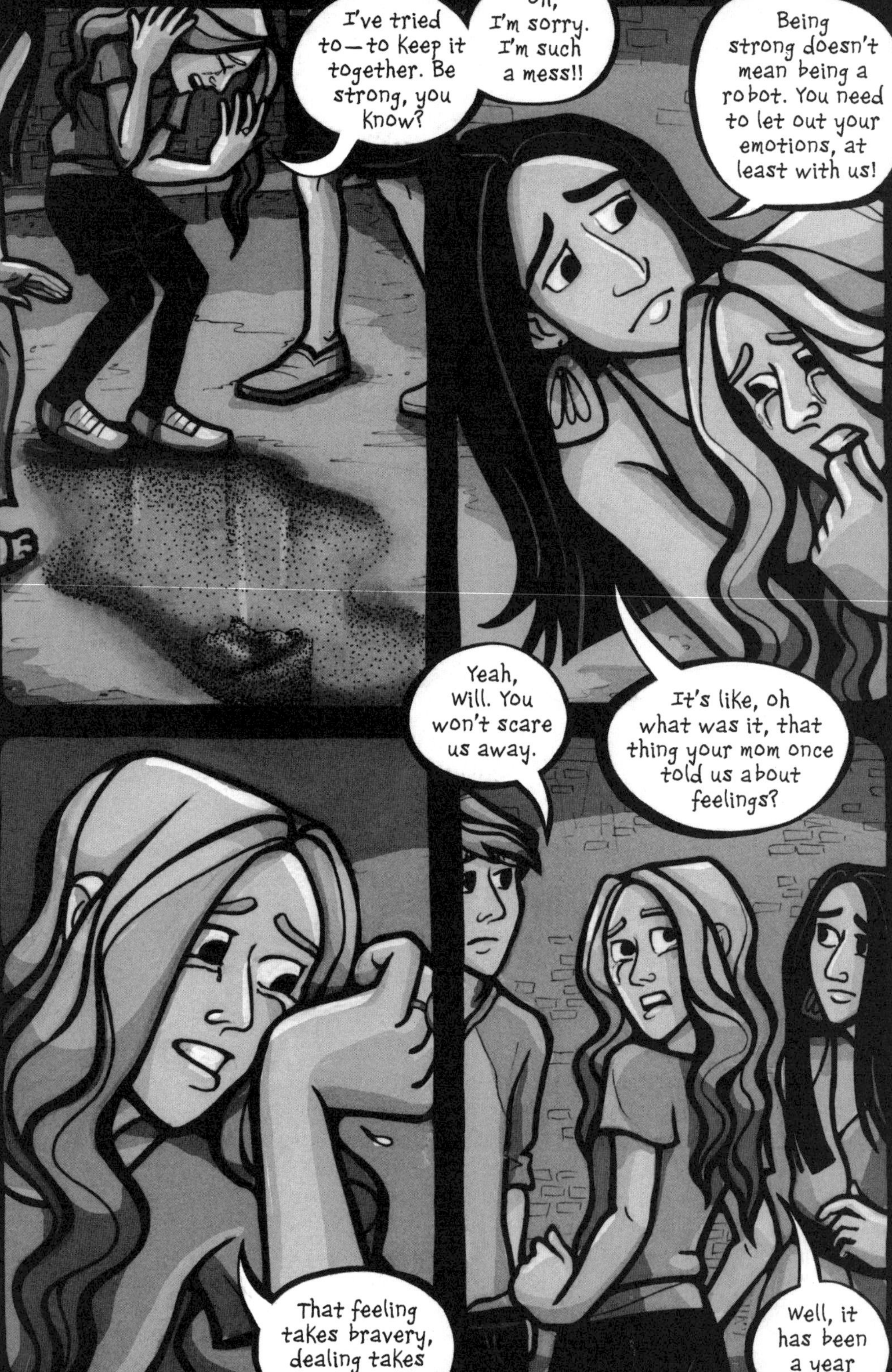
I've tried to—to keep it together. Be strong, you know?
Oh, I'm sorry. I'm such a mess!!
Being strong doesn't mean being a robot. You need to let out your emotions, at least with us!
It's like, oh what was it, that thing your mom once told us about feelings?
Yeah, Will. You won't scare us away.
That feeling takes bravery, dealing takes strength.
Well, it has been a year now.

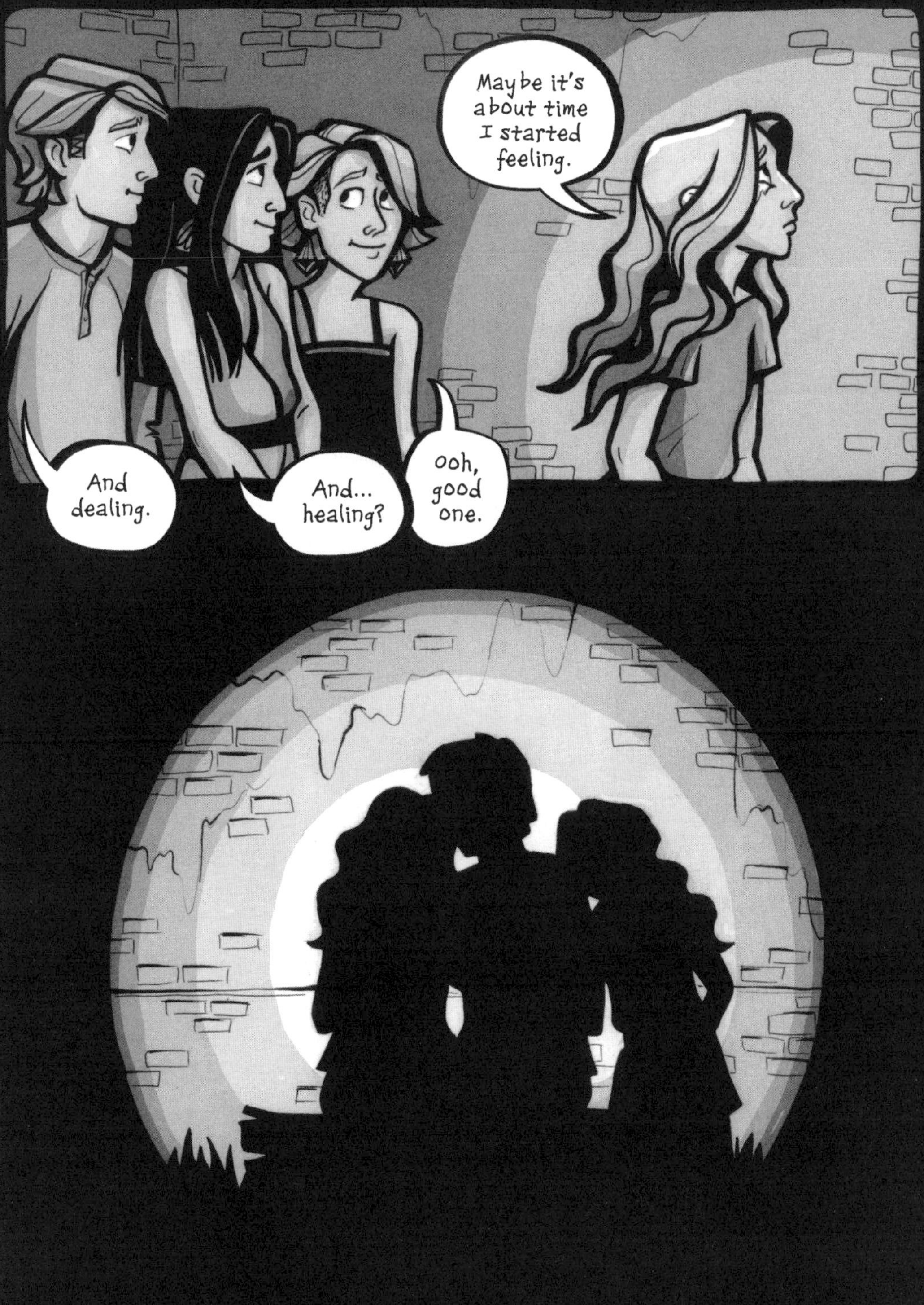
Maybe it's about time I started feeling.
And dealing.
And... healing?
ooh, good one.

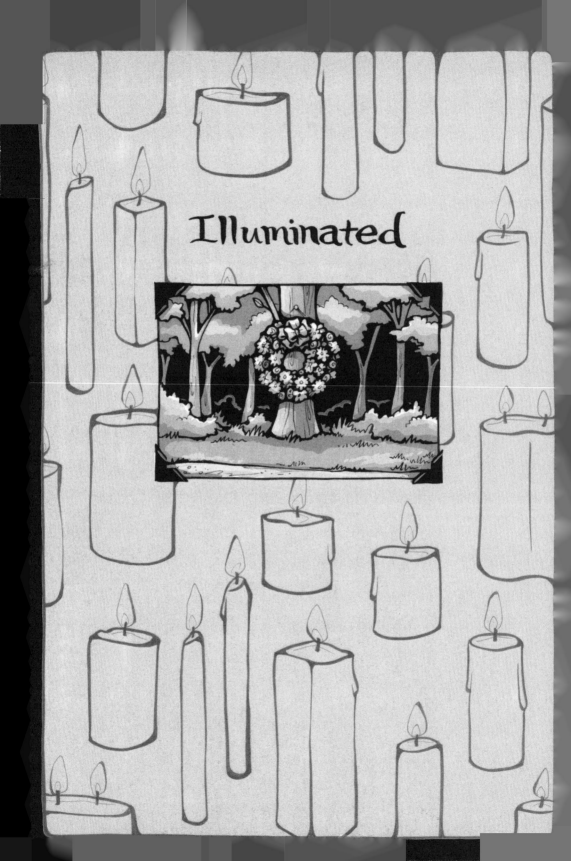

Illuminated

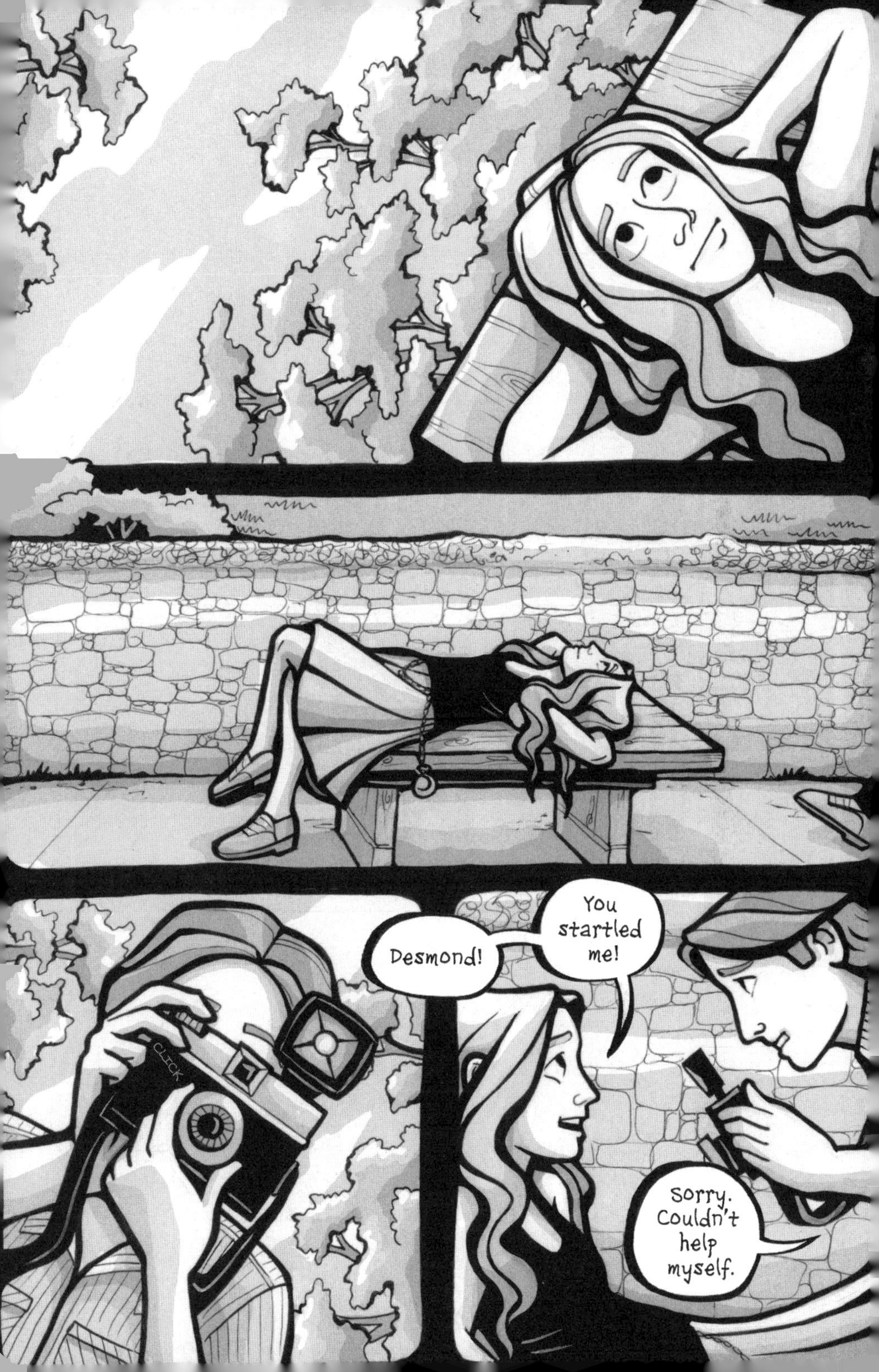
CLICK
Desmond!
You startled me!
Sorry. Couldn't help myself.

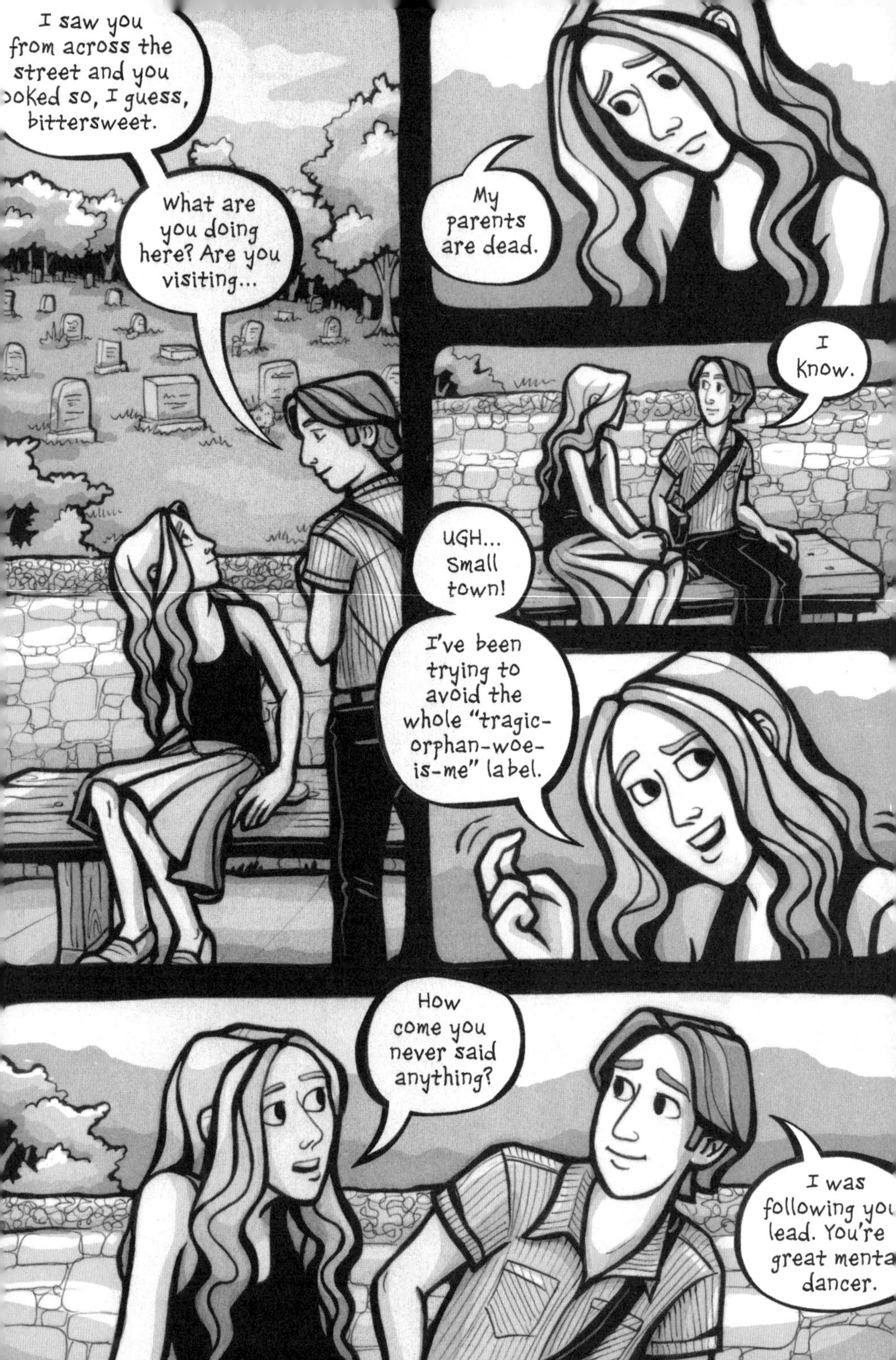

I saw you from across the street and you ooked so, I guess, bittersweet.
What are you doing here? Are you visiting...
My parents are dead.
I know.
UGH... Small town!
I've been trying to avoid the whole "tragic-orphan-woe-is-me" label.
How come you never said anything?
I was following yo lead. You're great menta dancer.

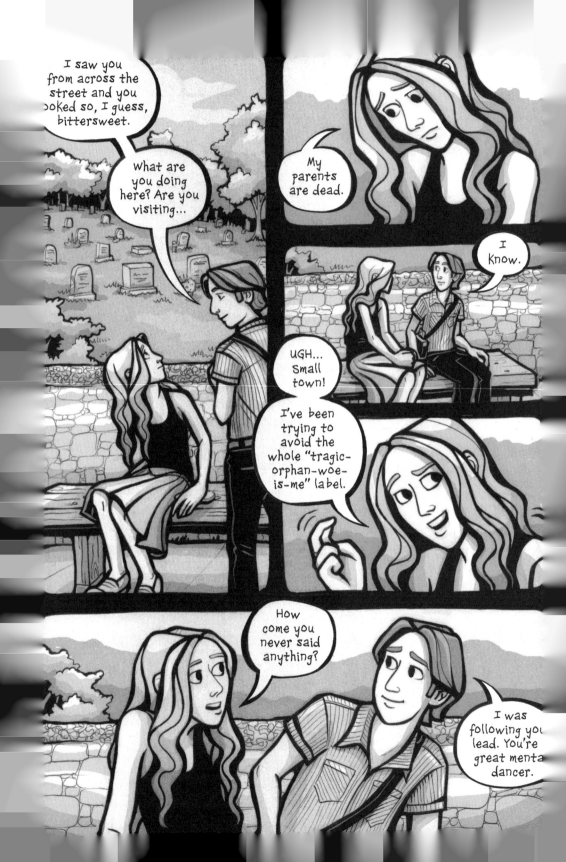

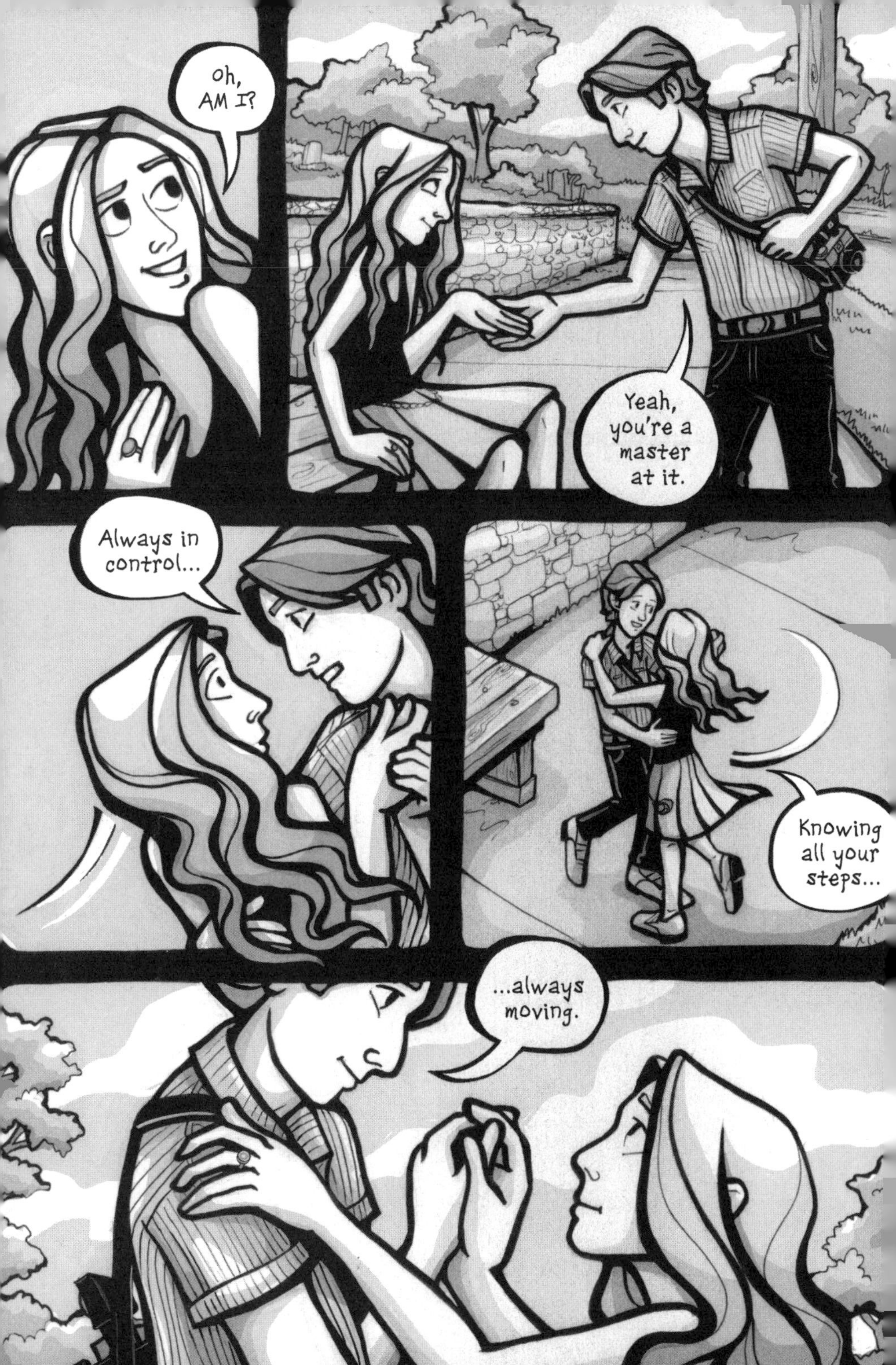
Oh, AM I?
Yeah, you're a master at it.
Always in control...
Knowing all your steps...
...always moving.

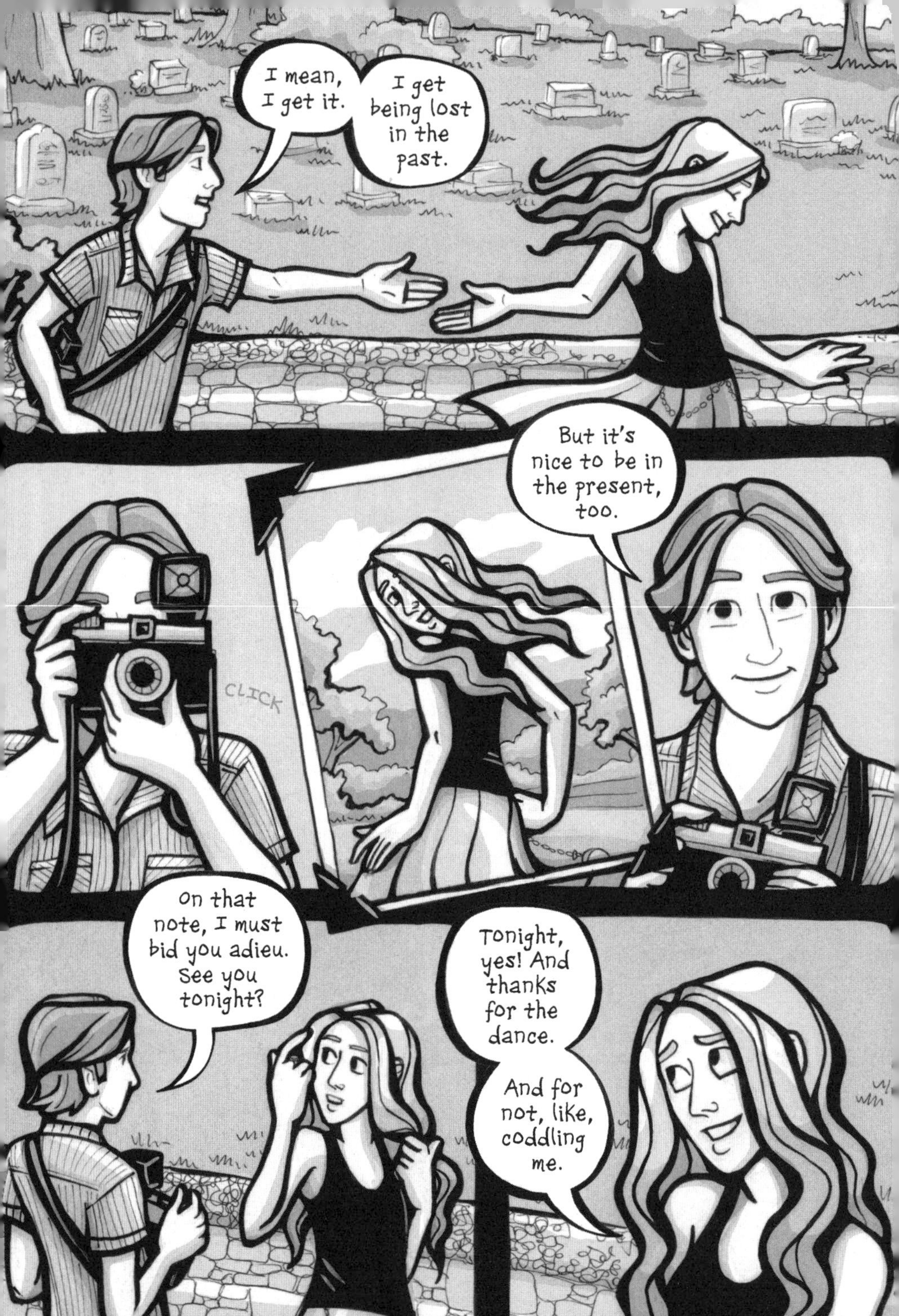
I mean, I get it.
I get being lost in the past.
But it's nice to be in the present, too.
CLICK
On that note, I must bid you adieu. See you tonight?
Tonight, yes! And thanks for the dance.
And for not, like, coddling me.

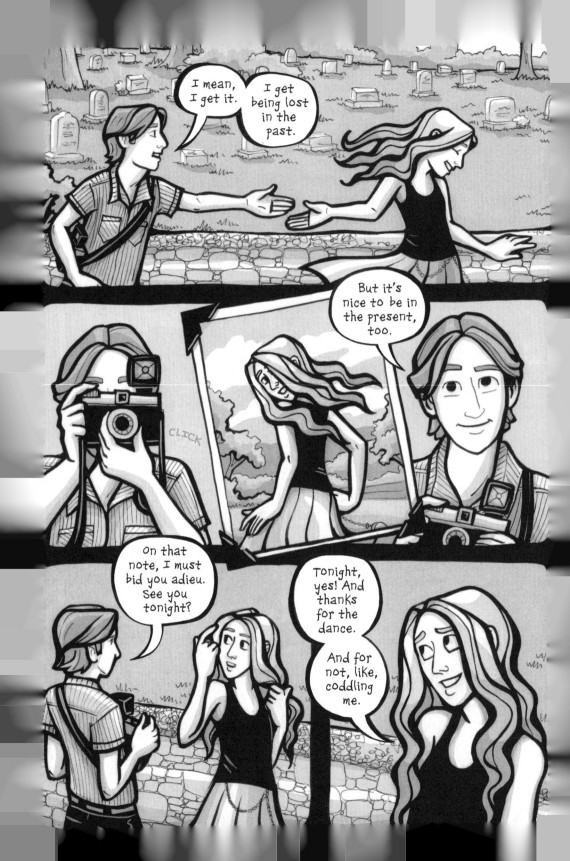

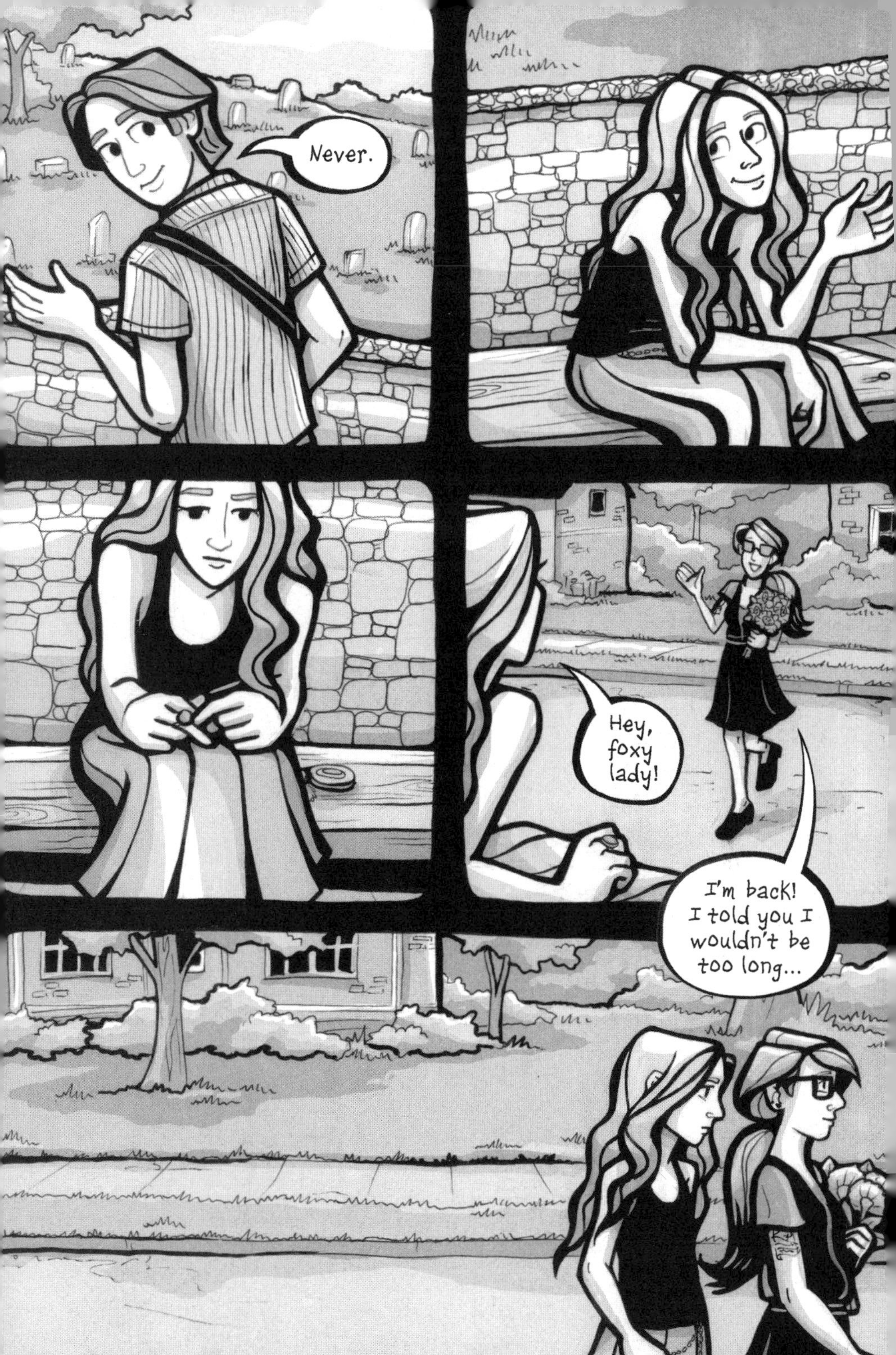
Never.
Hey, foxy lady!
I'm back! I told you I wouldn't be too long...

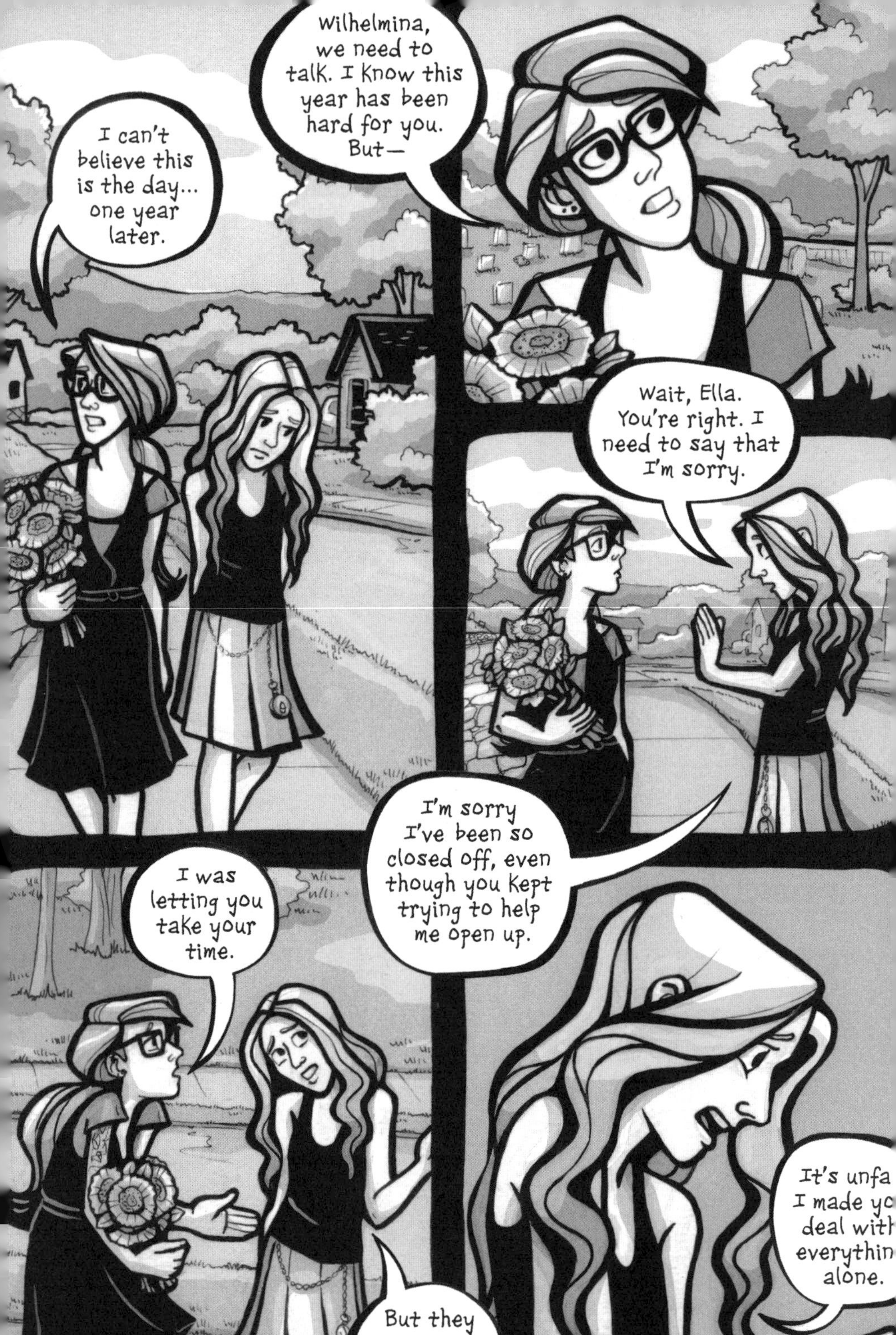
I can't believe this is the day... one year later.
Wilhelmina, we need to talk. I know this year has been hard for you. But—
Wait, Ella. You're right. I need to say that I'm sorry.
I'm sorry I've been so closed off, even though you kept trying to help me open up.
I was letting you take your time.
But they were your family,
It's unfa I made yo deal wit everythin alone.

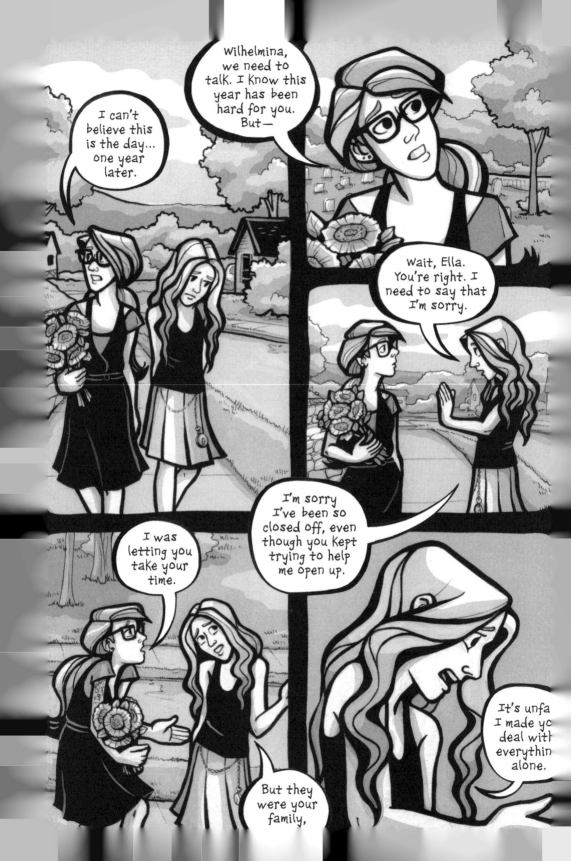

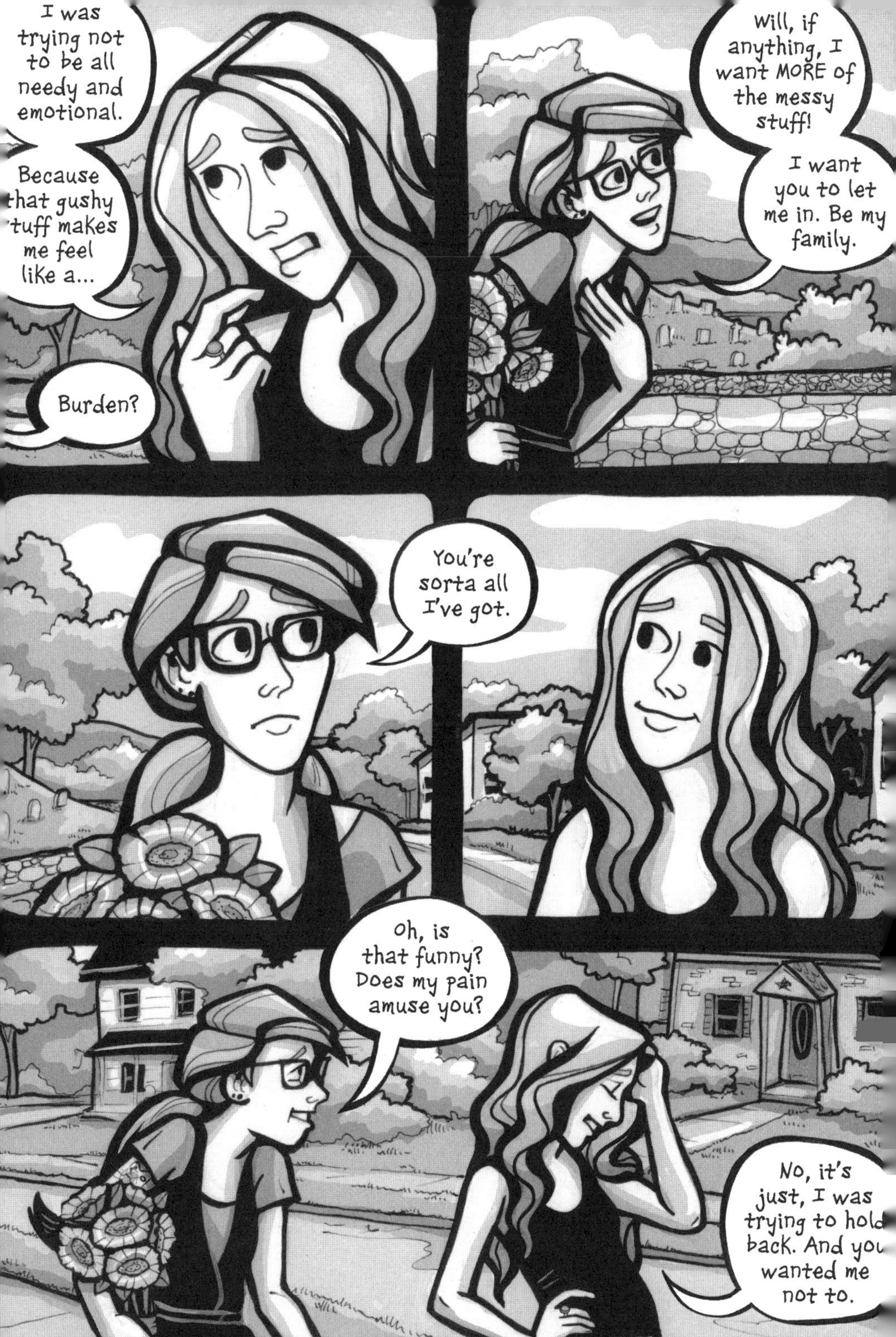
I was trying not to be all needy and emotional.
Because that gushy stuff makes me feel like a...
Burden?
Will, if anything, I want MORE of the messy stuff!
I want you to let me in. Be my family.
You're sorta all I've got.
Oh, is that funny? Does my pain amuse you?
No, it's just, I was trying to hold back. And you wanted me not to.

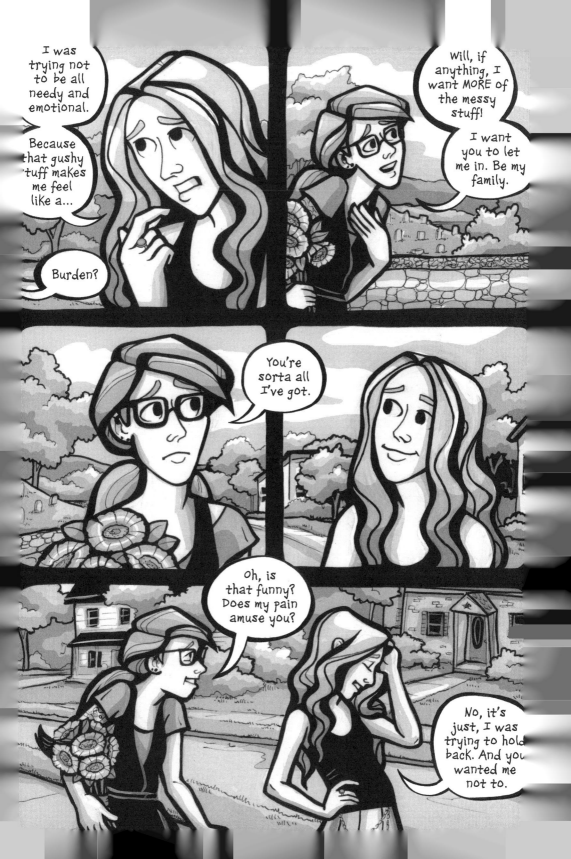

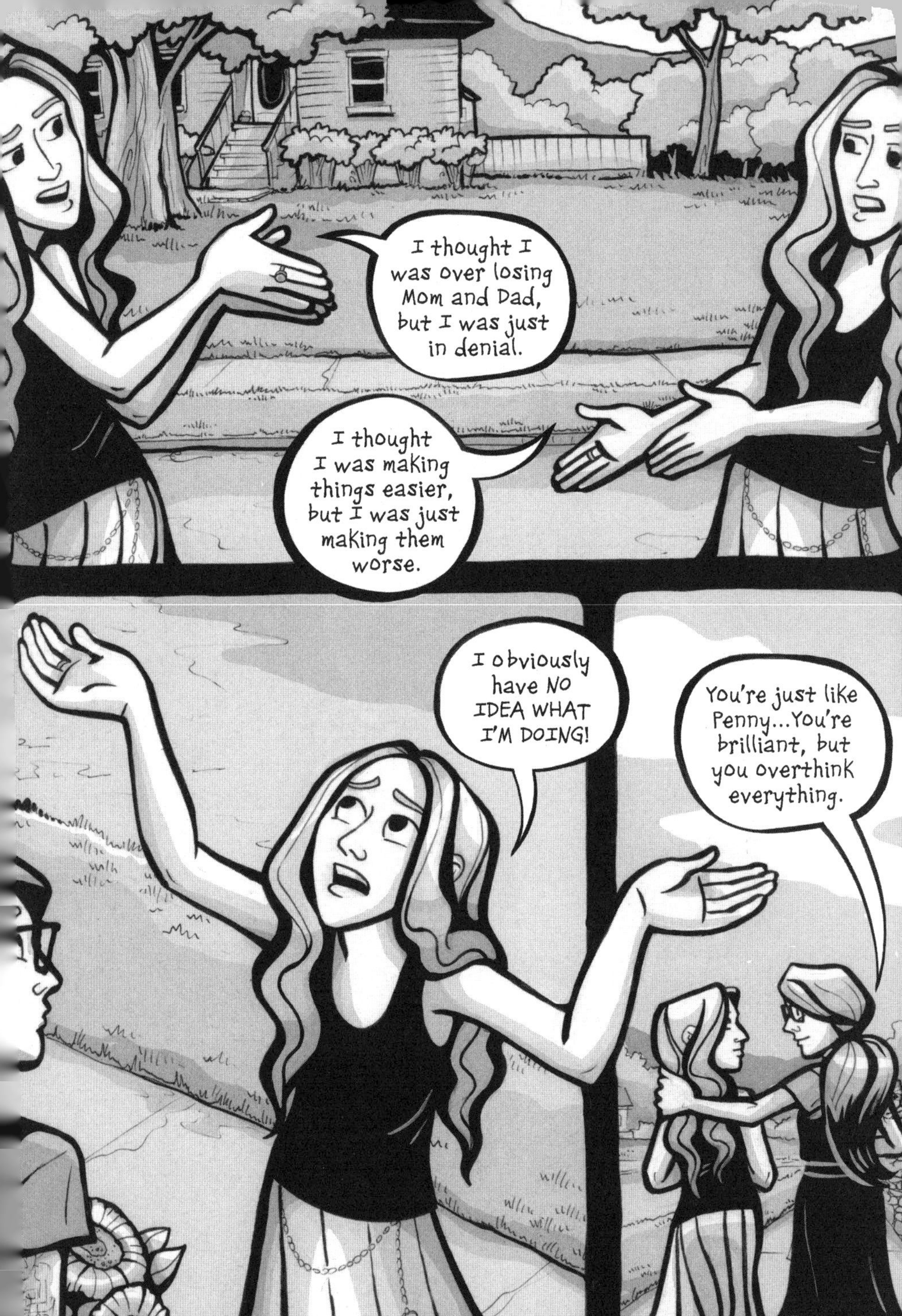
I thought I was over losing Mom and Dad, but I was just in denial.
I thought I was making things easier, but I was just making them worse.
I obviously have NO IDEA WHAT I'M DOING!
You're just like Penny...You're brilliant, but you overthink everything.

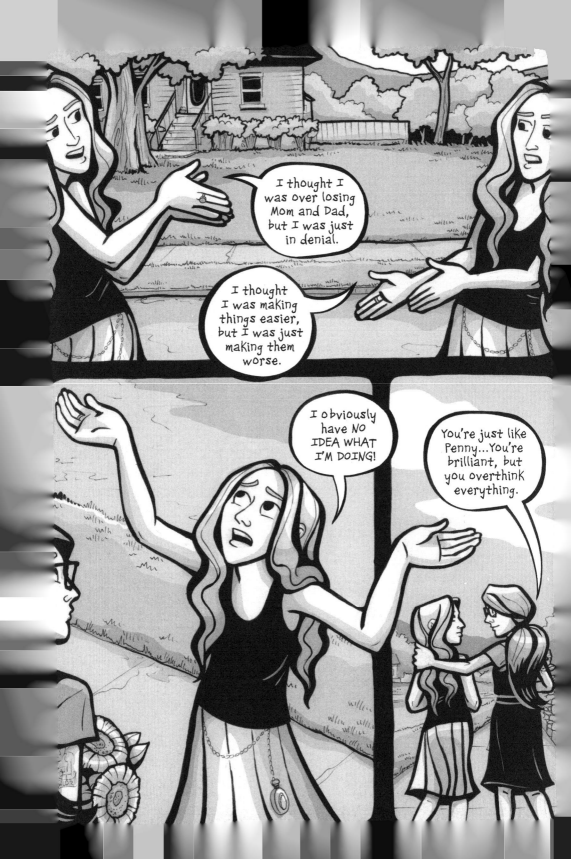

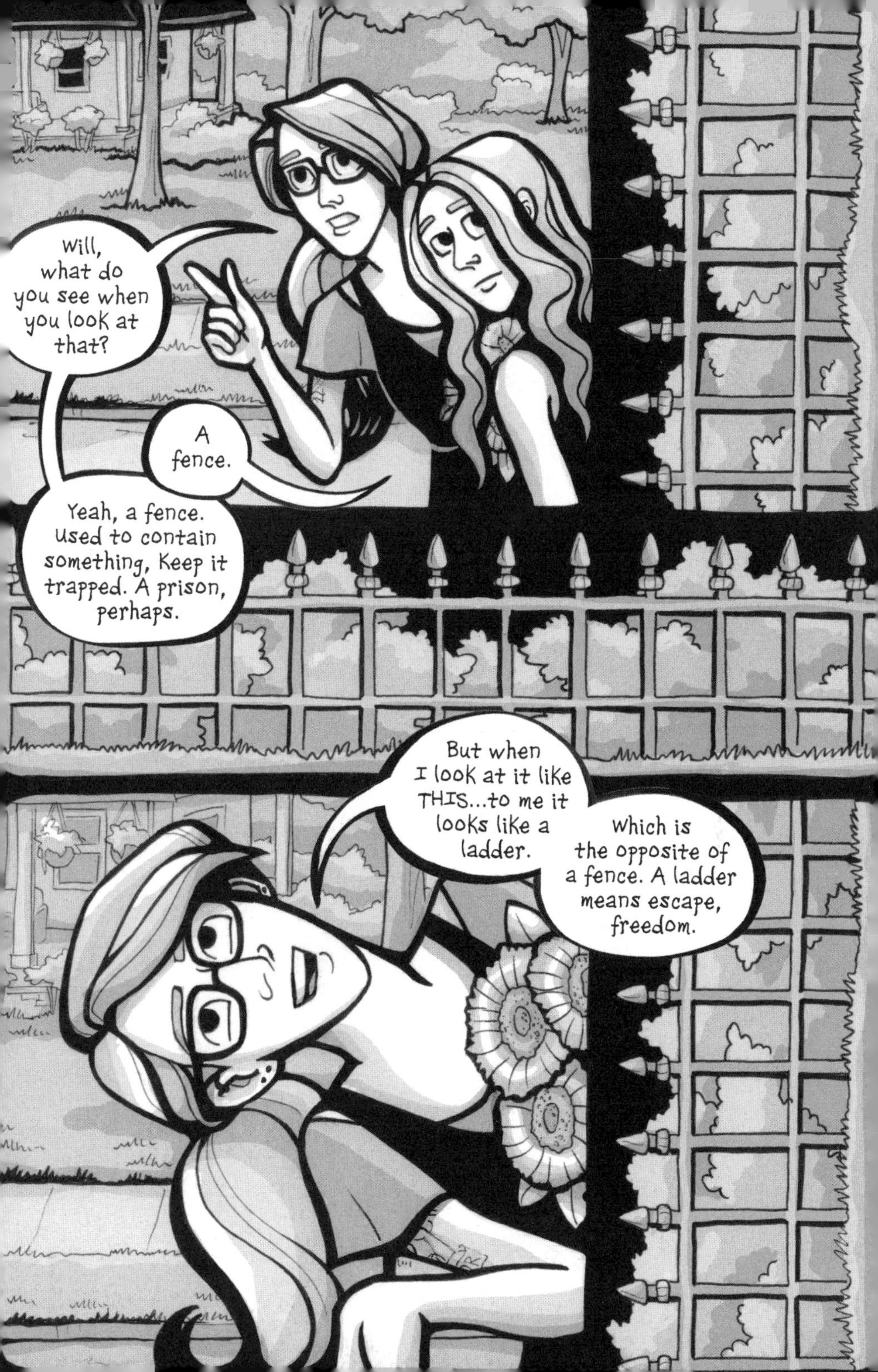
Will, what do you see when you look at that?
A fence.
Yeah, a fence. Used to contain something, Keep it trapped. A prison, perhaps.
But when I look at it like THIS...to me it looks like a ladder.
Which is the opposite of a fence. A ladder means escape, freedom.

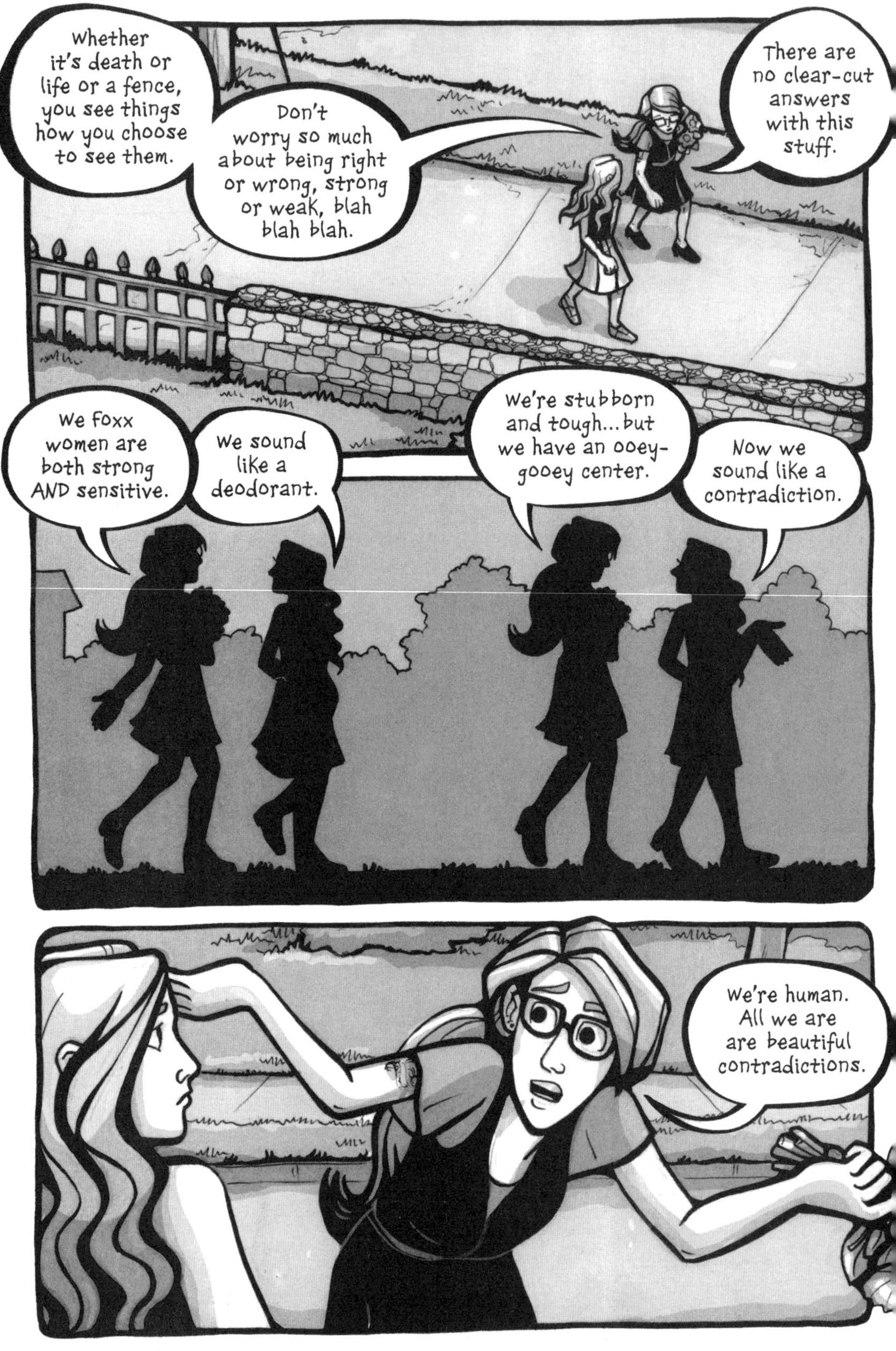
Whether it's death or life or a fence, you see things how you choose to see them.
Don't worry so much about being right or wrong, strong or weak, blah blah blah.
There are no clear-cut answers with this stuff.
We Foxx women are both strong AND sensitive.
We sound like a deodorant.
We're stubborn and tough... but we have an ooey-gooey center.
Now we sound like a contradiction.
We're human. All we are are beautiful contradictions.

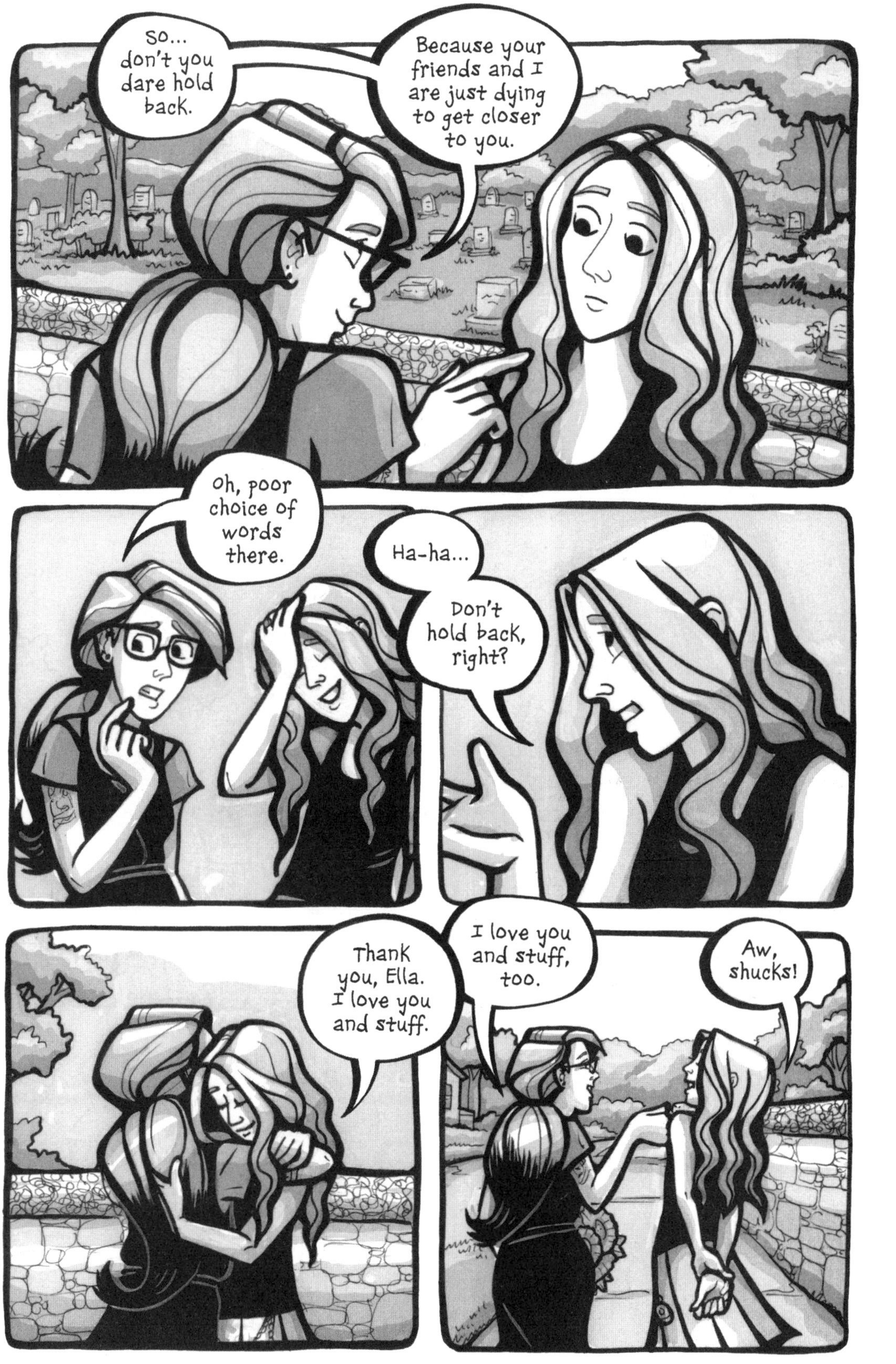
So... don't you dare hold back.
Because your friends and I are just dying to get closer to you.
Oh, poor choice of words there.
Ha-ha...
Don't hold back, right?
Thank you, Ella. I love you and stuff.
I love you and stuff, too.
Aw, shucks!

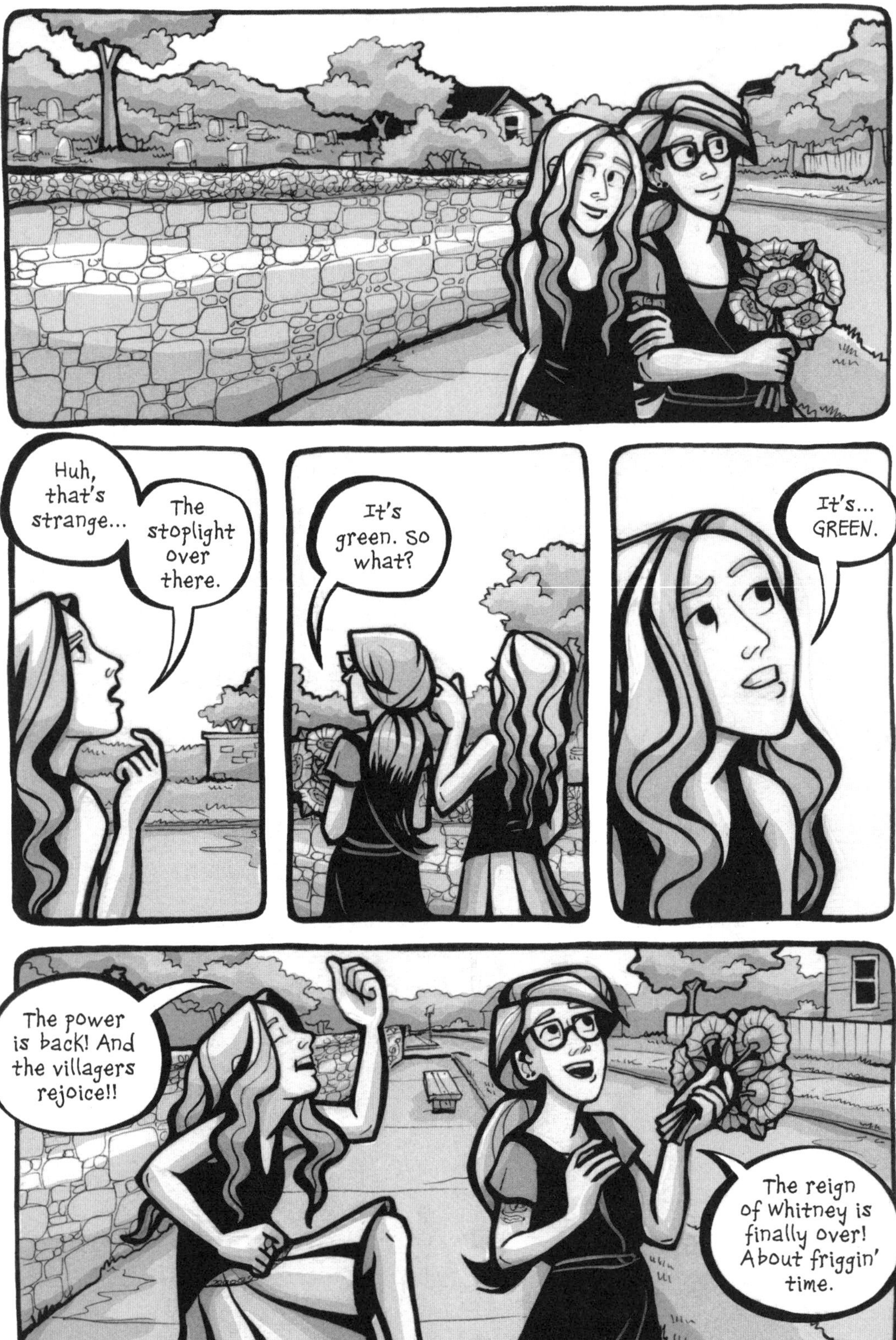
Huh, that's strange...
The stoplight over there.
It's green. So what?
It's... GREEN.
The power is back! And the villagers rejoice!!
The reign of Whitney is finally over! About friggin' time.

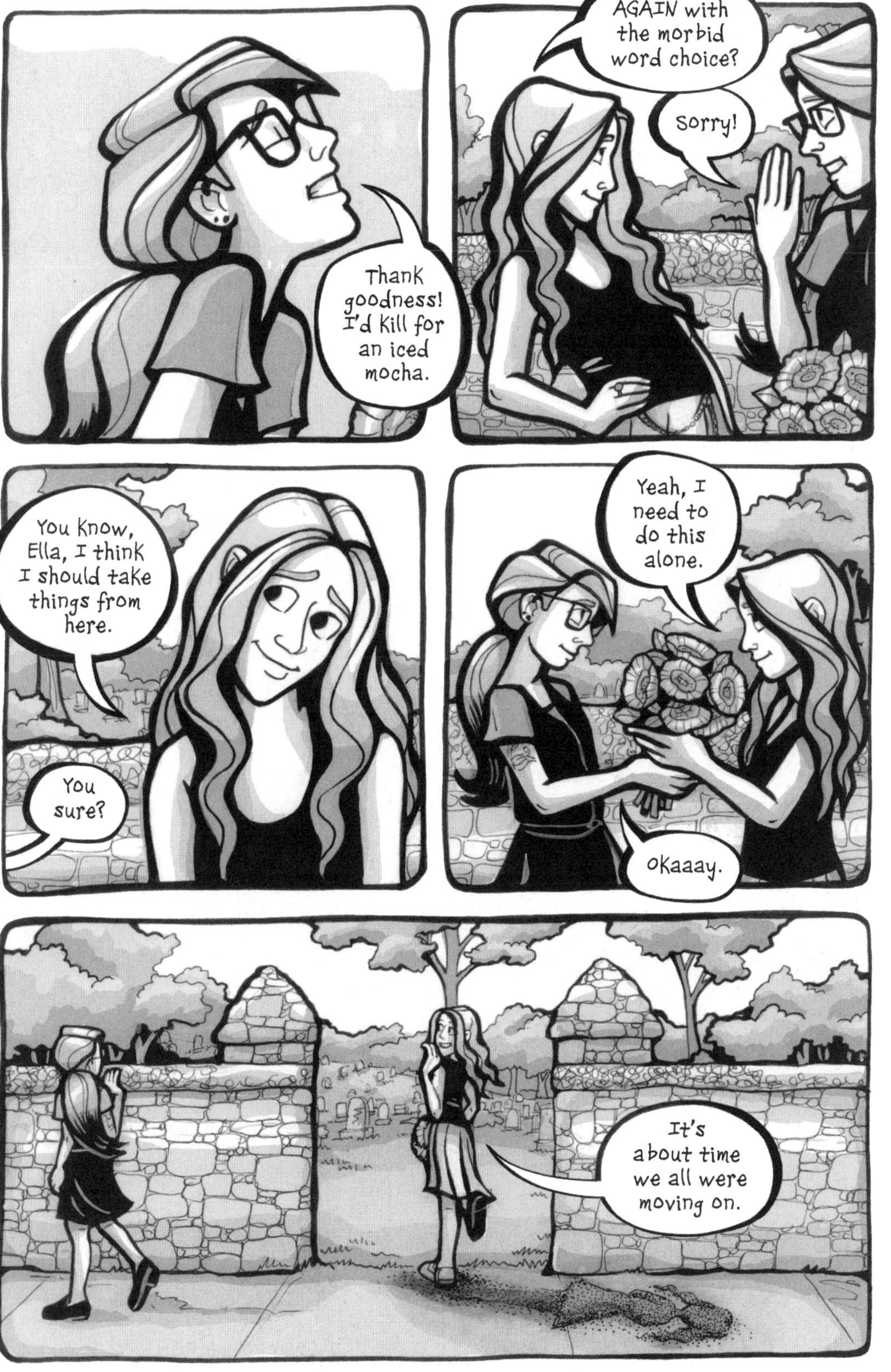
Thank goodness! I'd kill for an iced mocha.
AGAIN with the morbid word choice?
Sorry!
You know, Ella, I think I should take things from here.
You sure?
Yeah, I need to do this alone.
Okaaay.
It's about time we all were moving on.

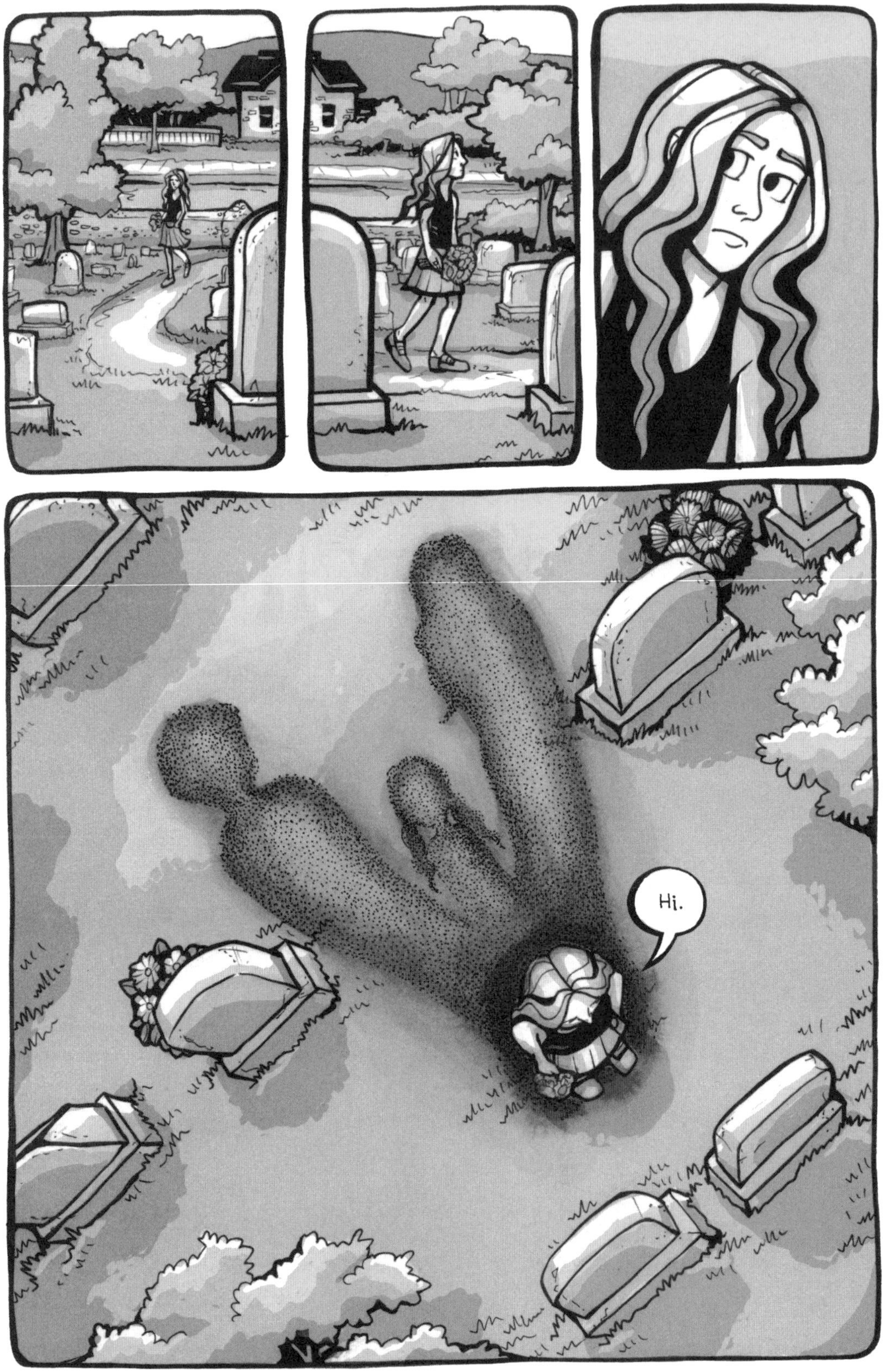
Hi.

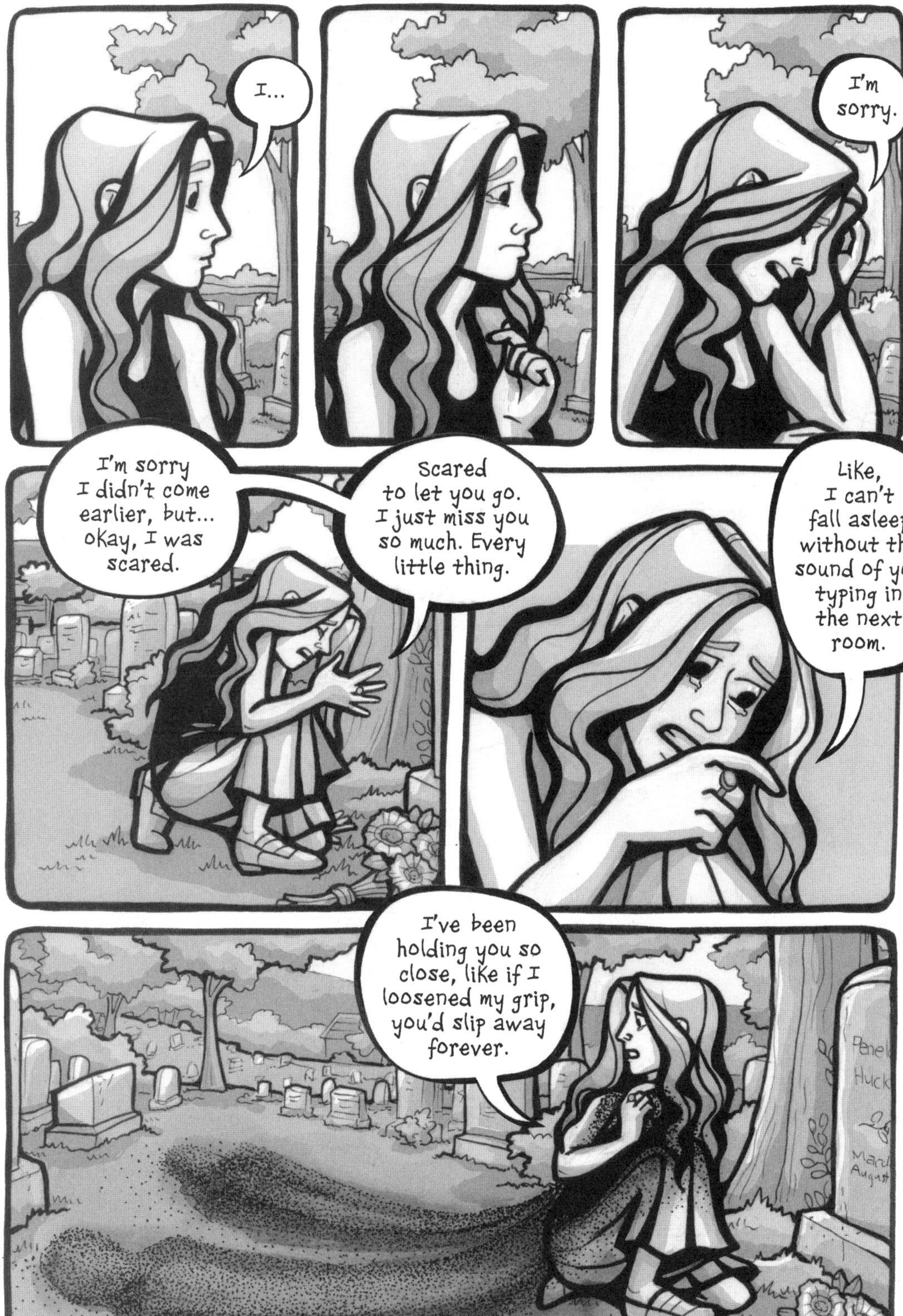
I...
I'm sorry.
I'm sorry I didn't come earlier, but... okay, I was scared.
Scared to let you go. I just miss you so much. Every little thing.
Like, I can't fall asleep without the sound of you typing in the next room.
I've been holding you so close, like if I loosened my grip, you'd slip away forever.

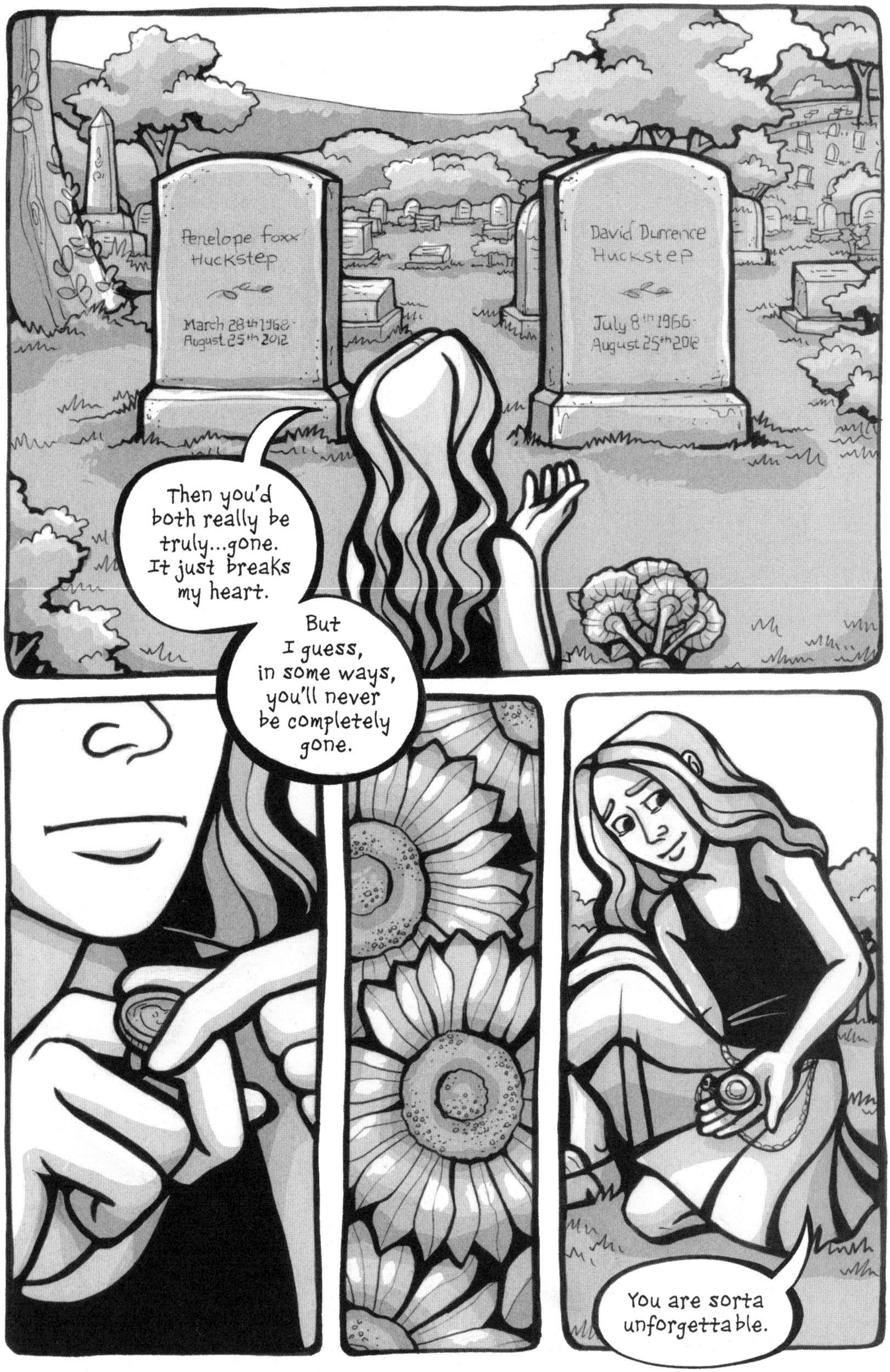
Penelope Foxx Huckstep
March 28th 1968 August 25th 2012
David Durrence Huckstep
July 8th 1966 August 25th 2012
Then you'd both really be truly...gone. It just breaks my heart.
But I guess, in some ways, you'll never be completely gone.
You are sorta unforgettable.

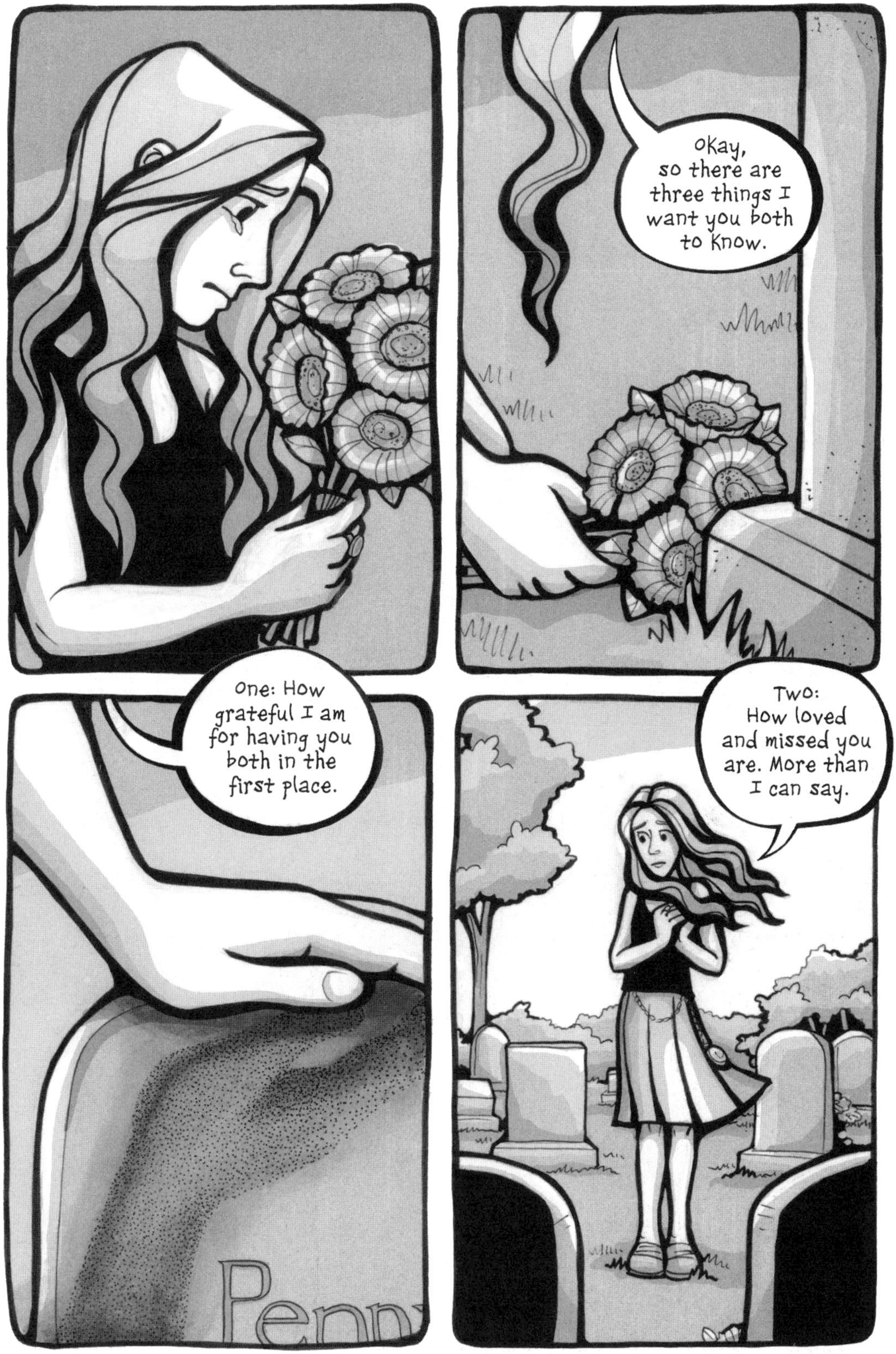
Okay, so there are three things I want you both to know.
One: How grateful I am for having you both in the first place.
Two: How loved and missed you are. More than I can say.
Penny

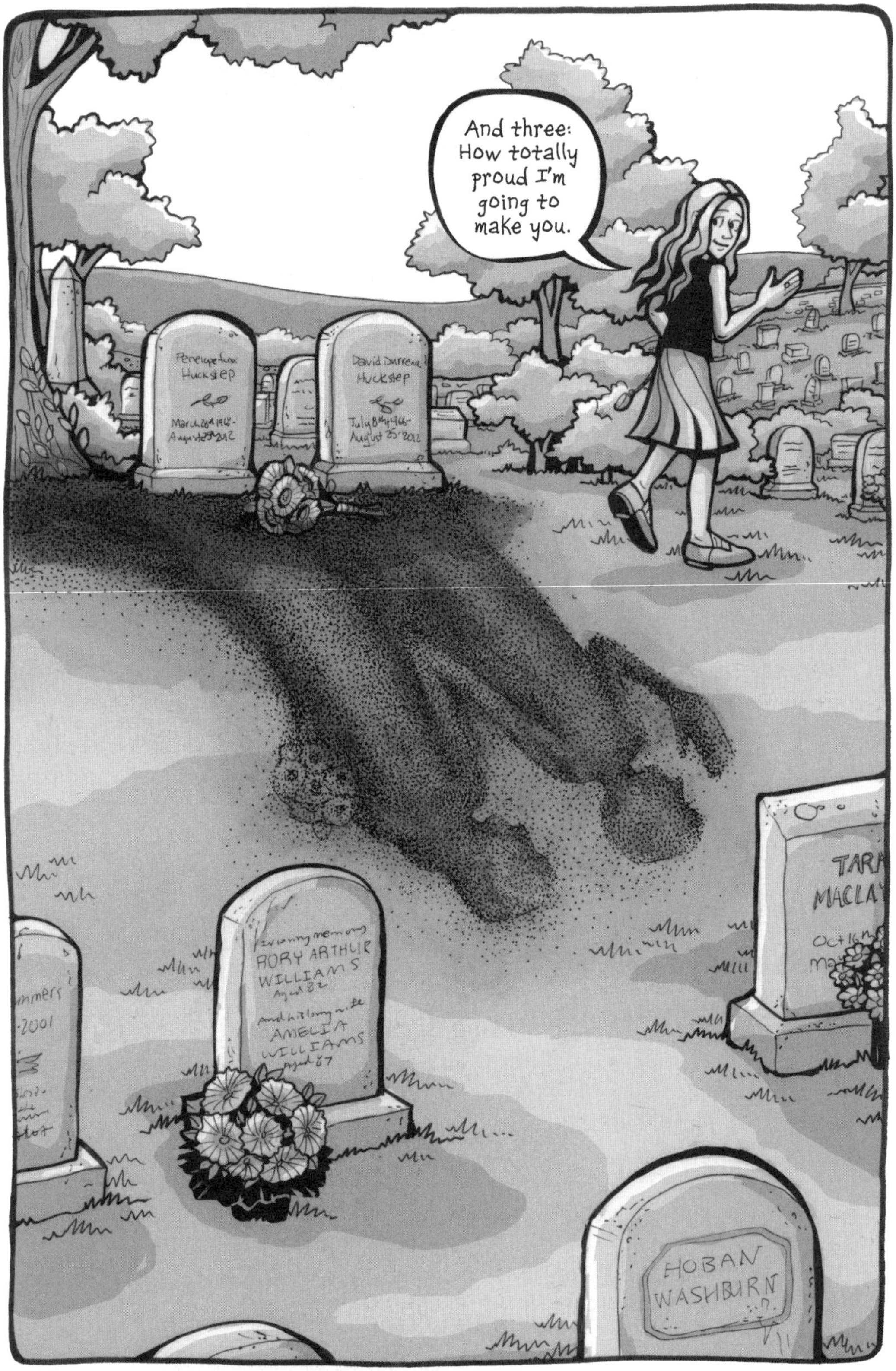
And three: How totally proud I'm going to make you.
RORY ARTHUR WILLIAMS
AMELIA WILLIAMS
HOBAN WASHBURN

Epilogue

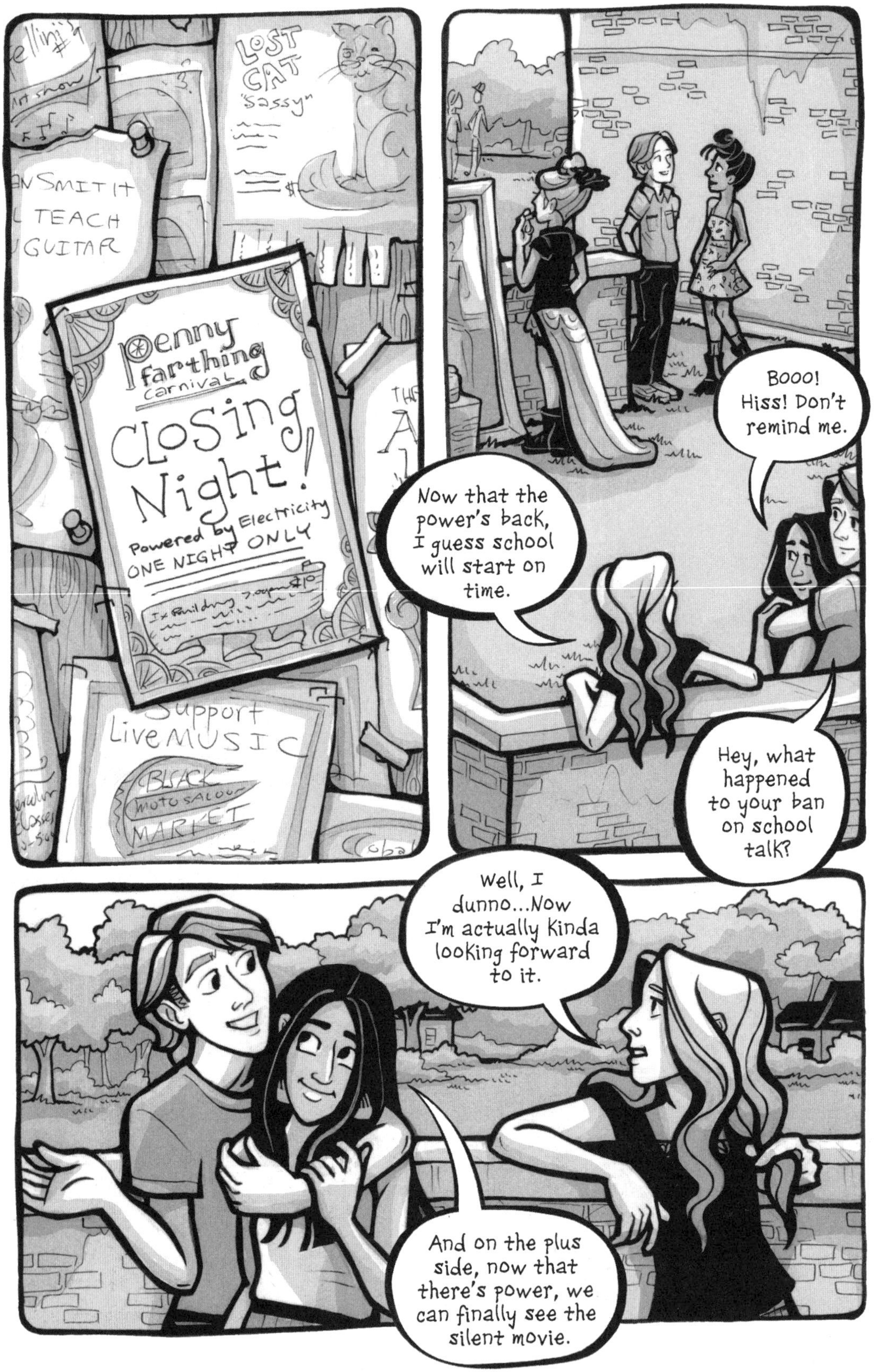
LOST CAT
"Sassy"
penny farthing carnival
CLOSING Night!
Powered by Electricity
ONE NIGHT ONLY
Support Live MUSIC
Booo! Hiss! Don't remind me.
Now that the power's back, I guess school will start on time.
Hey, what happened to your ban on school talk?
Well, I dunno...Now I'm actually kinda looking forward to it.
And on the plus side, now that there's power, we can finally see the silent movie.

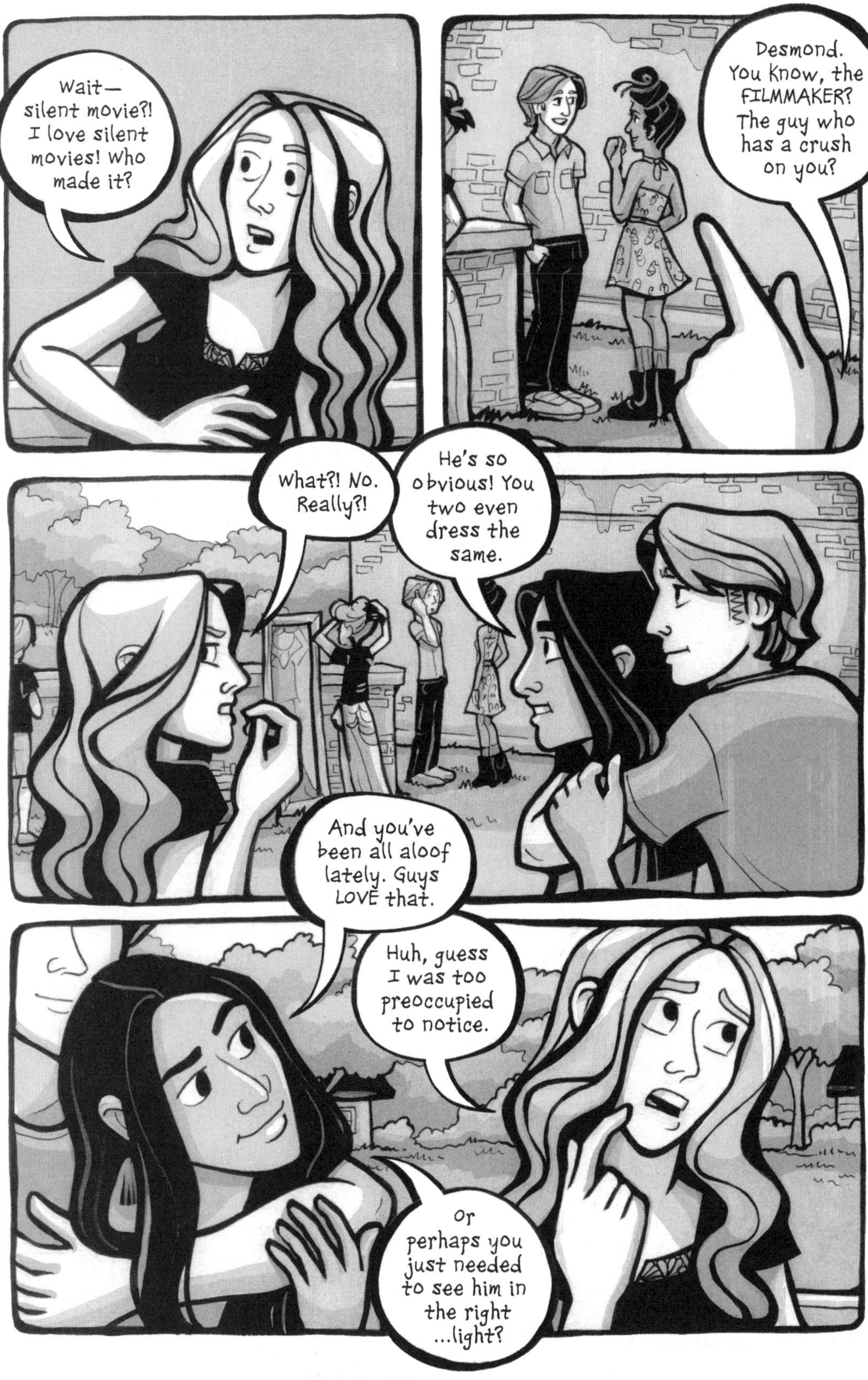
Wait— silent movie?! I love silent movies! Who made it?
Desmond. You know, the FILMMAKER? The guy who has a crush on you?
What?! No. Really?!
He's so obvious! You two even dress the same.
And you've been all aloof lately. Guys LOVE that.
Huh, guess I was too preoccupied to notice.
Or perhaps you just needed to see him in the right ...light?

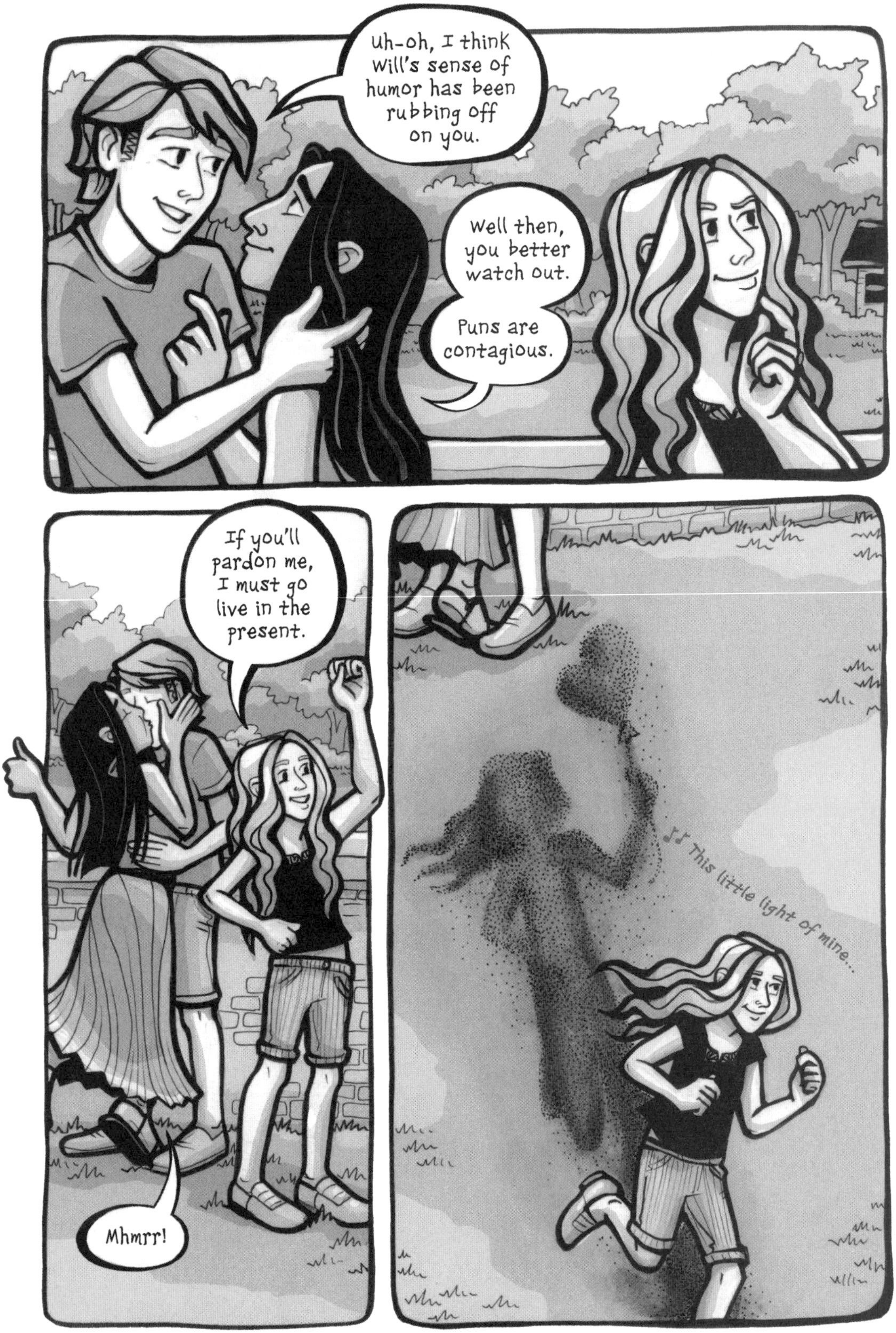
Uh-oh, I think Will's sense of humor has been rubbing off on you.
Well then, you better watch out.
Puns are contagious.
If you'll pardon me, I must go live in the present.
Mhmrr!
This little light of mine...

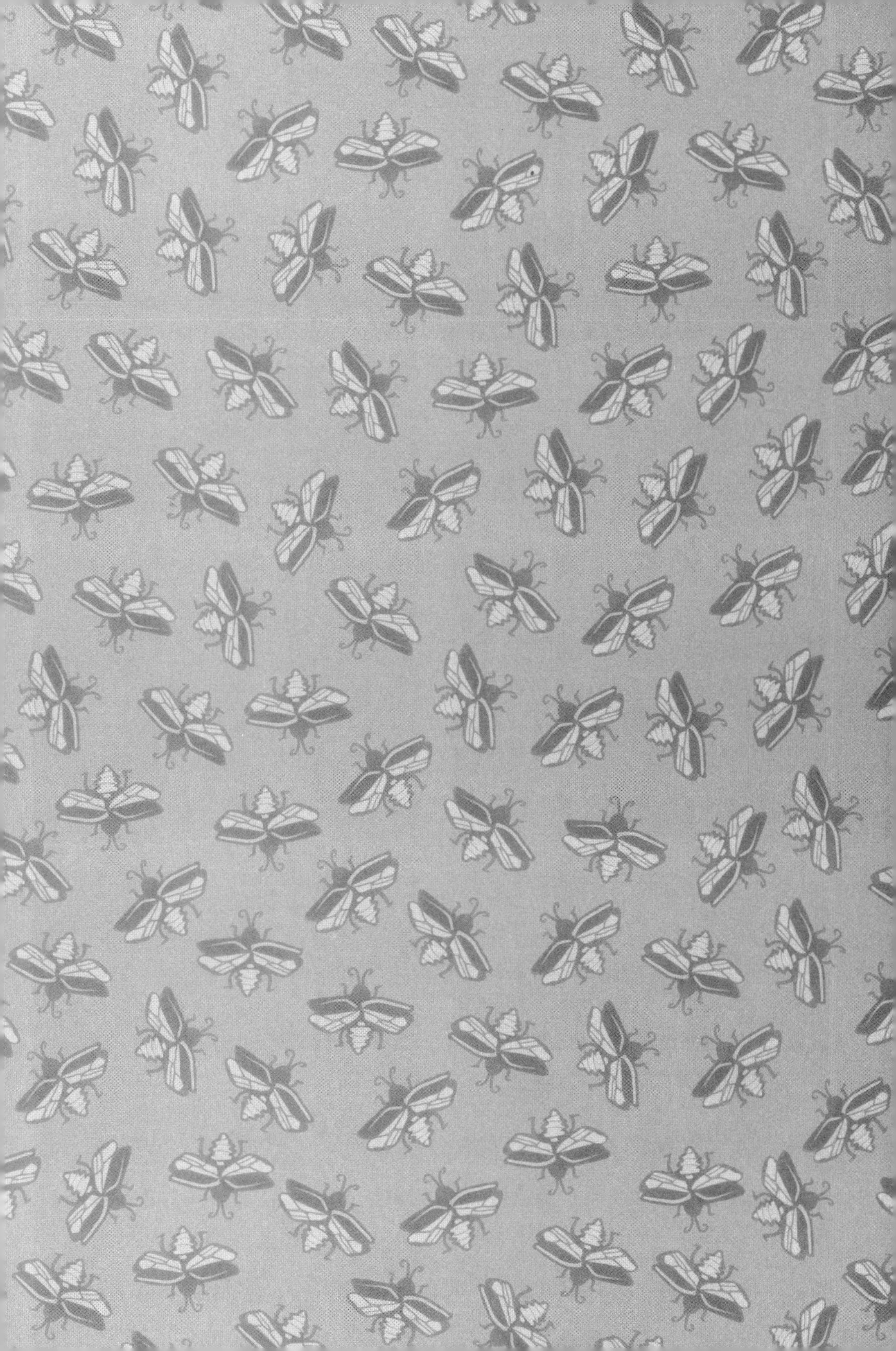

Acknowledgments

Special thanks to:

My dad, who became my official digital helper/intern for this book. I couldn't have made my deadline without his help. (PS—Happy retirement, Crazy Old Maurice!)

Chris Irving, Josh Gorfain, and Rob Richmond for helping me with technical jams. Juliet Trail, Andrea Sparacio, Kurt Christenson, and my Bushcrafters for helping me out of emotional ones. My mom and brother for being so very understanding.

Lauren Larken for writing Ava's birdcage song. Matt Lesser and Adam Jones for allowing cameos from their Stuft puppets. Maggie Lehrman, Chad Beckerman, Charlie Kochman, Mary Ann Zissimos, and Dan Lazar for all your support as this project evolved...especially when my confidence waned.

And high fives to my readers, artners, and fellow agents of whimsy. Thank you for your support and inspiration! Gold stars all around! Let's go make stuff.

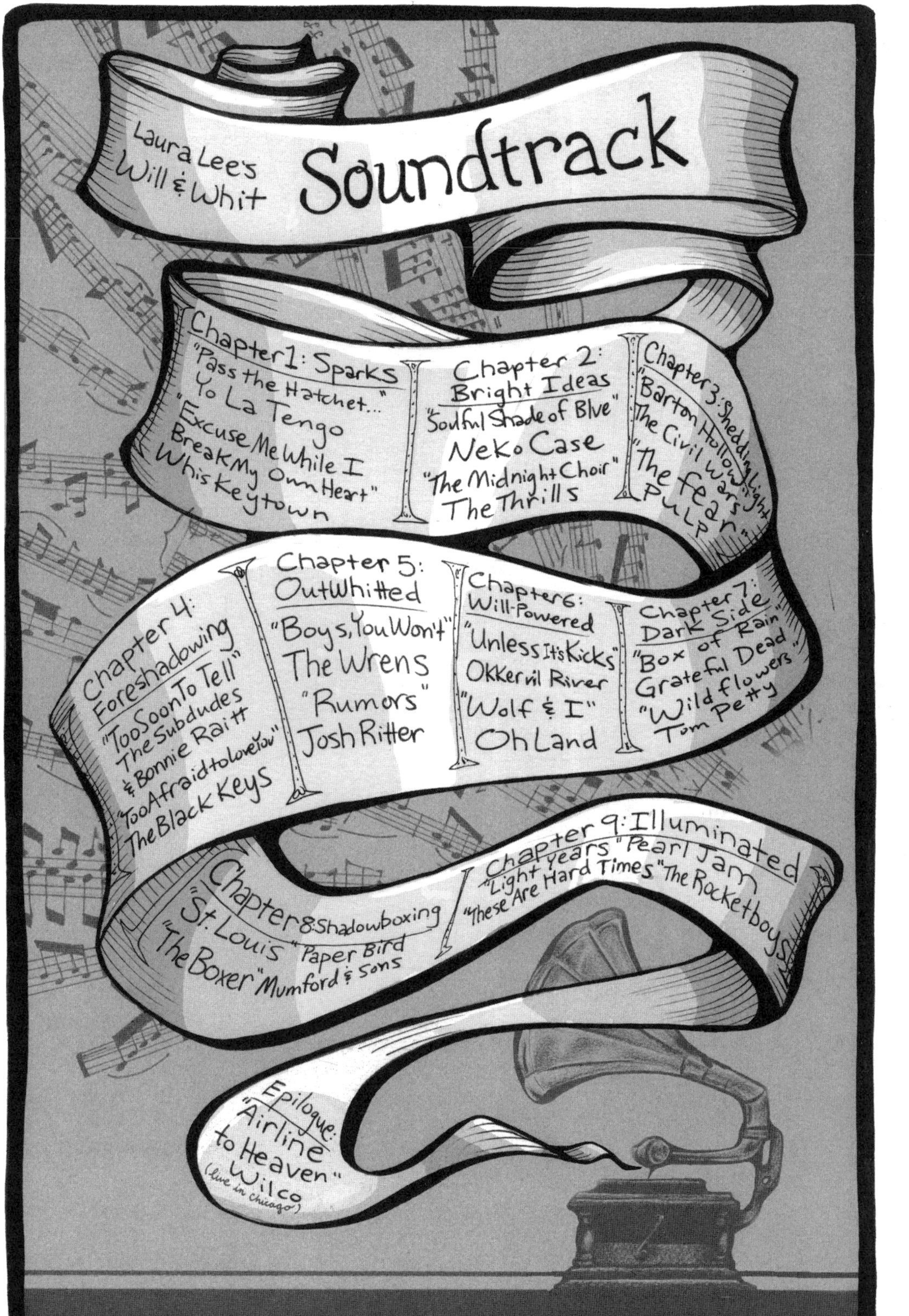
Laura Lee's
Will & Whit
Soundtrack
Chapter 1: Sparks
"Pass the Hatchet..." Yo La Tengo
"Excuse Me While I Break My Own Heart" Whiskeytown
Chapter 2: Bright Ideas
"Soulful Shade of Blue" Neko Case
"The Midnight Choir" The Thrills
Chapter 3: Shedding Light
"Barton Hollow" The Civil Wars
"The Fear" Pulp
Chapter 4: Foreshadowing
"Too Soon To Tell" The Subdudes & Bonnie Raitt
"Too Afraid to Love You" The Black Keys
Chapter 5: OutWhitted
"Boys, You Won't" The Wrens
"Rumors" Josh Ritter
Chapter 6: Will-Powered
"Unless It's Kicks" Okkervil River
"Wolf & I" Oh Land
Chapter 7: The Dark Side
"Box of Rain" Grateful Dead
"Wildflowers" Tom Petty
Chapter 8: Shadowboxing
"St. Louis" Paper Bird
"The Boxer" Mumford & Sons
Chapter 9: Illuminated
"Light Years" Pearl Jam
"These Are Hard Times" The Rocketboys
Epilogue: "Airline to Heaven" Wilco (live in Chicago)

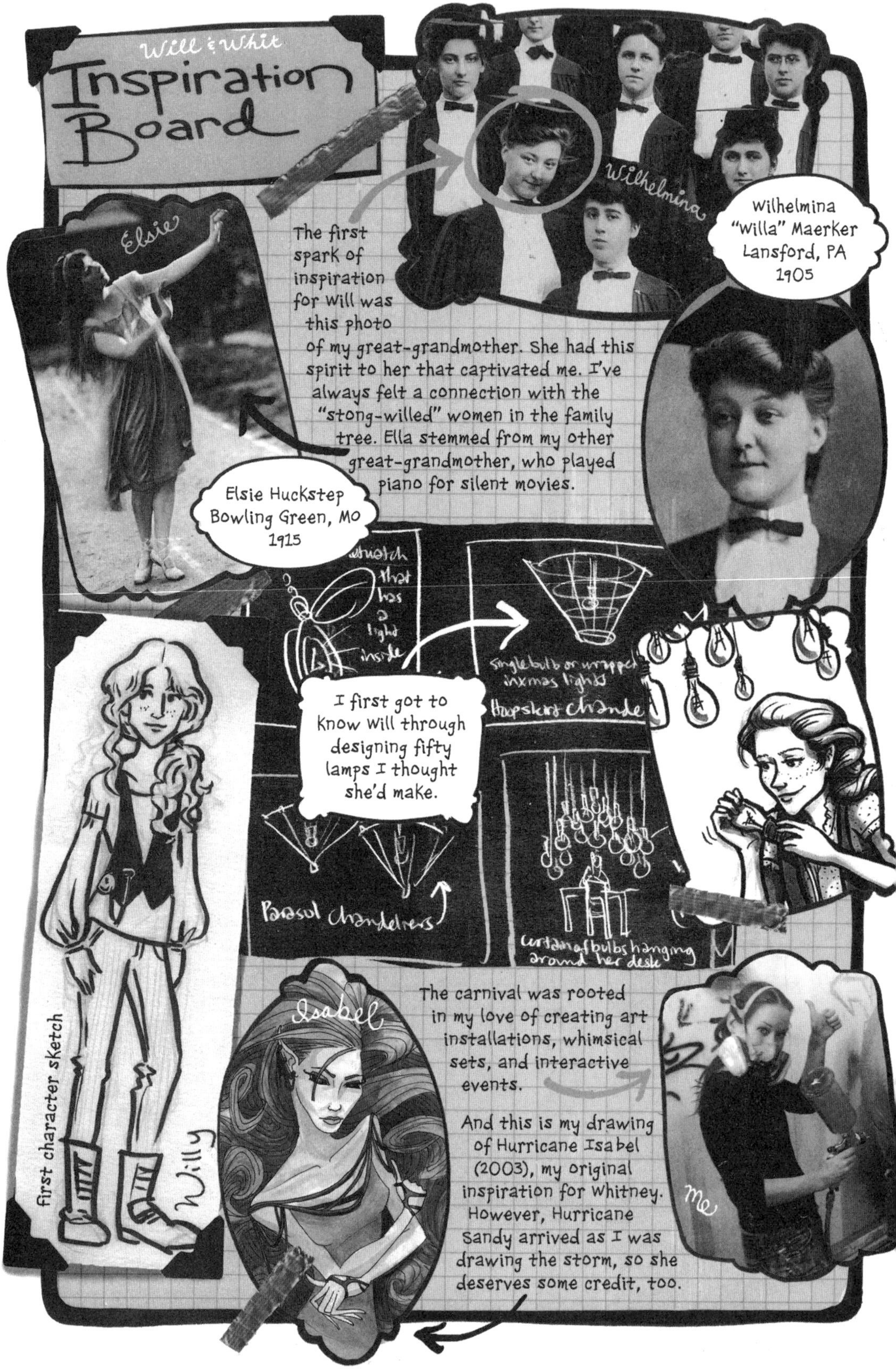

Will & Whit
Inspiration Board
Wilhelmina
Wilhelmina "Willa" Maerker Lansford, PA 1905
Elsie
The first spark of inspiration for Will was this photo of my great-grandmother. She had this spirit to her that captivated me. I've always felt a connection with the "stong-willed" women in the family tree. Ella stemmed from my other great-grandmother, who played piano for silent movies.
Elsie Huckstep Bowling Green, MO 1915
that has a light inside
single bulb or wrapped in xmas lights
Hoopskirt chande
I first got to know Will through designing fifty lamps I thought she'd make.
Parasol chandeliers
curtain of bulbs hanging around her desk
first character sketch
Willy
Isabel
The carnival was rooted in my love of creating art installations, whimsical sets, and interactive events.
And this is my drawing of Hurricane Isabel (2003), my original inspiration for Whitney. However, Hurricane Sandy arrived as I was drawing the storm, so she deserves some credit, too.
me

Cut Out Page

But only cut if this is YOUR book!

Blue Crush Cookies

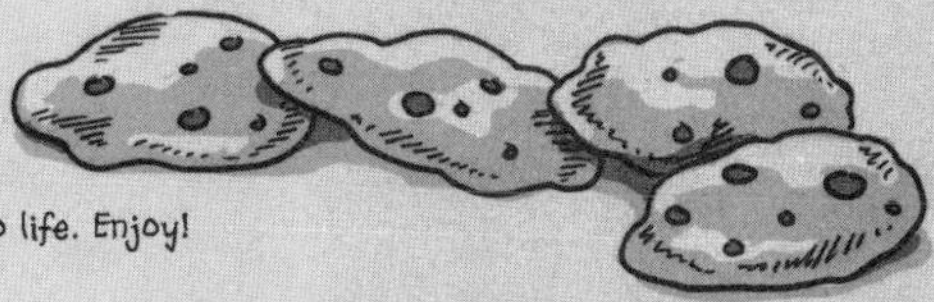

Anyone can use food coloring to dye a cookie blue. But if you're anything like Noel, you're willing to put in a little extra effort for someone you're sweet on. So our Blue Crush Cookies are colored naturally! Thank you, Paige and Anton Mikuriya, for bringing this recipe to life. Enjoy!

-INGREDIENTS-

*1 cup fresh blueberries, washed
*1 cup water
*1/2 cup sugar. White is ideal for color intensity
*Your favorite chocolate chip cookie recipe & ingredients

-DIRECTIONS-

*Step 1. Prepare your chocolate chip cookie recipe to the point where you'd add the chocolate chips.

*Step 2. Now for the blue part: Place the blueberries, water, and sugar in a small pot. Cook for 30 minutes on mid to low heat, stirring occasionally, and covered with a lid. You can use more or less sugar depending on the sweetness of your particular berries...and how strong your sweet tooth is.

*Step 3. Using a slotted spoon, remove the cooked berries and gently HAND MIX the blueberries into your cookie dough along with your chocolate chips. It's normal for the batter to look grey at this point, so don't fret.

*Step 4. And now bake 'em like usual, and behold as they turn blue! I personally like to sprinkle a little sea salt on top as a finishing touch, but feel free to come up with your own variation.

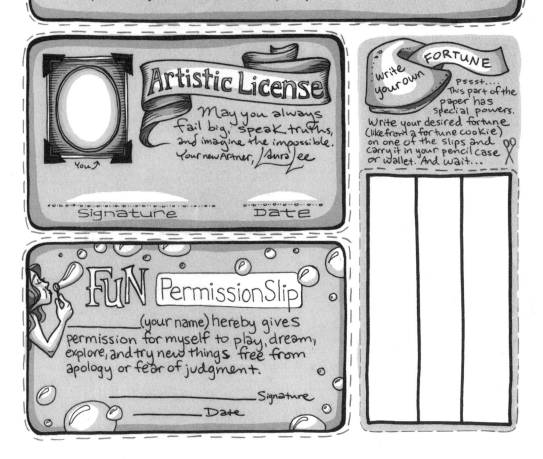

Artistic License

May you always fail big, speak truths, and imagine the impossible.
Your new Artmer, Laura Lee

You ↗

..........Signature..........   ....Date..........

write your own FORTUNE

Pssst.... This part of the paper has special powers. Write your desired fortune (like from a fortune cookie) on one of the slips and carry it in your pencil case or wallet. And wait...

FUN Permission Slip

_____ (your name) hereby gives permission for myself to play, dream, explore, and try new things free from apology or fear of judgment.

_____ Signature
_____ Date

About the Author

Laura Lee Gulledge

is the author of *Page by Paige*, which was nominated for the prestigious Eisner Award. She has worked in art education, scenic painting, and event production, among other pursuits. She's originally from Virginia but now makes her home in Brooklyn, where she is developing *Will & Whit* for the stage.

Visit her online at whoislauralee.com, where she regularly posts new and in-progress art.

2 1982 02004 3307

To COM from LLG

Library of Congress Control Number: 2012955192

ISBN: 978-1-4197-0546-5

Text and illustrations copyright © 2013 Laura Lee Gulledge
Book design by Laura Lee Gulledge and Chad W. Beckerman

Printed and bound in U.S.A
10 9 8 7 6 5 4 3 2 1

Amulet Books are available at special discounts when purchased in quantity for premiums and promotions as well as fundraising or educational use. Special editions can also be created to specification. For details, contact specialsales@abramsbooks.com or the address below.

ABRAMS
THE ART OF BOOKS SINCE 1949
115 West 18th Street
New York, NY 10011
www.amuletbooks.com